with Dr. David Jeremiah

SPECIAL TURNING POINT EDITION

COMMENTS FROM DR. DAVID JEREMIAH

"People Panic—Millions Missing Around the World"

The newspapers and television will not be able to report the magnitude of this news. Some will say this must be "The Rapture," because they heard about it in church or read about it in a book. Others will attempt to explain it scientifically.

When Jesus returns for His own, the world will not hear the voice nor the trumpet. The ears of the nonbelievers will be deaf and their eyes blind. It will take place so fast, "in the twinkling of an eye," that most will not understand what has happened.

What will the world be like for those left behind? The Bible tells us, and it doesn't take a theologian to understand it. Turmoil will reign on earth. People will wander through vacant rooms looking for their loved ones. As God's harsh judgments begin to unfold, many will look to a new world leader, a man described as a Dark Prince.

This novel portrays what may happen in that day. It is the first book in the *Left Behind* series, co-authored by my friend and former pastor of Shadow Mountain Community Church, Dr. Tim LaHaye. A phenomenon in the publishing industry, *Left Behind* has sold more copies than any other book series ever! Perhaps it is a precursor and God's final warning to those who yet disbelieve biblical prophecy. To that end, we offer it to our friends and supporters along with our prayer that none will be left behind.

David Jeremiah
Dr. David Jeremiah

Turning Point • P.O. Box 3838 • San Diego, CA 92163

Tyndale House books by
Tim LaHaye and Jerry B. Jenkins

The Left Behind series
Left Behind
Tribulation Force
Nicolae
Soul Harvest
Apollyon
Assassins
The Indwelling—available spring 2000

Left Behind: The Kids
#1: The Vanishings
#2: Second Chance
#3: Through the Flames
#4: Facing the Future
#5: Nicolae High
#6: The Underground
#7: Busted!—available spring 2000
#8: Death Strike—available spring 2000

Tyndale House books by Tim LaHaye
Are We Living in the End Times?
How to Be Happy Though Married
Spirit-Controlled Temperament
Transformed Temperaments
Why You Act the Way You Do

Tyndale House books by Jerry B. Jenkins
And Then Came You
As You Leave Home
Still the One

LEFT

A NOVEL OF THE EARTH'S LAST DAYS

BEHIND™

TIM LaHAYE
JERRY B. JENKINS

Tyndale House Publishers, Inc.
WHEATON, ILLINOIS

Visit Tyndale's exciting Web site at www.tyndale.com

For the latest Left Behind news visit the Left Behind Web site at www.leftbehind.com

Left Behind series designed by Catherine Bergstrom

Published in association with the literary agency of Alive Communications, Inc.,1465 Kelly Johnson Blvd., Suite 320, Colorado Springs, CO 80920.

ISBN 0-8423-4248-6

Printed in the United States of America

04 03 02 01 00
7   6   5   4   3   2   1

For Alice MacDonald and Bonita Jenkins,
who ensured we would not be left behind

ONE

RAYFORD Steele's mind was on a woman he had never touched. With his fully loaded 747 on autopilot above the Atlantic en route to a 6 A.M. landing at Heathrow, Rayford had pushed from his mind thoughts of his family.

Over spring break he would spend time with his wife and twelve-year-old son. Their daughter would be home from college, too. But for now, with his first officer dozing, Rayford imagined Hattie Durham's smile and looked forward to their next meeting.

Hattie was Rayford's senior flight attendant. He hadn't seen her in more than an hour.

Rayford used to look forward to getting home to his wife. Irene was attractive and vivacious enough, even at forty. But lately he had found himself repelled by her obsession with religion. It was all she could talk about.

God was OK with Rayford Steele. Rayford even

enjoyed church occasionally. But since Irene had hooked up with a smaller congregation and was into weekly Bible studies and church every Sunday, Rayford had become uncomfortable. Hers was not a church where people gave you the benefit of the doubt, assumed the best about you, and let you be. People there had actually asked him, to his face, what God was doing in his life.

"Blessing my socks off" had become the smiling response that seemed to satisfy them, but he found more and more excuses to be busy on Sundays.

Rayford tried to tell himself it was his wife's devotion to a divine suitor that caused his mind to wander. But he knew the real reason was his own libido.

Besides, Hattie Durham was drop-dead gorgeous. No one could argue that. What he enjoyed most was that she was a toucher. Nothing inappropriate, nothing showy. She simply touched his arm as she brushed past or rested her hand gently on his shoulder when she stood behind his seat in the cockpit.

It wasn't her touch alone that made Rayford enjoy her company. He could tell from her expressions, her demeanor, her eye contact that she at least admired and respected him. Whether she was interested in anything more, he could only guess. And so he did.

They had spent time together, chatting for hours over drinks or dinner, sometimes with coworkers, sometimes not. He had not returned so much as one brush of a finger, but his eyes had held her gaze, and he could only assume his smile had made its point.

Maybe today. Maybe this morning, if her coded tap on

the door didn't rouse his first officer, he would reach and cover the hand on his shoulder—in a friendly way he hoped she would recognize as a step, a first from his side, toward a relationship.

And a first it would be. He was no prude, but Rayford had never been unfaithful to Irene. He'd had plenty of opportunities. He had long felt guilty about a private necking session he enjoyed at a company Christmas party more than twelve years before. Irene had stayed home, uncomfortably past her ninth month carrying their surprise tagalong son, Ray Jr.

Though under the influence, Rayford had known enough to leave the party early. It was clear Irene noticed he was slightly drunk, but she couldn't have suspected anything else, not from her straight-arrow captain. He was the pilot who had once consumed two martinis during a snowy shutdown at O'Hare and then voluntarily grounded himself when the weather cleared. He offered to pay for bringing in a relief pilot, but Pan-Continental was so impressed that instead they made an example of his self-discipline and wisdom.

In a couple of hours Rayford would be the first to see hints of the sun, a teasing palette of pastels that would signal the reluctant dawn over the continent. Until then, the blackness through the window seemed miles thick. His groggy or sleeping passengers had window shades down, pillows and blankets in place. For now the plane was a dark, humming sleep chamber for all but a few wanderers, the attendants, and one or two responders to nature's call.

The question of the darkest hour before dawn, then, was whether Rayford Steele should risk a new, exciting relationship with Hattie Durham. He suppressed a smile. Was he kidding himself? Would someone with his reputation ever do anything but dream about a beautiful woman fifteen years his junior? He wasn't so sure anymore. If only Irene hadn't gone off on this new kick.

Would it fade, her preoccupation with the end of the world, with the love of Jesus, with the salvation of souls? Lately she had been reading everything she could get her hands on about the Rapture of the church. "Can you imagine, Rafe," she exulted, "Jesus coming back to get us before we die?"

"Yeah, boy," he said, peeking over the top of his newspaper, "that would kill me."

She was not amused. "If I didn't know what would happen to me," she said, "I wouldn't be glib about it."

"I *do* know what would happen to me," he insisted. "I'd be dead, gone, *finis*. But you, of course, would fly right up to heaven."

He hadn't meant to offend her. He was just having fun. When she turned away he rose and pursued her. He spun her around and tried to kiss her, but she was cold. "Come on, Irene," he said. "Tell me thousands wouldn't just keel over if they saw Jesus coming back for all the good people."

She had pulled away in tears. "I've told you and told you. Saved people aren't good people, they're—"

"Just forgiven, yeah, I know," he said, feeling

rejected and vulnerable in his own living room. He returned to his chair and his paper. "If it makes you feel any better, I'm happy for you that you can be so cocksure."

"I only believe what the Bible says," Irene said.

Rayford shrugged. He wanted to say, "Good for you," but he didn't want to make a bad situation worse. In a way he had envied her confidence, but in truth he wrote it off to her being a more emotional, more feelings-oriented person. He didn't want to articulate it, but the fact was, he was brighter—yes, more intelligent. He believed in rules, systems, laws, patterns, things you could see and feel and hear and touch.

If God was part of all that, OK. A higher power, a loving being, a force behind the laws of nature, fine. Let's sing about it, pray about it, feel good about our ability to be kind to others, and go about our business. Rayford's greatest fear was that this religious fixation would not fade like Irene's Amway days, her Tupper-ware phase, and her aerobics spell. He could just see her ringing doorbells and asking if she could read people a verse or two. Surely she knew better than to dream of his tagging along.

Irene had become a full-fledged religious fanatic, and somehow that freed Rayford to daydream without guilt about Hattie Durham. Maybe he would say something, suggest something, hint at something as he and Hattie strode through Heathrow toward the cab line. Maybe earlier. Dare he assert himself even now, hours before touchdown?

Next to a window in first class, a writer sat hunched over his laptop. He shut down the machine, vowing to get back to his journal later. At thirty, Cameron Williams was the youngest ever senior writer for the prestigious *Global Weekly*. The envy of the rest of the veteran staff, he either scooped them on or was assigned to the best stories in the world. Both admirers and detractors at the magazine called him Buck, because they said he was always bucking tradition and authority. Buck believed he lived a charmed life, having been eyewitness to some of the most pivotal events in history.

A year and two months earlier, his January 1 cover story had taken him to Israel to interview Chaim Rosenzweig and had resulted in the most bizarre event he had ever experienced.

The elderly Rosenzweig had been the only unanimous choice for Newsmaker of the Year in the history of *Global Weekly*. Its staff had customarily steered clear of anyone who would be an obvious pick as *Time*'s Man of the Year. But Rosenzweig was an automatic. Cameron Williams had gone into the staff meeting prepared to argue for Rosenzweig and against whatever media star the others would typically champion.

He was pleasantly surprised when executive editor Steve Plank opened with, "Anybody want to nominate someone stupid, such as anyone other than the Nobel prizewinner in chemistry?"

The senior staff members looked at each other, shook their heads, and pretended to begin leaving. "Put the chairs on the wagon, the meetin' is over," Buck said. "Steve, I'm not angling for it, but you know I know the guy and he trusts me."

"Not so fast, Cowboy," a rival said, then appealed to Plank. "You letting Buck assign himself now?"

"I might," Steve said. "And what if I do?"

"I just think this is a technical piece, a science story," Buck's detractor muttered. "I'd put the science writer on it."

"And you'd put the reader to sleep," Plank said. "C'mon, you know the writer for showcase pieces comes from this group. And this is not a science piece any more than the first one Buck did on him. This has to be told so the reader gets to know the man and understands the significance of his achievement."

"Like that isn't obvious. It only changed the course of history."

"I'll make the assignment today," the executive editor said. "Thanks for your willingness, Buck. I assume everyone else is willing as well." Expressions of eagerness filled the room, but Buck also heard grumbled predictions that the fair-haired boy would get the nod. Which he did.

Such confidence from his boss and competition from his peers made him all the more determined to outdo himself with every assignment. In Israel, Buck stayed in a military compound and met with Rosenzweig in the same kibbutz on the outskirts of Haifa where he had interviewed him a year earlier.

Rosenzweig was fascinating, of course, but it was his

discovery, or invention—no one knew quite how to cate-gorize it—that was truly the "newsmaker of the year." The humble man called himself a botanist, but he was in truth a chemical engineer who had concocted a synthetic fertilizer that caused the desert sands of Israel to bloom like a greenhouse.

"Irrigation has not been a problem for decades," the old man said. "But all that did was make the sand wet. My formula, added to the water, fertilizes the sand."

Buck was not a scientist, but he knew enough to shake his head at that simple statement. Rosenzweig's formula was fast making Israel the richest nation on earth, far more profitable than its oil-laden neighbors. Every inch of ground blossomed with flowers and grains, including produce never before conceivable in Israel. The Holy Land became an export capital, the envy of the world, with virtually zero unemployment. Everyone prospered.

The prosperity brought about by the miracle formula changed the course of history for Israel. Flush with cash and resources, Israel made peace with her neighbors. Free trade and liberal passage allowed all who loved the nation to have access to it. What they did not have access to, however, was the formula.

Buck had not even asked the old man to reveal the for-mula or the complicated security process that protected it from any potential enemy. The very fact that Buck was housed by the military evidenced the importance of secu-rity. Maintaining that secret ensured the power and inde-pendence of the state of Israel. Never had Israel enjoyed such tranquility. The walled city of Jerusalem was only a symbol now, welcoming everyone who embraced peace. The old guard believed God had rewarded them and compensated them for centuries of persecution.

Chaim Rosenzweig was honored throughout the world and revered in his own country. Global leaders sought him out, and he was protected by security systems as complex as those that protected heads of state. As heady as Israel became with newfound glory, the nation's leaders were not stupid. A kidnapped and tortured Rosenzweig could be forced to reveal a secret that would similarly revolutionize any nation in the world.

Imagine what the formula might do if modified to work on the vast tundra of Russia! Could regions bloom, though snow covered most of the year? Was this the key to resurrecting that massive nation following the shattering of the Union of Soviet Socialist Republics?

Russia had become a great brooding giant with a devastated economy and regressed technology. All the nation had was military might, every spare mark going into weaponry. And the switch from rubles to marks had not been a smooth transition for the struggling nation. Streamlining world finance to three major currencies had taken years, but once the change was made, most were happy with it. All of Europe and Russia dealt exclusively in marks. Asia, Africa, and the Middle East traded in yen. North and South America and Australia dealt in dollars. A move was afoot to go to one global currency, but those nations that had reluctantly switched once were loath to do it again.

Frustrated at their inability to profit from Israel's fortune and determined to dominate and occupy the Holy Land, the Russians had launched an attack against Israel in the middle of the night. The assault became known as the Russian Pearl Harbor, and because of his interview with Rosenzweig, Buck Williams was in Haifa when it happened. The Russians sent intercontinental ballistic missiles and nuclear-equipped MiG fighter-bombers into the region. The number of aircraft and warheads made it clear their mission was annihilation.

To say the Israelis were caught off guard, Cameron Williams had written, was like saying the Great Wall of China was long. When Israeli radar picked up the Russian planes, they were nearly overhead. Israel's frantic plea for support from her immediate neighbors and the United States was simultaneous with her demand to know the intentions of the invaders of her airspace. By the time Israel and her allies could have mounted anything close to a defense, it was obvious the Russians would have her outnumbered a hundred to one.

They had only moments before the destruction would begin. There would be no more negotiating, no more pleas for a sharing of the wealth with the hordes of the north. If the Russians meant only to intimidate and bully, they would not have filled the sky with missiles. Planes could turn back, but the missiles were armed and targeted.

So this was no grandstand play designed to bring Israel to her knees. There was no message for the victims. Receiving no explanation for war machines crossing her borders and descending upon her, Israel was forced to defend herself, knowing full well that the first volley would bring about her virtual disappearance from the face of the earth.

With warning sirens screaming and radio and tele- viion sending the doomed for what flimsy cover they might find, Israel defended herself for what would surely be the last time in history. The first battery of Israeli surface-to-air missiles hit their marks, and the sky was lit with orange-and-yellow balls of fire that would certainly do little to slow a Russian offensive for which there could be no defense.

Those who knew the odds and what the radar screens foretold interpreted the deafening explosions in the sky as the Russian onslaught. Every military leader who knew what was coming expected to be put out of his misery in seconds when the fusillade reached the ground and cov- ered the nation.

From what he heard and saw in the military com- pound, Buck Williams knew the end was near. There was no escape. But as the night shone like day and the horrific, deafening explosions continued, nothing on the ground suffered. The building shook and rattled and rumbled. And yet it was not hit.

Outside, warplanes slammed to the ground, digging craters and sending burning debris flying. Yet lines of communication stayed open. No other command posts had been hit. No reports of casualties. Nothing destroyed yet.

Was this some sort of a cruel joke? Sure, the first Israeli missiles had taken out Russian fighters and caused missiles to explode too high to cause more than fire damage on the ground. But what had happened to the rest of the Russian air corps? Radar showed they had clearly sent nearly every plane they had, leaving hardly anything in reserve for defense. Thousands of planes swooped down on the tiny country's most populated cities.

The roar and the cacophony continued, the explosions so horrifying that veteran military leaders buried their faces and screamed in terror. Buck had always wanted to be near the front lines, but his survival instinct was on full throttle. He knew beyond doubt that he would die, and he found himself thinking the strangest thoughts. Why had he never married? Would there be remnants of his body for his father and brother to identify? Was there a God? Would death be the end?

He crouched beneath a console, surprised by the urge to sob. This was not at all what he had expected war to sound like, to look like. He had imagined himself peeking at the action from a safe spot, recording in his mind the drama.

Several minutes into the holocaust, Buck realized he would be no more dead outside than in. He felt no bravado, only uniqueness. He would be the only person in this post who would see and know what killed him. He made his way to a door on rubbery legs. No one seemed to notice or care to warn him. It was as if they had all been sentenced to death.

He forced open the door against a furnace blast and had to shield his eyes from the whiteness of the blaze. The sky was afire. He still heard planes over the din and roar of the fire itself, and the occasional exploding missile sent new showers of flame into the air. He stood in stark terror and amazement as the great machines of war plummeted to the earth all over the city, crashing and burning. But they fell between buildings and in deserted streets and fields. Anything atomic and explosive erupted high in the atmosphere, and Buck stood there in the heat, his face blistering and his body pouring sweat. What in the world was happening?

Then came chunks of ice and hailstones big as golf balls, forcing Buck to cover his head with his jacket. The earth shook and resounded, throwing him to the ground. Facedown in the freezing shards, he felt rain wash over him. Suddenly the only sound was the fire in the sky, and it began to fade as it drifted lower. After ten minutes of thunderous roaring, the fire dissipated, and scattered balls of flame flickered on the ground. The firelight disappeared as quickly as it had come. Stillness settled over the land.

As clouds of smoke wafted away on a gentle breeze, the night sky reappeared in its blue-blackness and stars shone peacefully as if nothing had gone awry.

Buck turned back to the building, his muddy leather jacket in his fist. The doorknob was still hot, and inside, military leaders wept and shuddered. The radio was alive with reports from Israeli pilots. They had not been able to get airborne in time to do anything but watch as the entire Russian air offensive seemed to destroy itself.

Miraculously, not one casualty was reported in all of Israel. Otherwise Buck might have believed some mysterious malfunction had caused missile and plane to destroy each other. But witnesses reported that it had been a firestorm, along with rain and hail and an earthquake, that consumed the entire offensive effort.

Had it been a divinely appointed meteor shower? Perhaps. But what accounted for hundreds and thousands of chunks of burning, twisted, molten steel smashing to the ground in Haifa, Jerusalem, Tel Aviv, Jericho, even Bethlehem—leveling ancient walls but not so much as scratching one living creature? Daylight revealed the carnage and exposed Russia's secret alliance with Middle Eastern nations, primarily Ethiopia and Libya.

Among the ruins, the Israelis found combustible material that would serve as fuel and preserve their natural resources for more than six years. Special task forces competed with buzzards and vultures for the flesh of the enemy dead, trying to bury them before their bones were picked clean and disease threatened the nation.

Buck remembered it vividly, as if it were yesterday. Had he not been there and seen it himself, he would not have believed it. And it took more than he had in him to get any reader of *Global Weekly* to buy it either.

Editors and readers had their own explanations for the phenomenon, but Buck admitted, if only to himself, that he became a believer in God that day. Jewish scholars pointed out passages from the Bible that talked about God destroying Israel's enemies with a firestorm, earthquake, hail, and rain. Buck was stunned when he read Ezekiel 38 and 39 about a great enemy from the north invading Israel with the help of Persia, Libya, and Ethiopia. More stark was that the Scriptures foretold of weapons of war used as fire fuel and enemy soldiers eaten by birds or buried in a common grave.

Christian friends wanted Buck to take the next step and believe in Christ, now that he was so clearly spiritually attuned. He wasn't prepared to go that far, but he was certainly a different person and a different journalist from then on. To him, nothing was beyond belief.

Not sure whether he'd follow through with anything overt, Captain Rayford Steele felt an irresistible urge to see Hattie Durham right then. He unstrapped himself and squeezed his first officer's shoulder on the way out of the cockpit. "We're still on auto, Christopher," he said as the younger man roused and straightened his headphones. "I'm gonna make the sunup stroll."

Christopher squinted and licked his lips. "Doesn't look like sunup to me, Cap."

"Probably another hour or two. I'll see if anybody's stirring anyway."

"Roger. If they are, tell 'em Chris says, 'Hey.'"

Rayford snorted and nodded. As he opened the cockpit door, Hattie Durham nearly bowled him over.

"No need to knock," he said. "I'm coming."

The senior flight attendant pulled him into the galleyway, but there was no passion in her touch. Her fingers felt like talons on his forearm, and her body shuddered in the darkness.

"Hattie—"

She pressed him back against the cooking compartments, her face close to his. Had she not been clearly terrified, he might have enjoyed this and returned her embrace. Her knees buckled as she tried to speak, and her voice came in a whiny squeal.

"People are missing," she managed in a whisper, burying her head in his chest.

He took her shoulders and tried to push her back, but she fought to stay close. "What do you m—?"

She was sobbing now, her body out of control. "A whole bunch of people, just gone!"

"Hattie, this is a big plane. They've wandered to the lavs or—"

She pulled his head down so she could speak directly into his ear. Despite her weeping, she was plainly fighting to make herself understood. "I've been everywhere. I'm telling you, dozens of people are missing."

"Hattie, it's still dark. We'll find—"

"I'm not crazy! See for yourself! All over the plane, people have disappeared."

"It's a joke. They're hiding, trying to—"

"Ray! Their shoes, their socks, their clothes, everything was left behind. These people are gone!"

Hattie slipped from his grasp and knelt whimpering in the corner. Rayford wanted to comfort her, to enlist her help, or to get Chris to go with him through the plane. More than anything he wanted to believe the woman was crazy. She knew better than to put him on. It was obvious she really believed people had disappeared.

He had been daydreaming in the cockpit. Was he asleep now? He bit his lip hard and winced at the pain. So he was wide awake. He stepped into first class, where an elderly woman sat stunned in the predawn haze, her husband's sweater and trousers in her hands. "What in the world?" she said. "Harold?"

Rayford scanned the rest of first class. Most passengers were still asleep, including a young man by the window, his laptop computer on the tray table. But indeed several seats were empty. As Rayford's eyes grew accustomed to the low light, he strode quickly to the stairway. He started down, but the woman called to him.

"Sir, my husband—"

Rayford put a finger to his lips and whispered, "I know. We'll find him. I'll be right back."

What nonsense! he thought as he descended, aware of Hattie right behind him. *"We'll find him"?*

Hattie grabbed his shoulder and he slowed. "Should I turn on the cabin lights?"

"No," he whispered. "The less people know right now, the better."

Rayford wanted to be strong, to have answers, to be an example to his crew, to Hattie. But when he reached the lower level he knew the rest of the flight would be chaotic. He was as scared as anyone on board. As he scanned the seats, he nearly panicked. He backed into a secluded spot behind the bulkhead and slapped himself hard on the cheek.

This was no joke, no trick, no dream. Something was terribly wrong, and there was no place to run. There would be enough confusion and terror without his losing control. Nothing had prepared him for this, and he would be the one everybody would look to. But for what? What was he supposed to do?

First one, then another cried out when they realized their seatmates were missing but that their clothes were still there. They cried, they screamed, they leaped from their seats. Hattie grabbed Rayford from behind and wrapped her hands so tight around his chest that he could hardly breathe. "Rayford, what is this?"

He pulled her hands apart and turned to face her. "Hattie, listen. I don't know any more than you do. But we've got to calm these people and get on the ground. I'll make some kind of an announcement, and you and your people keep everybody in their seats. OK?"

She nodded but she didn't look OK at all. As he edged past her to hurry back to the cockpit, he heard her scream. *So much for calming the passengers,* he thought as he whirled to see her on her knees in the aisle. She lifted a blazer, shirt and tie still intact. Trousers lay at her feet. Hattie frantically turned the blazer to the low light and read the name tag. "Tony!" she wailed. "Tony's gone!"

Rayford snatched the clothes from her and tossed them behind the bulkhead. He lifted Hattie by her elbows and pulled her out of sight. "Hattie, we're hours from touchdown. We can't have a planeload of hysterical people. I'm going to make an announcement, but you have to do your job. Can you?"

She nodded, her eyes vacant. He forced her to look at him. "Will you?" he said.

She nodded again. "Rayford, are we going to die?"

"No," he said. "That I'm sure of."

But he wasn't sure of anything. How could he know? He'd rather have faced an engine fire or even an uncontrolled dive. A crash into the ocean had to be better than this. How would he keep people calm in such a nightmare?

By now keeping the cabin lights off was doing more harm than good, and he was glad to be able to give Hattie a specific assignment. "I don't know what I'm going to say," he said, "but get the lights on so we can make an accurate record of who's here and who's gone, and then get more of those foreign visitor declaration forms."

"For what?"

"Just do it. Have them ready."

Rayford didn't know if he had done the right thing by leaving Hattie in charge of the passengers and crew. As he raced up the stairs, he caught sight of another attendant backing out of a galleyway, screaming. By now poor Christopher in the cockpit was the only one on the plane unaware of what was happening. Worse, Rayford had told Hattie he didn't know what was happening any more than she did.

The terrifying truth was that he knew all too well. Irene had been right. He, and most of his passengers, had been left behind.

TWO

CAMERON Williams had roused when the old woman directly in front of him called out to the pilot. The pilot had shushed her, causing her to peek back at Buck. He dragged his fingers through his longish blonde hair and forced a groggy smile. "Trouble, ma'am?"

"It's my Harold," she said.

Buck had helped the old man put his herringbone wool jacket and felt hat in the overhead bin when they boarded. Harold was a short, dapper gentleman in penny loafers, brown slacks, and a tan sweater-vest over a shirt and tie. He was balding, and Buck assumed he would want the hat again later when the air-conditioning kicked in.

"Does he need something?"

"He's gone!"

"I'm sorry?"

"He's disappeared!"

"Well, I'm sure he slipped off to the washroom while you were sleeping."

"Would you mind checking for me? And take a blanket."

"Ma'am?"

"I'm afraid he's gone off naked. He's a religious person, and he'll be terribly embarrassed."

Buck suppressed a smile when he noticed the woman's pained expression. He climbed over the sleeping executive on the aisle, who had far exceeded his limit of free drinks, and leaned in to take a blanket from the old woman. Indeed, Harold's clothes were in a neat pile on his seat, his glasses and hearing aid on top. The pant legs still hung over the edge and led to his shoes and socks. *Bizarre,* Buck thought. *Why so fastidious?* He remembered a friend in high school who had a form of epilepsy that occasionally caused him to black out when he seemed perfectly conscious. He might remove his shoes and socks in public or come out of a washroom with his clothes open.

"Does your husband have a history of epilepsy?"

"No."

"Sleepwalking?"

"No."

"I'll be right back."

The first-class lavs were unoccupied, but as Buck headed for the stairs he found several other passengers in the aisle. "Excuse me," he said, "I'm looking for someone."

"Who isn't?" a woman said.

Buck pushed his way past several people and found lines to the washrooms in business and economy. The pilot brushed past him without a word, and Buck was soon met by the senior flight attendant. "Sir, I need to ask you to return to your seat and fasten your belt."

"I'm looking for—"

"Everybody is looking for someone," she said. "We hope to have some information for you in a few minutes. Now, please." She steered him back toward the stairs, then slipped past him and took the steps two at a time.

Halfway up the stairs Buck turned and surveyed the scene. It was the middle of the night, for heaven's sake, and as the cabin lights came on, he shuddered. All over the plane, people were holding up clothes and gasping or shrieking that someone was missing.

Somehow he knew this was no dream, and he felt the same terror he had endured awaiting his death in Israel. What was he going to tell Harold's wife? *You're not the only one? Lots of people left their clothes in their seats?*

As he hurried back to his seat, his mind searched its memory banks for anything he had ever read, seen, or heard of any technology that could remove people from their clothes and make them disappear from a decidedly secure environment. Whoever did this, were they on the plane? Would they make demands? Would another wave of disappearances be next? Would he become a victim? Where would he find himself?

Fear seemed to pervade the cabin as he climbed over

his sleeping seatmate again. He stood and leaned over the back of the chair ahead of him. "Apparently many people are missing," he told the old woman. She looked as puzzled and fearful as Buck himself felt.

He sat down as the intercom came on and the captain addressed the passengers. After instructing them to return to their assigned seats, the captain explained, "I'm going to ask the flight attendants to check the lavatories and be sure everybody is accounted for. Then I'll ask them to pass out foreign entry cards. If anyone in your party is missing, I would like you to fill out the card in his or her name and list every shred of detail you can think of, from date of birth to description.

"I'm sure you all realize that we have a very troubling situation. The cards will give us a count of those missing, and I'll have something to give authorities. My first officer, Mr. Smith, will now make a cursory count of empty seats. I will try to contact Pan-Continental. I must tell you, however, that our location makes it extremely difficult to communicate with the ground without long delays. Even in this satellite age, we're in a pretty remote area. As soon as I know anything, I'll convey it to you. In the meantime, I appreciate your cooperation and calm."

Buck watched as the first officer came rushing from the cockpit, hatless and flushed. He hurried down one aisle and up the other, eyes darting from seat to seat as the flight attendants passed out cards.

Buck's seatmate roused, drooling, when an attendant asked if anyone in his party was missing. "Missing? No.

And there's nobody in this party but me." He curled up again and went back to sleep, unaware.

The first officer had been gone only a few minutes when Rayford heard his key in the cockpit door and it banged open. Christopher flopped into his chair, ignored the seat belt, and sat with his head in his hands.

"What's going on, Ray?" he said. "We got us more than a hundred people gone with nothing but their clothes left behind."

"That many?"

"Yeah, like it'd be better if it was only fifty? How the heck are we gonna explain landing with less passengers than we took off with?"

Rayford shook his head, still working the radio, trying to reach someone, anyone, in Greenland or an island in the middle of nowhere. But they were too remote even to pick up a radio station for news. Finally he connected with a Concorde several miles away heading the other direction. He nodded to Christopher to put on his own earphones.

"You got enough fuel to get back to the States, over?" the pilot asked Rayford.

He looked at Christopher, who nodded and whispered, "We're halfway."

"I could make Kennedy," Rayford said.

"Forget it," came the reply. "Nothing's landing in New York. Two runways still open in Chicago. That's where we're going."

"We came from Chicago. Can't I put down at Heathrow?"

"Negative. Closed."

"Paris?"

"Man, you've got to get back where you came from. We left Paris an hour ago, got the word what's happening, and were told to go straight to Chicago."

"What's happening, Concorde?"

"If you don't know, why'd you put out the Mayday?"

"I've got a situation here I don't even want to talk about."

"Hey, friend, it's all over the world, you know?"

"Negative, I don't know," Rayford said. "Talk to me."

"You're missing passengers, right?"

"Roger. More than a hundred."

"Whoa! We lost nearly fifty."

"What do you make of it, Concorde?"

"First thing I thought of was spontaneous combustion, but there would have been smoke, residue. These people materially disappeared. Only thing I can compare it to is the old *Star Trek* shows where people got dematerialized and rematerialized, beamed all over the place."

"I sure wish I could tell my people their loved ones were going to reappear just as quickly and completely as they disappeared," Rayford said.

"That's not the worst of it, Pan Heavy. People everywhere have disappeared. Orly lost air-traffic controllers and ground controllers. Some planes have lost flight crews. Where it's daylight there are car pileups, chaos everywhere. Planes down all over and at every major airport."

"So this was a spontaneous thing?"

"Everywhere at once, just a little under an hour ago."

"I was almost hoping it was something on this plane. Some gas, some malfunction."

"That it was selective, you mean, over?"

Rayford caught the sarcasm.

"I see what you mean, Concorde. Gotta admit this is somewhere we've never been before."

"And never want to be again. I keep telling myself it's a bad dream."

"A nightmare, over."

"Roger, but it's not, is it?"

"What are you going to tell your passengers, Concorde?"

"No clue. You, over?"

"The truth."

"Can't hurt now. But what's the truth? What do we know?"

"Not a blessed thing."

"Good choice of words, Pan Heavy. You know what some people are saying, over?"

"Roger," Rayford said. "Better it's people gone to heaven than some world power doing this with fancy rays."

"Word we get is that every country has been affected. See you in Chicago?"

"Roger."

Rayford Steele looked at Christopher, who began

changing the settings to turn the monstrous wide-body around and get it headed back toward the States. "Ladies and gentlemen," Rayford said over the intercom, "we're not going to be able to land in Europe. We're headed back to Chicago. We're almost exactly halfway to our original destination, so we will not have a fuel problem. I hope this puts your minds at ease somewhat. I will let you know when we are close enough to begin using the telephones. Until I do, you will do yourself a favor by not trying."

———————

When the captain had come back on the intercom with the information about returning to the United States, Buck Williams was surprised to hear applause throughout the cabin. Shocked and terrified as everyone was, most were from the States and wanted at least to return to familiarity to sort this thing out. Buck nudged the businessman on his right. "I'm sorry, friend, but you're going to want to be awake for this."

The man peered at Buck with a disgusted look and slurred, "If we're not crashin', don't bother me."

———————

When the Pan-Continental 747 was finally within satellite communications range of the United States, Captain Rayford Steele connected with an all-news radio outlet and learned the far-reaching effects of the disappearance

of people from every continent. Communication lines
were jammed. Medical, technical, and service people
were among the missing all over the world. Every civil
service agency was on full emergency status, trying to
handle the unending tragedies. Rayford remembered the
El-train disaster in Chicago years before and how the
hospitals and fire and police units brought everyone in to
work. He could imagine that now, multiplied thousands
of times.

Even the newscasters' voices were terror filled, as
much as they tried to mask it. Every conceivable explanation was proffered, but overshadowing all such discussion and even coverage of the carnage were the practical
aspects. What people wanted from the news was simple
information on how to get where they were going and
how to contact their loved ones to determine if they were
still around. Rayford was instructed to get in a multistate
traffic pattern that would allow him to land at O'Hare at
a precise moment. Only two runways were open, and
every large plane in the country seemed headed that way.
Thousands were dead in plane crashes and car pileups.
Emergency crews were trying to clear expressways and
runways, all the while grieving over loved ones and
coworkers who had disappeared. One report said that so
many cabbies had disappeared from the cab corral at
O'Hare that volunteers were being brought in to move
the cars that had been left running with the former drivers' clothes still on the seats.

Cars driven by people who spontaneously disappeared
had careened out of control, of course. The toughest

chore for emergency personnel was to determine who had disappeared, who was killed, and who was injured, and then to communicate that to the survivors.

When Rayford was close enough to communicate to the tower at O'Hare, he asked if they would try to connect him by phone to his home. He was laughed off. "Sorry, Captain, but phone lines are so jammed and phone personnel so spotty that the only hope is to get a dial tone and use a phone with a redial button."

Rayford filled the passengers in on the extent of the phenomenon and pleaded with them to remain calm. "There is nothing we can do on this plane that will change the situation. My plan is to get you on the ground as quickly as possible in Chicago so you can have access to some answers and, I hope, some help."

The in-flight phone embedded in the back of the seat in front of Buck Williams was not assembled with external modular connections the way most phones were. Buck imagined that Pan Con Airlines would soon be replacing these relics to avoid complaints from computer users. But Buck guessed that inside the phone the connection was standard and that if he could somehow get in there without damaging the phone, he could connect his computer's modem directly to the line. His own cellular phone was not cooperating at this altitude.

In front of him, Harold's wife rocked and whimpered, her face buried in her hands. The executive next to Buck snored. Before drinking himself into oblivion soon after takeoff, he had said something about a major meeting in Scotland. Would he be surprised by the view upon landing!

All around Buck, people cried, prayed, and talked. Flight attendants offered snacks and drinks, but few accepted. Having preferred an aisle seat for a little more legroom, Buck was now glad he was partially hidden near the window. He removed from his computer bag a tiny tool kit he had never expected to use, and went to work on the phone.

Disappointed to find no modular connection even inside the housing, he decided to play amateur electrician. These phone lines always have the same color wires, he decided, so he opened his computer and cut the wire leading to the female connector. Inside the phone, he cut the wire and sliced off the protective rubber coating. Sure enough, the four inner wires from both computer and phone looked identical. In a few minutes, he had spliced them together.

Buck tapped out a quick message to his executive editor, Steve Plank, in New York, telling of his destination. "I will bang out all I know, and I'm sure this will be just one of many similar stories. But at least this will be up to the minute, as it happens. Whether it will be of any use, I don't know. The thought hits me, Steve, that you may be among the missing. How would I know? You know my computer address. Let me know you're still with us."

He stored the note and set up his modem to send it to New York in the background, while he was working on his own writing. At the top of the screen a status bar flashed every twenty seconds, informing him that the connection to his ramp on the information superhighway was busy. He kept working.

The senior flight attendant startled him several pages into his own reflections and feelings. "What in the world are you doing?" she said, leaning in to stare at the mess of wires leading from his laptop to the in-flight phone. "I can't let you do that."

He glanced at her name tag. "Listen, beautiful Hattie, are we or are we not looking at the end of the world as we know it?"

"Don't patronize me, sir. I can't let you sit here and vandalize airline property."

"I'm not vandalizing it. I'm adapting it in an emergency. With this I can hopefully make a connection where nothing else will work."

"I can't let you do it."

"Hattie, can I tell you something?"

"Only that you're going to put that phone back the way you found it."

"I will."

"Now."

"No, I won't do that."

"That's the only thing I want to hear."

"I understand that, but please listen."

The man next to Buck stared at him and then at Hattie. He swore, then used a pillow to cover his right ear, pressing his left against the seat back.

Hattie grabbed a computer printout from her pocket

and located Buck's name. "Mr. Williams, I expect you to cooperate. I don't want to bother the pilot with this."

Buck reached for her hand. She stiffened but didn't pull away. "Can we talk for just a second?"

"I'm not going to change my mind, sir. Now please, I have a plane full of frightened people."

"Aren't you one of them?" He was still holding her hand.

She pursed her lips and nodded.

"Wouldn't you like to make contact with someone? If this works, I can reach people who can make phone calls for you, let your family know you're all right, even get a message back to you. I haven't destroyed anything, and I promise I can put it back the way I found it."

"You can?"

"I can."

"And you'd help me?"

"Anything. Give me some names and phone numbers. I'll send them in with what I'm trying to upload to New York, and I'll insist that someone make the calls for you and report back to me. I can't guarantee I'll get through or that if I do they'll get back to me, but I will try."

"I'd be grateful."

"And can you protect me from other overly zealous flight attendants?"

Hattie managed a smile. "They might all want your help."

"This is a long shot as it is. Just keep everybody away from me, and let me keep trying."

"Deal," she said, but she looked troubled.

"Hattie, you're doing the right thing," he said. "It's OK in a situation like this to think of yourself a little. That's what I'm doing."

"But everybody's in the same boat, sir. And I have responsibilities."

"You have to admit, when people disappear, some rules go out the window."

———

Rayford Steele sat ashen faced in the cockpit. Half an hour from touchdown in Chicago, he had told the passengers everything he knew. The simultaneous disappearance of millions all over the globe had resulted in chaos far beyond imagination. He complimented everyone on remaining calm and avoiding hysterics, although he had received reports of doctors on board who handed out Valium like candy.

Rayford had been forthright, the only way he knew to be. He realized he had told the people more than he might have if he'd lost an engine or his hydraulics or even his landing gear. He had been frank with them that those who had not had loved ones disappear might get home to discover that they had been victims of the many tragedies that had ensued.

He thought, but didn't say, how grateful he was to have been in the air when this event had taken place. What confusion must await them on the ground! Here, in a literal sense, they were above it all. They had been affected, of course. People were missing from everywhere. But except for the staff shortage caused by the disappearance of three crew members, the passengers didn't suffer the way they might have had they been in traffic or if he and Christopher had been among those who had disappeared.

As he settled into a holding pattern miles from O'Hare, the full impact of the tragedy began to come into view. Flights from all over the country were being rerouted to Chicago. Planes were reorganized based on their fuel supplies. Rayford needed to stay in priority position after flying across the eastern seaboard and then over the Atlantic before turning back. It was not Rayford's practice to communicate with ground control until after he landed, but now the air-traffic control tower was recommending it. He was informed that visibility was excellent, despite intermittent smoke from wreckages on the ground, but that landing would be risky and precarious because the two open runways were crowded with jets. They lined either side, all the way down the runway. Every gate was full, and none were backing out. Every mode of human transport was in use, busing passengers from the ends of the runways back to the terminal.

But, Rayford was told, he would likely find that his people—at least most of them—would have to walk all the way. All remaining personnel had been called in to serve, but they were busy directing planes to safe areas. The few buses and vans were reserved for the handicapped, elderly, and flight crews. Rayford passed the word along that his crew would be walking.

Passengers reported that they had been unable to get through on the in-flight phones. Hattie Durham told Rayford that one enterprising passenger in first class had somehow hooked up the phone to his computer, and while he composed messages it was automatically dialing and redialing New York. If a line opened, this would be the guy who got through.

———

By the time the plane began its descent into Chicago, Buck had been able to squeeze onto only one briefly freed-up line to his computer service, which prompted him to download his waiting mail. This came just as Hattie announced that all electronic devices must be turned off.

With an acumen he didn't realize he possessed, Buck speed-tapped the keys that retrieved and filed all his messages, downloaded them, and backed him out of the linkup in seconds. Just when his machine might have interfered with flight communications, he was off-line and would have to wait to search his files for news from friends, coworkers, relatives, anyone.

Before her last-minute preparations for landing, Hattie hurried to Buck. "Anything?" He shook his head apologetically. "Thanks for trying," she said. And she began to weep.

He reached for her wrist. "Hattie, we're all going to go home and cry today. But hang in there. Get your passengers off the plane, and you can at least feel good about that."

"Mr. Williams," she sobbed, "you know we lost several old people, but not all of them. And we lost several middle-aged people, but not all of them. And we lost several people your age and my age, but not all of them. We even lost some teenagers."

He stared at her. What was she driving at?

"Sir, we lost every child and baby on this plane."

"How many were there?"

"More than a dozen. But all of them! Not one was left."

The man next to Buck roused and squinted at the late-morning sun burning through the window. "What in blazes are you two talking about?" he said.

"We're about to land in Chicago," Hattie said. "I've got to run."

"Chicago?"

"You don't want to know," Buck said.

The man nearly sat in Buck's lap to get a look out the window, his boozy breath enveloping Buck. "What, are we at war? Riots? What?"

Having just cut through the cloud bank, the plane allowed passengers a view of the Chicago area. Smoke. Fire. Cars off the road and smashed into each other and guardrails. Planes in pieces on the ground. Emergency vehicles, lights flashing, picking their way around the debris.

As O'Hare came into view, it was clear no one was going anywhere soon. There were planes as far as the eye could see, some crashed and burning, the others gridlocked in line. People trudged through the grass and between vehicles toward the terminal. The expressways that led to the airport looked like they had during the great Chicago blizzards, only without the snow.

Cranes and wreckers were trying to clear a path through the front of the terminal so cars could get in and out, but that would take hours, if not days. A snake of humanity wended its way slowly out of the great terminal buildings, between the motionless cars, and onto the ramps. People walking, walking, walking, looking for a cab or a limo. Buck began plotting how he would beat the new system. Somehow, he had to get moving and get out of such a congested area. The problem was, his goal was to get to a worse one: New York.

"Ladies and gentlemen," Rayford announced, "I want to thank you again for your cooperation today. We've been asked to put down on the only runway that will take this size plane and then to taxi to an open area about two miles from the terminal. I'm afraid I'm going to have to ask you to use our inflatable emergency chutes, because we will not be able to hook up to any gateways. If you are unable to walk to the terminal, please stay with the plane, and we will send someone back for you."

There was no thanking them for choosing Pan-Continental, no "We hope you'll make us your choice next time you need air service." He did remind them to stay seated with their belts fastened until he turned off the seat belt sign, because privately he knew this would be his most difficult landing in years. He knew he could do it, but it had been a long time since he had had to land a plane among other aircraft.

Rayford envied whoever it was in first class who had the inside track on communicating by modem. He was desperate to call Irene, Chloe, and Ray Jr. On the other hand, he feared he might never talk to them again.

THREE

HATTIE Durham and what was left of her cabin crew encouraged passengers to study the safety cards in their seat pockets. Many feared they would be unable to jump and slide down the chutes, especially with their carry-on luggage. They were instructed to remove their shoes and to jump seatfirst onto the chute. Then crew members would toss them their shoes and bags. They were advised not to wait in the terminal for their checked baggage. That, they were promised, would eventually be delivered to their homes. No guarantees when.

Buck Williams gave Hattie his card and got her phone number, "just in case I get through to your people before you do."

"You're with *Global Weekly?*" she said. "I had no idea."

"And you were going to send me to my room for tampering with the phone."

She appeared to be trying to smile. "Sorry," Buck said, "not funny. I'll let you go."

Always a light traveler, Buck was grateful he had checked no baggage. Never did, not even on international flights. When he opened the bin to pull down his leather bag, he found the old man's hat and jacket still perched atop it. Harold's wife sat staring at Buck, her eyes full, jaw set. "Ma'am," he said quietly, "would you want these?"

The grieving woman gratefully gathered in the hat and coat, and crushed them against her chest as if she would never let them go. She said something Buck couldn't hear. He asked her to repeat it. "I can't jump out of any airplane," she said.

"Stay right here," he said. "They'll send someone for you."

"But will I still have to jump and slide down that thing?"

"No, ma'am. I'm sure they'll have a lift of some sort."

Buck carefully laid his laptop and case in among his clothes. With his bag zipped, he hurried to the front of the line, eager to show others how easy it was. He tossed his shoes down first, watching them bounce and skitter onto the runway. Then he clutched his bag across his chest, took a quick step and threw his feet out in front of him.

A bit enthusiastic, he landed not on his seat but on his shoulders, which threw his feet over the top of his head. He picked up speed and hit the bottom with his weight shifting forward. The buggy-whip centripetal force slammed his stockinged feet to the ground and brought his torso up and over in a somersault that barely missed planting his face on the concrete. At the last instant, still hanging on to his bag for dear life, he tucked his head under and took the abrasion on the back of his head rather than on his nose. He fought the urge to say, "No problem," but he couldn't keep from rubbing the back of his head, already matted with blood. It wasn't a serious problem, only a nuisance. He quickly retrieved his shoes and began jogging toward the terminal, as much from embarrassment as need. He knew there would be no more hurrying once he hit the terminal.

———————

Rayford, Christopher, and Hattie were the last three off the 747. Before disembarking, they had made sure all able-bodied people got down the chutes and that the elderly and infirm were transported by bus. The bus driver insisted that the crew ride with him and the last passengers, but Rayford refused. "I can't see passing my own passengers as they walk to the terminal," he said. "How would that look?"

Christopher said, "Suit yourself, Cap. You mind if I take him up on his offer?"

Rayford glared at him. "You're serious?"

"I don't get paid enough for this."

"Like this was the airline's fault. Chris, you don't mean it."

"The heck I don't. By the time you get up there, you'll wish you'd ridden, too."

"I should write you up for this."

"Millions of people disappear into thin air and I should worry about getting written up for riding instead of walking? Later, Steele."

Rayford shook his head and turned to Hattie. "Maybe I'll see you up there. If you can get out of the terminal, don't wait for me."

"Are you kidding? If you're walking, I'm walking."

"You don't need to do that."

"After that dressing-down you just gave Smith? I'm walking."

"He's first officer. We ought to be last off the ship and first to volunteer for emergency duty."

"Well, do me a favor and consider me part of your crew, too. Just because I can't fly the thing doesn't mean I don't feel some ownership. And don't treat me like a little woman."

"I would never do that. Got your stuff?"

Hattie pulled her bag on wheels and Rayford carried his navigator's leather box. It was a long walk, and several times they waved off offers of rides from units speeding out to pick up the nonambulatory. Along the way they passed other passengers from their flight. Many thanked Rayford; he wasn't sure for what. For not panicking, he guessed. But they looked as terrified and shell-shocked as he felt.

They shielded their ears from flights screaming in to land. Rayford tried to calculate how long it would be before this runway was shut down, too. He couldn't imagine the other open strip holding many more planes, either. Would some have to try to put down on highways or open fields? And how far away from the big cities would they have to look for open stretches of highway unencumbered by bridges? He shuddered at the thought.

All around were ambulances and other emergency vehicles trying to get to ugly wreckage scenes.

Finally in the terminal, Rayford found crowds standing in lines behind banks of phones. Most had angry people waiting, yelling at callers who shrugged and redialed. Airport snack bars and restaurants were already sold out of or low on food, and all newspapers and magazines were gone. In shops where staffers had disappeared, looters walked off with merchandise.

Rayford wanted more than anything to sit and talk with someone about what to make of this. But everybody he saw—friend, acquaintance, or stranger—was busy trying to make arrangements. O'Hare was like a massive prison with resources dwindling and gridlock growing. No one slept. Everyone scurried about, trying to find some link to the outside world, to contact their families, and to get out of the airport.

At the flight center in the bowels of the place, Rayford found much the same thing. Hattie said she would try making her calls from the lounge and would meet him later to see if they could share a ride to the suburbs. He knew they were unlikely to find any rides going anywhere, and he didn't relish walking twenty miles. But all hotels in the area were already full.

Finally a supervisor asked for the attention of the fliers in the underground center. "We have some secure lines, about five," he said. "Whether you can get through, we don't know, but it's your best chance. They do bypass the normal trunk lines out of here, so you won't be competing with all the pay phones in the terminal. Streamline your calls. Also, there are a limited number of helicopter rides available to suburban hospitals and police departments, but naturally you're secondary to medical emergencies. Get in line over here for phones and rides to the suburbs. As of right now we have no word of the cancellation of any flights except for the remainder of today. It's your responsibility to be back here for your next flight or to call in and find out its status."

Rayford got in line, beginning to feel the tension of having flown too long and known too little. Worse was the knowledge that he had a better idea than most of what had happened. If he was right, if it were true, he would not be getting an answer when he dialed home. As he stood there, a TV monitor above him broadcast images of the chaos. From around the globe came wailing mothers, stoic families, reports of death and destruction. Dozens of stories included eyewitnesses who had seen loved ones and friends disappear before their eyes.

Most shocking to Rayford was a woman in labor, about to go into the delivery room, who was suddenly barren. Doctors delivered the placenta. Her husband had caught the disappearance of the fetus on tape. As he videotaped her great belly and sweaty face, he asked questions. How did she feel? "How do you think I feel, Earl? Turn that thing off." What was she hoping for? "That you'll get close enough for me to slug you." Did she realize that in a few moments they'd be parents? "In about a minute, you're going to be divorced."

Then came the scream and the dropping of the camera, terrified voices, running nurses, and the doctor. CNN reran the footage in superslow motion, showing the woman going from very pregnant to nearly flat stomached, as if she had instantaneously delivered. "Now, watch with us again," the newsman intoned, "and keep your eyes on the left edge of your screen, where a nurse appears to be reading a printout from the fetal heart monitor. There, see?" The action stopped as the pregnant woman's stomach deflated. "The nurse's uniform seems to still be standing as if an invisible person is wearing it. She's gone. Half a second later, watch." The tape moved ahead and stopped. "The uniform, stockings and all, are in a pile atop her shoes."

Local television stations from around the world reported bizarre occurrences, especially in time zones where the event had happened during the day or early evening. CNN showed via satellite the video of a groom disappearing while slipping the ring onto his bride's finger. A funeral home in Australia reported that nearly every mourner disappeared from one memorial service, including the corpse, while at another service at the same time, only a few disappeared and the corpse remained. Morgues also reported corpse disappearances. At a burial, three of six pallbearers stumbled and dropped a casket when the other three disappeared. When they picked up the casket, it too was empty.

Rayford was second in line for the phone, but what he saw next on the screen convinced him he would never see his wife again. At a Christian high school soccer game at a missionary headquarters in Indonesia, most of the spectators and all but one of the players disappeared in the middle of play, leaving their shoes and uniforms on the ground. The CNN reporter announced that, in his remorse, the surviving player took his own life.

But it was more than remorse, Rayford knew. Of all people, that player, a student at a Christian school, would have known the truth immediately. The Rapture had taken place. Jesus Christ had returned for his people, and that boy was not one of them. When Rayford sat at the phone, tears streamed down his face. Someone said, "You have four minutes," and he knew that would be more than he needed. His answering machine at home picked up immediately, and he was pierced to hear the cheerful voice of his wife. "Your call is important to us," she said. "Please leave a message after the beep."

Rayford punched a few buttons to check for messages. He ran through three or four mundane ones, then was startled to hear Chloe's voice. "Mom? Dad? Are you there? Have you seen what's going on? Call me as soon as you can. We've lost at least ten students and two profs, and all the married students' kids disappeared. Is

48

Raymie all right? Call me!" Well, at least he knew Chloe was still around. All he wanted was to hold her.

Rayford redialed and left a message on his own machine. "Irene? Ray? If you're there, pick up. If you get this message, I'm at O'Hare and trying to get home. It may take a while if I don't get a copter ride. I sure hope you're there."

"Let's go, Cap," someone said. "Everybody's got a call to make."

Rayford nodded and quickly dialed his daughter's dorm room at Stanford. He got the irritating message that his call could not be completed as dialed.

Rayford gathered his belongings and checked his mail slot. Besides a pile of the usual junk, he found a padded manila envelope from his home address. Irene had taken to mailing him little surprises lately, the result of a marriage book she had been urging him to read. He slipped the envelope into his case and went looking for Hattie Durham. Funny, he had no emotional attraction whatever to Hattie just now. But he felt obligated to be sure she got home.

As he stood in a crowd by the elevator, he heard the announcement that a helicopter was available for no more than eight pilots and would make a run to Mount Prospect, Arlington Heights, and Des Plaines. Rayford hurried to the pad. "Got room for one to Mount Prospect?"

"Yup."

"How about another to Des Plaines?"

"Maybe, if he gets here in about two minutes."

"It's not a he. She's a flight attendant."

"Pilots only. Sorry."

"What if you have room?"

"Well, maybe, but I don't see her."

"I'll have her paged."

"They're not paging anyone."

"Give me a second. Don't leave without me."

The chopper pilot looked at his watch. "Three minutes," he said. "I'm leavin' at one."

Rayford left his bag on the ground, hoping it would hold the helicopter pilot in case he was a little late. He charged up the stairs and into the corridor. Finding Hattie would be impossible. He grabbed a courtesy phone. "I'm sorry, we're unable to page anyone just now."

"This is an emergency and I am a Pan-Continental captain."

"What is it?"

"Have Hattie Durham meet her party at K-17."

"I'll try."

"Do it!"

Rayford stood on tiptoe to see Hattie coming, yet still somehow she surprised him. "I was fourth in line for the phone in the lounge," she said, appearing at his side. "Got a better deal?"

"Got us a helicopter ride if we hurry," he said.

As they skipped down the stairs she said, "Wasn't it awful about Chris?"

"What about him?"

"You really don't know?"

Rayford wanted to stop and tell her to quit making

him work so hard. That frustrated him about people her age. They enjoyed a volleying conversation game. He liked to get to the point. "Just tell me!" he said, sounding more exasperated than he intended.

As they burst through the door and onto the tarmac, the chopper blades whipped their hair and deafened them. Rayford's bag had already been put on board, and only one seat remained. The pilot pointed at Hattie and shook his head. Rayford grabbed her elbow and pulled her aboard as he climbed in. "Only way she's not coming is if you can't handle the weight!"

"What do you weigh, doll?" the pilot said.

"One-fifteen!"

"I can handle the weight!" he told Rayford. "But if she's not buckled in, I'm not responsible!"

"Let's go!" Rayford shouted.

He buckled himself in and Hattie sat in his lap. He wrapped his arms around her waist and clasped his wrists together. He thought how ironic it was that he had been dreaming of this for weeks, and now there was no joy, no excitement in it, nothing sensual whatever. He was miserable. Glad to be able to help her out, but miserable.

Hattie looked embarrassed and uncomfortable, and Rayford noticed she took a sheepish peek at the other seven pilots in the copter. None seemed to return her gaze. This disaster was still too fresh and there were too many unknowns. Rayford thought he heard or lip-read one of them saying, "Christopher Smith," but there was no way he could hear inside the raucous craft. He put his mouth next to Hattie's ear.

"Now what about Chris?" he said.

She turned and spoke into his ear. "They wheeled him past us while I was going into the lounge. Blood all over!"

"What happened?"

"I don't know, but, Rayford, he didn't look good!"

"How bad?"

"I think he was dead! I mean, they were working on him, but I'd be surprised if he made it."

Rayford shook his head. What next? "Did he get hit or something? Did that bus crash?" Wouldn't that be ironic!

"I don't know," she said. "The blood seemed like it was coming from his hand or his waist or both."

Rayford tapped the pilot on the shoulder. "Do you know anything about First Officer Christopher Smith?"

"He with Pan-Con?" the pilot said.

"Yes!"

"Was he the suicide?"

Rayford recoiled. "I don't think so! Was there a suicide?"

"Lots of 'em, I guess, but mostly passengers. Only crew member I heard about was a Smith from Pan. Slit his wrists."

Rayford quickly scanned the others in the chopper to see if he recognized anyone. He didn't, but one was nodding sadly, having overheard the pilot's shouting. He leaned forward. "Chris Smith! You know him?"

"My first officer!"

"Sorry."

"What'd you hear?"

"Don't know how reliable this is, but the rumor is he found out his boys had disappeared and his wife was killed in a wreck!"

For the first time the enormity of the situation became personal for Rayford. He didn't know Smith well. He vaguely remembered Chris had two sons. Seemed they were young teenagers, very close in age. He had never met the wife. But suicide! Was that an option for Rayford? No, not with Chloe still there. But what if he had discovered that Irene and young Ray were gone and Chloe had been killed? What would he have to live for?

He hadn't been living for them anyway, certainly not the last several months. He had been playing around on the edges of his mind with the girl in his lap, though he had never gone so far as touching her, even when she often touched him. Would he want to live if Hattie Durham were the only person he cared about? And why did he care about her? She was beautiful and sexy and smart, but only for her age. They had little in common. Was it only because he was convinced Irene was gone that he now longed to hold his own wife?

There was no affection in his embrace of Hattie Durham just now, nor in hers. Both were scared to death, and flirting was the last thing on their minds. The irony was not lost on him. He recalled that the last thing he daydreamed about—before Hattie's announcement—was finally making a move on her. How could he have known she would be in his lap hours later and that he would have no more interest in her than in a stranger?

The first stop was the Des Plaines Police Department, where Hattie disembarked. Rayford advised her to ask for a ride home with the police if a squad car was available. Most had been pressed into service in more congested areas, so that was unlikely. "I'm only about a mile from here anyway!" Hattie shouted above the roar as Rayford helped her from the chopper. "I can walk!" She wrapped her arms around his neck in a fierce embrace, and he felt her quiver in fear. "I hope everyone's OK at your place!" she said. "Call me and let me know, OK?"

He nodded.

"OK?" she insisted.

"OK!"

As they lifted off he watched her survey the parking lot. Spotting no squad cars, she turned and hurried off, pulling her suitcase on wheels. By the time the helicopter began to swing toward Mount Prospect, Hattie was trotting toward her condominium.

Buck Williams had been the first passenger from his flight to reach the terminal at O'Hare. He found a mess. No one waiting in line for a phone would put up with his trying to plug his modem into it, and he couldn't get his cellular phone to work, so he made his way to the exclusive Pan-Con Club. It, too, was jammed, but despite a loss of personnel, including the disappearance of several employees while on the job, some semblance of order prevailed. Even here people waited in line for the phones, but as each became available, it was understood that some might try faxing or connecting directly by modem. While Buck waited, he went to work again on his computer, reattaching the inside modem cord to the female connector. Then he called up the messages that he had quickly downloaded before landing.

The first was from Steve Plank, his executive editor, addressed to all field personnel:

> Stay put. Do not try to come to New York. Impossible here. Call when you can. Check your voice mail and your E-mail regularly. Keep in touch as possible. We have enough staff to remain on schedule, and we want personal accounts, on-the-scene stuff, as much as you can transmit. Not sure of transportation and communications lines between us and our printers, nor their employee levels. If possible, we'll print on time.
>
> Just a note: Begin thinking about the causes. Military? Cosmic? Scientific? Spiritual? But so far we're dealing mainly with what happened.
>
> Take care, and keep in touch.

The second message was also from Steve and was for Buck's eyes only.

> Buck, ignore general staff memo. Get to New York as soon as you can at any expense. Take care of

family matters, of course, and file any personal experience or reflections, just like everyone else. But you're going to head up this effort to get at what's behind the phenomenon. Ideas are like egos—everybody's got one.

Whether we'll come to any conclusions, I don't know, but at the very least we'll catalog the reasonable possibilities. You may wonder why we need you here to do this; I do have an ulterior motive. Sometimes I think because of the position I'm in, I'm the only one who knows these things; but three different department editors have turned in story ideas on various international groups meeting in New York this month. Political editor wants to cover a Jewish Nationalist conference in Manhattan that has something to do with a new world order government. What they care about that, I don't know and the political editor doesn't either. Religion editor has something in my in box about a conference of Orthodox Jews also coming for a meeting. These are not just from Israel but apparently all over, and they are no longer haggling over the Dead Sea Scrolls. They're still giddy over the destruction of Russia and her allies—which I know you still think was supernatural, but hey, I love you anyway. Religion editor thinks they're looking for help in rebuilding the temple. That may be no big deal or have anything to do with anything other than the religion department, but I was struck by the timing—with the other Jewish group meeting at pretty much the same time and at the same place about something entirely political. The other religious conference in town is among leaders of all the major religions, from the standard ones to the New Agers, also talking about a one-world religious order. They ought to get together with the Jewish Nationalists, huh? Need your brain on this. Don't know what to make of it, if anything.

I know all anybody cares about is the disappearances. But we need to keep an eye on the rest of the world. You know the United Nations has that international monetarist confab coming up, trying to gauge how we're all doing with the three-currency thing. Personally I like it, but I'm a little skittish about going to one currency unless it's dollars. Can you imagine trading in yen or marks here? Guess I'm still provincial.

Everybody's pretty enamored with this Carpathia guy from Romania who so impressed your friend Rosenzweig. He's got everybody in a bind in the upper house in his own country because he's been invited to speak at the U.N. in a couple of weeks. Nobody knows how he wangled an invitation, but his international popularity reminds me a lot of Walesa or even Gorbachev. Remember them? Ha!

Hey, friend, get word to me you didn't disappear. As far as I know right now, I lost a niece and two nephews, a sister-in-law I didn't like, and possibly a couple of other distant relatives. You think they'll be back? Well, save that till we get rolling on what's behind this. If I had to guess, I'm anticipating some God-awful ransom demand. I mean, it's not like these people who disappeared are dead. What in the world is going to happen to the life insurance industry? I'm not ready to start believing the tabloids. You just know they're going to be saying the space aliens finally got us.

Get in here, Buck.

FOUR

BUCK kept pressing a handkerchief soaked with cold water onto the back of his head. His wound had stopped bleeding, but it stung. He found another message in his E-mail in box and was about to call it up when he was tapped on the shoulder.

"I'm a doctor. Let me dress your wound."

"Oh, it's all right, and I—"

"Just let me do this, pal. I'm going crazy here with nothing to do, and I have my bag. I'm workin' free today. Call it a Rapture Special."

"A what?"

"Well, what would you call what happened?" the doctor said, removing a bottle and gauze from his bag. "This is gonna be pretty rudimentary, but we will be sterile. AIDS?"

"I'm sorry?"

"C'mon, you know the routine." He snapped on rubber gloves. "Have you got HIV or anything fun like that?"

"No. And, hey, I appreciate this." At that instant the doctor splashed a heavy dose of disinfectant on the gauze and held it against Buck's scraped head. "Yow! Take it easy!"

"Be a big boy there, stud. This'll hurt less than the infection you'd get otherwise." He roughly scraped the wound, cleansing it and causing it to ooze blood again. "Listen, I'm going to do a little shave job so I can get a bandage to hold. All right with you?"

Buck's eyes were watering. "Yeah, sure, but what was that you said about rapture?"

"Is there any other explanation that makes sense?" the doctor said, using a scalpel to tear into Buck's hair. A club attendant came by and asked if they could move the operation into one of the washrooms.

"I promise to clean up, hon," the doctor said. "Almost done here."

"Well, this can't be sanitary, and we do have other members to think about."

"Why don't you just give them their drinks and nuts, all right? You'll find this just isn't going to upset them that much on a day like this."

"I don't appreciate being spoken to that way."

The doctor sighed as he worked. "You're right. What's your name?"

"Suzie."

"Listen, Suzie, I've been rude and I apologize. OK?

Now let me finish this, and I promise not to perform any more surgery right out here in public." Suzie left, shaking her head.

"Doc," Buck said, "leave me your card so I can properly thank you."

"No need," the doctor said, putting his stuff away.

"Now give me your take on this. What did you mean about the Rapture?"

"Another time. Your turn for the phone."

Buck was torn, but he couldn't pass up the chance to communicate with New York. He tried dialing direct but couldn't get through. He hooked his modem up to the phone and initiated repeat dialing while he looked at the message from Steve Plank's secretary, the matronly Marge Potter.

> Buck, you scoundrel! Like I don't have enough to do and worry about today, I've got to check on your girlfriends' families? Where'd you meet this Hattie Durham? You can tell her I reached her mother out west, but that was before a flood or storm or something knocked phone lines out again. She's perfectly healthy but rattled, and she was very grateful to know her daughter hadn't disappeared. The two sisters are OK, too, according to Mom.
>
> You are a dear for helping people like this, Buck. Steve says you're going to try to come in. It'll be good to see you. This is so awful. So far we know of several staffers who disappeared, several more we haven't heard from, including some in Chicago.

Everybody from the senior staff is accounted for, now that we've heard from you. I hoped and prayed you'd be all right. Have you noticed it seems to have struck the innocents? Everyone we know who's gone is either a child or a very nice person. On the other hand, some truly wonderful people are still here. I'm glad you're one of them, and so is Steve. Call us.

No word whether she had been able to reach Buck's widowed father or married brother. Buck wondered if that was on purpose or if she simply had no news yet. His niece and nephew had to be gone if it was true that no children had survived. Buck gave up trying to reach the office directly but again successfully connected with his on-line service. He uploaded his files and a few hastily batted out messages of his whereabouts. That way, by the time the telephone system once again took on some semblance of normalcy, *Global Weekly* would have already gotten a head start on his stuff.

He hung up and disconnected to the grateful look of the next in line, then went looking for that doctor. No luck. Marge had referred to the innocents. The doctor assumed it was the Rapture. Steve had pooh-poohed space aliens. But how could you rule out anything at this point? His mind was already whirring with ideas for the story behind the disappearances. Talk about the assignment of a lifetime!

Buck got in line at the service desk, knowing his odds of getting to New York by conventional means were slim. While he waited he tried to remember what it was Chaim Rosenzweig, the Newsmaker of the Year, had told him about the young Nicolae Carpathia of Romania. Buck had told only Steve Plank about it, and Steve agreed it wasn't worth putting in the already tight story. Rosenzweig had been impressed with Carpathia, that was true. But why?

Buck sat on the floor in line and moved when he had to. He called up his archived files on the Rosenzweig interview and did a word search on Carpathia. He recalled having been embarrassed to admit to Rosenzweig that he had never heard of the man. As the taped interview transcripts scrolled past, he hit the pause button and read. When he noticed his low battery light flashing, he fished an extension cord out of his bag and plugged the computer into a socket along the wall. "Watch the cord," he called out occasionally as people passed. One of the women behind the counter hollered at him that he'd have to unplug.

He smiled at her. "And if I don't, are you going to have me thrown out? Arrested? Cut me some slack today, of all days!" Hardly anyone took note of the crazy man on the floor yelling at the counter woman. Such rarely happened in the Pan-Con Club, but nothing surprised anyone today.

Rayford Steele disembarked on the helipad at Northwest Community Hospital in Arlington Heights, where the pilots had to get off and make room so a patient could be flown to Milwaukee. The other pilots hung around the entrance, hoping to share a cab, but Rayford had a better idea. He began walking.

He was about five miles from home, and he was betting he could hitch a ride easier than finding a cab. He hoped his captain's uniform and his clean-cut appearance would set someone's mind at ease about giving him a ride.

As he trudged along, his trenchcoat over his arm and his bag in his hand, he had an empty, despairing feeling. By now Hattie would be getting to her condo, checking her messages, trying to get calls through to her family. If he was right that Irene and Ray Jr. were gone, where would they have been when it happened? Would he find evidence that they had disappeared rather than being killed in some related accident?

Rayford calculated that the disappearances would have taken place late evening, perhaps around 11 P.M. central time. Would anything have taken them away from home at that hour? He couldn't imagine what, and he doubted it.

A woman of about forty stopped for Rayford on Algonquin Road. When he thanked her and told her where he lived, she said she knew the area. "A friend of mine lives there. Well, lived there. Li Ng, the Asian girl on Channel 7 news?"

"I know her and her husband," Rayford said. "They still live on our street."

"Not anymore. They dedicated the noon newscast to her today. The whole family is gone."

Rayford exhaled loudly. "This is unbelievable. Have you lost people?"

"'Fraid so," she said, her voice quavery. "About a dozen nieces and nephews."

"Wow."

"You?"

"I don't know yet. I'm just getting back from a flight, and I haven't been able to reach anybody."

"Do you want me to wait for you?"

"No. I have a car. If I need to go anywhere, I'll be all right."

"O'Hare's closed, you know," she said.

"Really? Since when?"

"They just announced it on the radio. Runways are full of planes, terminals full of people, roads full of cars."

"Tell me about it."

As the woman drove, sniffling, into Mount Prospect, Rayford felt fatigue he had never endured before. Every few houses had driveways jammed with cars, people milling about. It appeared everyone everywhere had lost someone. He knew he would soon be counted among them.

"Can I offer you anything?" he asked the woman as she pulled into his driveway.

She shook her head. "I'm just glad to have been able to help. You could pray for me, if you think of it. I don't know if I can endure this."

"I'm not much for praying," Rayford admitted.

"You will be," she said. "I never was before either, but I am now."

"Then you can pray for me," he said.

"I will. Count on it."

Rayford stood in the driveway and waved to the woman till she was out of sight. The yard and the walk were spotless as usual, and the huge home, his trophy house, was sepulchral. He unlocked the front door. From the newspaper on the stoop to the closed drapes in the picture window to the bitter smell of burned coffee when he opened the door, everything pointed to what he dreaded.

Irene was a fastidious housekeeper. Her morning routine included the coffeepot on a timer kicking on at six, percolating her special blend of decaf with an egg. The radio was set to come on at 6:30, tuned to the local Christian station. The first thing Irene did when she came downstairs was open the drapes at the front and back of the house.

With a lump in his throat Rayford tossed the newspaper into the kitchen and took his time hanging up his coat and sliding his bag into the closet. He remembered the package Irene had mailed him at O'Hare and put it in his wide uniform pocket. He would carry it with him as he searched for evidence that she had disappeared. If she was gone, he sure hoped she had been right. He wanted above all else for her to have seen her dream realized, for her to have been taken away by Jesus in the twinkling of an eye—a thrilling, painless journey to his side in heaven, as she always loved to say. She deserved that if anybody did.

And Raymie. Where would he be? With her? Of

course. He went with her to church, even when Rayford didn't go. He seemed to like it, to get into it. He even read his Bible and studied it.

Rayford unplugged the coffeepot that had been turning itself off and then back on for seven hours and had ruined the brew. He dumped the mess and left the pot in the sink. He flicked off the radio, which was piping the Christian station's network news hookup into the air, droning on about the tragedy and mayhem that had resulted from the disappearances.

He looked about the living room, dining room, and kitchen, expecting to see nothing but the usual neatness of Irene's home. His eyes filling with tears, he opened the drapes as she would have. Was it possible she had gone somewhere? Visited someone? Left him a message? But if she had and he did find her, what would that say about her own faith? Would it prove this was not the Rapture she believed in? Or would it mean she was lost, just like he was? For her sake, if this was the Rapture, he hoped she *was* gone. But the ache and the emptiness were already overwhelming.

He switched on the answering machine and heard all the same messages he had heard when he had gotten through from O'Hare, plus the message he had left. His own voice sounded strange to him. He detected in it a fatalism, as if he knew he was not leaving a message for his wife and son, but only pretending to.

He dreaded going upstairs. He moseyed through the family room to the garage exit. If only one of the cars was missing. And one was! Maybe she had gone somewhere! But as soon as he thought of it, Rayford slumped onto the step just inside the garage. It was his own BMW that was gone. The one he had driven to O'Hare the day before. It would be waiting for him when the traffic cleared.

The other two cars were there, Irene's and the one Chloe used when she was home. And all those memories of Raymie were there, too. His four-wheeler, his snow-mobile, his bike. Rayford hated himself for his broken promises to spend more time with Raymie. He'd have plenty of time to regret that.

Rayford stood and heard the rattle of the envelope in his pocket. It was time to go upstairs.

It was nearly Buck Williams's turn at the head of the line at the Pan-Con Club counter when he found the material he had been looking for on disk. At some point during their several days of taping, Buck had raised the issue of every other country trying to curry favor with Dr. Rosenzweig and hoping to gain access to his formula for its own gain.

"This has been an interesting aspect," Rosenzweig had allowed, his eyes twinkling. "I was most amused by a visit from the vice president of the United States himself. He wanted to honor me, to bring me to the president, to have a parade, to confer a degree, all that. He diplomatically said nothing about my owing him anything in return, but I would owe him everything, would I not? Much was said about what a friend of

Israel the United States has been over the decades. And this has been true, no? How could I argue?

"But I pretended to see the awards and kindnesses as all for my own benefit, and I humbly turned them down. Because you see, young man, I am most humble, am I not?" The old man had laughed uproariously at himself and relayed several other stories of visiting dignitaries who worked at charming him.

"Was anyone sincere?" Buck had asked. "Did anyone impress you?"

"Yes!" Rosenzweig had said without hesitation. "From the most perplexing and surprising corner of the world—Romania. I do not know if he was sent or came on his own, but I suspect the latter because I believe he is the lowest-ranking official I entertained following the award. That is one of the reasons I wanted to see him. He asked for the audience himself. He did not go through typical political and protocol channels."

"And he was . . . ?"

"Nicolae Carpathia."

"Carpathia like the—?"

"Yes, like the Carpathian Mountains. A melodic name, you must admit. I found him most charming and humble. Not unlike myself!" Again he had laughed.

"I've not heard of him."

"You will! You will."

Buck had tried to lead the old man. "Because he's . . ."

"Impressive, that's all I can say."

"And he's some sort of a low-level diplomat at this point?"

"He is a member of the lower house of Romanian government."

"In the senate?"

"No, the senate is the upper house."

"Of course."

"Don't feel bad that you don't know, even though you are an international journalist. This is something only Romanians and amateur political scientists like me know. That is something I like to study."

"In your spare time."

"Precisely. But even I had not known of this man. I mean, I knew someone in the House of Deputies—that's what they call the lower house in Romania—was a peacemaker and leading a movement toward disarmament. But I did not know his name. I believe his goal is global disarmament, which we Israelis have come to distrust. But of course he must first bring about disarmament in his own country, which not even you will see in your lifetime. This man is about your age, by the way. Blonde and blue eyed, like the original Romanians, who came from Rome, before the Mongols affected their race."

"What did you like so much about him?"

"Let me count," Rosenzweig had said. "He knew my language as well as his own. And he speaks fluent English. Several others also, they tell me. Well educated but also widely self-taught. And I just like him as a person. Very bright. Very honest. Very open."

"What did he want from you?"

"That was what I liked the best. Because I found him

so open and honest, I asked him outright that question.
He insisted I call him Nicolae, and so I said, 'Nicolae'
(this is after an hour of pleasantries), 'what do you want
from me?' Do you know what he said, young man? He
said, 'Dr. Rosenzweig, I seek only your goodwill.' What
could I say? I said, 'Nicolae, you have it.' I am a bit of a
pacifist myself, you know. Not unrealistically. I did not
tell him this. I merely told him he had my goodwill.
Which is something you also have."

"I suspect that is not something you bestow easily."

"That is why I like you and why you have it. One day
you must meet Carpathia. You would like each other.
His goals and dreams may never be realized even in his
own country, but he is a man of high ideals. If he should
emerge, you will hear of him. And as you are emerging in
your own orbit, he will likely hear of you, or from you,
am I right?"

"I hope you are."

Suddenly it was Buck's turn at the counter. He gathered up his extension cord and thanked the young
woman for bearing with him. "Sorry about that,"
he said, pausing briefly for forgiveness that was not
forthcoming. "It's just that today, of all days, well, you
understand."

Apparently she did not understand. She'd had a rough
day, too. She looked at him tolerantly and said, "What
can I not do for you?"

"Oh, you mean because I did not do something you
asked?"

"No," she said. "I'm saying that to everybody. It's my little joke because there's really nothing I can do for anybody. No flights are scheduled today. The airport is going to close any minute. Who knows how long it will take to clear all the wreckage and get any kind of traffic moving again? I mean, I'll take your request and everything, but I can't get your luggage, book you a flight, get you a phone, book you a hotel room, anything we love to do for our members. You are a member, aren't you?"

"Am I a member!"

"Gold or platinum?"

"Lady, I'm, like, a kryptonite member."

He flashed his card, showing that he was among the top 3 percent of air travelers in the world. If any flight had one seat in the cheapest section, it had to be given to him and upgraded to first class at no charge.

"Oh, my gosh," she said, "tell me you're not the Cameron Williams from that magazine."

"I am."

"*Time?* Honest?"

"Don't blaspheme. I'm from the competition."

"Oh, I knew that. The reason I know is that I wanted to get into journalism. I studied it in college. I just read about you, didn't I? Youngest award winner or most cover stories by someone under twelve?"

"Funny."

"Or something."

"I can't believe we're joking on a day like this," he said.

She suddenly clouded over. "I don't even want to

think about it. So what could I do for you if I could do anything?"

"Here's the thing," Buck said. "I have to get to New York. Now don't give me that look. I know it's the worst place to try to get to right now. But you know people. You know pilots who fly on the side, charter stuff. You know what airports they would fly out of. Let's say I had unlimited resources and could pay whatever I needed to. Who would you send me to?"

She stared at him. "I can't believe you asked me that."

"Why?"

"Because I do know someone. He flies these little jets out of like Waukegan and Palwaukee airports. He's expensive and he's the type who would charge double during a crisis, especially if he knew who you were and how desperate."

"There won't be any hiding that. Give me the info."

———

Hearing it on the radio or seeing it on television was one thing. Encountering it for yourself was something else again. Rayford Steele had no idea how it would feel to find evidence that his own wife and son had vanished from the face of the earth.

At the top of the stairs he paused by the family photos. Irene, always one for order, had hung them chronologically, beginning with his and her great grandparents. Old, cracked black and whites of stern-faced, rawboned men and women of the Midwest. Then came the faded color shots of their grandparents on their fiftieth wedding anniversaries. Then their parents, their siblings, and themselves. How long had it been since he had studied their wedding photo, her with her flip hairstyle and him with his hair over his ears and muttonchops?

And those family pictures with Chloe eight years old, holding the baby! How grateful he was that Chloe was still here and that somehow he would connect with her! But what did this all say about the two of them? They were lost. He didn't know what to hope and pray for. That Irene and Raymie were still here and that this was not what it appeared?

He could wait no longer. Raymie's door was open a crack. His alarm was beeping. Rayford turned it off. On the bed was a book Raymie had been reading. Rayford slowly pulled the blankets back to reveal Raymie's Bulls pajama top, his underpants, and his socks. He sat on the bed and wept, nearly smiling at Irene's harping about Raymie's not wearing socks to bed.

He laid the clothes in a neat pile and noticed a picture of himself on the bed table. He stood smiling inside the terminal, his cap tucked under his arm, a 747 outside the window in the background. The picture was signed, "To Raymie with love, Dad." Under that he had written, "Rayford Steele, Captain, Pan-Continental Airlines, O'Hare." He shook his head. What kind of a dad autographs a picture for his own son?

Rayford's body felt like lead. It was all he could do to force himself to stand. And then he was dizzy, realizing he hadn't eaten in hours. He slowly made his way out of

Raymie's room without looking back, and he shut the door.

At the end of the hall he paused before the French doors that led to the master suite. What a beautiful, frilly place Irene had made it, decorated with needlepoint and country knickknacks. Had he ever told her he appreciated it? *Had* he ever appreciated it?

There was no alarm to turn off here. The smell of coffee had always roused Irene. Another picture of the two of them, him looking confidently at the camera, her gazing at him. He did not deserve her. He deserved this, he knew, to be mocked by his own self-centeredness and to be stripped of the most important person in his life.

He approached the bed, knowing what he would find. The indented pillow, the wrinkled covers. He could smell her, though he knew the bed would be cold. He carefully peeled back the blankets and sheet to reveal her locket, which carried a picture of him. Her flannel nightgown, the one he always kidded her about and which she wore only when he was not home, evidenced her now departed form.

His throat tight, his eyes full, he noticed her wedding ring near the pillow, where she always supported her cheek with her hand. It was too much to bear, and he broke down. He gathered the ring into his palm and sat on the edge of the bed, his body racked with fatigue and grief. He put the ring in his jacket pocket and noticed the package she had mailed. Tearing it open, he found two of his favorite homemade cookies with hearts drawn on the top in chocolate.

What a sweet, sweet woman! he thought. *I never deserved her, never loved her enough!* He set the cookies on the bedside table, their essence filling the air. With wooden fingers he removed his clothes and let them fall to the floor. He climbed into the bed and lay facedown, gathering Irene's nightgown in his arms so he could smell her and imagine her close to him.

And Rayford cried himself to sleep.

FIVE

BUCK Williams ducked into a stall in the Pan-Con Club
men's room to double-check his inventory. Tucked
in a special pouch inside his jeans, he carried thousands
of dollars' worth of traveler's checks, redeemable in
dollars, marks, or yen. His one leather bag contained
two changes of clothes, his laptop, cellular phone, tape
recorder, accessories, toiletries, and some serious,
insulated winter gear.

He had packed for a ten-day trip to Britain when
he left New York three days before the apocalyptic
disappearances. His practice overseas was to do his
own laundry in the sink and let it dry a whole day
while wearing one outfit and having one more in
reserve. That way he was never burdened with lots
of luggage.

Buck had gone out of his way to stop in Chicago first

to mend fences with the *Global Weekly*'s bureau chief there, a fiftyish black woman named Lucinda Washington. He had gotten crossways with her—what else was new?—when he scooped her staff on, of all things, a sports story that was right under their noses. An aging Bears legend had finally found enough partners to help him buy a professional football team, and Buck had somehow sniffed it out, tracked him down, gotten the story, and run with it.

"I admire you, Cameron," Lucinda Washington had said, characteristically refusing to use his nickname. "I always have, as irritating as you can be. But the very least you should have done was let me know."

"And let you assign somebody who should have been on top of this anyway?"

"Sports isn't even your gig, Cameron. After doing the Newsmaker of the Year and covering the defeat of Russia by Israel, or I should say by God himself, how can you even get interested in penny-ante stuff like this? You Ivy League types aren't supposed to like anything but lacrosse and rugby, are you?"

"This was bigger than a sports story, Lucy, and—"

"Hey!"

"Sorry, *Lucinda*. And wasn't that just a bit of stereotyping? Lacrosse and rugby?"

They had shared a laugh.

"I'm not even saying you should have told me you were in town," she had said. "All I'm saying is, at least let me know before the piece runs in the *Weekly*. My people and I were embarrassed enough to get beat like that, especially by the legendary Cameron Williams, but for it to be a, well—"

"That's why you squealed on me?"

Lucinda had laughed again. "That's why I told Plank it would take a face-to-face to get you back in my good graces."

"And what made you think I'd care about that?"

"Because you love me," she had said. "You can't help yourself." Buck had smiled. "But, Cameron, if I catch you in my town again, on my beat without my knowledge, I'm gonna whip your tail."

"Well, I'll tell you what, Lucinda. Let me give you a lead I don't have time to follow up on. I happen to know the NFL franchise purchase is not going to go through after all. The money was shaky and the league's gonna reject the offer. Your local legend is going to be embarrassed."

Lucinda had begun scribbling furiously. "You're not serious," she had said, reaching for her phone.

"No, I'm not, but it was sure fun to see you swing into action."

"You creep," she had said. "Anybody else I'd be throwing out of here on his can."

"But you love me. You can't help yourself."

"That wasn't even Christian," she had said.

"Don't start with that again."

"Come on, Cameron. You know you got your mind right when you saw what God did for Israel."

"Granted, but don't start calling me a Christian. Deist is as much as I'll cop to."

"Stay in town long enough to come to my church, and God'll getcha."

"He's already got me, Lucinda. But Jesus is another thing. The Israelis hate Jesus, but look what God did for them."

"The Lord works in—"

"—mysterious ways, yeah, I know. Anyway, I'm going to London Monday. Working on a hot tip from a friend there."

"Yeah? What?"

"Not on your life. We don't know each other that well yet."

She had laughed, and they had parted with a friendly embrace. That had been three days ago.

Buck had boarded the ill-fated flight to London prepared for anything. He was following a tip from a former Princeton classmate, a Welshman who had been working in the London financial district since graduate school. Dirk Burton had been a reliable source in the past, tipping off Buck about secret high-level meetings among international financiers. For years Buck had been slightly amused at Dirk's tendency to buy into conspiracy theories. "Let me get this straight," Buck had asked him once, "you think these guys are the real world leaders, right?"

"I wouldn't go that far, Cam," Dirk had said. "All I know is, they're big, they're private, and after they meet, major things happen."

"So you think they get world leaders elected, handpick dictators, that kind of a thing?"

"I don't belong to the conspiracy book club, if that's what you mean."

"Then where do you get this stuff, Dirk? Come on, you're a relatively sophisticated guy. Power brokers behind the scenes? Movers and shakers who control the money?"

"All I know is, the London Exchange, the Tokyo Exchange, the New York exchange—we all basically drift until these guys meet. Then things happen."

"You mean like when the New York Stock Exchange has a blip because of some presidential decision or some vote of Congress, it's really because of your secret group?"

"No, but that's a perfect example. If there's a blip in your market because of your president's health, imagine what it does to world markets when the real money people get together."

"But how does the market know they're meeting? I thought you were the only one who knew."

"Cam, be serious. OK, not a lot of people agree with me, but then I don't say this to just anyone. One of our muckety-mucks is part of this group. When they have a meeting, no, nothing happens right away. But a few days later, a week, changes occur."

"Like what?"

"You're going to call me crazy, but a friend of mine is related to a girl who works for the secretary of our guy in this group, and—"

"Whoa! Hold it! What's the trail here?"

"OK, maybe the connection is a little remote, but you

know the old guy's secretary is not going to say anything. Anyway, the scuttlebutt is that this guy is real hot on getting the whole world onto one currency. You know half our time is spent on exchange rates and all that. Takes computers forever to constantly readjust every day, based on the whims of the markets."

Buck was not convinced. "One global currency? Never happen," he had said.

"How can you flatly say that?"

"Too bizarre. Too impractical. Look what happened in the States when they tried to bring in the metric system."

"Should have happened. You Yanks are such rubes."

"Metrics were only necessary for international trade. Not for how far it is to the outfield wall at Yankee Stadium or how many kilometers it is from Indianapolis to Atlanta."

"I know, Cam. Your people thought you'd be paving the way for the Communists to take over if you made maps and distance markers easy for them to read. And where are your Commies now?"

Buck had passed off most of Dirk Burton's ideas until a few years later when Dirk had called him in the middle of the night. "Cameron," he had said, unaware of the nickname bestowed by his friend's colleagues, "I can't talk long. You can pursue this or you can just watch it happen and wish it had been your story. But you remember that stuff I was saying about the one world currency?"

"Yeah. I'm still dubious."

"Fine, but I'm telling you the word here is that our

guy pushed the idea at the last meeting of these secret financiers and something's brewing."

"What's brewing?"

"Well, there's going to be a major United Nations Monetary Conference, and the topic is going to be streamlining currency."

"Big deal."

"It *is* a big deal, Cameron. Our guy got shot down. He, of course, was pushing for world currency to become pounds sterling."

"What a surprise that that won't happen. Look at your economy."

"But listen, the big news, if you can believe any leak out of the secret meeting, is that they have it down to three currencies for the entire world, hoping to go to just one inside a decade."

"No way. Won't happen."

"Cameron, if my information is correct, the initial stage is a done deal. The U.N. conference is just window dressing."

"And the decision has already been made by your secret puppeteers."

"That's right."

"I don't know, Dirk. You're a buddy, but I think you would rather be doing what I'm doing."

"Who wouldn't?"

"Well, that's true. I sure wouldn't want to be doing what you're doing."

"But I'm not wrong, Cameron. Test my information."

"How?"

"I'll predict what's going to come out of the U.N. within two weeks, and if I'm right, you start treating me with a little deference, a little respect."

Buck realized that he and Dirk had been sparring the way everyone at Princeton had during weekend pizza and beer bashes in the dorms. "Dirk, listen. That sounds interesting, and I'm listening. But you do know, don't you, all kidding aside, that I wouldn't think any less of you even if you were way off base here?"

"Well, thanks, Cam. Really. That means a lot to me. And for that little tidbit, I'm going to give you a bonus. I'm not only going to tell you that the U.N. resolution is going to be for dollars, marks, and yen within five years, but I'm also going to tell you that the real power behind the power is an American."

"What do you mean, the power behind the power?"

"The mightiest of the secret group of international money men."

"This guy runs the group, in other words?"

"He's the one who shot down sterling as one of the currencies and has dollars in mind for the one world commodity in the end."

"I'm listening."

"Jonathan Stonagal."

Buck had hoped Dirk would name someone ludicrous so he could burst into laughter. But he had to admit, if only to himself, that if there was anything to this, Stonagal would be a logical choice. One of the richest men in the world and long known as an American power broker, Stonagal would have to be involved if serious global finance was being discussed. Though he was already in his eighties and appeared infirm in news photos, he not only owned the biggest banks and financial institutions in the United States, but he also owned or had huge interests in the same throughout the world.

Though Dirk was a friend, Buck had felt the need to play him along a bit, to keep him eager to provide information. "Dirk, I'm going back to bed. I appreciate all this and find it very interesting. I'm going to see what comes out of this U.N. deal, and I'm also going to see if I can trace the movements of Jonathan Stonagal. If it happens the way you think, you'll be my best informant. Meanwhile, see if you can find out for me how many are in this secret group and where they meet."

"That's easy," Dirk had said. "There are at least ten, though more than that sometimes come to the meetings, including some heads of state."

"U.S. presidents?"

"Occasionally, believe it or not."

"That's sort of one of the popular conspiracy theories here, Dirk."

"That doesn't mean it isn't true. And they usually meet in France. I don't know why. Some kind of private chalet or something there gives them a sense of security."

"But nothing escapes your friend of a friend of a relative of a subordinate of a secretary, or whatever."

"Laugh all you want, Cam. Our guy in the group, Joshua Todd-Cothran, may just not be quite as buttoned-down as the rest."

"Todd-Cothran? Doesn't he run the London Exchange?"

"That's the guy."

"Not buttoned-down? How could he have that position and not be? Plus, who ever heard of a Brit who was not buttoned-down?"

"It happens."

"Good night, Dirk."

Of course, it had all proven correct. The U.N. made its resolution. Buck discovered that Jonathan Stonagal had lived in the Plaza Hotel in New York during the ten days of the confab. Mr. Todd-Cothran of London had been one of the more eloquent speakers, expressing such eagerness to see the matter through that he volunteered to carry the torch back to the prime minister regarding Great Britain moving to the mark from the pound.

Many Third World countries fought the change, but within a few years the three currencies had swept the globe. Buck had told only Steve Plank of his tip on the U.N. meetings, but he didn't say where he'd gotten the information, and neither he nor Plank felt it worth a speculative article. "Too risky," Steve had said. Soon they both wished they had run with it in advance. "You'd have become even more of a legend, Buck."

Dirk and Buck had become closer than ever, and it wasn't unusual for Buck to visit London on short notice. If Dirk had a serious lead, Buck packed and went. His trips had often turned into excursions into countries and climates that surprised him, thus he had packed the emergency gear. Now, it appeared, it was superfluous. He was stuck in Chicago after the most electrifying phenomenon in world history, trying to get to New York.

Despite the incredible capabilities of his laptop, there was still no substitute for the pocket notebook. Buck scribbled a list of things to do before setting off again:

Call Ken Ritz, charter pilot
Call Dad and Jeff
Call Hattie Durham with news of family
Call Lucinda Washington about local hotel
Call Dirk Burton

The phone awakened Rayford Steele. He had not moved for hours. It was early evening and beginning to get dark. "Hello?" he said, unable to mask the sleepy huskiness in his voice.

"Captain Steele?" It was the frantic voice of Hattie Durham.

"Yes, Hattie. Are you all right?"

"I've been trying to reach you for hours! My phone was dead for the longest time, then everything was busy. I thought I was getting a ring on your phone, but you never answered. I don't know anything about my mother or my sisters. What about you?"

Rayford sat up, dizzy and disoriented. "I got a message from Chloe," he said.

"I knew that," she said. "You told me at O'Hare. Are your wife and son all right?"

"No."

"No?"

Rayford was silent. What else was there to say?

"Do you know anything for sure?" Hattie asked.

"I'm afraid I do," he said. "Their bedclothes are here."

"Oh, no! Rayford, I'm sorry! Is there anything I can do?"

"No, thanks."

"Do you want some company?"

"No, thanks."

"I'm scared."

"So am I, Hattie."

"What are you going to do?"

"Keep trying to get Chloe. Hope she can come home or I can get to her."

"Where is she?"

"Stanford. Palo Alto."

"My people are in California, too," Hattie said. "They've got all kinds of trouble out there, even worse than here."

"I imagine it's because of the time difference," Rayford said. "More people on the roads, that sort of thing."

"I'm scared to death of what's become of my family."

"Let me know what you find out, Hattie, OK?"

"I will, but you were supposed to call me. 'Course my phone was dead, and then I couldn't get through to you."

"I wish I could say I tried to call you, Hattie, but I didn't. This is hard for me."

"Let me know if you need me, Rayford. You know, just someone to talk to or be with."

"I will. And you let me know what you find out about your family."

He almost wished he hadn't added that. Losing his wife and child made him realize what a vapid relationship he had been pursuing with a twenty-seven-year-old woman. He hardly knew her, and he certainly didn't much care what happened to her family any more than he cared when he heard about a remote tragedy on the news. He knew Hattie was not a bad person. In fact, she was nice and friendly. But that was not why he had been interested in her. It had merely been a physical attraction, something he had been smart enough or lucky enough or naive enough not to have acted upon. He felt guilty for having considered it, and now his own grief would obliterate all but the most common courtesy of simply caring for a coworker.

"There's my call waiting," she said. "Can you hold?"

"No, just go ahead and take it. I'll call you later."

"I'll call you back, Rayford."

"Well, OK."

———

Buck Williams had gotten back in line and gained access to a pay phone. This time he wasn't trying to hook up his computer to it. He simply wanted to see how many personal calls he could make. He reached Ken Ritz's answering machine first.

"This is Ritz's Charter Service. Here's the deal in light of the crisis: I've got Learjets at both Palwaukee and Waukegan, but I've lost my other flyer. I can get to either airport, but right now they're not lettin' anyone into any of the major strips. Can't get into Milwaukee, O'Hare, Kennedy, Logan, National, Dulles, Dallas, Atlanta. I can get into some of the smaller, outlying airports, but it's a seller's market. Sorry to be so opportunistic, but I'm asking two dollars a mile, cash up front. If I can find someone who wants to come back from where you're goin', I might be able to give you a little discount. I'm checkin' this tape tonight and will take off first thing in the morning. Longest trip with guaranteed cash gets me. If your stop is on the way, I'll try to squeeze you in. Leave me a message and I'll get back to you."

That was a laugh. How would Ken Ritz get hold of Buck? With his cellular phone unreliable, the only thing he could think of was to leave his New York voice-mail number. "Mr. Ritz, my name is Buck Williams, and I need to get as close to New York City as you can get me. I'll pay the full fare you're asking in traveler's checks, redeemable in whatever currency you want." Sometimes that was attractive to private contractors because they kept up with the differences in currency and could make a little margin on the exchange. "I'm at O'Hare and will try to find a place to stay in the suburbs. Just to save you time, let me just pick somewhere between here and Waukegan. If I get a new number in the meantime, I'll call it in. Meanwhile, you may leave a message for me at the following New York number."

Buck was still unable to get through to his office directly, but his voice-mail number worked. He retrieved his new messages, mostly from coworkers checking on him and lamenting the loss of mutual friends. Then there was the welcome message from Marge Potter, who was a genius to think of leaving it there for him. "Buck, if you get this, call your father in Tucson. He and your brother are together, and I hate to tell you here, but they're having trouble reaching Jeff's wife and the kids. They should have news by the time you call. Your father was most grateful to hear that you were all right."

Buck's voice mail also noted that he still had a saved message. That was the one from Dirk Burton that had spurred his trip in the first place. He would need to listen to it again when he had time. Meanwhile, he left a message for Marge that if she had time and an open line, she needed to let Dirk know Buck's flight never made it to Heathrow. Of course, Dirk would know that by now, but he needed to know Buck wasn't among the missing and that he would get there in due time.

Buck hung up and dialed his father. The line was busy, but it was not the same kind of a tone that tells you the lines are down or that the whole system is kaput. Neitherwas it that irritating recording he'd grown so used to. He knew it would be only a matter of time before he could get through. Jeff must be beside himself not knowing about his wife, Sharon, and the kids. They'd had their differences and had even been separated before the children came along, but for several years the marriage had been better. Jeff's wife had proven forgiving and conciliatory. Jeff himself admitted he was puzzled that she would take him back. "Call me undeserving, but grateful," he once told Buck. Their son and daughter, who both looked like Jeff, were precious.

Buck pulled out the number the beautiful blonde flight attendant had given him and chastised himself for not trying again to reach her earlier. It took a while for her to answer.

"Hattie Durham, this is Buck Williams."

"Who?"

"Cameron Williams, from the *Global*—"

"Oh yes! Any news?"

"Yes, ma'am, good news."

"Oh, thank God! Tell me."

"Someone from my office tells me they reached your mother and that she and your sisters are fine."

"Oh, thank you, thank you, thank you! I wonder why they haven't called here? Maybe they've tried. My phone has been haywire."

"There are other problems in California, ma'am. Lines down, that kind of a thing. It may be a while before you can talk to them."

"I know. I heard. Well, I sure appreciate this. How about you? Have you been able to reach your family?"

"I got word that my dad and brother are OK. We still don't know about my sister-in-law and the kids."

"Oh. How old are the kids?"

"Can't remember. Both under ten, but I don't know exactly."

"Oh." Hattie sounded sad, guarded.

"Why?" Buck asked.

"Oh, nothing. It's just that—"

"What?"

"You can't go by what I say."

"Tell me, Miss Durham."

"Well, you remember what I told you on the plane. And on the news it looks like all children are gone, even unborn ones."

"Yeah."

"I'm not saying that means your brother's children are—"

"I know."

"I'm sorry I brought that up."

"No, it's OK. This is too strange, isn't it?"

"Yeah. I just got off the phone with the captain who piloted the flight you were on. He lost his wife and son, but his daughter is OK. She's in California, too."

"How old is she?"

"About twenty, I guess. She's at Stanford."

"Oh."

"Mr. Williams, what did you call yourself?"

"Buck. It's a nickname."

"Well, Buck, I know better than to say what I said about your niece and nephew. I hope there are exceptions and that yours are OK." She began to cry.

"Miss Durham, it's OK. You have to admit, no one is thinking straight right now."

"You can call me Hattie."

That struck him as humorous under the circumstances. She had been apologizing for being inappropriate, yet she didn't want to be too formal. If he was Buck, she was Hattie.

"I suppose I shouldn't tie up this line," he said. "I just wanted to get the news to you. I thought maybe by now you already knew."

"No, and thanks again. Would you mind calling me again sometime, if you think of it? You seem like a nice person, and I appreciate what you did for me. It would be nice to hear from you again. This is kind of a scary, lonely time."

He couldn't argue with that understatement. Funny, her request had sounded like anything but a come-on. She seemed wholly sincere, and he was sure she was. A nice, scared, lonely woman whose world had been skewed, just like his and everyone's he knew.

When Buck got off the phone, he saw the young woman at the counter flagging him down. "Listen," she whispered, "they don't want me making an announcement that would start a stampede, but we just heard something interesting. The livery companies have gotten together and moved their communications center out to a median strip near the Mannheim Road interchange."

"Where's that?"

"Just outside the airport. There's no traffic coming into the terminals anyway. Total gridlock. But if you can walk as far as that interchange, supposedly you'll find all those guys with walkie-talkies trying to get limos in and out from there."

"I can imagine the prices."

"No, you probably can't."

"I can imagine the wait."

"Like standing in line for a rental car in Orlando," she said.

Buck had never done that, but he could imagine that, too. And she was right. After he had hiked, with a crowd, to the Mannheim interchange, he found a mob surrounding the dispatchers. Intermittent announcements got everyone's attention.

"We're filling every car. A hundred bucks a head to any suburb. Cash only. Nothing's going to Chicago."

"No cards?" someone shouted.

"I'll say it again," the dispatcher said. "Cash only. If you know you've got cash or a checkbook at home, you can plead with the driver to trust you till you get there." He called out a listing of which companies were heading which directions. Passengers ran to fill the cars as they lined up on the shoulder of the expressway.

Buck handed a hundred-dollar traveler's check to the dispatcher for the northern suburbs. An hour and a half later, he joined several others in a limo. After checking his cellular phone again to no avail, he offered the driver fifty dollars to use his phone. "No guarantees," the driver said. "Sometimes I get through, sometimes I don't."

Buck checked the phone log in his laptop for Lucinda Washington's home number and dialed. A teenage boy answered, "Washingtons."

"Cameron Williams of *Global Weekly* calling for Lucinda."

"My mom's not here," the young man said.

"Is she still at the office? I need a recommendation where to stay near Waukegan."

"She's nowhere," the boy said. "I'm the only one left. Mama, Daddy, everybody else is gone. Disappeared."

"Are you sure?"

"Their clothes are here, right where they were sitting. My daddy's contact lenses are still on top of his bathrobe."

"Oh, man! I'm sorry, son."

"That's all right. I know where they are, and I can't even say I'm surprised."

"You know where they are?"

"If you know my mama, you know where she is, too. She's in heaven."

"Yeah, well, are you all right? Is there someone to look after you?"

"My uncle's here. And a guy from our church. Probably the only one who's still around."

"You're all right then?"

"I'm all right."

Cameron folded the phone and handed it back to the driver. "Any idea where I should stay if I'm trying to fly out of Waukegan in the morning?"

"The chain hotels are probably full, but there's a couple of flea bags on Washington you might sneak into. You'd be close enough to the airport. You'd be my last drop-off."

"Fair enough. They got phones in those dives?"

"More likely a phone and a TV than running water."

SIX

IT HAD been ages since Rayford Steele had been drunk. Irene had never been much of a drinker, and she had become a teetotaler during the last few years. She insisted he hide any hard stuff if he had to have it in the house at all. She didn't want Raymie even knowing his daddy still drank.

"That's dishonest," Rayford had countered.

"It's prudent," she said. "He doesn't know everything, and he doesn't have to know everything."

"How does that jibe with your insistence that we be totally truthful?"

"Telling the whole truth doesn't always mean telling everything you know. You tell your crew you're taking a bathroom break, but you don't go into detail about what you're doing in there, do you?"

"Irene!"

"I'm just saying you don't have to make it obvious to your preteen son that you drink hard liquor."

He had found her point hard to argue, and he had kept his bourbon stashed high and out of sight. If ever there was a moment that called for a stiff drink, this was it. He reached behind the empty cake cover in the highest cabinet over the sink and pulled down a half-finished fifth of whiskey. His inclination, knowing no one he cared about would ever see, was to tip it straight up and guzzle. But even at a time like this there were conventions and manners. Guzzling booze from the bottle was simply not his style.

Rayford poured three inches into a wide crystal glass and threw it back like a veteran. That was about as out of character as he could find comfortable. The stuff hit the back of his throat and burned all the way down, giving him a chill that made him shudder and groan. *What an idiot!* he thought. *And on an empty stomach, too.*

He was already getting a buzz when he replaced the bottle, then thought better of it. He slipped it into the garbage under the sink. Would this be a nice memorial to Irene, giving up even the occasional hard drink? There would be no benefit to Raymie now, but he didn't feel right about drinking alone anyway. Did he have the capacity to become a closet drunk? *Who doesn't?* he wondered. Regardless, he wasn't going to cash in his maturity because of what had happened.

Rayford's sleep had been deep but not long enough. He had few immediate chores. First he had to connect with Chloe. Second he had to find out what Pan-Con wanted from him in the next week. Normal regulations would have grounded him after an overly long flight and a rerouted emergency landing. But who knew what was going on now?

How many pilots had they lost? When would runways be cleared? Flights scheduled? If he knew anything about the airlines, it would all be about dollars. As soon as they could get those machines airborne, they could start being profitable again. Well, Pan-Con had been good to him. He would hang in there and do his part. But what was he supposed to do about this grief, this despair, this empty ache?

Finally he understood the bereaved who complained when their loved one was too mangled to see or whose body had been destroyed. They often complained that there was no sense of closure and that the grieving process was more difficult because they had a hard time imagining their loved one actually dead.

That had always seemed strange to him. Who would want to see a wife or child stretched out and made up for a funeral? Wouldn't you want to remember them alive and happy as they were? But he knew better now. He had no doubt that his wife and son were gone as surely as if they had died, as his own parents had years before. Irene and Ray would not be coming back, and he didn't know if he would ever see them again, because he didn't know if there were second chances on this heaven thing.

He longed to be able to see their bodies, at least—in bed, in a casket, anywhere. He would have given anything for one last glimpse. It wouldn't have made them any less dead to him, but maybe he wouldn't feel so abandoned, so empty.

Rayford knew there would not likely be phone connections between Illinois and California for hours, maybe days. Yet he had to try. He dialed Stanford, the main administration number, and didn't even get a busy signal or a recorded message. He dialed Chloe's room. Still nothing. Every half hour or so he hit the redial button. He refused to hope she would answer; if she did, it would be a wonderful surprise.

Rayford found himself ravenous and knew he'd better get something in his stomach before the few ounces of booze did a number on him. He mounted the stairs again, stopping in Raymie's room to pick up the little pile of clothes by which he would remember the boy. He put them in a cardboard gift box he found in Irene's closet, then placed her nightgown, locket, and ring in another.

He took the boxes downstairs, along with the two cookies she had mailed him. The rest of that batch of cookies had to be around somewhere. He found them in a Tupperware bowl in the cupboard. He was grateful that their smell and taste would remind him of her until they were gone.

Rayford added a couple to the two he had brought down, put them on a paper plate, and poured himself a glass of milk. He sat at the kitchen table next to the phone but couldn't force himself to eat. He felt paralyzed. To busy himself, he erased the calls on the answering machine and added a new outgoing message. He said, "This is Rayford Steele. If you must, please leave a very brief message. I am trying to leave this line open for my daughter. Chloe, if it's you, I'm either sleeping or close by, so give me a chance to pick up. If we don't connect for some reason, do whatever you have to, to get home. Any airline can charge it to me. I love you."

And with that he slowly ate his cookies, the smell and taste bringing images to him of Irene in the kitchen, and the milk making him long for his boy. This was going to be hard, so hard.

He was exhausted, and yet he couldn't bring himself to go upstairs again. He knew he would have to force himself to sleep in his own bedroom that night. For now he would stretch out on the couch in the living room and hope Chloe would get through. He idly pushed the redial button again, and this time he got the quick busy signal that told him something was happening. At the very least, lines were being worked on. That was progress. He knew she was thinking of him while he was thinking of her. But she had no idea what might have happened to her mother or her brother. Would he have to tell her by phone? He feared he would. She would surely ask.

He lumbered to the couch and lay down, a sob in his throat but no more tears to accompany it. If only Chloe would somehow get his message and get started home, he could at least tell her face-to-face.

Rayford lay there grieving, knowing the television would be full of scenes he didn't want to see, dedicated around the clock to the tragedy and mayhem all over the world. And then it hit him. He sat up, staring out the window in the darkness. He owed it to Chloe not to fail her. He loved her and she was all he had left. He had to find out how they had missed everything Irene had been trying to tell them, why it had been so hard to accept and believe. Above all, he had to study, to learn, to be prepared for whatever happened next.

If the disappearances were of God, if they had been his doing, was this the end of it? The Christians, the real believers, get taken away, and the rest are left to grieve and mourn and realize their error? Maybe so. Maybe that was the price. *But then what happens when* we *die?* he thought. *If heaven is real, if the Rapture was a fact, what does that say about hell and judgment? Is that our fate? We go through this hell of regret and remorse, and then we literally go to hell, too?*

Irene had always talked of a loving God, but even God's love and mercy had to have limits. Had everyone who denied the truth pushed God to his limit? Was there no more mercy, no second chance? Maybe there wasn't, and if that was so, that was so.

But if there were options, if there was still a way to find the truth and believe or accept or whatever it was Irene said one was supposed to do, Rayford was going to find it. Would it mean admitting that he didn't know everything? That he had relied on himself and that now he felt stupid and weak and worthless? He could admit that. After a lifetime of achieving, of excelling, of being better than most and the best in most circles, he had been as humbled as was possible in one stroke.

There was so much he didn't know, so much he didn't understand. But if the answers were still there, he would find them. He didn't know whom to ask or where to start, but this was something he and Chloe could do together. They'd always gotten along all right. She'd gone through the typical teenage independence, but she had never done anything stupid or irreparable as far as he knew. In fact, they had probably been too close; she was too much like him.

It was simply Raymie's age and innocence that had allowed his mother's influence to affect him so. It was his spirit. He didn't have the killer instinct, the "me first" attitude Rayford thought he would need to succeed in the real world. He wasn't effeminate, but Rayford had worried that he might be a mama's boy—too compassionate, too sensitive, too caring. He was always looking out for someone else when Rayford thought he should be looking out for number one.

How grateful he was now that Raymie took after his mother more than he took after his father. And how he wished there had been some of that in Chloe. She was competitive, a driver, someone who had to be convinced and persuaded. She could be kind and generous when it suited her purpose, but she was like her dad. She took care of herself.

Good job, big shot, Rayford told himself. *The girl you were so proud of because she was so much like you is in your same predicament.*

That, he decided, would have to change. As soon as they reconnected, that *would* change. They would be on a mission, a quest for truth. If he was already too late, he would have to accept and deal with that. He'd always been one who went for a goal and accepted the consequences. Only these consequences were eternal. He hoped against all hope that there was another chance at truth and knowledge out there somewhere. The only problem was that the ones who knew were gone.

The Midpoint Motel on Washington Street, a few miles from the tiny Waukegan Airport, was tacky enough that there wasn't a waiting list. Buck Williams was pleasantly surprised they had not even raised their rates for the crisis. When he saw the room, he knew why, and he wondered what two places in the world this dive was midpoint *between*. Whatever they were, either had to be better. There was a phone, however, and a shower, a bed, and a TV. Run-down as it was, it would suffice. First Buck called his voice mail in New York. Nothing from this Ritz character or anything else new, so he listened to his saved message from Dirk Burton, which reminded him why he had felt it so important to get to London. Buck tapped it into his laptop as he listened:

> Cameron, you always tell me this message center is confidential, and I hope you're right. I'm not even going to identify myself, but you know who it is. Let me tell you something major and encourage you to come here as quickly as possible. The big man,

your compatriot, the one I call the supreme power broker internationally, met here the other day with the one I call our muckety-muck. You know who I mean. There was a third party at the meeting. All I know is that he's from Europe, probably Eastern Europe. I don't know what their plans are for him, but apparently something on a huge scale.

My sources say your man has met with each of his key people and this same European in different locations. He introduced him to people in China, the Vatican, Israel, France, Germany, here, and the States. Something is cooking, and I don't even want to suggest what it is other than in person. Visit me as soon as you can. In case that's not possible, let me just encourage this: Watch the news for the installation of a new leader in Europe. If you say, as I did, that no elections are scheduled and no changes of power are imminent, you'll get my drift. Come soon, friend.

Buck called Ken Ritz's machine to tell him where he was. Then he tried calling west once again and finally got through. Buck was surprised at what a relief it was to hear his father's voice, though he sounded tired, discouraged, and not a little panicky.

"Everybody OK out there, Dad?"

"Well, not everybody. Jeff was here with me, but he's taken the four-wheel drive to see if he can get to the accident site where Sharon was last seen."

"Accident?"

"She was pickin' up the kids at a retreat or something, something to do with her church. She doesn't go with us anymore, you know. Story is, she never got there. Car flipped over. No trace of her, 'cept her clothes, and you know what that means."

"She's gone?"

"Looks that way. Jeff can't accept it. He's takin' it hard. Wants to see for himself. Trouble is, the kids are gone, too, all of 'em. All their friends, everybody at that retreat thing in the mountains. State police found all the kids' clothes, about a hundred sets of them, and some kind of a late-night snack burning on the stove."

"Whew, boy! Tell Jeff I'm thinking of him. If he wants to talk, I'm here."

"I can't imagine he'll want to talk, Cameron, unless you have some answers."

"That's one thing I haven't got, Dad. I don't know who does. I have this feeling that whoever had the answers is gone."

"This is awful, Cam. I wish you were out here with us."

"Yeah, I'll bet."

"You bein' sarcastic?"

"Just expressing the truth, Dad. If you wanted me out there, it'd be the first time."

"Well, this is the kind of time when maybe we change our minds."

"About me? I doubt it."

"Cameron, let's not get into this, huh? For once, think of somebody other than yourself. You lost a sister-in-law and a niece and a nephew yesterday, and your brother'll probably never get over it."

Buck bit his tongue. Why did he always have to do this, and especially right now? His dad was right. If only Buck could admit that, maybe they could move on. He had been resented by the family ever since he'd gone on to college, following his academic prowess to the Ivy League. Where he came from, the kids were supposed to follow their parents into the business. His dad's was trucking fuel into the state, mostly from Oklahoma and Texas. It was a tough business with local people thinking the resources ought to all come from their own state. Jeff had worked his way up in the little business, starting in the office, then driving a truck, now running the day-to-day operations.

There had been a lot of bad blood, especially since Cameron was away at school when his mother fell ill. She had insisted he stay in school, but when he missed coming home for Christmas due to money problems, his dad and brother never really forgave him. His mother died while he was away, and he got the cold shoulder even at her funeral.

Some healing had occurred over the years, mostly because his family loved to claim him and brag about him once he became known as a journalistic prodigy. He had let bygones be bygones but resented that he was now welcome because he was somebody. And so he rarely went home. There was too much baggage to reconcile completely, but he was still angry with himself for opening old wounds when his family was suffering.

"If there's some kind of memorial service or something, I'll try to make it, Dad. All right?"

"You'll *try?*"

"That's all I can promise. You can imagine how busy things are at *Global* right now. Needless to say, this is the story of the century."

"Will you be writing the cover story?"

"I'll have a lot to do with the coverage, yeah."

"But the cover?"

Buck sighed, suddenly tired. It was no wonder. He'd been awake nearly twenty-four hours. "I don't know, Dad. I've already filed a lot of stuff. My guess is this next issue will be a huge special with lots of stuff from all over. It's unlikely my piece would be the sole cover article. It looks like I do have the assignment for a pretty major treatment two weeks from now."

He hoped that would satisfy his dad. He wanted to get off and get some sleep. But it didn't.

"What's that mean? What's the story?"

"Oh, I'll be pulling together several writers' pieces on the theories behind what's happened."

"That'll be a big job. Everybody I talk to has a different idea. You know your brother is afraid it was like the last judgment of God or something."

"He does?"

"Yeah. But I don't think so."

"Why not, Dad?" He didn't really want to get into a lengthy discussion, but this surprised him.

"Because I asked our pastor. He said if it was Jesus Christ taking people to heaven, he and I and you and Jeff would be gone, too. Makes sense."

"Does it? I've never claimed any devotion to the faith."

"The heck you haven't. You always get into this liberal, East Coast baloney. You know good and well we
had you in church and Sunday school from the time you
were a baby. You're as much a Christian as any one of
us."

Cameron wanted to say, "Precisely my point." But he
didn't. It was the lack of any connection between his
family's church attendance and their daily lives that
made him quit going to church altogether the day it
became his choice.

"Yeah, well, tell Jeff I'm thinking about him, huh?
And if I can work it out at all, I'll get back there for
whatever he's going to do about Sharon and the kids."

Buck was grateful the Midpoint at least had plenty of
hot water for a long shower. He had forgotten about the
nagging throb at the back of his head until the water hit
it and loosened the bandage. He didn't have anything to
redress it, so he just let it bleed a while, then found some
ice. In the morning he would find a bandage, just for
looks. For now, he had had it. He was bone weary.

There was no remote control for the TV and no way
he would get up once he stretched out. He turned CNN
on low so it wouldn't interrupt his sleep, and he watched
the world roundup before dozing off. Images from
around the globe were almost more than he could take,
but news was his business. He remembered the many
earthquakes and wars of the last decade and the nightly
coverage that was so moving. Now here was a thousand
times more of the same, all on the same day. Never in
history had more people been killed in one day than

those who disappeared all at once. Had they been killed? Were they dead? Would they be back?

Buck couldn't take his eyes, heavy as they were, off the screen as image after image showed disappearances caught on home videotape. From some countries came professional tapes of live television shows in progress, a host's microphone landing atop his empty clothes, bouncing off his shoes, and making a racket as it rolled across the floor. The audience screamed. One of the cameras panned the crowd, which had been at capacity a moment before. Now several seats were empty, clothes draped across them.

Nothing could have been scripted like this, Buck thought, blinking slowly. If somebody tried to sell a screenplay about millions of people disappearing, leaving everything but their bodies behind, it would be laughed off.

Buck was not aware that he was asleep until the cheap phone jangled so loudly it sounded as if it would rattle itself off the table. He groped for it.

"Sorry to bother you, Mr. Williams, but I just noticed you was off the phone there. While you was talkin', you got a call. Guy name of Ritz. Says you can call him or you can just be waitin' for him outside at six in the mornin'."

"OK. Thanks."

"What're you gonna do? Call him or meet him?"

"Why do you need to know?"

"Oh, I ain't bein' nosy or nothin'. It's just that if you're leavin' here at six, I gotta get payment in advance. You got the long-distance call and all. And I don't get up till seven."

"I'll tell you what, uh, what was your name?"

"Mack."

"I'll tell you what, Mack. I left you my charge card number, so you know I'm not going to sneak out on you. But in the morning I'm going to leave a traveler's check in the room for you, covering the price of the room and a lot more than enough for the phone call. You get my meaning?"

"A tip?"

"Yes, sir."

"That would be nice."

"What I need for you to do for me is slip a bandage under my door."

"I got one. You need it right now? You all right?"

"I'm fine. Not now. When you turn in. Nice and quiet like. And turn off my phone, OK, just in case? If I have to get up that early, I've got to do some serious sleeping right now. Can you handle that for me, Mack?"

"I sure can. I'll turn it off right now. You want a wake-up call?"

"No, thanks," Buck said, and he smiled when he realized the phone was dead in his hand. Mack was as good as his word. If he found that bandage in the morning, he would leave Mack a good tip. Buck forced himself to get up and shut off the TV set and the light. He was the type who could look at his watch before retiring and wake up precisely when he told himself to. It was nearly midnight. He would be up at five-thirty.

By the time he hit the mattress, he was out. When he awoke five and a half hours later, he had not moved a muscle.

Rayford felt as if he were sleepwalking as he padded through the kitchen to head upstairs. He couldn't believe how tired he still was after his long nap and his fitful dozing on the couch. The newspaper was still rolled up and rubber-banded on a chair where he had tossed it. If he had any trouble sleeping upstairs, maybe he would glance at the paper. It should be interesting to read the meaningless news of a world that didn't realize it was going to suffer the worst trauma in its history just after the paper had been set in type.

Rayford punched the redial button on the phone and walked slowly toward the stairs, only half listening. What was that? The dial tone had been interrupted, and the phone in Chloe's dorm room was ringing. He hurried to the phone as a girl answered.

"Chloe?"

"No. Mr. Steele?"

"Yes!"

"This is Amy. Chloe's trying to find a way back there. She'll try to call you along the way, sometime tomorrow. If she can't get through, she'll call you when she gets there or she'll get a cab home."

"She's on her way?"

"Yeah. She didn't want to wait. She tried calling and calling, but—"

"Yeah, I know. Thanks, Amy. Are you all right?"

"Scared to death, like everybody else."

"I can imagine. Did you lose anyone?"

"No, and I feel kinda guilty about that. Seems like everyone I know lost somebody. I mean I lost a few friends, but nobody close, no family."

Rayford didn't know whether to express congratulations or remorse. If this was what he now believed it had been, this poor child hardly knew anyone who'd been taken to heaven.

"Well," he said, "I'm glad you're all right."

"How about you?" she said. "Chloe's mom and brother?"

"I'm afraid they're gone, Amy."

"Oh, no!"

"But I would appreciate your letting me tell Chloe, just in case she reaches you before she reaches me."

"Oh, don't worry. I don't think I could tell her even if you wanted me to."

Rayford lay in bed several minutes, then idly thumbed through the first section of the paper. Hmm. A surprise move in Romania.

Democratic elections became passé when, with the seeming unanimous consensus of the people and both the upper and lower houses of government, a popular young businessman/politician assumed the role of president of the country. Nicolae Carpathia, a 33-year-old born in Cluj, had in recent months taken the nation by storm with his popular, persuasive speaking, charming the populace, friend and foe alike. Reforms he proposed for the country saw him swept to prominence and power.

Rayford glanced at the photo of the young Carpathia, a strikingly handsome blond who looked not unlike a young Robert Redford. *Wonder if he would've wanted the job had he known what was about to happen?* Rayford thought. *Whatever he has to offer won't amount to a hill of beans now.*

SEVEN

KEN Ritz roared up to the Midpoint precisely at six, rolled down his window, and said, "You Williams?"

"I'm your man," Buck said. He climbed into the late model four-wheel drive with his one bag. Fingering his freshly bandaged head, Buck smiled at the thought of Mack enjoying his extra twenty bucks.

Ritz was tall and lean with a weathered face and a shock of salt-and-pepper hair. "Let's get down to business," he said. "It's 740 miles from O'Hare to JFK and 746 from Milwaukee to JFK. I'm gonna get you as close to JFK as I can, and we're about equidistant between O'Hare and Milwaukee, so let's call it 743 air miles. Multiply that by two bucks, you're talkin' fourteen hundred and eighty-six. Round it off to fifteen hundred for the taxi service, and we got us a deal."

"Deal," Buck said, pulling out his checks and starting to sign. "Pretty expensive taxi."

Ritz laughed. "Especially for a guy coming out of the Midpoint."

"It was lovely."

Ritz parked in a metal Quonset hut at the Waukegan airport and chatted while running through preflight procedures. "No crashes here," he said. "There were two at Palwaukee. They lost a couple of staff people here though. Weirder than weird, wasn't it?"

Buck and Ritz shared stories of lost relatives, where they were when it happened, and exactly who they were. "Never flew a writer before," Ken said. "Charter, I mean. Must've flown a bunch of your types when I was commercial."

"Better money on your own?"

"Yeah, but I didn't know that when I switched. It wasn't my choice."

They were climbing into the Lear. Buck shot him a double take. "You were grounded?"

"Don't worry, partner," the pilot said. "I'll get you there."

"You owe it to me to tell me if you were grounded."

"I was fired. There's a difference."

"Depends on what you were fired for, doesn't it?"

"True enough. This ought to make you feel real good. I was fired for bein' too careful. Beat that."

"Talk to me," Buck said.

"You remember a lot of years ago when there was all that flak about puddle jumpers goin' down in icy weather?"

116

"Yeah, until they made some adjustments or something."

"Right. Well, you remember that one pilot refused to fly even after he was told to and the public was assured everything up to that point was explainable or a fluke?"

"Uh-huh."

"And you remember that there was another crash right after that, which proved the pilot right?"

"Vaguely."

"Well, I remember it plain as day, because you're lookin' at him."

"I do feel better."

"You know how many of those same model puddle jumpers are in the air today? Not a one. When you're right, you're right. But was I reinstated? No. Once a troublemaker, always a troublemaker. Lots of my colleagues were grateful though. And some pilots' widows were pretty angry that I got ignored and then canned, too late for their husbands."

"Ouch."

As the jet screamed east, Ritz wanted to know what Buck thought of the disappearances. "Funny you should ask," Buck said. "I've got to start working on that in earnest today. What's your read of it? And do you mind if I flip on a tape recorder?"

"Fine," Ritz said. "Dangedest thing I've ever seen. 'Course, that doesn't make me unique. I have to say, though, I've always believed in UFOs."

"You're kidding! A levelheaded, safety-conscious pilot?"

Ritz nodded. "I'm not talking about little green men or space aliens who kidnap people. I'm talking about some of the more documentable stuff, like some astronauts have seen, and some pilots."

"You ever see anything?"

"Nope. Well, a couple of unexplainable things. Some lights or mirages. Once I thought I was flying too close to a squad of helicopters. Not too far from here either. Glenview Naval Air Station. I radioed a warning, then lost sight of them. I suppose that's explainable. I could have been going faster than I realized and not been as close as I thought. But I never got an answer, no acknowledgment that they were even airborne. Glenview wouldn't confirm it. I shrugged it off, but a few weeks later, close to the same spot, my instruments went wacky on me. Dials spinning, meters sticking, that kind of thing."

"What did you make of that?"

"Magnetic field or some force like that. Could be explainable, too. You know there's no sense reporting strange occurrences or sightings near a military base, because they just reject 'em out of hand. They don't even take seriously anything strange within several miles of a commercial airport. That's why you never hear stories of UFOs near O'Hare. Not even considered."

"So, you don't buy the kidnapping space aliens, but you connect the disappearances with UFOs?"

"I'm just sayin' it's not like E.T., with creatures and all that. I think our ideas of what space people would look like is way too simple and rudimentary. If there is intelligent life out there, and there has to be just because of the sheer odds—"

"What do you mean?"

"The vastness of space."

"Oh, so many stars and so much area that something has to be out there somewhere."

"Exactly. And I agree with people who think those beings are more intelligent than we are. Otherwise, they wouldn't have made it here, if they are here. And if they are, I'm thinking they're sophisticated and advanced enough that they can do things to us we've never dreamed of."

"Like making people disappear right out of their clothes."

"Sounded pretty silly until the other night, didn't it?" Buck nodded.

"I've always laughed about people assuming these beings could read our thoughts or get into our heads and stuff," Ritz continued. "But look who's missing. Everybody I've read about or heard about or knew who's now gone was either under twelve years old or was an unusual personality."

"With all the people who disappeared, you think they had something in common?"

"Well, they've got something in common now, wouldn't you say?"

"But something set them apart, made them easier to snatch?" Buck asked.

"That's what I think."

"So we're still here because we were strong enough to resist, or maybe we weren't worth the trouble."

Ritz nodded. "Something like that. It's almost like some force or power was able to read the level of resistance or weakness, and once that force got sunk in, it was able to rip those people right off the earth. They disappeared in an instant, so they had to be dematerialized. The question is whether they were destroyed in the process or could be reassembled."

"What do you think, Mr. Ritz?"

"At first I would have said no. But a week ago I would have told you that millions of people all over the world disappearing into thin air sounds like a B movie. When I allow for the fact that it actually happened, I have to allow for the next logical step. Maybe they're somewhere specific in some form, and maybe they can return."

"That's a comforting thought," Buck said. "But is it more than wishful thinking?"

"Hardly. That idea and fifty cents would be worth half a dollar. I fly planes for money. I haven't got a clue. I'm still as much in shock as the next guy, and I don't mind tellin' you, I'm scared."

"Of?"

"That it might happen again. If it was anything like I think it was, maybe all this force needs to do now is crank up the power somehow and they can get older people, smarter people, people with more resistance that they ignored the first time around."

Buck shrugged and sat in silence for a few minutes. Finally he said, "There's a little hole in your argument. I know of some people who are missing who seem as strong as anyone."

"I wasn't talking physical strength."

"Neither was I." Buck thought about Lucinda Washington. "I lost a friend and coworker who was bright, healthy, happy, strong, and a forceful personality."

"Well, I'm not saying I know everything or even anything. You wanted my theory, there it is."

———

Rayford Steele lay on his back, staring at the ceiling. Sleep had come hard and intermittently, and he hated the logy feeling. He didn't want to watch the news. He didn't want to read the paper, even knowing a new one had flopped up onto the porch before dawn. All he wanted was for Chloe to get home so they could grieve together. There was nothing, he decided, more lonely than grief.

He and his daughter would have work to do, too. He wanted to investigate, to learn, to know, to act. He started by searching for a Bible, not the family Bible that had collected dust on his shelf for years, but Irene's. Hers would have notes in it, maybe something that would point him in the right direction.

It wasn't hard to find. It was usually within arm's reach of where she slept. He found it on the floor, next to the bed. Would there be some guide? An index? Something that referred to the Rapture or the judgment or something? If not, maybe he'd start at the end. If *genesis* meant "beginning," maybe *revelation* had something to do with the end, even though it didn't mean that. The only Bible verse Rayford could quote by heart was Genesis 1:1: "In the beginning God created the heavens and the earth." He hoped there'd be some corresponding verse at the end of the Bible that said something like, "In the end God took all his people to heaven and gave everybody else one more chance."

But no such luck. The very last verse in the Bible meant nothing to him. It said, "The grace of the Lord Jesus be with you all. Amen." And it sounded like the religious mumbo jumbo he had heard in church. He backed up a verse and read, "He who testifies to these things says, 'Yes, I am coming quickly.' Amen. Come, Lord Jesus."

Now he was getting somewhere. Who was this who testified of these things, and what were these things? The quoted words were in red. What did that mean? He looked through the Bible and then noticed on the spine, "Words of Christ in red." So Jesus said he was coming quickly. Had he come? And if the Bible was as old as it seemed, what did "quickly" mean? It must not have meant soon, unless it was from the perspective of someone with a long view of history. Maybe Jesus meant that when he came, he would do it quickly. Was that what this was all about? Rayford glanced at the last chapter as a whole. Three other verses had red letters, and two of those repeated the business about coming quickly.

Rayford could make no sense of the text of the chapter. It seemed old and formal. But near the end of the chapter was a verse that ended with words that had a strange impact on him. Without a hint of their meaning, he read, "Let the one who is thirsty come; let the one who wishes take the water of life without cost."

Jesus wouldn't have been the one who was thirsty. He would not have been the one who wished to take the water of life. That, Rayford assumed, referred to the reader. It struck him that he was thirsty, soul thirsty. But what was the water of life? He had already paid a terrible cost for missing it. Whatever it was, it had been in this book for hundreds of years.

Rayford idly leafed through the Bible to other passages, none of which made sense to him. They discouraged him because they didn't seem to flow together, to refer to each other, to have a direction. Language and concepts foreign to him were not helping.

Here and there he saw notes in the margins in Irene's delicate handwriting. Sometimes she simply wrote, "Precious." He was determined to study and find someone who could explain those passages to him. He was tempted to write, "precious," next to that verse in Revelation about taking the water of life without cost. It sounded precious to him, though he couldn't yet make it compute.

Worst of all, he feared he was reading the Bible too late. Clearly he was too late to have gone to heaven with his wife and son. But was he too late, period?

In the front flyleaf was last Sunday's church bulletin. What was this, Wednesday morning? Three days ago he had been where? In the garage. Raymie had begged him to go with them to church. He promised he would next Sunday. "That's what you said last week," Raymie had said.

"Do you want me to fix this four-wheeler for you or not? I don't have all the time in the world."

Raymie was not one for pushing a guilt trip. He just repeated, "Next Sunday?"

"For sure," Rayford had said. And now he wished next Sunday were here. He wished even more that Raymie were there to go with him because he *would* go. Or would he? Would he be off work that day? And would there be church? Was anyone left in that congregation? He pulled the bulletin from Irene's Bible and circled the phone number. Later that day, after he checked in with Pan-Continental, he would call the church office and see if anything was going on.

He was about to set the Bible on the bed table when he grew curious and opened the front flyleaf again. On the first white-papered page he saw the inscription. He had given this Bible to Irene on their first wedding anniversary. How could he have forgotten, and what had he been thinking? She was no more devout than he back then, but she talked about wanting to get serious about church attendance before the children came along. He had been angling for something or trying to impress her. Maybe he thought she would think him spiritual if he gave her a gift like that. Maybe he was hoping she would let him off the hook and go to church by herself if he proved his spiritual sensitivity with this gift.

For years he had tolerated church. They had gone to one that demanded little and offered a lot. They made many friends and had found their doctor, dentist, insurance man, and even country club entrée in that church. Rayford was revered, proudly introduced as a 747 captain to newcomers and guests, and even served on the church board for several years.

When Irene discovered the Christian radio station and what she called "real preaching and teaching," she grew disenchanted with their church and began searching for a new one. That gave Rayford the opportunity to quit going at all, telling her that when she found one she really liked, he would start going again. She found one, and he tried it occasionally, but it was a little too literal and personal and challenging for him. He was not revered. He felt like a project. And he pretty much stayed away.

Rayford noticed another bit of Irene's handwriting. It was labeled her prayer list, and he was at the top. She had written, "Rafe, for his salvation and that I be a loving wife to him. Chloe, that she come to Christ and live in purity. Ray Jr., that he never stray from his strong, childlike faith." Then she had listed her pastor, political leaders, missionaries, world conflict, and several friends and other relatives.

"For his salvation," Rayford whispered. "Salvation." Another ten-dollar church word that had never really impressed him. He knew Irene's new church was interested in the salvation of souls, something he'd never heard in the previous church. But the closer he had gotten to the concept, the more he had been repelled. Didn't salvation have something to do with confirmation, baptism, testifying, getting religion, being holy? He hadn't wanted to deal with it, whatever it was. And now he was desperate to know exactly what it meant.

Ken Ritz radioed ahead to airports in suburban New York, finally getting clearance to touch down at Easton, Pennsylvania. "You know," Ritz said, "these are the old stompin' grounds of Larry Holmes, once the heavy-weight champion of the world."

"The guy that beat Ali?"

"One and the same. If he was still around, whoever was takin' people might've got a knock on the noggin from ol' Larry. You can bet on that."

The pilot asked personnel in Easton if they could arrange a ride to New York City for his passenger.

"You're joking, right, Lear?"

"Didn't mean to, over."

"We got a guy can get him to within a couple of miles of the subway. No cars in or out of the city yet, and even the trains have some kind of a complicated route that takes them around bad sites."

"Bad sites?" Buck repeated.

"Say again," Ritz radioed.

"Haven't you been watching the news? Some of the worst disasters in the city were the result of disappearing motor-men and dispatchers. Six trains were involved in head-ons with lots of deaths. Several trains ran up the back of other ones. It'll be days before they clear all the tracks and replace cars. You sure your man wants to get into midtown?"

"Roger. Seems like the type who can handle it."

"Hope he's got good hiking boots, over."

It cost Buck another premium for a ride close enough to the train that he could walk the rest of the way. His driver had not even been a cabbie, nor the vehicle a cab. But it might as well have been. It was just as decrepit and unsafe.

A two-mile walk got him to the train platform at about noon, where he waited more than forty minutes with a mass of humanity, only to find himself among the last half who had to wait another half an hour for the next train. The zigzag ride took two hours to get to Manhattan, and all during the trip Buck tapped at the keys on his laptop or stared out the window at the gridlock that went on for miles. He knew many of his locally based colleagues would have already filed similar reports, so his only hope of scoring with Steve Plank and having this see publication was if his were more powerfully or eloquently written. He was in such awe of the scene that he doubted he could pull it off. At the very least he was adding drama to his own memoirs. New York City was at a standstill, and the biggest surprise was that they were letting people in at all. No doubt many of these, like him, lived here and needed to get to their homes and apartments.

The train lurched to a stop, far short of where he had been told it would reach. The garbled announcement, the best he could make out, informed passengers that this was the new last stop. Their next jog would have put them in the middle of a crane site where cars were being lifted off the track. Buck calculated about a fifteen-mile walk to his office and another five to his apartment.

Fortunately, Buck was in great shape. He put everything into his bag and shortened the strap so he could carry it close to his body without it swinging. He set off at what he guessed was a four-mile-per-hour pace, and three hours later he was hurting. He was sure he had blisters, and his neck and shoulders were tired from the bag and strap. He was sweating through his clothes, and there was no way he was going to get to his apartment before stopping in at the office.

"Oh, God, help me," Buck breathed, more exasperated than praying. But if there was a God, he decided, God had a sense of humor. Leaning against a brick wall in an alley in plain sight was a yellow bicycle with a cardboard sign clipped to it. It read, "Borrow this bike. Take it where you like. Leave it for someone else in need. No charge."

Only in New York, he thought. *Nobody steals something that's free.*

He thought about breathing a prayer of thanks, but somehow the world he was looking at didn't show any other evidence of a benevolent Creator. He mounted the bike, realized how long it had been since he had been aboard one, and wobbled off till he found his balance. It wasn't long before he cruised into midtown between the snarl of wreckage and wreckers. Only a few other people were traveling as efficiently as he was—couriers on bikes, two others on yellow bikes just like his, and cops on horseback.

Security was tight at the *Global Weekly* building, which somehow didn't surprise him. After identifying himself to a new desk clerk, he rode to the twenty-seventh floor, stopped in the public washroom to freshen up, and finally entered the main suites of the magazine. The receptionist immediately buzzed Steve Plank's office, and both Steve and Marge Potter hurried out to embrace and welcome him.

Buck Williams was hit with a strange, new emotion. He nearly wept. He realized he, along with everyone else, was enduring a hideous trauma and that he had no doubt been running on adrenaline. But somehow, getting back to familiar territory—especially with the expense and effort it had taken—made him feel as if he had come home. He was with people who cared about him. This was his family. He was really, really glad to see them, and it appeared the feeling was mutual.

He bit his lip to keep from clouding up, and as he followed Steve and Marge down the hall past his tiny, cluttered office and into Steve's spacious office/conference room, he asked if they had heard about Lucinda Washington.

Marge stopped in the corridor, bringing her hands to her face. "Yes," she managed, "and I wasn't going to do this again. We've lost several. Where does the grieving start and end?"

With that, Buck lost it. He couldn't pretend any longer, though he was as surprised as anyone at his own sensitivity. Steve put an arm around his secretary and guided her and Buck into his office, where others from the senior staff waited.

They cheered when they saw Buck. These people, the ones he had worked with, fought with, feuded with, irritated, and scooped, now seemed genuinely glad to see him. They could have no idea how he felt. "Boy, it's good to be back here," he said, then sat and buried his head in his hands. His body began to shake, and he could fight the tears no longer. He began to sob, right there in front of his colleagues and competitors.

He tried to wipe the tears away and compose himself, but when he looked up, forcing an embarrassed smile, he noticed everyone else was emotional, too. "It's all right, Bucky," one said. "If this is your first cry, you'll discover it won't be your last. We're all just as scared and stunned and grief stricken as you are."

"Yeah," another said, "but his personal account will no doubt be more compelling." Which made everyone laugh and cry all the more.

Rayford talked himself into calling the Pan-Con Flight Center early in the afternoon. He learned that he was to report in for a Friday flight two days later. "Really?" he said.

"Don't count on actually flying it," he was told. "Not too many flights are expected to be lifting off by then. Certainly none till late tomorrow, and maybe not even then."

"There's a chance I'll get called off before I leave home?"

"More than a chance, but that's your assignment for now."

"What's the route?"

"ORD to BOS to JFK."

"Hmm. Chicago, Boston, New York. Home when?"

"Saturday night."

"Good."

"Why? Got a date?"

"Not funny."

"Oh, gosh, I'm sorry, Captain. I forgot who I was talking to."

"You know about my family?"

"Everybody here knows, sir. We're sorry. We heard it from the senior flight attendant on your aborted Heathrow run. You got the word on your first officer on that flight, didn't you?"

"I heard something but never got any official word."

"What'd you hear?"

"Suicide."

"Right. Awful."

"Can you check on something for me?"

"If it's in my power, Captain."

"My daughter is trying to get back this way from California."

"Unlikely."

"I know, but she's on her way. Trying anyway. She'll more than likely try to fly Pan. Can you check and see if she's on any of the manifests coming east?"

"Shouldn't be too hard. There are precious few, and you know none of them will be landing here."

"How about Milwaukee?"

"Don't think so." He was tapping computer keys. "Where would she originate?"

"Somewhere near Palo Alto."

"Not good."

"Why?"

"Hardly anything coming out of there. Let me check."

Rayford could hear the man talking to himself, trying things, suggesting options. "Air California to Utah. Hey! Found her! Name Chloe with your last name?"

"That's her!"

"She checked in at Palo Alto. Pan put her on a bus to some outlying strip. Flew her to Salt Lake City on Air California. First time out of the state for that plane, I'll bet. She got on a Pan-Con plane, oh, an oldie, and they took her to, um, oh brother. Enid, Oklahoma."

"Enid? That's never been on our routes."

"No kidding. They were overrun with Dallas's spill-over, too. Anyway, she's flying Ozark to Springfield, Illinois."

"Ozark!"

"I just work here, Cap."

"Well, somebody's trying to make it work, aren't they?"

"Yeah, the good news is, we've got a turboprop or two down there that can get her up into the area, but it doesn't say where she might land. It might not even come up on this screen because they won't know till they get close."

"How will I know where to pick her up?"

"You may not. I'm sure she'll call you when she lands. Who knows? Maybe she'll just show up."

"That would be nice."

"Well, I'm sorry for what you're going through, sir, but you can be grateful your daughter didn't get on Pan-Con directly out of Palo Alto. The last one out of there went down last night. No survivors."

"And this was after the disappearances?"

"Just last night. Totally unrelated."

"Wouldn't that have been a kick in the teeth?" Rayford said.

"Indeed."

EIGHT

WHEN the other senior writers and editors drifted back to their offices, Steve Plank insisted Buck Williams go home and rest before coming back for an eight o'clock meeting that evening.

"I'd rather get done now and go home for the night."

"I know," the executive editor said, "but we've got a lot to do and I want you sharp."

Still, Buck was reluctant. "How soon can I get to London?"

"What have you got there?"

Buck filled Steve in on his tip about a major U.S. financier meeting with international colleagues and introducing a rising European politico. "Oh, man, Buck," Steve said, "we're all over that. You mean Carpathia."

Buck was stunned. "I do?"

"He was the guy Rosenzweig was so impressed with."

"Yeah, but you think he's the one my informant is—"

"Man, you *have* been out of touch," Steve said. "It's not that big a deal. The financier has to be Jonathan Stonagal, who seems to be sponsoring him. I told you Carpathia was coming to address the U.N., didn't I?"

"So he's the new Romanian ambassador to the U.N.?" Buck said.

"Hardly."

"What then?"

"President of the country."

"Didn't they just elect a leader, what, eighteen months ago?" Buck said, remembering Dirk's tip that a new leader would seem out of place and time.

"Big shake-up there," Steve said. "Better check it out."

"I will."

"I don't mean you. I really don't think there's much of a story. The guy is young and dashing and all that, charming and persuasive as I understand it. He had been a meteoric business star, making a killing when Romanian markets opened to the West years ago. But as of last week he wasn't even in their senate yet. He was only in the lower house."

"The House of Deputies," Buck said.

"How did you know that?"

Buck grinned. "Rosenzweig educated me."

"For a minute there I thought you really did know everything. That's what you get accused of around here, you know."

"What a crime."

"But you play it with such humility."

"That's me. So, Steve, why don't you think it's important that a guy like Carpathia comes from nowhere to unseat the president of Romania?"

"He didn't exactly come from nowhere. His businesses were built on Stonagal financing. And Carpathia has been a disarmament crusader, very popular with his colleagues and the people."

"But disarmament doesn't fit with Stonagal. Isn't he a closet hawk?"

Plank nodded.

"So there are mysteries."

"Some, but, Buck, what could be bigger than the story you're on? You haven't got time to fool with a guy who becomes president of a nonstrategic country."

"There's something there, though, Steve. My guy in London tips me off. Carpathia's tied in with the most influential nonpolitician in the world. He goes from lower house to president without a popular election."

"And—"

"There's more? Which side of this argument are you on? Did he have the sitting president killed or something?"

"Interesting you should say that, because the only wrinkle in Carpathia's history are some rumors that he was ruthless with his business competition years ago."

"How ruthless?"

"People took dirt naps."

"Ooh, Steve, you talk just like a mobster."

"And listen, the previous president stepped down for Carpathia. Insisted on his installation."

"And you say there's no story here?"

"This is like the old South American coups, Buck. A new one every week. Big deal. So Carpathia's beholden to Stonagal. All that means is that Stonagal will have free rein in the financial world of an Eastern European country that thinks the best thing that ever happened to it was the destruction of Russia."

"But, Steve, this is like a freshman congressman becoming president of the United States in an off-election year, no vote, president steps aside, and everybody's happy."

"No, no, no, big difference. We're talking Romania here, Buck. *Romania.* Nonstrategic, scant gross national product, never invaded anybody, never anyone's strategic ally. There's nothing there but low-level internal politics."

"It still smells major to me," Buck said. "Rosenzweig was high on this guy, and he's an astute observer. Now Carpathia's coming to speak at the U.N. What next?"

"You forget he was coming to the U.N. *before* he became president of Romania."

"That's another puzzle. He was a nobody."

"He's a new name and face in disarmament. He gets his season in the sun, his fifteen minutes of fame. Trust me, you're not going to hear of him again."

"Stonagal had to be behind the U.N. gig, too," Buck said. "You know Diamond John is a personal friend of our ambassador."

"Stonagal is a personal friend of every elected official from the president to the mayors of most medium-sized cities, Buck. So what? He knows how to play the game. He reminds me of old Joe Kennedy or one of the Rockefellers, all right? What's your point?"

"Just that Carpathia is speaking at the U.N. on Stonagal's influence."

"Probably. So what?"

"He's up to something."

"Stonagal's always up to something, keeping the skids greased for one of his projects. OK, so he gets a businessman into Romanian politics, maybe even gets him installed as president. Who knows, maybe he even got him his little audience with Rosenzweig, which never amounted to anything. Now he gets Carpathia a little international exposure. That happens all the time because of guys like Stonagal. Would you rather chase this nonstory than tie together a cover piece that tries to make sense of the most monumental and tragic phenomenon in the history of the world?"

"Hmm, let me think about that," Buck said, smiling, as Plank punched him.

"Man, you can sure chase rabbit trails," the executive editor said.

"You used to like my instincts."

"I still do, but you're a little sleep-deprived right now."

"I'm definitely not going to London? Because I've got to tell my guy."

"Marge tried to reach the guy who was supposed to meet your plane. She can tell you how to get through and all that. But be back here by eight. I'm bringing in the department editors interested in the various international

meetings coming here this month. You're going to be
tying that coverage together, so—"

"So they can all hate me in the same meeting?" Buck
said.

"They'll feel important."

"But *is* it important? You want me to ignore
Carpathia, but you're going to complicate my life with,
what was it, an ecumenical religious convention and a
one-world-currency confab?"

"You *are* short on sleep, aren't you, Buck? This is why
I'm still your boss. Don't you get it? Yes, I want coordination and I want a well-written piece. But think about
it. This gives you automatic entrée to all these dignitaries. We're talking Jewish Nationalist leaders interested in
one world government—"

"Unlikely and hardly compelling."

"—Orthodox Jews from all over the world looking at
rebuilding the temple, or some such—"

"I'm being overrun by Jews."

"—international monetarists setting the stage for one
world currency—"

"Also unlikely."

"But this will let you keep an eye on your favorite
power broker—"

"Stonagal."

"Right, and heads of various religious groups looking
to cooperate internationally."

"Bore me to death, why don't you? These people are
discussing impossibilities. Since when have religious
groups been able to get along?"

"You're still not getting it, Buck. You're going to have access to all these people—religious, monied, political—while trying to write a piece about what happened and why it happened. You can get the thinking of the greatest minds from the most diverse viewpoints."

Buck shrugged in surrender. "You've got a point. I still say our department editors are going to resent me."

"There's something to be said for consistency."

"I still want to try to get to Carpathia."

"That won't be hard. He's already a media darling in Europe. Eager to talk."

"And Stonagal."

"You know he never talks to the press, Buck."

"I like a challenge."

"Go home and take a load off. See you at eight."

Marge Potter was preparing to leave as Buck approached. "Oh yes," Marge said, setting down her stuff and flipping through her notebook. "I tried Dirk Burton several times. Got through once to his voice mail and left him your message. Received no confirmation. OK?"

"Thanks."

Buck wasn't sure he'd be able to rest at home with everything flying through his brain. He was pleasantly surprised when he reached street level to find that representatives of various cab companies were posted outside office buildings, directing people to cabs that could reach certain areas via circuitous routes. For premium fares, of course. For thirty dollars, in a shared cab, Buck was let off two blocks from his apartment. In three hours he would have to be back at the office, so he made arrangements with the cabbie to meet him at the same spot at seven forty-five. That, he decided, would be a miracle. With all the cabs in New York, he had never before had to make such an arrangement, and to his knowledge had never even seen the same cabbie twice.

Rayford was pacing, miserable. He came to the painful realization that this was the worst season of his life. He had never even come close before. His parents had been older than those of his peers. When they had died within two years of each other, it had been a relief. They were not well, not lucid. He loved them and they were no burden, but they had virtually died to him years before, due to strokes and other ailments. When they did pass, Rayford had grieved in a way, but mostly he was just sentimental about them. He had good memories, he appreciated the kindness and sympathy he received at their funerals, and he got on with his life. Whatever tears he shed were not from remorse or heartache. He felt primarily nostalgic and melancholy.

The rest of his life had been without complication or pain. Becoming a pilot was akin to rising to any other highly paid professional level. You had to be intelligent and disciplined, accomplished. He came through the ranks in the usual way—military-reserve duty, small planes, then bigger ones, then jets and fighters. Finally he had reached the pinnacle.

He had met Irene in Reserve Officer Training Corps in college. She had been an army brat who had never rebelled. Many of her chums had turned their backs on military life and didn't even want to own up to it. Her father had been killed in Vietnam and her mother married another military man, so Irene had seen or lived on nearly every army base in the United States.

They were married when Rayford was a senior in college and Irene a sophomore. She dropped out when he went into the military, and everything had been on schedule since. They had Chloe during their first year of marriage but, due to complications, waited another eight years for Ray Jr. Rayford was thrilled with both children, but he had to admit he had longed for a namesake boy.

Unfortunately, Raymie came along during a bleak period for Rayford. He was thirty and feeling older, and he didn't enjoy having a pregnant wife. Many people thought, because of his premature but not unattractive gray hair, that he was older, and so he endured the jokes about being an old father. It was a particularly difficult pregnancy for Irene, and Raymie was a couple of weeks late. Chloe was a spirited eight-year-old, so Rayford disengaged as much as possible.

Irene, he believed, slipped into at least some mild depression during that time and was short tempered with him and weepy. At work Rayford was in charge, listened to, and admired. He had been rated for the biggest, latest, and most sophisticated planes in the Pan-Continental stable. His work life was going swimmingly; he didn't enjoy going home.

He had drunk more during that period than ever before or since, and the marriage had gone through its most trying time. He was frequently late getting home and at times even fibbed about his schedule so he could leave a day early or come back a day late. Irene accused him of all manner of affairs, and because she was wrong, he denied them with great vigor and, he felt, justified anger.

The truth was, he was hoping for and angling for just what she was charging. What frustrated him so was that, despite his looks and bearing, it just wasn't in him to pull it off. He didn't have the moves, the patter, the style. A flight attendant had once called him a hunk, but he felt like a geek, an egghead. Sure, he had access to any woman with a price, but that was beneath him. While he toyed with and hoped for an old-fashioned affair, he somehow couldn't bring himself to stoop to something as tawdry as paying for sex.

Had Irene known how hard he was trying to be unfaithful, she would have left him. As it was, he had indulged in that make-out session at the Christmas party before Raymie was born, but he was so inebriated he could hardly remember it.

The guilt and nearly spoiling his image straightened him up and made him cut down on his drinking. Seeing Raymie born sobered him even more. It was time to grow up and take as much responsibility as a husband and father as he did as a pilot.

But now, as Rayford ran all those memories through his throbbing head, he felt the deepest regret and remorse a man can feel. He felt like a failure. He was so unworthy of Irene. Somehow he knew now, though he had never allowed himself to consider it before, that she couldn't in any way have been as naive or stupid as he had hoped and imagined. She had to have known how vapid he was, how shallow, and yes, cheap. And yet she had stayed by him, loved him, fought to keep the marriage together.

He couldn't argue that she became a different person after she switched churches and got serious about her faith. She preached at him at first, sure. She was excited and wanted him to discover what she had found. He ran. Eventually she either gave up or resigned herself to the fact that he was not going to come around by her pleading or cajoling. Now he knew from seeing her list that she had never given up. She had simply taken to praying for him.

No wonder Rayford had never gotten that close to ultimately defiling his marriage with Hattie Durham. Hattie! How ashamed he was of that silly pursuit! For all he knew, Hattie was innocent. She had never bad-mouthed his wife or the fact that he was married. She had never suggested anything inappropriate, at least for her age. Young people were more touchy and flirtatious, and she claimed no moral or religious code. That Rayford had obsessed over the possibilities with Hattie, while she probably hardly knew it, made him feel all the more foolish.

Where was this guilt coming from? He had locked eyes with Hattie numerous times, and they had spent hours alone together over dinners in various cities. But she had never asked him to her room or tried to kiss him or even hold his hand. Maybe she would have responded had he been the aggressor, but maybe not. She might just as easily have been offended, insulted, disappointed.

Rayford shook his head. Not only was he guilty of lusting after a woman to whom he had no right, but he was still such a klutz he hadn't even known how to pursue her.

And now he faced the darkest hours of his soul. He was nervous about Chloe. He wanted her home and safe in the worst way, hoping that having his own flesh and blood in the house would somehow assuage his grief and pain. He knew he should be hungry again, but nothing appealed. Even the fragrant and tasty cookies he thought he would have to ration had become painful reminders of Irene. Maybe tomorrow.

Rayford switched on the television, not out of interest in seeing more mayhem, but with the hope of some news of order, traffic clearing, people connecting. After a minute or two of the same old same old, he turned it off again. He rejected the idea of calling O'Hare about the likelihood of getting in to get his car, because he didn't want to tie up the phone for even a minute in case Chloe was trying to get through. It had been hours since he'd heard she left Palo Alto. How long would it take to make all those crazy connections and finally get on an Ozark flight from Springfield to the Chicago area? He remembered the oldest joke in the airline industry: Ozark spelled backward is Krazo. Only it didn't amuse him just then.

He leaped when the phone rang, but it was not Chloe.

"I'm sorry, Captain," Hattie said. "I promised to call you back, but I fell asleep after the call I took and have been out ever since."

"That's quite all right, Hattie. In fact, I need to—"

"I mean, I didn't want to bother you anyway at a time like this."

"No, that's OK, I just—"

"Have you talked to Chloe?"

"I'm waiting for her to call right now, so I really have to get off!"

Rayford had been more curt than he intended and Hattie was, at first, silent. "Well, all right then. I'm sorry."

"I'll call you, Hattie. OK?"

"OK."

She had sounded hurt. He was sorry about that, but not sorry that he had gotten rid of her for the time being. He knew she was only trying to help and be kind, but she hadn't been listening. She was alone and afraid just like he was, and no doubt by now she had found out about her family. Oh, no! He hadn't even asked about them! She would hate him, and why shouldn't she? *How selfish could I be?* he wondered.

Eager as he was to hear from Chloe, he had to risk a couple more minutes on the phone. He dialed Hattie, but her line was busy.

———

Buck tried calling Dirk Burton in London as soon as he got home, not wanting to wait longer with the time difference overseas. He got a puzzling response. Dirk's personal answering machine ran through its usual message, but as soon as the leave-a-message beep sounded, a longer tone indicated that the tape was full. Strange. Dirk was either sleeping through it all or—

Buck had not considered that Dirk could have disappeared. Besides leaving Buck with a million questions about Stonagal, Carpathia, Todd-Cothran, and the whole phenomenon, Dirk was one of his best friends from Princeton. *Oh, please let this be a coincidence,* he thought. *Let him be traveling.*

As soon as Buck hung up, his phone rang. Of all people, it was Hattie Durham. She was crying. "I'm sorry to bother you, Mr. Williams, and I had promised myself I would never use your home number—"

"That's all right, Hattie. What is it?"

"Well, it's silly really, but I just went through something, and I don't have anybody to talk to about it. I couldn't get through to my mother and sisters, and well, I just thought maybe you'd understand."

"Try me."

She told Buck about her call to Captain Steele and brought him up to date on who Steele was, that he had lost his wife and son, and that she had been late calling him back after hearing her good news from Buck. "And then he just brushed me off because he's waiting for a call from his daughter."

"I can understand that," Buck tried, rolling his eyes. How did he get into this lonely hearts club? Didn't she have any girlfriends to unload on?

"I can, too," she said. "That's just it. And I know he's grieving because it's like his wife and son are dead, but he knew I was on pins and needles about my family, and he never even asked."

"Well, I'm sure it is all just part of the tension of the moment, the grief, like you say, and—"

"Oh, I know it. I just wanted to talk to somebody, and I thought of you."

"Well, hey, anytime," Buck lied. *Oh, boy,* he thought. *My home number is definitely going to come off that next batch of business cards.* "Listen, I'd better let you go. I've got an evening meeting tonight myself, and—"

"Well, thanks for listening."

"I understand," he said, though he doubted he ever would. Maybe Hattie showed more depth and sense when she wasn't under stress. He hoped so.

Rayford was glad Hattie's line was busy, because he could tell her he had tried to call her right back, but he didn't have to tie up his phone any longer. A minute later, his phone rang again.

"Captain, it's me again. I'm sorry, I won't keep you long, but I thought you might have tried to call me, and I've been on the phone, so—"

"As a matter of fact, I did, Hattie. What have you found out about your family?"

"They're fine." She was crying.

"Oh, thank God," he said.

Rayford wondered what had gotten into him. He said he was happy for her, but he had come to the conclusion that those who had not disappeared had missed out on the greatest event of cosmic history. But what was he supposed to say—"Oh, I'm sorry your family was left behind, too"?

When he hung up, Rayford sat next to the phone with a nagging feeling that he had for sure missed Chloe's call this time. It made him mad. His stomach was growling and he knew he should eat, but he had decided he would hold off as long as possible, hoping to eat with Chloe when she arrived. Knowing her, she wouldn't have eaten a thing.

NINE

BUCK's subconscious waking system failed him that evening, but by 8:45 P.M. he was back in Steve Plank's office, disheveled and apologetic. And he had been right. He felt the resentment from veteran department editors. Juan Ortiz, chief of the international politics section, was incensed that Buck should have anything to do with the summit conference Juan planned to cover in two weeks.

"The Jewish Nationalists are discussing an issue I have been following for years. Who would have believed they would consider warming to one world government? That they would even entertain the discussion is monumental. They're meeting here, rather than in Jerusalem or Tel Aviv, because their idea is so revolutionary. Most Israeli Nationalists think the Holy Land has gone too far with its bounty already. This is historic."

"Then what's your problem," Plank said, "with my adding our top guy to the coverage?"

"Because *I* am your top guy on this."

"I'm trying to make sense of all these meetings," Plank said.

Jimmy Borland, the religion editor, weighed in. "I understand Juan's objections, but I've got two meetings at the same time. I welcome the help."

"Now we're getting somewhere," Plank said.

"But I'll be frank, Buck," Borland added. "I want a say in the final piece."

"Of course," Plank said.

"Not so fast," Buck said. "I don't want to be treated like a pool reporter here. I'm going to have my own take on these meetings, and I'm not trying to horn in on your expert territories. I wouldn't want to do the coverages of the individual meetings themselves. I want to bring some coordination, find the meaning, the common denominators. Jimmy, your two groups—the religious Jews who want to rebuild the temple and the ecumenicalists who want some sort of one-world religious order—are they going to be at odds with each other? Will there be religious Jews—"

"Orthodox."

"OK, Orthodox Jews at the ecumenical meeting? Because that seems at cross purposes with rebuilding the temple."

"Well, at least you're thinking like a religion editor," Jimmy said. "That's encouraging."

"But what's your thought?"

"I don't know. That's what makes this so interesting. That they should meet at the same time in the same city is too good to be true."

Financial editor Barbara Donahue brought closure to the discussion. "I've dealt with you before on these kinds of efforts, Steve," she said. "And I appreciate the way you let everybody vent without threat. But we all know your mind is made up about Buck's involvement, so let's lick our wounds and get on with it. If we each get to put our own spin on the coverage in our departments and have some input on the overall piece that I assume goes in the main well, let's get on with it."

Even Ortiz nodded, though to Buck he seemed reluctant.

"Buck's the quarterback," Plank said, "so keep in touch with him. He'll report to me. You want to say anything, Buck?"

"Just thanks a lot," he said ruefully, causing everyone to chuckle. "Barbara, your monetarists are meeting right at the U.N., like they did when they went to the three-currency thing?"

She nodded. "Same place and pretty much the same people."

"How involved is Jonathan Stonagal?"

"Overtly, you mean?" she said.

"Well, everybody knows he's circumspect. But is there a Stonagal influence?"

"Does a duck have lips?"

Buck smiled and jotted a note. "I'll take that as a yes. I'd like to hang around that one, maybe try to get to Diamond John."

"Good luck. He probably won't show his face."

"But he'll be in town, won't he, Barbara? Wasn't he at the Plaza for the duration last time?"

"You do get around, don't you?" she said.

"Well, he only had each of the principals up to his suite every day."

Juan Ortiz raised a hand. "I'm going along with this, and I have nothing personal against you, Buck. But I don't believe there is a way to coordinate this story without inventing some tie-in. I mean, if you want to lead off a feature story by saying there were four important international meetings in town almost all at once, fine. But to make them interrelated would be stretching."

"If I find that they aren't interrelated, there won't be an overall story," Buck said. "Fair enough?"

Rayford Steele was nearly beside himself with worry, compounded by his grief. Where was Chloe? He had been inside all day, pacing, mourning, thinking. He felt stale and claustrophobic. He had called Pan-Continental and was told his car might be released by the time he got back from his weekend flight. The news on TV showed the amazing progress being made at clearing the roadways and getting mass transportation rolling again. But the landscape would appear tacky for months. Cranes and wreckers had run out of junkyards, so the twisted wreckages remained in hazardous piles at the sides of roads and expressways.

By the time Rayford got around to calling his wife's church, it was after hours, and he was grateful he wouldn't have to talk to anyone. As he hoped, a new message was on their answering machine, though it was communicated by a stunned-sounding male voice.

"You have reached New Hope Village Church. We are planning a weekly Bible study, but for the time being we will meet just once each Sunday at 10 A.M. While our entire staff, except me, and most of our congregation are gone, the few of us left are maintaining the building and distributing a videotape our senior pastor prepared for a time such as this. You may come by the church office anytime to pick up a free copy, and we look forward to seeing you Sunday morning."

Well, of course, Rayford thought, *that pastor had often spoken of the Rapture of the church.* That was why Irene was so enamored with it. What a creative idea, to tape a message for those who had been left behind! He and Chloe would have to get one the next day. He hoped she would be as interested as he was in discovering the truth.

Rayford gazed out the front window in the darkness, just in time to see Chloe, one big suitcase on the ground next to her, paying a cabdriver. He ran from the house in his stocking feet and gathered her into his arms. "Oh, Daddy!" she wailed. "How's everybody?"

He shook his head.

"I don't want to hear this," she said, pulling away from him and looking to the house as if expecting her mother or brother to appear in the doorway.

"It's just you and me, Chloe," Rayford said, and they stood together in the darkness, crying.

———————

It was Friday before Buck Williams was able to track down Dirk Burton. He reached the supervisor in Dirk's area of the London Exchange. "You must tell me precisely who you are and your specific relationship to Mr. Burton before I am allowed to inform you as to his disposition," Nigel Leonard said. "I am also constrained to inform you that this conversation shall be taped, beginning immediately."

"I'm sorry?"

"I'm taping our conversation, sir. If that is a problem for you, you may disconnect."

"I don't follow."

"What's to follow? You understand what a tape is, do you?"

"Of course, and I'm turning mine on now as well, if you don't mind."

"Well, I *do* mind, Mr. Williams. Why on earth would *you* be taping?"

"Why would *you?*"

"We are the ones with a most unfortunate situation, and we need to investigate all leads."

"What situation? Was Dirk among those who disappeared?"

"Nothing so tidy as that, I'm afraid."

"Tell me."

"First your reason for asking."

"I'm an old friend. We were college classmates."

"Where?"

"Princeton."

"Very well. When?"

Buck told him.

"Very well. The last time you spoke to him?"

"I don't recall, OK? We've been trading voice-mail messages."

"Your occupation?"

Buck hesitated. "Senior writer, *Global Weekly,* New York."

"Would your interest be journalistic in nature?"

"I won't preclude that," Buck said, trying not to let his anger seep through, "but I can't imagine that my friend, important as he is to me, is of interest to my readers."

"Mr. Williams," Nigel said carefully, "allow me to state categorically, on both our tapes apparently, that what I am about to say is strictly off the record. Do you understand?"

"I—"

"Because I am aware that both in your country and in the British Commonwealth, anything said following an assertion that we are off the record is protected."

"Granted," Buck said.

"Beg pardon?"

"You heard me. Granted. We're off the record. Now where is Dirk?"

"Mr. Burton's body was discovered in his flat this morning. He had suffered a bullet wound to the head. I'm sorry, as you were a friend, but suicide has been determined."

Buck was nearly speechless. "By whom?" he managed.

"The authorities."

"What authorities?"

"Scotland Yard and security personnel here at the exchange."

Scotland Yard? Buck thought. *We'll see about that.* "Why is the exchange involved?"

"We're protective of our information and our personnel, sir."

"Suicide is impossible, you know," Buck said.

"Do I?"

"If you are his supervisor, you know."

"There have been countless suicides since the disappearances, sir."

Buck was shaking his head as if Nigel could see him from across the Atlantic. "Dirk didn't kill himself, and you know it."

"Sir, I can appreciate your sentiments, but I don't know any more than you did what was in Mr. Burton's mind. I was partial to him, but I would not be in a position to question the conclusion of the medical examiner."

Buck slammed the phone down and marched into Steve Plank's office. He told Steve what he had heard.

"That's terrible," Steve said.

"I have a contact at Scotland Yard who knows Dirk, but I don't dare talk to him about it by phone. Can I have Marge book me on the next flight to London? I'll be back in time for all these summits, but I've got to go."

"If you can get a flight. I don't know that JFK is even open yet."

"How about La Guardia?"

"Ask Marge. You know Carpathia will be here tomorrow."

"You said yourself he was small potatoes. Maybe he'll still be here when I get back."

Rayford Steele hadn't been able to talk his grieving daughter into leaving the house. Chloe had spent hours in her little brother's room, and then in her parents' bedroom, picking through their personal effects to add to the boxes of memories her father had put together. Rayford felt so bad for her. He had secretly hoped she would be of comfort to him. He knew she would be eventually. But for now she needed time to face her own loss. Once she had cried herself out, she was ready to talk. And after she had reminisced to the point where Rayford didn't know if his heart could take any more, she finally changed the subject to the phenomenon of the disappearances themselves.

"Daddy, in California they're actually buying into the space invasion theory."

"You're kidding."

"No. Maybe it's because you were always so practical and skeptical about all that tabloid newspaper stuff, but I just can't get into it. I mean, it has to be something supernatural or otherworldly, but—"

"But what?"

"It just seems that if some alien life force was capable of doing this, they would also be capable of communicating to us. Wouldn't they want to take over now or demand ransom or get us to do something for them?"

"Who? Martians?"

"Daddy! I'm not saying I believe it. I'm saying I don't. But doesn't my reasoning make sense?"

"You don't have to convince me. I admit I wouldn't have dreamed any of this even possible a week ago, but my logic has been stretched to the breaking point."

Rayford hoped Chloe would ask his theory. He didn't want to start right in on a religious theme. She had always been antagonistic about that, having stopped going to church in high school when both he and Irene gave up fighting with her over it. She was a good kid, never in trouble. She made grades good enough to get her a partial academic scholarship, and though she occasionally stayed out too late and went through a boy-crazy period in high school, they had never had to bail her out of jail and there was never any evidence of drug use. He didn't take that lightly.

Rayford and Irene knew Chloe had come home from more than one party drunk enough to spend the night vomiting. The first time, he and Irene chose to ignore it, to act as if it didn't happen. They believed she was level-headed enough to know better the next time. When the next time came, Rayford had a chat with her.

"I know, I know, I know, OK, Dad? You don't need to start in on me."

"I'm not starting in on you. I want to make sure you know enough to not drive if you drink too much."

"Of course I do."

"And you know how stupid and dangerous it is to drink too much."

"I thought you weren't starting in on me."

"Just tell me you know."

"I think I already said that."

He had shaken his head and said nothing.

"Daddy, don't give up on me. Go ahead, give me both barrels. Prove you care."

"Don't make fun of me," he had said. "Someday you're going to have a child and you won't know what to say or do either. When you love somebody with all your heart and all you care about is her welfare—"

Rayford hadn't been able to continue. For the first time in his adult life, he had choked up. It had never happened during his arguments with Irene. He had always been too defensive, concerned too much about making his point to think about how much he cared for her. But with Chloe, he really wanted to say the right thing, to protect her from herself. He wanted her to know how much he loved her, and it was coming out all wrong. It was as if he were punishing, lecturing, reprimanding, condescending. That had caused him to break.

Though he hadn't planned it, that involuntary show of emotion got through to Chloe. For months she had been drifting from him, from both her parents. She had been sullen, cold, independent, sarcastic, challenging. He knew it was all part of growing up and becoming one's own person, but it was a painful, scary time.

As he bit his lip and breathed deeply, hoping to regain composure and not embarrass himself, Chloe had come to him and wrapped her arms around his neck, just as she had as a little girl. "Oh, Daddy, don't cry," she had said. "I know you love me. I know you care. Don't worry about me. I learned my lesson and I won't be stupid again, I promise."

He had dissolved into tears, and so had she. They had bonded as never before. He didn't recall ever having to discipline her again, and though she had not come back to church, he had started to drift by then himself. They had become buddies, and she was growing up to be just like him. Irene had kidded him that their children each had their own favorite parent.

Now, just days after Irene and Raymie had disappeared, Rayford hoped the relationship that had really begun with an emotional moment when Chloe was in high school would blossom so they could talk. What was more important than what had happened? He knew now what her crazy college friends and the typical Californian believed. What else was new? He always generalized that people on the West Coast afforded the tabloids the same weight Midwesterners gave the *Chicago Tribune* or even the *New York Times*.

Late in the day, Friday, Rayford and Chloe reluctantly agreed they should eat, and they worked together in the kitchen, rustling up a healthy mixture of fruits and vegetables. There was something calming and healing about working with her in silence. It was painful on the one hand, because anything domestic reminded him of Irene. And when they sat to eat, they automatically sat in their customary spots at either end of the table—which made the other two open spots that much more conspicuous.

Rayford noticed Chloe clouding up again, and he knew she was feeling what he was. It hadn't been that many years since they had enjoyed three or four meals a week together as a family. Irene had always sat on his left, Raymie on his right, and Chloe directly across. The emptiness and the silence were jarring.

Rayford was ravenous and finished a huge salad. Chloe stopped eating soon after she had begun and wept silently, her head down, tears falling in her lap. Her father took her hand, and she rose and sat in his lap, hiding her face and sobbing. His heart aching for her, Rayford rocked her until she was silent. "Where are they?" she whined at last.

"You want to know where I think they are?" he said. "Do you really want to know?"

"Of course!"

"I believe they are in heaven."

"Oh, Daddy! There were some religious nuts at school who were saying that, but if they knew so much about it, how come they didn't go?"

"Maybe they realized they had been wrong and had missed their opportunity."

"You think that's what we've done?" Chloe said, returning to her chair.

"I'm afraid so. Didn't your mother tell you she

believed that Jesus could come back some day and take his people directly to heaven before they died?"

"Sure, but she was always more religious than the rest of us. I thought she was just getting a little carried away."

"Good choice of words."

"Hm?"

"She got carried away, Chloe. Raymie too."

"You don't really believe that, do you?"

"I do."

"That's about as crazy as the Martian invasion theory."

Rayford felt defensive. "So what's *your* theory?"

Chloe began to clear the table and spoke with her back to him. "I'm honest enough to admit I don't know."

"So now I'm not being honest?"

Chloe turned to face him, sympathy on her face. "Don't you see, Dad? You've gravitated to the least painful possibility. If we were voting, my first choice would be that my mom and my little brother are in heaven with God, sitting on clouds, playing their harps."

"So I'm deluding myself, is that what you're saying?"

"Daddy, I don't fault you. But you have to admit this is pretty far-fetched."

Now Rayford was angry. "What's more far-fetched than people disappearing right out of their clothes? Who else could have done that? Years ago we'd have blamed it on the Soviets, said they had developed some super new technology, some death ray that affected only human flesh and bone. But there's no Soviet threat anymore, and the Russians lost people, too. And how did this . . . this whatever it was—how did it choose who to take and who to leave?"

"You're saying the only logical explanation is God, that he took his own and left the rest of us?"

"That's what I'm saying."

"I don't want to hear this."

"Chloe, our own family is a perfect picture of what happened. If what I'm saying is right, the logical two people are gone and the logical two were left."

"You think I'm that much of a sinner?"

"Chloe, listen. Whatever you are, I am. I'm not judging you. If I'm right about this, we missed something. I always called myself a Christian, mostly because I was raised that way and I wasn't Jewish."

"Now you're saying you're not a Christian?"

"Chloe, I think the Christians are gone."

"So I'm not a Christian either?"

"You're my daughter and the only other member of my family still left; I love you more than anything on earth. But if the Christians are gone and everyone else is left, I don't think anyone is a Christian."

"Some kind of a super Christian, you mean."

"Yeah, a true Christian. Apparently those who were taken were recognized by God as truly his. How else can I say it?"

"Daddy, what does this make God? Some sick, sadistic dictator?"

"Careful, honey. You think I'm wrong, but what if I'm right?"

"Then God is spiteful, hateful, mean. Who wants to go to heaven with a God like that?"

"If that's where your mom and Raymie are, that's where I want to be."

"I want to be with them, too, Daddy! But tell me how this fits with a loving, merciful God. When I went to church, I got tired of hearing how loving God is. He never answered *my* prayers and I never felt like he knew me or cared about me. Now you're saying I was right. He didn't. I didn't qualify, so I got left behind? You'd better hope you're not right."

"But if I'm not right, who is right, Chloe? Where are they? Where is everybody?"

"See? You've latched onto this heaven thing because it makes you feel better. But it makes me feel worse. I don't buy it. I don't even want to consider it."

Rayford dropped the subject and went to watch television. Limited regular programming had resumed, but he was still able to find continuing news coverage. He was struck by the unusual name of the new Romanian president he had recently read about. Carpathia. He was scheduled to arrive at La Guardia in New York on Saturday and hold a press conference Monday morning before addressing the United Nations.

So La Guardia was open. That was where Rayford was supposed to fly later that evening with an oversold flight. He called Pan-Continental at O'Hare. "Glad you called," a supervisor said. "I was about to call you. Is your 757 rating up to date?"

"No. I used to fly them regularly, but I prefer the 747 and haven't been rated this year on the '57."

"That's all we're flying east this weekend. We'll have to get somebody else. And you need to get rated soon, just so we have flexibility."

"Duly noted. What's next for me?"

"You want a Monday run to Atlanta and back the same day?"

"On a . . . ?"

"'47."

"Sounds perfect. Can you tell me if there'll be room on that flight?"

"For?"

"A family member."

"Let me check." Rayford heard the computer keys and the distracted voice. "While I'm checking, ah, we got a request from a crew member to be assigned to your next flight, only I think she was thinking you'd be going on that run tonight, Logan to JFK and back."

"Who? Hattie Durham?"

"Let me see. Right."

"So is she assigned to Boston and New York?"

"Uh-huh."

"And I'm not, so that question is moot, right?"

"I guess so. You got any leanings one way or the other?"

"I'm sorry?"

"She's gonna ask again, is my guess. You have any objection to her being assigned to one of your upcoming flights?"

"Well, it won't be Atlanta, right? That's too soon."

"Right."

Rayford sighed. "No objections, I guess. No, wait. Let's just let it happen if it happens."

"I'm not following you, Captain."

"I'm just saying if she gets assigned in the normal course, I have no objection. But let's not go through any gymnastics to make it happen."

"Gotcha. And your flight to Atlanta looks like it could handle your freebie. Name?"

"Chloe Steele."

"I'll put her in first class, but if they sell out, you know I've got to bump her back."

When Rayford got off the phone, Chloe drifted into the room. "I'm not flying tonight," he said.

"Is that good news or bad news?"

"I'm relieved. I get to spend more time with you."

"After the way I talked to you? I figured you'd want me out of sight and out of mind."

"Chloe, we can talk frankly to each other. You're my family. I hate to think of being away from you at all. I've got a down-and-back flight to Atlanta Monday and have you booked in first class if you want to go."

"Sure."

"And I only wish you hadn't said one thing."

"Which?"

"That you don't even want to consider my theory. You've always liked my theories. I don't mind your saying you don't buy it. I don't know enough to articulate it in a way that makes any sense. But your mother talked about this. Once she even warned me that if I didn't know for sure I'd be going if Christ returned for his people, I shouldn't be flip about it."

"But you were?"

"I sure was. But never again."

"Well, Daddy, I'm not being flip about it. I just can't accept it, that's all."

"That's fair. But don't say you won't even consider it."

"Well, did you consider the space invaders theory?"

"As a matter of fact, I did."

"You're kidding."

"I considered everything. This was so far beyond human experience, what were we supposed to think?"

"OK, so if I take back that I won't even consider it, what does that mean? We become religious fanatics all of a sudden, start going to church, what? And who says it's not too late? If you're right, maybe we missed our chance forever."

"That's what we have to find out, don't you think? Let's check this out, see if there's anything to it. If there is, we should want nothing more than to know if there's still a chance we can be with Mom and Raymie again someday."

Chloe sat shaking her head. "Gee, Dad. I don't know."

"Listen, I called the church your mom was going to."

"Oh, brother."

He told her about the recording and the offer of the tape.

"Dad! A tape for those left behind? Please!"

"You're coming at this as a skeptic, so sure it sounds ridiculous to you. I see no other logical explanation, so I can't wait to hear the tape."

"You're desperate."

"Of course I am! Aren't you?"

"I'm miserable and scared, but I'm not so desperate that I'm going to lose my faculties. Oh, Daddy, I'm sorry. Don't look at me like that. I don't blame you for checking this out. Go ahead, and don't worry about me."

"Will you go with me?"

"I'd rather not. But if you want me to . . ."

"You can wait in the car."

"It's not that. I'm not afraid of meeting someone I disagree with."

"We'll go over there tomorrow," Rayford said, disappointed in her reaction but no less determined to follow through, for her sake as much as his. If he was right, he did not want to fail his own daughter.

TEN

CAMERON Williams convinced himself he should not call his and Dirk Burton's mutual friend at Scotland Yard before leaving New York. With communications as difficult as they had been for days and after the strange conversation with Dirk's supervisor, Buck didn't want to risk someone listening in. The last thing he wanted was to compromise his Scotland Yard contact's integrity.

Buck took both his real and his phony passport and visa—a customary safety precaution—caught a late flight to London out of La Guardia Friday night, and arrived at Heathrow Saturday morning. He checked into the Tavistock Hotel and slept until midafternoon. Then he set out to find the truth about Dirk's death.

He started by calling Scotland Yard and asking for his friend Alan Tompkins, a midlevel operative. They were almost the same age, and Tompkins was a thin, dark-

haired, and slightly rumpled investigator Buck had interviewed for a story on British terrorism.

They had taken to each other and even enjoyed an
evening at a pub with Dirk. Dirk, Alan, and Buck had
become pals, and whenever Buck visited, the three got
together. Now, by phone, he tried to communicate to
Tompkins in such a way that Alan would catch on
quickly and not give away that they were friends—in
case the line was tapped.

"Mr. Tompkins, you don't know me, but my name is
Cameron Williams of *Global Weekly.*" Before Alan could
laugh and greet his friend, Buck quickly continued, "I'm
here in London to do a story preliminary to the international monetary conference at the United Nations."

Alan sounded suddenly serious. "How can I help you,
sir? What does that have to do with Scotland Yard?"

"I'm having trouble locating my interview subject, and
I suspect foul play."

"And your subject?"

"His name is Burton. Dirk Burton. He works at the
exchange."

"Let me do some checking and call you back."

A few minutes later, Buck's phone rang.

"Yes, Tompkins from the Yard. I wonder if you would
be so kind as to come in and see me."

———————

Early on Saturday morning in Mount Prospect, Illinois,
Rayford Steele phoned the New Hope Village Church

again. This time a man answered the phone. Rayford
introduced himself as the husband of a former parishioner. "I know you, sir," the man said. "We've met.
I'm Bruce Barnes, the visitation pastor."

"Oh, yes, hi."

"By former parishioner, I assume you're telling me
that Irene is no longer with us?"

"That's right, and our son."

"Ray Jr., wasn't it?"

"Right."

"You also had an older daughter, did you not, a
nonattender?"

"Chloe."

"And she—?"

"Is here with me. I was wondering what you all make
of this—how many people have disappeared, are you still
meeting, that kind of thing. I know you have a service on
Sundays and that you're offering this tape."

"Well, you know just about everything then, Mr.
Steele. Nearly every member and regular attender of this
church is gone. I am the only person on the staff who
remains. I have asked a few women to help out in the
office. I have no idea how many will show up Sunday,
but it would be a privilege to see you again."

"I'm very interested in that tape."

"I'd be happy to give you one in advance. It's what I
will be discussing Sunday morning."

"I don't know how to ask this, Mr. Barnes."

"Bruce."

"Bruce. You'll be teaching or preaching or what?"

"Discussing. I will be playing the tape for any who have not heard it, and then we will discuss it."

"But you . . . I mean, how do you account for the fact that you are still here?"

"Mr. Steele, there is only one explanation for that, and I would prefer to discuss it with you in person. If I know when you might come by for the tape, I'll be sure to be here."

Rayford told him he and perhaps Chloe would come by that afternoon.

Alan Tompkins waited just inside the vestibule at Scotland Yard. When Buck arrived, Alan formally shook his hand and led him to a rundown compact, which he drove quickly to a dark pub a few miles away. "Let's not talk till we get there," Alan said, continually checking his mirrors. "I need to concentrate." Buck had never seen his friend so agitated and, yes, scared.

The pair took pints of dark ale to a booth in a secluded corner, but Alan never touched his. Buck, who hadn't eaten since the flight, switched his empty mug for Alan's full one and downed it, too. When the waitress came for the mugs, Buck ordered a sandwich. Alan declined and Buck, knowing his limit, ordered a soda.

"I know this will be like pouring petrol on a flame," Alan began, "but I need to tell you this is a nasty business and that you want to stay as far away from it as you can."

"Darn right you're fanning my flame," Buck said. "What's going on?"

"Well, they say it's suicide, but—"

"But you and I both know that's nonsense. What's the evidence? Have you been to the scene?"

"I have. Shot through the temple, gun in his hand. No note."

"Anything missing?"

"Didn't appear to be, but, Cameron, you know what this is about."

"I don't!"

"Come, come, man. Dirk was a conspiracy theorist, always sniffing around Todd-Cothran's involvement with international money men, his role in the three-currency conference, even his association with your Stonagal chap."

"Alan, there are books about this stuff. People make a hobby of ascribing all manner of evil to the Tri-Lateral Commission, the Illuminati, even the Freemasons, for goodness sake. Dirk thought Todd-Cothran and Stonagal were part of something he called the Council of Ten or the Council of Wise Men. So what? It's harmless."

"But when you have an employee, admittedly several levels removed from the head of the exchange, trying to connect his boss to conspiracy theories, he has a problem."

Buck sighed. "So he gets called on the carpet, maybe he gets fired. But tell me how he gets dead or pushed to suicide."

"I'm going to tell you something, Cameron," Alan said. "I know he was murdered."

"Well, I'm pretty sure he was, too, because I think I'd have had a clue if he was suicidal."

"They're trying to pin it on his remorse over losing people in the great disappearance, but it won't wash. He didn't lose anybody close as far as I know."

"But you *know* he was murdered? Pretty strong words for an investigator."

"I know because I knew him, not because I'm an investigator."

"That won't hold up," Buck said. "I can also say I knew him and that he couldn't have committed suicide, but I'm prejudiced."

"Cameron, this is so simple it would be a cliché if Dirk wasn't our friend. What did we always kid him about?"

"Lots of things. Why?"

"We kidded him about being such a klutz."

"Yeah. So?"

"If he was with us right now, where would he be sitting?"

It suddenly dawned on Buck what Alan was driving at. "He would be sitting to one of our lefts, and he was such a klutz because he was left-handed."

"He was shot through the right temple and the so-called suicide weapon was found in his right hand."

"So what did your bosses say when you told them he was left-handed and that this had to be murder?"

"You're the first person I've told."

"Alan! What are you saying?"

"I'm saying I love my family. My parents are still

living and I have an older brother and sister. I have a former wife I'm still fond of. I wouldn't mind snuffing her myself, but I certainly wouldn't want anyone else harming her."

"What are you afraid of?"

"I'm afraid of whoever was behind Dirk's murder, of course."

"But you'd have all of Scotland Yard behind you, man! You call yourself a law-enforcement officer and you're going to let this slide?"

"Yes, and that's just what you're going to do!"

"I am not. I wouldn't be able to live with myself."

"Do something about this and you won't be alive at all."

Buck waved the barmaid over and asked for chips. She brought him a heaping, greasy mass. It was just what he wanted. The ale had worked on him and the sandwich had not been enough to counteract it. He felt lightheaded, and he was afraid he might not be hungry again for a long time.

"I'm listening," he whispered. "What are you trying to tell me. Who's gotten to you?"

"If you believe me, you won't like it."

"I have no reason not to believe you and I already don't like it. Now spill."

"Dirk's death was ruled a suicide and that was that. Scene cleared, body cremated. I asked about an autopsy and was laughed off. My superior officer, Captain Sullivan, asked what I thought an autopsy would show. I told him abrasions, scrapes, signs of a struggle. He asked if I thought it made sense that a bloke would wrestle with himself before shooting himself. I kept the personal knowledge to myself."

"Why?"

"I smelled something."

"What if I put a story in an international magazine that pointed out the discrepancies? Something would have to happen."

"I have been told to tell you to go home and forget you ever heard about this suicide."

Buck squinted in disbelief. "Nobody knew I was coming."

"I think that's true, but somebody assumed you might show up. I wasn't surprised you came."

"Why should you be? My friend is dead, ostensibly by his own hand. I wasn't going to ignore that."

"You're going to ignore it now."

"You think I'm going to turn coward just because you did?"

"Cameron, you know me better than that."

"I wonder if I know you at all! I thought we were kindred spirits. We were justice freaks, Alan. Seekers of truth. I'm a journalist, you're an investigator. We're skeptics. What is this running from the truth, especially when it concerns our friend?"

"Did you hear me? I said I was told to call you off, if and when you showed up."

"Then why did you let me come to the Yard?"

"I'd have been in trouble if I had tipped you off."

"With whom?"

"I thought you'd never ask. I was visited by what you in America call a goon."

"A heavy?"

"Precisely."

"He threatened you?"

"He did. He said if I didn't want what had happened to my friend to happen to me or to my family, I would do as he said. I was afraid he was the same guy who had murdered Dirk."

"And he probably was. So, why didn't you report the threat?"

"I was going to. I started by trying to handle it myself. I told him he didn't have to worry about me. The next day I went to the exchange and asked for a meeting with Mr. Todd-Cothran."

"The big man himself?"

"In the flesh. I don't have an appointment, of course, but I insist it's Scotland Yard business, and he allows me in. His very office is intimidating. All mahogany and dark green draperies. Well, I get right down to business. I tell him, 'Sir, I believe you've had an employee murdered.' And just as calm as you like, he says, 'Tell you what, governor'—which is a term cockneys use on each other, not something people of his station usually call people of mine. Anyway, he says, 'Tell you what, governor, the next time somebody visits your flat at ten o'clock at night, as a certain gentleman did last night, greet him for me, won't you?'"

"What did you say?"

"What could I say? I was stunned to silence! I just

looked at him and nodded. 'And let me tell you something else,' he says. 'Tell your friend Williams to keep out of this.' I say, 'Williams?' like I don't know who he's talking about. He ignores that because, of course, he knows better."

"Somebody listened to Dirk's voice mail."

"No question. And he says, 'If he needs convincing, just tell him I'm as partial as he is to Dad and Jeff.' That your brother?"

Buck nodded. "So you caved?"

"What was I supposed to do? I tried playing Mr. Brave Boy. I said, 'I could be wired. I could be recording this conversation.' Cool as can be, he said, 'Metal detector would have picked it up.' 'I've got a good memory. I'll expose you,' I told him. He said, 'At your own risk, governor. Who's going to believe you over me? Marianne wouldn't even believe you—of course, she might not be healthy enough to understand.'"

"Marianne?"

"My sister. But that's not the half of it. As if he needs to drive the point home, he called my captain on his speakerphone. He said to him, 'Sullivan, if one of your men was to come to my office and harass me about anything, what should I do?' And Sullivan, one of my idols, sounded like a little baby. He said, 'Mr. Todd-Cothran, sir, you do whatever you need to do.' And Todd-Cothran said, 'What if I was to kill him where he sits?' And Sullivan said, 'Sir, I'm sure it would be justifiable homicide.' Now get this. Todd-Cothran said, right over the phone to Scotland Yard, where you know they tape every incoming call, and Todd-Cothran knows it just as well, 'What if his name happened to be Alan Tompkins?' Just like that, plain as day. And Sullivan said, 'I'd come over there and dispose of the body myself.' Well, I got the picture."

"So you have no one to turn to."

"Nobody I can think of."

"And I'm supposed to just turn tail and run."

Alan nodded. "I have to report back to Todd-Cothran that I've delivered the message. He'll expect you on the next plane out."

"And if I'm not?"

"No guarantees, but I wouldn't push it."

Buck shoved the plates aside and pushed his chair back. "Alan, you don't know me well, but you have to know I'm not the type of guy who takes this stuff sitting down."

"That's what I was afraid of. I'm not either, but where do I turn? What do I do? You'd think someone somewhere can be trusted, but what can anyone do? If this proves Dirk was right, that he got too close to some clandestine thing Todd-Cothran was into, where does it end? Does it include your man Stonagal? And how about the others on the international team of financiers they meet with? Have you considered that they may own everybody? I grew up reading the stories about your Chicago mobsters who had paid off cops and judges and even politicians. No one could touch them."

Buck nodded. "No one could touch them except the ones who couldn't be bought."

"The Untouchables?"

"Those were my heroes," Buck said.

"Mine too," Alan said. "That's why I'm an investigator. But if the Yard is dirty, who do I turn to?"

Buck rested his chin in his hand. "Do you think you're being watched? Followed?"

"I've been looking for that. So far, no."

"Nobody knows where we are now?"

"I tried to keep an eye out for a tail. In my professional opinion, we're here unnoticed. What are you going to do, Cameron?"

"There's precious little I can do here, apparently. Maybe I'll head back right away under a different name and make it look, to whoever cares, like I'm being obstinate and staying here."

"What's the use?"

"I may be scared, Alan, but I will look for my angle. And somehow I will find the person with the clout to help. I don't know your country well enough to know whom to trust. Of course I trust you, but you've been incapacitated."

"Am I weak, Cameron? Do you see that I have a choice?"

Buck shook his head. "I feel for you," he said. "I can't say what I'd do in your place."

The barmaid was making some sort of an announcement, asking people a question at every other table or so. As she neared them, Buck and Alan fell silent to hear. "Anyone drivin' a light green sedan? Fella says the inside light is on."

"That's mine," Alan said. "I don't remember even having the inside light on."

"Me either," Buck said, "but it was light out when we got here. Maybe we didn't notice."

"I'll get it. Probably won't hurt anything, but that old beater's battery can't take much."

"Careful," Buck said. "Be sure no one was tampering with it."

"Unlikely. We're right in front, remember."

Buck leaned out of his chair and followed Alan with his eyes as the investigator strolled out. Sure enough, the car's inside light could be seen from inside the pub. Alan went around to the driver's side and reached in to turn the light off. When he came back he said, "Gettin' daft in my old age. Next I'll be leavin' the headlights on."

Buck was sad, thinking of his friend's predicament. What a spot, working at something you'd wanted all your life to do and knowing that your superiors were beholden to what amounted to an international thug. "I'm going to call the airport and see if I can get a flight tonight."

"Nothin's going your way this time of the evening," Alan said.

"I'll take something to Frankfurt and head back from there in the morning. I don't think I should test my luck here."

"There's a phone up by the door. I'll pay the girl."

"I insist," Buck said, sliding a fifty-mark bill across the table.

Buck was on the phone to Heathrow while Alan

counted the change from the barmaid. Buck got a seat on a flight to Frankfurt forty-five minutes later that would allow him to catch a Sunday morning flight to JFK.

"Oh, Kennedy's open, is it?" he said.

"Just an hour ago," the woman said. "Limited flights, but your Pan-Continental out of Germany goes there in the morning. How many passengers?"

"One."

"Name?"

Buck peeked in his wallet to remind himself of the name on his phony British passport. "Pardon?" he said, stalling, as Alan approached.

"Name, sir."

"Oh, sorry. Oreskovich. George Oreskovich."

Alan mouthed that he would be in the car. Buck nodded.

"All right, sir," the woman said. "You're all set with a flight to Frankfurt this evening, continuing to JFK in New York tomorrow. Can I do anything else for you?"

"No, thank you."

As Buck hung up, the door of the pub was blown into the room and a blinding flash and deafening crash sent patrons screaming to the floor. As people crept to the door to see what had happened, Buck stared in horror at the frame and melted tires of what had been Alan's Scotland Yard–issue sedan. Windows had been blown out all up and down the street and a siren was already sounding. A leg and part of a torso lay on the sidewalk—the remains of Alan Tompkins.

As the patrons surged out to get a look at the burning wreckage, Buck elbowed his way through them, pulling his real passport and identification from his wallet. In the confusion he flipped the documents near what was left of the car and hoped they wouldn't get burned beyond readability. Whoever wanted him dead could assume him dead. Then he slipped through the crowd into the now-empty pub and sprinted to the back. But there was no back door, only a window. He raised it and crawled through, finding himself in a two-foot alleyway between buildings. Scraping his clothes on both sides as he hurried to a side street, he ran two blocks and hailed a cab. "The Tavistock," he said.

A few minutes later, when the cabbie was within three blocks of his hotel, Buck saw squad cars in front of the place and blocking traffic. "Just run me out to Heathrow, please," he said. He realized he had left his laptop among his things, but he had no choice. He had transferred the best stuff electronically already, but who knew who would have access to his material now?

"You don't need anything at the hotel then?" the cabbie said.

"No. I was just going to see someone."

"Very good, sir."

More authorities seemed to be combing Heathrow. "You wouldn't know where a fellow could get a hat like yours, would you?" Buck asked the cabbie as he paid.

"This old thing? I might be persuaded to part with it. I've got more than one other just like it. A souvenir, eh?"

"Will this do?" Buck said, pressing a large bill into his hand.

"It'll more than do, sir, and thank you kindly." The driver removed his official London cabbie pin and handed over the cap.

Buck pressed the too-large fisherman's style hat down over his ears and hurried into the terminal. He paid cash for his tickets in the name of George Oreskovich, a naturalized Englishman from Poland on his way to a holiday in the States, via Frankfurt. He was in the air before the authorities knew he was gone.

ELEVEN

RAYFORD was glad he could take Chloe out for a drive Saturday after having been cooped up with their grief. He was glad she had agreed to accompany him to the church.

Chloe had been sleepy and quiet all day. She had mentioned the idea of dropping out of the university for a semester and taking some classes locally. Rayford liked it. He was thinking of her. Then he realized she was thinking of him, and he was touched.

As they chatted on the short drive, he reminded her that after their day trip to Atlanta Monday they would have to drive home separately from O'Hare so he could get his car back. She smiled at him. "I think I can handle that, now that I'm twenty."

"I do treat you like a little girl sometimes, don't I?" he said.

"Not too much anymore," she said. "You can make up for it, though."

"I know what you're going to say."

"You don't either," she said. "Guess."

"You're going to say I can make up for treating you like a little girl by letting you have your own mind today, by not trying to talk you into anything."

"That goes without saying, I hope. But you're wrong, smart guy. I was going to say you could convince me you see me as a responsible adult by letting me drive *your* car back from the airport Monday."

"That's easy," Rayford said, suddenly switching to a babyish voice. "Would that make you feel like a big girl? OK, Daddy will do that."

She punched him and smiled, then quickly sobered. "It's amazing what amuses me these days," she said. "Good grief, I feel like an awful person."

Rayford let that comment hang in the air as he turned the corner and the tasteful little church came into view. "Don't make too much of what I just said," Chloe said. "I don't have to come in, do I?"

"No, but I'd appreciate it."

She pursed her lips and shook her head, but when he parked and got out, she followed.

Bruce Barnes was short and slightly pudgy, with curly hair and wire-rimmed glasses. He dressed casually but with class, and Rayford guessed him to be in his early thirties. He emerged from the sanctuary with a small vacuum in his hands. "Sorry," he said. "You must be the Steeles. I'm kind of the whole staff around here now, except for Loretta."

"Hello," an older woman said from behind Rayford and Chloe. She stood in the doorway of the church offices sunken-eyed and disheveled, as if she'd come through a war. After pleasantries she retreated to a desk in the outer office.

"She's putting together a little program for tomorrow," Barnes said. "Tough thing is, we have no idea how many to expect. Will you be here?"

"Not sure yet," Rayford said. "I probably will be."

They both looked at Chloe. She smiled politely. "I probably won't be," she said.

"Well, I've got the tape for you," Barnes said. "But I'd like to ask for a few more minutes of your time."

"I've got time," Rayford said.

"I'm with him," Chloe said resignedly.

Barnes led them to the senior pastor's office. "I don't sit at his desk or use his library," the younger man said, "but I do work in here at his conference table. I don't know what's going to happen to me or to the church, and I certainly don't want to be presumptuous. I can't imagine God would call me to take over this work, but if he does, I want to be ready."

"And how will he call you?" Chloe said, a smile playing at her mouth. "By phone?"

Barnes didn't respond in kind. "To tell you the truth, it wouldn't surprise me. I don't know about you, but he got my attention last week. A phone call from heaven would have been less traumatic."

Chloe raised her eyebrows, apparently in surrender to his point.

"Folks, Loretta there looks like I feel. We're shell-shocked and we're devastated, because we know exactly what happened."

"Or you think you do," Chloe said. Rayford tried to catch her eye to encourage her to back off, but she seemed unwilling to look at him. "There's every kind of theory you want on every TV show in the country."

"I know that," Barnes said.

"And each is self-serving," she added. "The tabloids say it was space invaders, which would prove the stupid stories they've been running for years. The government says it's some sort of enemy, so we can spend more on high-tech defense. You're going to say it was God so you can start rebuilding your church."

Bruce Barnes sat back and looked at Chloe, then at her father. "I'm going to ask you something," he said, turning to her again. "Could you let me tell you my story briefly, without interrupting or saying anything, unless there's something you don't understand?"

Chloe stared at him without responding.

"I don't want to be rude, but I don't want you to be either. I asked for a few moments of your time. If I still have it, I want to try to make use of it. Then I'll leave you alone. You can do anything you want with what I tell you. Tell me I'm crazy, tell me I'm self-serving. Leave and never come back. That's up to you. But can I have the floor for a few minutes?"

Rayford thought Barnes was brilliant. He had put Chloe in her place, leaving her no smart remark. She merely waved a hand of permission, for which Barnes thanked her, and he began.

"May I call you by your first names?"

Rayford nodded. Chloe didn't respond.

"Ray, is it? And Chloe? I sit here before you a broken man. And Loretta? If anyone has a right to feel as bad as I do, it's Loretta. She's the only person in her whole clan who is still here. She had six living brothers and sisters, I don't know how many aunts and uncles and cousins and nieces and nephews. They had a wedding here last year and she must have had a hundred relatives alone. They're all gone, every one of them."

"That's awful," Chloe said. "We lost my mom and my little brother, you know. Oh, I'm sorry. I wasn't going to say anything."

"It's all right," Barnes said. "My situation is almost as bad as Loretta's, only on a smaller scale. Of course it's not small for me. Let me tell you my story." As soon as he began with seemingly innocuous details, his voice grew thick and quiet. "I was in bed with my wife. She was sleeping. I was reading. Our children had been down for a couple of hours. They were five, three, and one. The oldest was a girl, the other two boys. That was normal for us—me reading while my wife slept. She worked so hard with the kids and a part-time job that she was always knocked out by nine or so.

"I was reading a sports magazine, trying to turn the pages quietly, and every once in a while she would sigh. Once she even asked how much longer I would be. I knew I should go in the other room or just turn the light off and try to sleep myself. But I told her, 'Not long,' hoping she'd fall asleep and I could just read the whole magazine. I can usually tell by her breathing if she's sleeping soundly enough that my light doesn't bother her. And after a while I heard that deep breathing.

"I was glad. My plan was to read till midnight. I was propped up on an elbow with my back to her, using a pillow to shield the light a little. I don't know how much longer I had been reading when I felt the bed move and sensed she had gotten up. I assumed she was going to the bathroom and only hoped she didn't wake up to the point where she'd bug me about still having the light on when she got back. She's a tiny little thing, and it didn't hit me that I didn't hear her walk to the bathroom. But, like I say, I was engrossed in my reading.

"After a few more minutes I called out, 'Hon, you OK?' And I didn't hear anything. I began wondering, was it just my imagination that she had gotten up? I reached behind me and she was not there, so I called out again. I thought maybe she was checking on the kids, but usually she's such a sound sleeper that unless she's heard one of them she doesn't do that.

"Well, probably another minute or two went by before I turned over and noticed that she was not only gone, but that it also appeared she had pulled the sheet and covers back up toward her pillow. Now you can imagine what I thought. I thought she was so frustrated at me for still reading that she had given up waiting for me to turn off the light and decided to go sleep on the couch. I'm a fairly decent husband, so I went out to apologize and bring her back to bed.

"You know what happened. She wasn't out on the

couch. She wasn't in the bathroom. I poked my head into each of the kids' rooms and whispered for her, thinking maybe she was rocking one of them or sitting in there. Nothing. The lights were off all over the house, except for my bedside. I didn't want to wake the kids by yelling for her, so I just turned on the hall light and checked their rooms again.

"I'm ashamed to say I still didn't have a clue until I noticed my oldest two kids weren't in their beds. My first thought was that they had gone into the baby's room, like they do sometimes, to sleep on the floor. Then I thought my wife had taken one or both of them to the kitchen for something. Frankly I was just a little perturbed that I didn't know what was going on in the middle of the night.

"When the baby was not in his crib, I turned the light on, stuck my head out the door and called down the hall for my wife. No answer. Then I noticed the baby's footie pajamas in the crib, and I knew. I just knew. It hit me all of a sudden. I ran from room to room, pulling back the covers and finding the kids' pajamas. I didn't want to, but I tore the cover back from my wife's side of the bed and there was her nightgown, her rings, and even her hair clips on the pillow."

Rayford was fighting the tears, remembering his own similar experience. Barnes took a deep breath and exhaled, wiping his eyes. "Well, I started phoning around," he said. "I started with the pastor, but of course I got his answering machine. A couple of other places I got answering machines, too, so I grabbed the church directory and started looking up older folks, the people I thought might not like answering machines and wouldn't have one. I let their phones ring off the hook. No answers.

"Of course I knew it was unlikely I'd find anybody. For some reason I ran out and jumped in my car and raced over here to the church. There was Loretta, sitting in her car in her robe, hair up in curlers, crying her eyes out. We came into the foyer and sat by the potted plants, crying and holding each other, knowing exactly what had happened. Within about half an hour, a few others showed up. We basically commiserated and wondered aloud what we were supposed to do next. Then somebody remembered Pastor's Rapture tape."

"His what?" Chloe asked.

"Our senior pastor loved to preach about the coming of Christ to rapture his church, to take believers, dead and alive, to heaven before a period of tribulation on the earth. He was particularly inspired once a couple of years ago."

Rayford turned to Chloe. "You remember your mother talking about that. She was so enthusiastic about it."

"Oh yeah, I do."

"Well," Barnes said, "the pastor used that sermon and had himself videotaped in this office speaking directly to people who were left behind. He put it in the church library with instructions to get it out and play it if most everyone seemed to have disappeared. We all watched it a couple of times the other night. A few people wanted to argue with God, trying to tell us that they really had been believers and should have been taken with the others, but we all knew the truth. We had been phony. There wasn't a one of us who didn't know what it meant to be a true Christian. We knew we weren't and that we had been left behind."

Rayford had trouble speaking, but he had to ask. "Mr. Barnes, you were on the staff here."

"Right."

"How did you miss it?"

"I'm going to tell you, Ray, because I no longer have anything to hide. I'm ashamed of myself, and if I never really had the desire or the motivation to tell others about Christ before, I sure have it now. I just feel awful that it took the most cataclysmic event in history to reach me. I was raised in the church. My parents and brothers and sisters were all Christians.

"I loved church. It was my life, my culture. I thought I believed everything there was to believe in the Bible. The Bible says that if you believe in Christ you have eternal life, so I assumed I was covered.

"I especially liked the parts about God being forgiving. I was a sinner, and I never changed. I just kept getting forgiveness because I thought God was bound to do that. He had to. Verses that said if we confessed our sins he was faithful and just to forgive us and to cleanse us. I knew other verses said you had to believe *and* receive, to trust and to abide, but to me that was sort of theological mumbo jumbo. I wanted the bottom line, the easiest route, the simplest path. I knew other verses said that we are not to continue in sin just because God shows grace.

"I thought I had a great life. I even went to Bible college. In church and at school, I said the right things and prayed in public and even encouraged people in their Christian lives. But I was still a sinner. I even said that. I told people I wasn't perfect; I was forgiven."

"My wife said that," Rayford said.

"The difference is," Bruce said, "she was sincere. I lied. I told my wife that we tithed to the church, you know, that we gave ten percent of our income. I hardly ever gave any, except when the plate was passed I might drop in a few bills to make it look good. Every week I would confess that to God, promising to do better next time.

"I encouraged people to share their faith, to tell other people how to become Christians. But on my own I never did that. My job was to visit people in their homes and nursing homes and hospitals every day. I was good at it. I encouraged them, smiled at them, talked with them, prayed with them, even read Scripture to them. But I never did that on my own, privately.

"I was lazy. I cut corners. When people thought I was out calling, I might be at a movie in another town. I was also lustful. I read things I shouldn't have read, looked at magazines that fed my lusts."

Rayford winced. That hit too close to home.

"I had a real racket going," Barnes was saying, "and I bought into it. Down deep, way down deep, I knew better. I knew it was too good to be true. I knew that true Christians were known by what their lives produced and that I was producing nothing. But I comforted myself that there were worse people around who called themselves Christians.

"I wasn't a rapist or a child molester or an adulterer, though many times I felt unfaithful to my wife because of my lusts. But I could always pray and confess and feel as though I was clean. It should have been obvious to me. When people found out I was on the pastoral staff at New Hope, I would tell them about the cool pastor and the neat church, but I was shy about telling them about Christ. If they challenged me and asked if New Hope was one of those churches that said Jesus was the only way to God, I did everything but deny it. I wanted them to think I was OK, that I was with it. I may be a Christian and even a pastor, but don't lump me with the weirdos. Above all, don't do that.

"I see now, of course, that God *is* a sin-forgiving God, because we're human and we need that. But we are to receive his gift, abide in Christ, and allow him to live through us. I used what I thought was my security as a license to do what I wanted. I could basically live in sin and pretend to be devout. I had a great family and a nice work environment. And as miserable as I was privately most of the time, I really believed I would go to heaven when I died.

"I hardly ever read my Bible except when preparing a talk or lesson. I didn't have the 'mind of Christ.' *Christian,* I knew vaguely, means 'Christ one' or 'one like Christ.' That sure wasn't me, and I found out in the worst way possible.

"Let me just say to you both—this is your decision.

These are your lives. But I know, and Loretta knows, and a few others who were playing around the edges here at this church know exactly what happened a few nights ago. Jesus Christ returned for his true family, and the rest of us were left behind."

Bruce looked Chloe in the eyes. "There is no doubt in my mind that we have witnessed the Rapture. My biggest fear, once I realized the truth, was that there was no more hope for me. I had missed it, I had been a phony, I had set up my own brand of Christianity that may have made for a life of freedom but had cost me my soul. I had heard people say that when the church was raptured, God's Spirit would be gone from the earth. The logic was that when Jesus went to heaven after his resurrection, the Holy Spirit that God gave to the church was embodied in believers. So when they were taken, the Spirit would be gone, and there would be no more hope for anyone left. You can't know the relief when Pastor's tape showed me otherwise.

"We realize how stupid we were, but those of us in this church—at least the ones who felt drawn to this building the night everyone else disappeared—are now as zealous as we can be. No one who comes here will leave without knowing exactly what we believe and what we think is necessary for them to have a relationship with God."

Chloe stood and paced, her arms folded across her chest. "That's a pretty interesting story," she said. "What was the deal with Loretta? How did she miss it if her whole extended family were true Christians?"

"You should have her tell you sometime," Bruce said. "But she tells me it was pride and embarrassment that kept her from Christ. She was a middle child in a very religious family, and she said she was in her late teens before she even thought seriously about her personal faith. She had just drifted along with the family to church and all the related activities. As she grew up, got married, became a mother and a grandmother, she just let everyone assume she was a spiritual giant. She was revered around here. Only she had never believed and received Christ for herself."

"So," Chloe said, "this believing and receiving stuff, this living for Christ or letting him live through you, that's what my mother meant when she talked about salvation, getting saved?"

Bruce nodded. "From sin and hell and judgment."

"Meantime, we're not saved from all that."

"That's right."

"You really believe this."

"I do."

"It's pretty freaky stuff, you have to admit."

"Not to me. Not anymore."

Rayford, always one for precision and order, asked, "So, what did you do? What did my wife do? What made her more of a Christian, or, ah . . . what, uh—"

"Saved her?" Bruce said.

"Yes," Rayford said. "That's exactly what I want to know. If you're right, and I've already told Chloe that I think I see this now, we need to know how it works.

How it goes. How does a person get from one situation to the other? Obviously, we were not saved from being left, and we're here to face life without our loved ones who were true Christians. So, how do we become true Christians?"

"I'm going to walk you through that," Bruce said. "And I'm going to send you home with the tape. And I'm going to go through this all in detail tomorrow morning at ten for whoever shows up. I'll probably do the same lesson every Sunday morning for as long as people need to know. One thing I'm sure of, as important as all the other sermons and lessons are, nothing matters like this one."

While Chloe stood with her back to the wall, arms still folded, watching and listening, Bruce turned to Rayford. "It's really quite simple. God made it easy. That doesn't mean it's not a supernatural transaction or that we can pick and choose the good parts—as I tried to do. But if we see the truth and act on it, God won't withhold salvation from us.

"First, we have to see ourselves as God sees us. The Bible says all have sinned, that there is none righteous, no not one. It also says we can't save ourselves. Lots of people thought they could earn their way to God or to heaven by doing good things, but that's probably the biggest misconception ever. Ask anyone on the street what they think the Bible or the church says about get-ting to heaven, and nine of ten would say it has some-thing to do with doing good and living right.

"We're to do that, of course, but not so we can earn

our salvation. We're to do that in *response* to our salvation. The Bible says that it's not by works of righteousness that we have done, but by his mercy God saved us. It also says that we are saved by grace through Christ, not of ourselves, so we can't brag about our goodness.

"Jesus took our sins and paid the penalty for them so we wouldn't have to. The payment is death, and he died in our place because he loved us. When we tell Christ that we acknowledge ourselves as sinners and lost, and receive his gift of salvation, he saves us. A transaction takes place. We go from darkness to light, from lost to found; we're saved. The Bible says that to those who receive him, he gives the power to become sons of God. That's what Jesus is—the Son of God. When we become sons of God, we have what Jesus has: a relationship with God, eternal life, and because Jesus paid our penalty, we also have forgiveness for our sins."

Rayford sat stunned. He sneaked a peek at Chloe. She looked frozen, but she didn't appear antagonistic. Rayford felt he had found exactly what he was looking for. It was what he had suspected and had heard bits and pieces of over the years, but he had never put it all together. In spite of himself, he was still reserved enough to want to mull it over, to see and hear the tape, and to discuss it with Chloe.

"I have to ask you," Bruce said, "something I never wanted to ask people before. I want to know if you're ready to receive Christ right now. I would be happy to pray with you and lead you in how to talk to God about this."

"No," Chloe said quickly, looking at her dad as if afraid he was going to do something foolish.

"No?" Bruce was clearly surprised. "Need more time?"

"At least," Chloe said. "Surely this isn't something you rush into."

"Well, let me tell you," Bruce said. "It's something I wish I had rushed into. I believe God has forgiven me and that I have a job to do here. But I don't know what's going to happen now, with the true Christians all gone. I'd sure rather have come to this point years ago than now, when it was nearly too late. You can imagine that I would much rather be in heaven with my family right now."

"But then who would tell us about this?" Rayford asked.

"Oh, I'm grateful for that opportunity," Bruce said. "But it has cost me dearly."

"I understand." Rayford could feel Bruce's eyes burning into him as if the young man knew Rayford was nearly ready to make a commitment. But he had never rushed into anything in his life. And while he didn't put this on the same scale as dealing with a salesman, he needed time to think, a cooling-off period. He was analytical, and while this suddenly made a world of sense to him and he didn't doubt at all Bruce's theory of the disappearances, he would not act immediately. "I'd appreciate the tape, and I can guarantee you, I will be back tomorrow."

Bruce looked at Chloe. "No guarantees from me," she

said, "but I appreciate your time and I will watch the tape."

"That's all I can ask," Bruce said. "But let me leave you with one little reminder of urgency. You may have heard this off and on your whole lives, the way I did. Maybe you haven't. But I need to tell you that you don't have any guarantees. It's too late for you to disappear like your loved ones did a few days ago. But people die every day in car accidents, plane crashes—oh, sorry, I'm sure you're a good pilot—all kinds of tragedies. I'm not going to push you into something you're not ready for, but just let me encourage you that if God impresses upon you that this is true, don't put it off. What would be worse than finally finding God and then dying without him because you waited too long?"

TWELVE

Buck checked into the Frankfurt Hilton at the airport under his phony name, knowing he had to call the States before his family and his colleagues heard he was dead. He started by finding a pay phone in the lobby and dialing his father's number in Arizona. With the time difference, it was shortly after noon on Saturday there.

"I'm really sorry about this, Dad, but you're going to hear I was killed in some sort of a car bombing, terrorist attack, that kind of thing."

"What the devil is going on, Cameron?"

"I can't get into it now, Dad. I just want you to know I'm all right. I'm calling from overseas, but I'd rather not say where. I'll be back tomorrow, but I'm going to have to lay low for a while."

"Your sister-in-law and niece and nephew's memorial services are tomorrow evening," Mr. Williams said.

"Oh, no. Dad, it would really be obvious if I showed up there. I'm sorry. Tell Jeff how really sorry I am."

"Well, do we have to play this charade out? I mean should we make it a memorial for you, too?"

"No, I'm not going to be able to play dead that long. Once the people at the *Global* find out I'm all right, the secret won't hold for long."

"Are you going to be in danger when whoever thinks they killed you finds out?"

"Probably, but Dad, I've got to get off now. Tell Jeff for me, huh?"

"I will. Be careful."

Buck switched to another phone and called the *Global*. Disguising his voice, he asked the receptionist to plug him into Steve Plank's after-hours voice mail. "Steve, you know who this is. No matter what you hear in the next twenty-four hours, I'm all right. I will call you tomorrow and we can meet. Let the others believe what they hear for now. I'm going to need to remain incognito until I can find someone who can really help. Talk to you soon, Steve."

Chloe was silent in the car. Rayford fought the urge to jabber. That was not his nature, but he felt the same urgency he had sensed in Bruce Barnes. He wanted to remain sensible, yes, analytical. He wanted to study, to pray, to be sure. But wasn't that just insurance? Could he be more sure?

What had he done in his raising of Chloe that could make her so cautious, so careful, that she might look down her nose at what was so obvious to him? He had found the truth, and Bruce was right. They needed to act on it before anything happened to them.

The news was full of crime, looting, people taking advantage of the chaos. People were being shot, maimed, raped, killed. The roadways were more dangerous than ever. Emergency units were understaffed, fewer air- and ground-traffic controllers manned the airports, fewer qualified pilots and crews flew the planes.

People checked the graves of loved ones to see if their corpses had disappeared, and unscrupulous types pretended to do the same while looking for valuables that might have been buried with the wealthy. It had become an ugly world overnight, and Rayford was worried about his and Chloe's safety. He didn't want to go much longer without watching the tape and making good on the decision he had already made.

"Can we watch it together?" he suggested.

"I'd really rather not, Dad. I can see where you're going with this, and I'm not comfortable with it yet. This is very personal. It isn't a group or family thing."

"I'm not so sure about that."

"Well, don't push me. You deal with it on your own, and I will later."

"You know I'm just worried about you and that I love you and care about you, don't you?"

"Of course."

"Will you watch it before the church meeting tomorrow?"

"Daddy, please. You're going to push me away if you keep bugging me about it. I'm not sure I even want to go to that. I heard his pitch today and he said himself it's going to be the same thing tomorrow."

"Well, what if I decide to become a Christian tomorrow? I'd kind of like you there."

Chloe looked at him. "I don't know, Dad. It's not like graduation or something."

"Maybe it is. I feel like your mother and your brother got promoted and I didn't."

"Gross."

"I'm serious. They qualified for heaven. I didn't."

"I don't want to talk about this now."

"OK, but let me just say one more thing. If you don't go tomorrow, I wish you'd watch the tape while I'm gone."

"Oh, I—"

"Because I'd really like to have you settle this thing before our flight Monday. Air travel is becoming more dangerous, and you never know what might happen."

"Daddy, come on! All my life all I've heard you do is set people straight about how safe flying is. Every time there's a crash, someone asks if you aren't afraid or if you've ever had a close call, and you rattle off all these statistics about how flying is so many times safer than riding in a car. So don't start with that."

Rayford gave up. He would deal with his own soul and pray for his daughter, but clearly there would be no badgering her into the faith.

Chloe went to bed early Saturday night while Rayford settled in front of the television and popped in the video. "Hello," came the pleasant voice of the pastor Rayford had met several times. As he spoke he sat on the edge of the desk in the very office Rayford had just visited. "My name is Vernon Billings, and I'm pastor of the New Hope Village Church of Mount Prospect, Illinois. As you watch this tape, I can only imagine the fear and despair you face, for this is being recorded for viewing only after the disappearance of God's people from the earth.

"That you are watching indicates you have been left behind. You are no doubt stunned, shocked, afraid, and remorseful. I would like you to consider what I have to say here as instructions for life following Christ's rapture of his church. That is what has happened. Anyone you know or knew of who had placed his or her trust in Christ alone for salvation has been taken to heaven by Christ.

"Let me show you from the Bible exactly what has happened. You won't need this proof by now, because you will have experienced the most shocking event of history. But as this tape was made beforehand and I am confident that I will be gone, ask yourself, how did he know? Here's how, from 1 Corinthians 15:51-57."

The screen began to scroll with the passage of Scripture. Rayford hit the pause button and ran to get Irene's Bible. It took him a while to find 1 Corinthians, and though it was slightly different in her translation, the meaning was the same.

The pastor said, "Let me read to you what the great missionary evangelist, the apostle Paul, wrote to the Christians at the church in the city of Corinth:

"Behold, I tell you a mystery: We shall not all sleep, but we shall all be changed—in a moment, in the twinkling of an eye, at the last trumpet. For the trumpet will sound, and the dead will be raised incorruptible, and we shall be changed. For this corruptible must put on incorruption, and this mortal must put on immortality. So when this corruptible has put on incorruption, and this mortal has put on immortality, then shall be brought to pass the saying that is written: 'Death is swallowed up in victory. O Death, where is your sting? O Hades, where is your victory?' The sting of death is sin, and the strength of sin is the law. But thanks be to God, who gives us the victory through our Lord Jesus Christ."

Rayford was confused. He could follow some of that, but the rest was like gibberish to him. He let the tape roll. Pastor Billings continued, "Let me paraphrase some of that so you'll understand it clearly. When Paul says we shall not all sleep, he means that we shall not all die. And he's saying that this corruptible being must put on an incorruptible body which is to last for all of eternity. When these things have happened, when the Christians who have already died and those that are still living receive their immortal bodies, the Rapture of the church will have taken place.

"Every person who believed in and accepted the sacrificial death, burial, and resurrection of Jesus Christ anticipated his coming again for them. As you see this tape, all those will have already seen the fulfillment of the promise of Christ when he said, 'I will come again and receive you unto Myself; that where I am, there you may be also.'

"I believe that all such people were literally taken from the earth, leaving everything material behind. If you have discovered that millions of people are missing and that babies and children have vanished, you know what I am saying is true. Up to a certain age, which is probably different for each individual, we believe God will not hold a child accountable for a decision that must be made with heart and mind, fully cognizant of the ramifications. You may also find that unborn children have disappeared from their mothers' wombs. I can only imagine the pain and heartache of a world without precious children, and the deep despair of parents who will miss them so.

"Paul's prophetic letter to the Corinthians said this would occur in the twinkling of an eye. You may have seen a loved one standing before you, and suddenly they were gone. I don't envy you that shock.

"The Bible says that men's hearts will fail them for fear. That means to me that there will be heart attacks due to shock, people will commit suicide in their despair, and you know better than I the chaos that will result from Christians disappearing from various modes of transportation, with the loss of firefighters and police officers and emergency workers of all sorts.

"Depending on when you're viewing this tape, you may have already found that martial law is in effect in many places, emergency measures trying to keep evil elements from looting and fighting over the spoils of what is left. Governments will tumble and there will be international disorder.

"You may wonder why this has happened. Some believe this is the judgment of God on an ungodly world. Actually, that is to come later. Strange as this may sound to you, this is God's final effort to get the attention of every person who has ignored or rejected him. He is allowing now a vast period of trial and tribulation to come to you who remain. He has removed his church from a corrupt world that seeks its own way, its own pleasures, its own ends.

"I believe God's purpose in this is to allow those who remain to take stock of themselves and leave their frantic search for pleasure and self-fulfillment, and turn to the Bible for truth and to Christ for salvation.

"Let me encourage you that your loved ones, your children and infants, your friends, and your acquaintances have not been snatched away by some evil force or some invasion from outer space. That will likely be a common explanation. What sounded ludicrous to you before might sound logical now, but it is not.

"Also, Scripture indicates that there will be a great lie, announced with the help of the media and perpetrated by a self-styled world leader. Jesus himself prophesied about such a person. He said, 'I have come in My Father's name, and you do not receive Me; if another comes in his own name, him you will receive.'

"Let me warn you personally to beware of such a

leader of humanity who may emerge from Europe. He will turn out to be a great deceiver who will step forward with signs and wonders that will be so impressive that many will believe he is of God. He will gain a great following among those who are left, and many will believe he is a miracle worker.

"The deceiver will promise strength and peace and security, but the Bible says he will speak out against the Most High and will wear down the saints of the Most High. That's why I warn you to beware now of a new leader with great charisma trying to take over the world during this terrible time of chaos and confusion. This person is known in the Bible as Antichrist. He will make many promises, but he will not keep them. You must trust in the promises of God Almighty through his Son, Jesus Christ.

"I believe the Bible teaches that the Rapture of the church ushers in a seven-year period of trial and tribulation, during which terrible things will happen. If you have not received Christ as your Savior, your soul is in jeopardy. And because of the cataclysmic events that will take place during this period, your very life is in danger. If you turn to Christ, you may still have to die as a martyr."

Rayford paused the tape. He had been prepared for the salvation stuff. But tribulation and trial? Losing his loved ones, facing the pride and self-centeredness that had kept him out of heaven—wasn't that enough? There would be *more?*

And what of this "great deceiver" the pastor had

talked about? Maybe he had taken this prophecy business too far. But this was no snake-oil salesman. This was a sincere, honest, trustworthy man—a man of God. If what the pastor said about the disappearances was true—and Rayford knew in his heart that it was—then the man deserved his attention, his respect.

It was time to move beyond being a critic, an analyst never satisfied with the evidence. The proof was before him: the empty chairs, the lonely bed, the hole in his heart. There was only one course of action. He punched the play button.

"It doesn't make any difference, at this point, why you're still on earth. You may have been too selfish or prideful or busy, or perhaps you simply didn't take the time to examine the claims of Christ for yourself. The point now is, you have another chance. Don't miss it.

"The disappearance of the saints and children, the chaos left behind, and the despairing of the heartbroken are evidence that what I'm saying is true. Pray that God will help you. Receive his salvation gift right now. And resist the lies and efforts of the Antichrist, who is sure to rise up soon. Remember, he will deceive many. Don't be counted among them.

"Nearly eight hundred years before Jesus came to earth the first time, Isaiah in the Old Testament prophesied that the kingdoms of nations will be in great conflict and their faces shall be as flames. To me, this portends World War III, a thermonuclear war that will wipe out millions.

"Bible prophecy is history written in advance. I urge

you to find books on this subject or find people who may
have been experts in this area but who for some reason
did not receive Christ before and were left behind. Study
so you'll know what is coming and you can be prepared.

"You'll find that government and religion will change,
war and inflation will erupt, there will be widespread
death and destruction, martyrdom of saints, and even
a devastating earthquake. Be prepared.

"God wants to forgive you your sins and assure you
of heaven. Listen to Ezekiel 33:11: 'I have no pleasure in
the death of the wicked, but that the wicked turn from
his way and live.'

"If you accept God's message of salvation, his Holy
Spirit will come in unto you and make you spiritually
born anew. You don't need to understand all this theo-
logically. You can become a child of God by praying to
him right now as I lead you—"

Rayford paused the tape again and saw the concern
on the pastor's face, the compassion in his eyes. He knew
friends and acquaintances would think him crazy, perhaps even his own daughter would. But this rang true
with him. Rayford didn't understand about the seven
years of tribulation and this new leader, the liar who was
supposed to emerge. But he knew he needed Christ in his
life. He needed forgiveness of sin and the assurance that
one day he would join his wife and son in heaven.

Rayford sat with his head in his hands, his heart
pounding. There was no sound from upstairs where
Chloe rested. He was alone with his thoughts, alone with
God, and he felt God's presence. Rayford slid to his knees

on the carpet. He had never knelt in worship before, but he sensed the seriousness and the reverence of the moment. He pushed the play button and tossed the remote control aside. He set his hands palms down before him and rested his forehead on them, his face on the floor. The pastor said, "Pray after me," and Rayford did. "Dear God, I admit that I'm a sinner. I am sorry for my sins. Please forgive me and save me. I ask this in the name of Jesus, who died for me. I trust in him right now. I believe that the sinless blood of Jesus is sufficient to pay the price for my salvation. Thank you for hearing me and receiving me. Thank you for saving my soul."

As the pastor continued with words of assurance, quoting verses that promised that whoever called upon the name of the Lord would be saved and that God would not cast out anyone who sought him, Rayford stayed where he was. As the tape finished the pastor said, "If you were genuine, you are saved, born again, a child of God." Rayford wanted to talk to God more. He wanted to be specific about his sin. He knew he was forgiven, but in a childlike way, he wanted God to know that he knew what kind of a person he had been.

He confessed his pride. Pride in his intelligence. Pride in his looks. Pride in his abilities. He confessed his lusts, how he had neglected his wife, how he had sought his own pleasure. How he had worshiped money and things. When he was through, he felt clean. The tape had scared him, all that talk about the tough times ahead, but he knew he would rather face them as a true believer than in the state he had been.

His first prayer following that was for Chloe. He would worry about her and pray for her constantly until he was sure she had joined him in this new life.

Buck arrived at JFK and immediately called Steve Plank. "Stay right where you are, Buck, you renegade. Do you know who wants to talk with you?"

"I couldn't guess."

"Nicolae Carpathia himself."

"Yeah, right."

"I'm serious. He's here and he's got your old friend Chaim Rosenzweig with him. Apparently Chaim sang your praises, and with all the media after him, he's asking for you. So I'll come get you, you'll tell me what in the world you've gotten yourself into, we'll get you undead, and you can have that great interview you've been looking for."

Buck hung up and clapped. *This is too good to be true,* he thought. *If there's one guy who's above these international terrorists and bullies and even the dirt at the London Exchange and Scotland Yard, it will be this Carpathia. If Rosenzweig likes him, he's got to be all right.*

Rayford couldn't wait to go to New Hope the next morning. He began reading the New Testament, and he scrounged around the house for any books or study guides Irene had collected. Though much of it was still difficult to understand, he found himself so hungry and thirsty for the story of the life of Christ that he read through all four Gospels until it was late and he fell asleep.

All Rayford could think of throughout the reading was that he was now part of this family that included his wife and son. Though he was scared of what the pastor had predicted on the tape about all the bad things that would happen in the world now that the church had been raptured, he was also excited about his new faith. He knew he would one day be with God and Christ, and he wanted that for Chloe more than ever.

Rayford kept himself from bugging her. He determined not to tell her what he had done unless she asked. She didn't ask before he left for church in the morning, but she apologized for not going with him. "I will go with you sometime," she said. "I promise. I'm not being antagonistic. I'm just not ready."

Rayford fought the urge to warn her not to wait too long. He also wanted to plead with her to watch the tape, but she knew he had watched it and she asked him nothing about it. He had rewound it and left it in the VCR, hoping and praying she would watch it while he was gone.

Rayford got to the church just before ten o'clock and was shocked to have to park nearly three blocks away. The place was packed. Few were carrying Bibles, and hardly anyone was dressed up. These were scared, desperate people who filled every pew, including in the balcony. Rayford wound up standing in the back with nowhere to sit.

Right at ten o'clock, Bruce began, but he asked Loretta to stand by the door and make sure any latecomers were welcomed. Despite the crowd, he did not use the platform spotlights, nor did he stand in the pulpit. He had placed a single microphone stand in front of the first pew, and he simply talked to the people.

Bruce introduced himself and said, "I'm not in the pulpit because that is a place for people who are trained and called to it. I am in a place of leadership and teaching today by default. Normally we at this church would be thrilled to see a crowd like this," he said. "But I'm not about to tell you how great it is to see you here. I know you're here seeking to know what happened to your children and loved ones, and I believe I have the answer. Obviously, I didn't have it before, or I too would be gone. We'll not be singing or making any announcements, except to tell you we have a Bible study scheduled for Wednesday night at seven. We will not be taking any offering, though we will have to start doing that next week to meet our expenses. The church has some money in the bank, but we do have a mortgage and I have living expenses."

Bruce then told the same story he had told Rayford and Chloe the day before, and his voice was the only sound in the place. Many wept. He showed the videotape, and more than a hundred people prayed along with the pastor at the end. Bruce urged them to begin coming to New Hope.

He added, "I know many of you may still be skeptical. You may believe what happened was of God, but you still don't like it and you resent him for it. If you would like to come back and vent and ask questions this evening, I will be here. But I choose not to offer that opportunity this morning because so many here are brand-new in their faith and I don't want to confuse the issue. Rest assured we will be open to any honest question.

"I do want to open the floor to anyone who received Christ this morning and would like to confess it before us. The Bible tells us to do that, to make known our decision and our stand. Feel free to come to the microphone."

Rayford was the first to move, but as he came down the aisle he sensed many falling in behind him. Dozens waited to tell their stories, to say where they'd been on their spiritual journey. Most were just like he was, having been on the edges of the truth through a loved one or friend, but never fully accepting the truth about Christ.

Their stories were moving and hardly anyone left, even when the clock swept past noon and forty or fifty more still stood in line. All seemed to need to tell of the ones who had left them. At two o'clock, when everyone was hungry and tired, Bruce said, "I'm going to have to bring this to a close. One thing I wasn't going to do today was anything traditionally churchy, including singing. But I feel we need to praise the Lord for what has happened here today. Let me teach you a simple chorus of adoration."

Bruce sang a brief song from Scripture, honoring God

the Father, Jesus his Son, and the Holy Spirit. When the people joined in, quietly and reverently and heartfelt, Rayford was too choked up to sing. One by one people stopped singing and mouthed the words or hummed, they were so overcome. Rayford believed it was the most moving moment of his life. How he longed to share it with Irene and Raymie and Chloe.

People seemed reluctant to leave, even after Bruce closed in prayer. Many stayed to get acquainted, and it became obvious a new congregation had begun. The name of the church was more appropriate than ever. New Hope. Bruce shook hands with people as they left, and no one ducked him or hurried past. When Rayford shook his hand, Bruce asked, "Are you busy this afternoon? Would you be able to join me for a bite?"

"I'd want to call my daughter first, but sure."

Rayford let Chloe know where he'd be. She didn't ask about the church meeting, except to say, "It went long, huh? Lot of people there?" And he simply told her yes on both counts. He was committed to not saying more unless she asked. He hoped and prayed her curiosity would get the best of her, and if he then could do justice to what had happened that day, maybe she would wish she'd been in on it. At the very least, she would have to recognize how it had affected him.

At a small restaurant in nearby Arlington Heights, Bruce looked exhausted but happy. He told Rayford he felt such a mix of emotions he hardly knew what to make of them. "My grief over the loss of my family is still so raw I can hardly function. I still feel shame over my phoniness. And yet since I repented of my sins and truly received Christ, in just a few days he has blessed me beyond anything I could have imagined. My house is lonely and cold and carries painful memories. And yet look what happened today. I've been given this new flock to shepherd, a reason for living."

Rayford merely nodded. He sensed Bruce simply needed someone to talk to.

"Ray," Bruce said, "churches are usually built by seminary-trained pastors and elders who have been Christians most of their lives. We don't have that luxury. I don't know what kind of leadership model we're going to have. It doesn't make sense to have elders when the interim pastor, which is all I can call myself, is himself a brand-new Christian and so is everybody else. But we're going to need a core of people who care about each other and are committed to the body. Loretta and a few of the people I met with the night of the Rapture are already part of that team, along with a couple of older men who were in the church for years but somehow missed the point as well.

"I know this is very new to you, but I feel as if I should ask you to join our little core group. We will be at the church for the Sunday morning meeting, the occasional Sunday evening meeting, the Wednesday night Bible study, and we will meet at my home one other evening every week. That's where we will pray for each other, keep each other accountable, and study a little deeper to stay ahead of the new congregation. Are you willing?"

Rayford sat back. "Wow," he said. "I don't know. I'm so new at this."

"We all are."

"Yeah, but you were raised in it, Bruce. You know this stuff."

"I only missed the most important point."

"Well, I'll tell you what appeals to me about it. I'm hungry for knowledge of the Bible. And I need a friend."

"So do I," Bruce said. "That's the risk. We could wind up grating on each other."

"I'm willing to take the risk if you are," Rayford said. "As long as I'm not expected to take any leadership role."

"Deal," Barnes said, thrusting out his hand. Rayford shook it. Neither smiled. Rayford had the feeling this was the beginning of a relationship born of tragedy and need. He just hoped it worked out. When Rayford finally arrived home, Chloe was eager to hear all about it. She was amazed at what her father told her and said she was embarrassed to say she had not watched the tape yet. "But I will now, Dad, before we go to Atlanta. You're really into this, aren't you? It sounds like something I want to check out, even if I don't do anything about it."

Rayford had been home about twenty minutes and had changed into his pajamas and robe to relax for the rest of the evening when Chloe called out to him. "Dad, I almost forgot. A Hattie Durham called for you several times. She sounded pretty agitated. Said she works with you."

"Yeah," Rayford said. "She wanted to be assigned to

my next flight and I ducked her. She probably found out and wants to know why."

"Why *did* you duck her?"

"It's a long story. I'll tell you sometime."

Rayford was reaching for the phone when it rang. It was Bruce. "I forgot to confirm," he said. "If you've agreed to be part of the core team, the first responsibility is tonight's meeting with the disenchanted and the skeptics."

"You *are* going to be a tough taskmaster, aren't you?"

"I'll understand if you weren't planning on it."

"Bruce," Rayford said, "except for heaven, there's no place I'd rather be. I wouldn't miss it. I might even be able to get Chloe to come to this one."

"What one?" Chloe asked when he hung up.

"In a minute," he said. "Let me call Hattie and calm the waters."

Rayford was surprised that Hattie said nothing about their flight assignments. "I just got some disconcerting news," she said. "You remember that writer from *Global Weekly* who was on our flight, the one who had his computer hooked up to the in-flight phone?"

"Vaguely."

"His name was Cameron Williams, and I talked to him by phone a couple of times since the flight. I tried calling him from the airport in New York last night but couldn't get through."

"Uh-huh."

"I just heard on the news that he was killed in England in a car bombing."

"You're kidding!"

"I'm not. Isn't that too bizarre? Rayford, sometimes I don't know how much of this I can take. I hardly knew this guy, but I was so shocked I just broke down when I heard. I'm sorry to bother you with it, but I thought you might remember him."

"No, that's all right, Hattie. And I know how overwhelming this is for you because it has been for me, too. I've got a lot to talk to you about, actually."

"You do?"

"Could we get together sometime soon?"

"I've put in to work one of your flights," she said. "Maybe if that works out."

"Maybe," he said. "And if it doesn't, maybe you could come over for dinner with Chloe and me."

"I'd like that, Rayford. I really would."

THIRTEEN

BUCK Williams sat near an exit at JFK Airport reading his own obituary. "Magazine Writer Assumed Dead," the headline read.

> Cameron Williams, 30, the youngest senior writer on the staff of any weekly newsmagazine, is feared dead after a mysterious car bombing outside a London pub Saturday night that took the life of a Scotland Yard investigator.
>
> Williams, a five-year employee of *Global Weekly*, had won a Pulitzer as a reporter for the *Boston Globe* before joining the magazine as a staff reporter at 25. He quickly rose to the position of senior writer and has since written more than three dozen cover stories, four times assigned the *Weekly*'s Newsmaker of the Year story.

The journalist won the prestigious Ernest Hemingway Prize for war correspondence when he chronicled the destruction of the Russian air force over Israel 14 months ago. According to Steve Plank, executive editor of *Global Weekly,* the administration of the magazine is refusing to confirm the report of Williams's death "until we see hard evidence."

Williams's father and a married brother reside in Tucson, where Williams lost his sister-in-law, niece, and nephew in last week's disappearances.

Scotland Yard reports that the London bombing appeared to be the work of Northern Ireland terrorists and might have been a case of retribution. Captain Howard Sullivan called his 29-year-old subordinate, victim Alan Tompkins, "one of the finest men and brightest investigators it has been my privilege to work with."

Sullivan added that Williams and Tompkins had become friends after the writer had interviewed the investigator for an article on terrorism in England several years ago. The two had just emerged from the Armitage Arms Pub in London when a bomb exploded in Tompkins's Scotland Yard vehicle.

Tompkins's remains have been identified, though only items of personal identification of Williams were recovered from the scene.

Rayford Steele had a plan. He had decided to be honest with Chloe about his attraction to Hattie Durham and how guilty he felt about it. He knew it would disappoint Chloe, even if it didn't shock her. He intended to talk about his new desire to share his faith with Hattie, hoping he could make some progress with Chloe without her feeling threatened. Chloe had gone with him to the church meeting for skeptics the night before, as she promised. But she had left a little over halfway through. She also fulfilled her promise to watch the video the former pastor had taped. They had discussed neither the meeting nor the video.

They wouldn't have much time together once they arrived at O'Hare, so Rayford broached the subject in the car as they gaped at the wreckage and debris lining the roadways. Between their house and the airport, they saw more than a dozen homes that had been gutted by fire. Rayford's theory was that families had disappeared, leaving something on the stove.

"And you think this was God's doing?" Chloe said, not disrespectfully.

"I do."

"I thought he was supposed to be a God of love and order," she said.

"I believe he is. This was his plan."

"There were plenty of tragedies and senseless deaths before this."

"I don't understand all that either," Rayford said. "But like Bruce said last night, we live in a fallen world. God left control of it pretty much to Satan."

"Oh, brother," she said. "Do you wonder why I walked out?"

"I figured it was because the questions and answers were hitting a little too close to home."

"Maybe they were, but all this stuff about Satan and the Fall and sin and all that . . ." She stopped and shook her head.

"I don't claim to understand it any better than you do, honey," Rayford said. "But I know I'm a sinner and that this world is full of them."

"And you consider me one."

"If you're part of everybody, then, yes, I do. Don't you?"

"Not on purpose."

"You're never selfish, greedy, jealous, petty, spiteful?"

"I try not to be, at least not at anyone else's expense."

"But you think you're exempt from what the Bible says about everybody being a sinner, about there not being one righteous person anywhere, 'No not one'?"

"I don't know, Daddy. I just have no idea."

"You know what I'm worried about, of course."

"Yeah, I know. You think the time is short, that in this new dangerous world I'm going to wait too long to decide what I'm going to do, and then it'll be too late."

"I couldn't have said it better myself, Chloe. I just hope you know I'm thinking only of you, nothing else."

"You don't have to worry about that, Daddy."

"What did you think of the video? Did it make sense to you?"

"It made a lot of sense if you buy into all that. I mean, you have to start with that as a foundation. Then it all works neatly. But if you're not sure about God and the

Bible and sin and heaven and hell, then you're still
wondering what happened and why."

"And that's where you are?"

"I don't know where I am, Dad."

Rayford fought the urge to plead with her. If they
had enough time over lunch in Atlanta, he would try
the approach of telling her about Hattie. The plane was
supposed to sit only about forty-five minutes before the
return to O'Hare. Rayford wondered if it was fair to
pray for a delay.

"Nice cap," Steve Plank said as he hurried into JFK and
slapped Buck on the shoulder. "And what's this? Two
day's growth?"

"I was never too much for disguises," Buck said.

"You're not famous enough to need to hide," Steve said.
"You staying away from your apartment for a while?"

"Yeah, and probably yours. You sure you weren't followed?"

"You're being a little paranoid, aren't you, Buck?"

"I have a right," Buck said as they climbed into a cab.
"Central Park," he informed the driver. Then he told
Steve the entire story.

"What makes you think Carpathia is going to help?"
Plank asked later as they walked through the park. "If the
Yard and the exchange are behind this, and you think
Carpathia is linked to Todd-Cothran and Stonagal, you
might be asking Carpathia to turn against his own angels."

They strolled under a bridge to elude the hot spring

sun. "I have a hunch about this guy," Buck said, his voice echoing off the cobblestone walls. "It wouldn't surprise me to discover that he met with Stonagal and Todd-Cothran in London the other day. But I have to believe he's a pawn."

Steve pointed to a bench and they sat. "Well, I met Carpathia this morning at his press conference," Steve said, "and all I can say is that I hope you're right."

"Rosenzweig was impressed with him, and that's one insightful old scientist."

"Carpathia's impressive," Steve conceded. "He's handsome as a young Robert Redford, and this morning he spoke in nine languages, so fluently you'd have thought each was his native tongue. The media is eating him up."

"You say that as if you're not the media," Buck said.

Steve shrugged. "I'm proving my own point. I've learned to be a skeptic, to let *People* and the tabloids chase the personalities. But here's a guy with substance, with a brain, with something to say. I liked him. I mean, I saw him only in a press conference setting, but he seems to have a plan. You'll like him, and you're a bigger skeptic than I am. Plus he wants to see you."

"Tell me about that."

"I told you. He's got a little entourage of nobodies, with one exception."

"Rosenzweig."

"Right."

"What's Chaim's connection?"

"Nobody's sure yet, but Carpathia seems to attract experts and consultants who keep him up to speed on technology, politics, finances, and all that. And you know, Buck, he's not that much older than you are. I think they said this morning he's thirty-three."

"Nine languages?"

Plank nodded.

"Do you remember which ones?"

"Why would you ask that?"

"Just thinking."

Steve pulled a reporter's notebook from his side pocket. "You want 'em in alphabetical order?"

"Sure."

"Arabic, Chinese, English, French, German, Hungarian, Romanian, Russian, and Spanish."

"One more time," Buck said, thinking.

Steve repeated them. "What's on your mind?"

"This guy's the consummate politician."

"He is not. Trust me, this was no trick. He knew these languages well and used them effectively."

"But don't you see which languages they are, Steve? Think about it."

"Spare me the effort."

"The six languages of the United Nations, plus the three languages of his own country."

"No kidding?"

Buck nodded. "So am I gonna get to meet him soon?"

The flight to Atlanta was full and busy, and Rayford had to change altitudes continually to avoid choppy air. He got to see Chloe for only a few seconds while his first officer was in the cockpit and the plane was on autopilot. Rayford made a hurried walk-through but had no time to chat.

He got his wish in Atlanta. Another 747 had to be flown back to Chicago in the middle of the afternoon, and the only other pilot available had to be back earlier. Chicago coordinated with Atlanta, switched the two assignments, and found a seat for Chloe, too. That gave Rayford and Chloe more than two hours for lunch, enough time to get away from the airport.

Their cab driver, a young woman with a beautiful lilt to her voice, asked if they wanted to see "a truly unbelievable sight."

"If it's not out of the way."

"It's just a couple of blocks from where y'all are going," she said.

She maneuvered around several detours and construction horses, then through two streets manned by traffic cops. "Over yonder," she said, pointing, and she pulled into a sandy parking lot rimmed by three-foot concrete-block walls. "Can you see that parking garage 'cross the way?"

"What in the world?" Chloe said.

"Strange, isn't it?" the cabbie said.

"What happened?" Rayford asked.

"This has been going on since the vanishings," she said.

They peered at a six-story garage with cars seemingly jammed into each other at all angles in a gridlock so tight and convoluted that cranes worked to lift them out through the open sides of the structure.

"They were all in there after a late ballgame that night," she said. "The police say it was bad anyway, long lines of cars trying to get out, people taking turns merging and lots of 'em not taking turns at all. So some people who got tired of waiting just tried to edge in and make other people let 'em in, you know."

"Yeah."

"And then, poof, they say more than a third of the cars ain't got drivers, just like that. If they had room, they kept going till they hit other cars or the wall. If they didn't have room, they just pushed up against the car in front of 'em. The ones that were left couldn't go one way or the other. It was such a mess that people just left their cars and climbed over other cars and went looking for help. They started at dawn moving the cars on the ground levels with tow trucks, then they got them cranes in there by noon, and they been at it ever since."

Rayford and Chloe sat and watched, shaking their heads. Cranes normally used for hoisting beams up to new buildings were wrapping cables around cars, tugging, yanking, dragging them past each other and through openings in the concrete to clear the garage. It appeared it would take several more days.

"How about you?" Rayford asked the driver. "Did you lose people?"

"Yes, sir. My mama and my grandmama and two baby sisters. But I know where they are. They're in heaven, just like my mama always said."

"I believe you're right," Rayford said. "My wife and son are gone, too."

"Are you saved now?" the girl asked.

Rayford was shocked by her forthrightness, but he knew exactly what she meant. "I am," he said.

"I am, too. You got to be blind or somethin' to not see the light now."

Rayford wanted to peek at Chloe, but he did not. He tipped the young woman generously when they got to the restaurant. Over lunch he told Chloe of his history with Hattie, such as it was.

She was silent a long time, and when she spoke her voice was weak. "So you never actually acted on it?" she said.

"Thankfully, no. I never would have been able to live with myself."

"It would have broken Mom's heart, that's for sure."

He nodded miserably. "Sometimes I feel as bad as if I had been unfaithful to her. But I justified my considering it because your mom was so obsessed with her faith."

"I know. Funny thing, though. That kept me straighter at school than I might have been otherwise. I mean, I'm sure Mom would be disappointed to know a lot of the things I've said and done while I've been away—don't ask. But knowing how sincere and devout she was, and what high hopes and expectations she had for me, kept me from doing something really stupid. I knew she was praying for me. She told me every time she wrote."

"Did she also tell you about the end times, Chloe?"

"Sure. All the time."

"But you still don't buy it?"

"I want to, Dad. I really do. But I have to be intellectually honest with myself."

It was all Rayford could do to stay calm. Had he been this pseudosophisticated at that age? Of course he had. He had run everything through that maddening intellectual grid—until recently, when the supernatural came crashing through his academic pretense. But like the cabbie had said, you'd have to be blind not to see the light now, no matter how educated you thought you were.

"I'm going to invite Hattie to dinner with us this week," he said.

Chloe narrowed her eyes. "What, you feel like you're available now?"

Rayford was stunned at his own reaction. He had to keep himself from slapping his own daughter, something he had never done. He gritted his teeth. "How can you say that after all I've just told you?" he said. "That's insulting."

"So was what you were hoping for with this Hattie Durham, Dad. Do you think she was unaware of what was going on? How do you think she'll interpret this? She may come on like gangbusters."

"I'm going to make it clear what my intentions are, and they are totally honorable, more honorable than they ever could have been before, because I had nothing of worth to offer her."

"So, now you're going to switch from hitting on her to preaching at her."

He wanted to argue, but he couldn't. "I care about her

237

as a person, and I want her to know the truth and be able to act on it."

"And what if she doesn't?"

"That's her choice. I can only do my part."

"Is that how you feel about me, too? If I don't act on it the way you want, you'll be satisfied that you've done your part?"

"I should, but obviously I care much more about you than I do Hattie."

"You should have thought of that before you risked everything to chase her."

Rayford was offended again, but he had brought this on himself and felt he deserved it. "Maybe that's why I never did anything about it," he said. "Ever think of that?"

"This is all news to me," she said. "I hope you restrained yourself because of your wife and kids."

"I almost didn't."

"So I gather. What if this strategy with Hattie just makes you all the more attractive to her? What's to keep you from being attracted to her, too? It's not like you're still married, if you're convinced Mom is in heaven."

Rayford ordered dessert and laid his napkin on the table. "Maybe I'm being naive, but your mother being in heaven is just like losing her to sudden death. The last thing on my mind is another woman, and certainly not Hattie. She's too young and immature, and I'm too disgusted with myself for having been tempted by her in the first place. I want to be up front with her and see what she says. It'll be instructive to know whether all this was just in my mind."

"You mean for future reference?"

"Chloe, I love you, but you're being bratty."

"I know. I'm sorry. That was uncalled for. But seriously, how will you know if she tells you the truth? If you tell her you were interested for the wrong reasons and that you aren't interested anymore, why should she be vulnerable enough to admit she thought you two had possibilities?"

Rayford shrugged. "You may be right. But I have to be honest with her even if she's not honest with me. I owe her that much. I want her to take me seriously when I tell her what I think she needs now."

"I don't know, Dad. I think it's a little too soon to be pushing her toward God."

"How soon is too soon, Chloe? There are no guarantees, not now."

Steve pulled from his breast pocket two sets of press credentials, permitting the bearers to attend Nicolae Carpathia's speech to the General Assembly of the United Nations that very afternoon. Buck's credentials were in the name of George Oreskovich.

"Do I take care of you, or what?"

"Unbelievable," Buck said. "How much time do we have?"

"A little over an hour," Steve said, rising to hail a cab. "And like I said, he wants to meet you."

"He reads, doesn't he? He's got to think I'm dead."

"I suppose. But he'll remember me from this morning and I'll be able to assure him it will be just as valuable for him to be interviewed by George Oreskovich as by the legendary Cameron Williams."

"Yeah, but Steve, if he's like the other politicians I know, he's hung up on image, on high-profile journalists. Like it or not, that's what I've become. How are you going to get him to settle for an unknown?"

"I don't know. Maybe I'll tell him it's really you. Then, while you're with him, I'll release the report that your obit was wrong and that right now you're doing a cover-story interview with Carpathia."

"A cover story? You've come a long way from calling him a low-level bureaucrat from a nonstrategic country."

"I was at the press conference, Buck. I met him. And I can at least gauge the competition. If we don't feature him prominently, we'll be the only national magazine that doesn't."

"Like I say, if he's like the typical politician—"

"You can put that out of your mind, Buck. You're going to find this guy the farthest thing you've ever seen from the typical politician. You're going to thank me for getting you the exclusive interview with him."

"I thought that was his idea because of my colossal name," Buck said, smiling.

"So? I could have turned him down."

"Yeah, and been the executive editor of the only national magazine that fails to cover the most exciting new face to visit the States."

"Believe me, Buck," Steve said during the ride to the

U.N. building, "this is going to be a refreshing change from the doom and gloom we've been writing and reading for days."

The two used their press credentials to get in, but Buck hung back out of sight of his colleagues and the competition until all were seated in the General Assembly. Steve held a seat for him in the back, where he would not draw attention when he slipped in at the last minute. Meanwhile, Steve would use his cellular phone to call in the story of Buck's reappearance, so it would hit the news by the end of the day.

Carpathia entered the assembly in a dignified yet inauspicious manner, though he had an entourage of a half dozen, including Chaim Rosenzweig and a financial wizard from the French government. Carpathia appeared an inch or two over six feet tall, broad shouldered, thick chested, trim, athletic, tanned, and blond. His thick shock of hair was trimmed neatly around the ears, sideburns, and neck, and his navy-on-navy pinstripe suit and matching tie were exquisitely conservative.

Even from a distance, the man seemed to carry himself with a sense of humility and purpose. His presence dominated the room, and yet he did not seem preoccupied or impressed with himself. His jewelry was understated. His jaw and nose were Roman and strong, his piercing blue eyes set deep under thick brows.

Buck was struck that Carpathia carried no notebook, and he assumed the man must have his speech notes in his breast pocket. Either that or they were being carried by an aide. Buck was wrong on both counts.

Secretary-General Mwangati Ngumo of Botswana announced that the assembly was privileged to hear briefly from the new president of the nation of Romania and that the formal introduction of their guest would be made by the Honorable Dr. Chaim Rosenzweig, with whom they were all familiar.

Rosenzweig hurried to the podium with a vigor that belied his age, and he initially received a more enthusiastic response than did Carpathia. The popular Israeli statesman and scholar said simply that it gave him great pleasure to introduce "to this worthy and august body a young man I respect and admire as much as anyone I've ever met. Please welcome His Honor, President Nicolae Carpathia of Romania."

Carpathia rose, turned to the assembly, and nodded humbly, then shook hands warmly with Rosenzweig. With courtly manners he remained at the side of the lectern until the older man was seated, then stood relaxed and smiling before speaking extemporaneously. Not only did he not use notes, but he also never hesitated, misspoke, or took his eyes off his audience.

He spoke earnestly, with passion, with a frequent smile, and with occasional, appropriate humor. He mentioned respectfully that he was aware that it had not been a full week yet since the disappearance of millions all over the world, including many who would have been "in this very room." Carpathia spoke primarily in perfectEnglish with only a hint of a Romanian accent. He used no contractions and enunciated every syllable of every word. Once again he employed all nine languages with which he was fluent, each time translating himself into English.

In one of the most touching scenes Buck had ever witnessed, Carpathia began by announcing that he was humbled and moved to visit "for the first time this historic site, where nation after nation has set its sights. One by one they have come from all over the globe on pilgrimages as sacred as any to the Holy Lands, exposing their faces to the heat of the rising sun. Here they have taken their stand for peace in a once-and-for-all, rock-solid commitment to putting behind them the insanity of war and bloodshed. These nations, great and small, have had their fill of the death and maiming of their most promising citizens in the prime of their youth.

"Our forebears were thinking globally long before I was born," Carpathia said. "In 1944, the year the International Monetary Fund and the World Bank were established, this great host nation, the United States of America, along with the British Commonwealth and the Union of Soviet Socialist Republics, met at the famous Dumbarton Oaks Conference to propose the birth of this body."

Displaying his grasp of history and his photographic memory of dates and places, Carpathia intoned, "From its official birth on October 24, 1945, and that first meeting of your General Assembly in London, January 10, 1946, to this day, tribes and nations have come together to pledge their wholehearted commitment to peace, brotherhood, and the global community."

He began in almost a whisper, "From lands distant

and near they have come: from Afghanistan, Albania, Algeria . . ." He continued, his voice rising and falling dramatically with the careful pronunciation of the name of each member country of the United Nations. Buck sensed a passion, a love for these countries and the ideals of the U.N. Carpathia was clearly moved as he plunged on, listing country after country, not droning but neither in any hurry.

A minute into his list, representatives noticed that with each name, someone from that country rose in dignity and stood erect, as if voting anew for peace among nations. Carpathia smiled and nodded at each as they rose, and nearly every country was represented. Because of the cosmic trauma the world had endured, they had come looking for answers, for help, for support. Now they had been given the opportunity to take their stand once again.

Buck was tired and felt grimy, wearing two-day-old clothes. But his worries were a distant memory as Carpathia moved along. By the time he got into the Ss in his alphabetical listing, those standing had begun to quietly applaud each new country mentioned. It was a dignified, powerful thing, this show of respect and admiration, this re-welcome into the global village. The applause was not so loud that it kept anyone from hearing Carpathia, but it was so heartfelt and moving that Buck couldn't suppress the lump in his throat. Then he noticed something peculiar. The press representatives from various countries were standing with their ambassadors and delegations. Even the objectivity of the world press had temporarily vanished in what they might previously have written off as jingoism, superpatriotism, or sanctimony.

Buck found himself eager to stand as well, ruing the fact that his country was near the end of the alphabet, but feeling pride and anticipation welling up within him. As more and more countries were named and their people stood proudly, the applause grew louder, merely because of the increased numbers. Carpathia was up to the task, his voice growing more emotional and powerful with each new country name.

On and on he thundered as people stood and clapped. "Somalia! South Africa! Spain! Sri Lanka! Sudan! Suriname! Swaziland! Sweden! Syria!"

More than five minutes into the recitation, Carpathia had not missed a beat. He had never once hesitated, stammered, or mispronounced a syllable. Buck was on the edge of his seat as the speaker swept through the Ts and reached "Uganda! Ukraine! The United Arab Emirates! The United Kingdom! The United States of America!" And Buck leaped to his feet, Steve right with him, along with dozens of other members of the press.

Something had happened in the disappearances of loved ones all over the globe. Journalism might never be the same. Oh, there would be skeptics and those who worshiped objectivity. But what had happened to brotherly love? What had become of depending on one another? What had happened to the brotherhood of men and nations?

It was back. And while no one expected that the press might become the public-relations agency for a new political star, Carpathia certainly had them in his corner this afternoon. By the end of his litany of nearly two hundred nations, young Nicolae was at an emotional, fevered pitch. With such electricity and power in the simple naming of all the countries who had longed to be united with each other, Carpathia had brought the entire crowd to its feet in full voice and applause, press and representative alike. Even the cynical Steve Plank and Buck Williams continued to clap and cheer, never once appearing embarrassed at their loss of detached objectivity.

And there was more, as the Nicolae Carpathia juggernaut sailed on. Over the next half hour he displayed such an intimate knowledge of the United Nations that it was as if he had invented and developed the organization himself. For someone who had never before set foot on American soil, let alone visited the United Nations, he displayed amazing understanding of its inner workings.

During his speech he casually worked in the name of every secretary-general from Trygve Lie of Norway to Ngumo and mentioned their terms of office not just by year but also by specific day and date of their installation and conclusion. He displayed awareness and understanding of each of the six principal organs of the U.N., their functions, their current members, and their particular challenges.

Then he swept through the eighteen U.N. agencies, mentioning every one, its current director, and its headquarters city. This was an amazing display, and suddenly it was no wonder this man had risen so quickly in his own nation, no wonder the previous leader had stepped aside. No wonder New York had already embraced him.

After this, Buck knew, Nicolae Carpathia would be embraced by all of America. And then the world.

FOURTEEN

RAYFORD'S plane touched down in Chicago during rush hour late Monday afternoon. By the time he and Chloe got to their cars, they had not had the opportunity to continue their conversation. "Remember, you promised to let me drive your car home," Chloe said.

"Is it that important to you?" he asked.

"Not really. I just like it. May I?"

"Sure. Just let me get my phone out of it. I want to see when Hattie can join us for dinner. That's all right with you, isn't it?"

"As long as you don't expect me to cook or something sexist and domestic like that."

"I hadn't even thought of it. She loves Chinese. We'll order some."

"She loves Chinese?" Chloe repeated. "You are familiar with this woman, aren't you?"

Rayford shook his head. "It's not like that. I mean, yes, I probably know more about her than I should. But I can tell you the culinary preferences of a dozen crew members, and I hardly know anything else about them."

Rayford retrieved his phone from the BMW and turned the ignition switch far enough to read the gas gauge. "You picked the right car," he said. "It's almost full. You'll beat me home. Your mother's car is on empty. You going to be all right there by yourself for a few minutes? I think I'll pick up a few groceries while I'm out."

Chloe hesitated. "It's eerie in there when you're by yourself, isn't it?" she said.

"A little. But we've got to get used to it."

"You're right," she said quickly. "They're gone. And I don't believe in ghosts. I'll be fine. But don't be long."

————————

At the post-U.N.-appearance press conference for Nicolae Carpathia of Romania, Buck briefly found himself the center of attention. Someone recognized him and expressed surprise and pleasure that he was alive. Buck tried to quiet everyone and tell them that it had all been a misunderstanding, but the furor continued as Chaim Rosenzweig saw him and hurried over, covering Buck's hand with both of his and pumping vigorously. "Oh, I am so glad to see you alive and well," he said. "I heard dreadful news about your demise. And President Carpathia was also disappointed to hear of it. He had so wanted to meet you and had agreed to an exclusive interview."

"Can we still do that?" Buck whispered, to the boos and catcalls of the competition.

"You'll do anything to get a scoop," someone groused. "Even have yourself blown up."

"It will probably not be possible until late tonight," Rosenzweig said. His hand swept the room, crowded with TV cameras, lights, microphones, and the press. "His schedule is full all day, and he has a photo shoot at *People* magazine early this evening. Perhaps following that. I'll speak to him."

"What's your connection?" Buck asked, but the old man put a finger to his lips and pulled away to return and sit near Carpathia as the press conference began.

The young Romanian was no less impressive and persuasive up close, beginning the session with his own statement before fielding questions. He conducted himself like an old pro, though Buck knew his press relations in Romania and the limited other areas of Europe he had visited would not have provided him this experience.

At one point or another, Buck noticed, Carpathia met the eyes of every person in the room, at least briefly. He never looked down, never looked away, never looked up. It was as if he had nothing to hide and nothing to fear. He was in command of himself and seemingly unaffected by the fuss and attention.

He seemed to have unusually good eyesight; it was clear he could see people's name tags from across the room. Anytime he spoke to a member of the press, he referred to them by name as Mr. or Ms. so-and-so. He insisted that people call him by whatever name made them comfortable. "Even Nick," he said, smiling. But no one did. They followed his lead and called him "Mr. President" or "Mr. Carpathia."

Carpathia spoke in the same impassioned and articulate tones he had used in his speech. Buck wondered if this was always the same, in public or private. Whatever else he brought to the world scene, he had a mastery of spoken communication second to none.

"Let me begin by saying what an honor it is for me to be in this country and at this historic site. It has been a dream of mine since I was a small boy in Cluj to one day see this place."

The initial pleasantries over, Carpathia launched into another minispeech, again showing incredible knowledge and grasp of the U.N. and its mission. "You will recall," he said, "that in the previous century the U.N. seemed to be in decline. U.S. president Ronald Reagan escalated the East-West controversies, and the U.N. seemed a thing of the past with its emphasis on North-South conflicts. This organization was in trouble financially, with few members willing to pay their share. With the end of the Cold War in the 1990s, however, your next president, Mr. Bush, recognized what he called the 'new world order,' which resonated deep within my young heart. The original basis for the U.N. charter promised cooperation among the first fifty-one members, including the great powers."

Carpathia went on to discuss the various peacekeeping military actions the U.N. had taken since the Korean conflict of the 1950s. "As you know," he said, speaking again of things long before he was born, "the U.N. has its legacy in the League of Nations, which I believe was the first international peacekeeping body. It came about at the end of the First World War, but when it failed to prevent a second, it became anachronistic. Out of that failure came the United Nations, which must remain strong to prevent World War III, which would result in the end of life as we know it."

After Carpathia outlined his eagerness to support the U.N. in any way possible, someone interjected a question about the disappearances. He became suddenly serious and unsmiling, and spoke with compassion and warmth.

"Many people in my country lost loved ones to this horrible phenomenon. I know that many people all over the world have theories, and I wish not to denigrate any one of them, the people or their ideas. I have asked Dr. Chaim Rosenzweig of Israel to work with a team to try to make sense of this great tragedy and allow us to take steps toward preventing anything similar from ever happening again.

"When the time is appropriate I will allow Dr. Rosenzweig to speak for himself, but for now I can tell you that the theory that makes the most sense to me is briefly as follows: The world has been stockpiling nuclear weapons for innumerable years. Since the United States dropped atomic bombs on Japan in 1945 and the Soviet

Union first detonated its own devices September 23, 1949, the world has been at risk of nuclear holocaust. Dr. Rosenzweig and his team of renowned scholars is close to the discovery of an atmospheric phenomenon that may have caused the vanishing of so many people instantaneously."

"What kind of a phenomenon?" Buck asked.

Carpathia glanced briefly at his name tag and then into his eyes. "I do not want to be premature, Mr. Oreskovich," he said. Several members of the press snickered, but Carpathia never lost pace. "Or I should say, 'Mr. Cameron Williams of *Global Weekly*.'" This elicited amused applause throughout the room. Buck was stunned.

"Dr. Rosenzweig believes that some confluence of electromagnetism in the atmosphere, combined with as yet unknown or unexplained atomic ionization from the nuclear power and weaponry throughout the world, could have been ignited or triggered—perhaps by a natural cause like lightning, or even by an intelligent life-form that discovered this possibility before we did—and caused this instant action throughout the world."

"Sort of like someone striking a match in a room full of gasoline vapors?" a journalist suggested.

Carpathia nodded thoughtfully.

"How is that different from the idea of aliens from outer space zapping everybody?"

"It is not wholly different," Carpathia conceded, "but I am more inclined to believe in the natural theory, that lightning reacted with some subatomic field."

"Why would the disappearances be so random? Why some people and not others?"

"I do not know," Carpathia said. "And Dr. Rosenzweig tells me they have come to no conclusions on that either. At this point they are postulating that certain people's levels of electricity made them more likely to be affected. That would account for all the children and babies and even fetal material that vanished. Their electromagnetism was not developed to the point where it could resist whatever happened."

"What do you say to people who believe this was the work of God, that he raptured his church?"

Carpathia smiled compassionately. "Let me be careful to say that I do not and will not criticize any sincere person's belief system. That is the basis for true harmony and brotherhood, peace and respect among peoples. I do not accept that theory because I know many, many more people who should be gone if the righteous were taken to heaven. If there is a God, I respectfully submit that this is not the capricious way in which he would operate. By the same token, you will not hear me express any disrespect for those who disagree."

Buck was then astonished to hear Carpathia say that he had been invited to speak at the upcoming ecumenical religious confab scheduled that month in New York. "There I will discuss my views of millenarianism, eschatology, the Last Judgment, and the second coming of Christ. Dr. Rosenzweig was kind enough to arrange that invitation, and until then I think it would be best if I did not attempt to speak on those subjects informally."

"How long will you be in New York?"

"If the people of Romania will permit me, I may be here an entire month. I hate to be away from my people, but they understand that I am concerned for the greater global good, and with technology as it is today and the wonderful people in positions of influence in Romania, I feel confident I can keep in contact and that my nation will not suffer for my brief absence."

By the time of the evening network news, a new international star had been born. He even had a nickname: Saint Nick. More than sound bites had been taken from the floor of the U.N. and the press conference. Carpathia enjoyed several minutes on each telecast, rousing the U.N. audience with the recitation of countries, urgently calling for a recommitment to world peace.

He had carefully avoided specific talk of global disarmament. His was a message of love and peace and understanding and brotherhood, and to quit fighting seemed to go without saying. No doubt he would be back to hammer home that point, but in the meantime, Carpathia was on the charmed ride of his life.

Broadcast commentators urged that he be named an adjunct adviser to the U.N. secretary-general and that he visit each headquarters of the various U.N. agencies around the world. By late that evening, he was invited to make appearances at each of the international meetings coming up within the next few weeks.

He was seen in the company of Jonathan Stonagal, no surprise to Buck. And immediately following the press conference he was whisked away to other appointments. Dr.

Rosenzweig found Buck. "I was able to get a commitment from him for late this evening," the old man said. "He has several interviews, mostly with the television people, and then he will be live on ABC's *Nightline* with Wallace Theodore. Following that, he will return to his hotel and will be happy to give you an uninterrupted half hour."

Buck told Steve he wanted to hurry home to his apartment, get freshened up, get his messages, run to the office and educate himself as quickly as possible from the files, and be totally prepared for the interview. Steve agreed to accompany him.

"But I'm still paranoid," Buck admitted. "If Stonagal is related in any way to Todd-Cothran, and we know he is, who knows what he thinks about what happened in London?"

"That's a long shot," Steve said. "Even if that dirt goes into the exchange and Scotland Yard, that doesn't mean Stonagal would have any interest in it. I would think he'd want to stay as far from it as possible."

"But, Steve, you have to agree it's likely that Dirk Burton was murdered because he got too close to Todd-Cothran's secret connections with Stonagal's international group. If they wipe out people they see as their enemies— even friends of their enemies like Alan Tompkins and I were—where will they stop?"

"But you're assuming Stonagal was aware of what happened in London. He's bigger than that. Todd-Cothran or the guy at the Yard may have seen you as a threat, but Stonagal has probably never heard of you."

"You don't think he reads the *Weekly?*"

"Don't be hurt. You're like a gnat to him if he even knows your name."

"You know what a swat with a magazine can do to a gnat, Steve?"

"There's one big hole in your argument," Steve said later as they entered Buck's apartment. "If Stonagal *is* dangerous to you, what does that make Carpathia?"

"Like I said, Carpathia can be only a pawn."

"Buck! You just heard him. Did I overrate him?"

"No."

"Were you blown away?"

"Yes."

"Does he look like anybody's pawn?"

"No. So I can assume only that he knows nothing about this."

"You're pretty sure he met with Todd-Cothran and Stonagal in London before coming here?"

"That had to be business," Buck said. "Planning for the trip and his involvement with international advisers."

"You're taking a big risk," Steve said.

"I have no choice. Anyway, I'm willing. Until he proves otherwise, I'm going to trust Nicolae Carpathia."

"Hmph," Steve said.

"What?"

"It's just that usually you work the other way around. You distrust someone until they prove otherwise."

"Well, it's a new world, Steve. Nothing's the same as it was last week, is it?"

And Buck pushed the button on his answering machine while beginning to undress for his shower.

Rayford pulled into his driveway with a sack of groceries on the seat beside him. He had gotten a hold of Hattie Durham, who wanted to keep him on the phone talking until he begged off. She was delighted with the dinner invitation and said she could come three nights later, on Thursday.

Rayford guessed he was half an hour behind Chloe, and he was impressed that she had left the garage door open for him. When he found the door locked between the garage and the house, however, he was concerned. He knocked. No answer.

Rayford reopened the garage door to go around to the front, but just before shutting it on his way out, he stopped. Something was different in the garage. He flipped on the light to add to the single bulb of the door opener. All three cars were in their places, but—

Rayford walked around the Jeep at the end. Raymie's stuff was missing! His bike. His four-wheeler. What was this?

Rayford jogged to the front door. The window of the storm door was broken and the door hung on one hinge. The main door had been kicked in. No small feat, as the door was huge and heavy with a dead bolt. The entire frame had been obliterated and lay in pieces on the floor of the entryway. Rayford rushed in, calling for Chloe.

He ran from room to room, praying nothing had happened to the only family member he had left. Everything of immediate material value seemed to be gone. Radios, televisions, VCRs, jewelry, CD players, video games, the silver, even the china. To his relief there was no sign of blood or struggle.

Rayford was on the phone to the police when his call waiting clicked. "I hate to put you on hold," he said, "but that may be my daughter."

It was. "Oh, Daddy!" she said, crying. "Are you all right? I came in through the garage and saw all that stuff missing. I thought maybe they'd come back, so I locked the door to the garage and was going to lock the front, but I saw the glass and wood and everything, so I ran out the back. I'm three doors down."

"They're not coming back, hon," he said. "I'll come get you."

"Mr. Anderson said he would walk me home."

A few minutes later Chloe sat rocking on the couch, her arms folded across her stomach. She told the police officer what she had told her father; then he took Rayford's statement. "You folks don't use your burglar alarm?"

Rayford shook his head. "That's my fault. We used it for years when we didn't need it, and I got tired of being awakened in the middle of the night with the false alarms and the . . . the, uh—"

"Calls from us, I know," the cop said. "That's what everybody says. But this time it would have been worth it, huh?"

"Hindsight and all that," Rayford said. "Never really thought we needed the security in this neighborhood."

"This kind of crime is up two hundred percent here in the last week alone," the officer said. "The bad guys know we don't have the time or manpower to do a blessed thing about it."

"Well, will you put my daughter's mind at ease and tell her they aren't interested in hurting us and that they won't be back?"

"That's right, miss," he said. "Your dad should get this door boarded up till it can be fixed, and I would arm that security system. But I wouldn't expect a repeat visit, at least not by the same bunch. We talked to the people across the street. They saw some kind of a carpet-service minivan here for about half an hour this afternoon. They went in the front, came through, opened the garage door, backed into the empty space in there, and carted your stuff off almost under your noses."

"Nobody saw them break in the front?"

"Your neighbors don't have a clear view of your entrance. Nobody really does. Slick job."

"I'm just glad Chloe didn't walk in on them," Rayford said.

The cop nodded on his way out. "You can be grateful for that. I imagine your insurance will take care of a lot of this. I don't expect to be recovering any of it. We haven't had any luck with the other cases."

Rayford embraced Chloe, who was still shaking. "Can you do me a favor, Dad?" she said.

"Anything."

"I want another copy of that video, the one from the pastor."

"I'll call Bruce, and we'll pick one up tonight."

Suddenly Chloe laughed.

"Now this is funny?" Rayford said.

"I just had a thought," she said, smiling through her tears. "What if the burglars watch that tape?"

FIFTEEN

ONE of the first messages on Buck's answering machine was from the flight attendant he had met the week before. "Mr. Williams, this is Hattie Durham," she said. "I'm in New York on another flight and thought I'd call to say hi and thanks again for helping me make contact with my family. I'll wait a second and keep jabbering here, in case you're screening your calls. It would be fun to get together for a drink or something, but don't feel obligated. Well, maybe another time."

"So who's that?" Steve called out as Buck hesitated near the bathroom door, waiting to hear all the messages before getting into the shower.

"Just a girl," he said.

"Nice?"

"Better than nice. Gorgeous."

"Better call her back."

"Don't worry."

Several other messages were unimportant. Then came two that had been left that very afternoon. The first was from Captain Howard Sullivan of Scotland Yard. "Ah yes, Mr. Williams. I hesitate to leave this message on your machine, but I would like to speak with you at your earliest convenience. As you know, two gentlemen with whom you were associated have met with untimely demises here in London. I would like to ask you a few questions. You may be hearing from other agencies, as you were seen with one of the victims just before his unfortunate end. Please call me." And he left the number.

The next message had come less than half an hour later and was from Georges Lafitte, an operative with Interpol, the international police organization headquartered in Lyons, France. "Mr. Williams," he said in a thick French accent, "as soon as you get this message, I would like you to call me from the nearest police station. They will know how to contact us directly, and they will have a printout of information on why we need to speak with you. For your own sake, I would urge you not to delay."

Buck leaned out to stare at Steve, who looked as puzzled as Buck was. "What are you now?" Steve asked. "A suspect?"

"I'd better not be. After what I heard from Alan about Sullivan and how he's in Todd-Cothran's pocket, there's no way I'm going to London and voluntarily put myself in their custody. These messages aren't binding, are they? I don't have to act on them just because I heard them, do I?"

Steve shrugged. "Nobody but me knows you heard them. Anyway, international agencies have no jurisdiction here."

"You think I might be extradited?"

"If they try to link you with either of those deaths."

Chloe didn't want to stay home alone that evening. She rode with her father to the church where Bruce Barnes met them and gave them another video. He shook his head when he heard about the break-in. "It's becoming epidemic," he said. "It's as if the inner city has moved to the suburbs. We're no safer here anymore."

It was all Rayford could do to keep from telling Bruce that replacing the stolen tape was Chloe's idea. He wanted to tell Bruce to keep praying, that she must still be thinking about things. Maybe the invasion of the house had made her feel vulnerable. Maybe she was getting the point that the world was much more dangerous now, that there were no guarantees, that her own time could be short. But Rayford also knew he could offend her, insult her, push her away if he used this situation to sic Bruce on her. She had enough information; he just had to let God work on her. Still, he was encouraged and wanted to let Bruce know what was going on. He supposed he would have to wait for a more opportune time.

While they were out, Rayford bought items that needed to be replaced right away, including a TV and

VCR. He arranged to have the front door fixed and got the insurance paperwork started. Most important, he armed the security system. Still, he knew, neither he nor Chloe would sleep soundly that night.

They came home to a phone call from Hattie Durham. Rayford thought she sounded lonely. She didn't seem to have a real reason to call. She simply told him she was grateful for the dinner invitation and was looking forward to it. He told her what had happened at their home, and she sounded genuinely troubled.

"Things are getting so strange," she said. "You know I have a sister who works in a pregnancy clinic."

"Uh-huh," Rayford said. "You've mentioned it."

"They do family planning and counseling and referrals for terminating pregnancies."

"Right."

"And they're set up to do abortions right there."

Hattie seemed to be waiting for some signal of affirmation or acknowledgment that he was listening. Rayford grew impatient and remained silent.

"Anyway," she said, "I won't keep you. But my sister told me they have zero business."

"Well, that would make sense, given the disappearances of unborn babies."

"My sister didn't sound too happy about that."

"Hattie, I imagine everyone's horrified by that. Parents are grieving all over the world."

"But the women my sister and her people were counseling *wanted* abortions."

Rayford groped for a pertinent response. "Yes, so

maybe those women are grateful they didn't have to go through the abortion itself."

"Maybe, but my sister and her bosses and the rest of the staff are out of work now until people start getting pregnant again."

"I get it. It's a money thing."

"They have to work. They have expenses and families."

"And aside from abortion counseling and abortions, they have nothing to do?"

"Nothing. Isn't that awful? I mean, whatever happened put my sister and a lot of people like her out of business, and nobody really knows yet whether anyone will be able to get pregnant again."

Rayford had to admit he had never found Hattie guilty of brilliance, but now he wished he could look into her eyes. "Hattie, um, I don't know how to ask this. But are you saying your sister is hoping women can get pregnant again so they'll need abortions and she can keep working?"

"Well, sure. What is she going to do otherwise? Counseling jobs in other fields are pretty hard to come by, you know."

He nodded, feeling stupid, knowing she couldn't see him. What kind of lunacy was this? He shouldn't waste his energy arguing with someone who clearly didn't have a clue, but he couldn't help himself.

"I guess I always thought clinics like the one where your sister works considered these unwanted pregnancies a nuisance. Shouldn't they be glad if such problems disappear, and even happier—except for the small complication that the human race will eventually cease to exist—if pregnancies never happen again?"

The irony was lost on her. "But Rayford, that's her job. That's what the center is all about. It's sort of like owning a gas station and nobody needing gas or oil or tires anymore."

"Supply and demand."

"Exactly! See? They need unwanted pregnancies because that's their business."

"Sort of like doctors wanting people to be sick or injured so they have something to do?"

"Now you've got it, Rayford."

———

After Buck had shaved and showered, Steve told him, "I was paged a minute ago. New York City detectives are looking for you at the office. Unfortunately, someone told them you would be at the Plaza with Carpathia later."

"Brilliant!"

"I know. Maybe you ought to just face this."

"Not yet, Steve. Let me get the Carpathia interview and get that piece started. Then I can extricate myself from this mess."

"You're hoping Carpathia can help."

"Precisely."

"What if you can't get to him before somebody gets to you?"

"I've got to. I've still got my Oreskovich press credentials and identification. If the cops are waiting for me at the Plaza, maybe they won't recognize me at first."

"C'mon, Buck. You think they aren't on to your phony ID by now, after you slipped out of Europe with it? Let me switch with you. If they think I'm you trying to pass yourself off as Oreskovich, that may buy you enough time to get in to see Carpathia."

Buck shrugged. "Worth a try," he said. "I don't want to stay here, but I want to see Carpathia on *Nightline*."

"Want to come to my place?"

"They'll probably look for me there before long."

"Let me call Marge. She and her husband don't live far away."

"Don't use my phone."

Steve grimaced. "You act like you're in a spy movie." Steve used his own cellular phone. Marge insisted they come over right away. She said her husband liked to watch his *M*A*S*H* rerun at that time of night but that she could talk him into taping it tonight.

Buck and Steve saw two unmarked squad cars pull up in front of Buck's apartment building as they climbed into a cab. "It *is* like a spy movie," Buck said.

Marge's husband was none too pleased to be displaced from his favorite spot and his favorite show, but even he was intrigued when *Nightline* began. Carpathia was either a natural or well-coached. He looked directly into the camera whenever possible and appeared to be speaking to individual viewers.

"Your speech at the United Nations," Wallace Theodore began, "which was sandwiched between two press conferences today, seems to have electrified New York, and because so much of it has been aired on both early evening and late night local newscasts, you've become a popular man in this country seemingly all at once."

Carpathia smiled. "Like anyone from Europe, particularly Eastern Europe, I am amazed at your technology. I—"

"But isn't it true, sir, that your roots are actually in Western Europe? Though you were born in Romania, are you not by heritage actually Italian?"

"That is true, as it is true of many native Romanians. Thus the name of our country. But as I was saying about your technology. It is amazing, but I confess I did not come to your country to become or to be made into a celebrity. I have a goal, a mission, a message, and it has nothing to do with my popularity or my personal—"

"But is it not true that you just came from a photo session with *People* magazine?"

"Yes, but I—"

"And is it not also true that they have already named you their newest Sexiest Man Alive?"

"I do not know what that means, really. I submitted to an interview that was mostly about my childhood and my business and political career, and I was under the impression that they do this sexy-man coverage in January each year, so it is too early for next year and too close to this year's."

"Yes, and I'm sure, Mr. Carpathia, that you were as thrilled as we were over the young singing star who was so named two months ago, but—"

"I regret to say I was not aware of the young man before I saw his photograph on the cover of the magazine."

"But, sir, are you saying you are not aware that *People* magazine is breaking tradition by, in effect, unseating their current sexiest man and installing you in his place with next week's issue?"

"I believe they tried to tell me that, but I do not understand. The young man did some damage to a hotel or some such thing, and so—"

"And so you were a convenient replacement for him."

"I know nothing about that, and to be perfectly honest, I might not have submitted to the interview under those circumstances. I do not consider myself sexy. I am on a crusade to see the peoples of the world come together. I do not seek a position of power or authority. I simply ask to be heard. I hope my message comes through in the article in the magazine as well."

"You already have a position of both power and authority, Mr. Carpathia."

"Well, our little country asked me to serve, and I was willing."

"How do you respond to those who say you skirted protocol and that your elevation to the presidency in Romania was partially effected by strong-arm tactics?"

"I would say that that is the perfect way to attack a pacifist, one who is committed to disarmament not only in Romania and the rest of Europe but also globally."

"So you deny having a business rival murdered seven years ago and using intimidation and powerful friends in America to usurp the president's authority in Romania?"

"The so-called murdered rival was one of my dearest friends, and I mourn him bitterly to this day. The few American friends I have may be influential here, but they could not have any bearing on Romanian politics. You must know that our former president asked me to replace him for personal reasons."

"But that completely ignores your constitution's procedure for succession to power."

"This was voted upon by the people and by the government and ratified with a huge majority."

"After the fact."

"In a way, yes. But in another way, had they not ratified it, both popularly and within the houses of government, I would have been the briefest reigning president in our nation's history."

Marge's husband growled, "This Roman kid is light on his feet."

"Romanian," Marge corrected.

"I heard him say he's a full-blood Eye-talian," her husband said. Marge winked at Steve and Buck.

Buck was amazed at Carpathia's thought processes and command of language. Theodore asked him, "Why the United Nations? Some would say you would have more impact and get more mileage out of an appearance before our Senate and House of Representatives."

"I would not even dream of such a privilege," Carpathia said. "But, you see, I was not looking for mileage. The U.N. was envisioned originally as a peacekeeping effort. It must return to that role."

"You hinted today, and I hear it in your voice even

now, that you have a specific plan for the U.N. that would make it better and which would be of some help during this unusually horrific season in history."

"I do. I did not feel it was my place to suggest such changes when I was a guest; however, I have no hesitationin this context. I am a proponent of disarmament. That is no secret. While I am impressed with the wide-ranging capabilities, plans, and programs of the United Nations, I do believe, with a few minor adjustments and the cooperation of its members, it can be all it was meant to be. We can truly become a global community."

"Can you briefly outline that in a few seconds?"

Carpathia's laugh appeared deep and genuine. "That is always dangerous," he said, "but I will try. As you know, the Security Council of the United Nations has five permanent members: the United States, the Russian Federation, Britain, France, and China. There are also ten temporary members, two each from five different regions of the world, which serve for two-year terms.

"I respect the proprietary nature of the original five. I propose choosing another five, just one each from the five different regions of the world. Drop the temporary members. Then you would have ten permanent members of the Security Council, but the rest of my plan is revolutionary. Currently the five permanent members have veto power. Votes on procedure require a nine-vote majority; votes on substance require a majority, including all five permanent members. I propose a tougher system. I propose unanimity."

"I beg your pardon?"

"Select carefully the representative ten permanent members. They must get input and support from all the countries in their respective regions."

"It sounds like a nightmare."

"But it would work, and here is why. A nightmare is what happened to us last week. The time is right for the peoples of the world to rise up and insist that their governments disarm and destroy all but ten percent of their weapons. That ten percent would be, in effect, donated to the United Nations so it could return to its rightful place as a global peacekeeping body, with the authority and the power and the equipment to do the job."

Carpathia went on to educate the audience that it was in 1965 that the U.N. amended its original charter to increase the Security Council from 11 to 15. He said that the original veto power of the permanent members had hampered military peace efforts, such as in Korea and during the Cold War.

"Sir, where did you get your encyclopedic knowledge of the U.N. and world affairs?"

"We all find time to do what we really want to do. This is my passion."

"What is your personal goal? A leadership role in the European Common Market?"

"Romania is not even a member, as you know. But no, I have no personal goal of leadership, except as a voice. We must disarm, we must empower the United Nations, we must move to one currency, and we must become a global village."

Rayford and Chloe sat in silence before their new television, taken with the fresh face and encouraging ideas of Nicolae Carpathia. "What a guy!" Chloe said at last. "I haven't heard a politician with anything to say since I was a little girl, and I didn't understand half of it then."

"He is something," Rayford agreed. "It's especially nice to see somebody who doesn't seem to have a personal agenda."

Chloe smiled. "So you're not going to start comparing him with the liar the pastor's tape warned us of, somebody from Europe who tries to take over the world?"

"Hardly," Rayford said. "There's nothing evil or self-seeking about this guy. Something tells me the deceiver the pastor talked about would be a little more obvious."

"But," Chloe said, "if he's a deceiver, maybe he's a good one."

"Hey, which side of this argument are you on? Does this guy look like the Antichrist to you?"

She shook her head. "He looks like a breath of fresh air to me. If he starts trying to weasel his way into power, I might be suspicious, but a pacifist, content to be president of a small country? His only influence is his wisdom, and his only power is his sincerity and humility."

The phone rang. It was Hattie, eager to talk to Rayford. She was nearly manic with praise for Carpathia. "Did you see that guy? He's so handsome! I just have to meet him. Do you have any flights scheduled to New York?"

"Wednesday I have a late morning flight and come back the next morning. Then we're going to see you for dinner that night, right?"

"Yeah, and that's great, but Rayford, would you mind if I tried to work that flight? I heard on the news that the death report on that magazine writer was wrong and he's in New York. I'm going to see if I can meet with him and get him to introduce me to this Carpathia."

"You think he knows him?"

"Buck knows everybody. He does all these big international stories. He's got to. Even if he doesn't, I wouldn't mind seeing Buck."

That was a relief to Rayford. So Hattie wasn't afraid to talk about two younger guys she was clearly interested in seeing, or at least meeting. He was sure she wasn't just saying it to test his level of interest. Surely she knew he wasn't interested in anyone with his wife so recently gone. Rayford wondered whether he should follow through on his plan to be honest with her about his past feelings for her. Maybe he should just jump right into urging that she watch the pastor's videotape.

"Well, good luck with it," Rayford said lamely.

"But can I apply for your flight?"

"Why don't you just see if it comes up that way on the schedule?"

"Rayford!"

"What?"

"You don't want me on your flight! Why? Have I said or done something?"

"Why do you think that?"

"You think I don't know you squashed my last request?"

"I didn't exactly squash it. I just said—"

"You might as well have."

"I said what I just told you. I'm not opposed to your working my flights, but why don't you just let them come as they come?"

"You know the odds of that! If I wait, the odds are against me. If I push for certain ones, with my seniority I can usually get them. Now what's the deal, Rayford?"

"Can we talk about this when you come for dinner?"

"Let's talk about it now."

Rayford paused, groping for words. "Look what your special requests do to the schedules, Hattie. Everybody else has to slide to accommodate you."

"That's your reason? You're worried about everybody else?"

He didn't want to lie. "Partly," he said.

"That never bothered you before. You used to encourage me to request your flights and sometimes you checked with me to make sure I had done it."

"I know."

"So, what's changed?"

"Hattie, please. I don't want to discuss this by phone."

"Then meet me somewhere."

"I can't do that. I can't leave Chloe so soon after we've had a burglary."

"Then I'll come there."

"It's late."

"Rayford! Are you brushing me off?"

"If I was brushing you off, I wouldn't have invited you to dinner."

"With your daughter at your home? I think I'm getting set up for the royal brush."

"Hattie, what are you saying?"

"Only that you enjoyed running around with me in private, pretending like something was going on."

"I'll admit that."

"And I do feel bad about your wife, Rayford, I really do. You're probably feeling guilty, even though we never did anything to feel guilty about. But don't cast me aside before you have a chance to get over your loss and start living again."

"That's not it. Hattie, what's to cast aside? It's not like we had a relationship. If we did, why are you so interested in this magazine guy and the Romanian?"

"Everybody's interested in Carpathia," she said. "And Buck is the only way I know of to get to him. You can't think I have designs on him. Really! An international newsmaker? Come on, Rayford."

"I don't care if you do. I'm only saying, how does that jibe with whatever you thought we had going?"

"You want me to not go to New York and to forget about both of them?"

"Not at all. I'm hardly saying that."

"Because I will. If I had ever thought there was really a chance with you, I'd have pursued it, believe me."

Rayford was taken aback. His fears and assumptions were correct, but now he felt defensive. "You never thought there was a chance?"

"You hardly gave me any indication. For all I knew you thought I was a cute kid, way too young, fun to be with, but don't touch."

"There's some truth to that."

"But you never once wished it was something more, Rayford?"

"That's something I would like to talk with you about, Hattie."

"You can answer it right now."

Rayford sighed. "Yes, there were times I wished it was something more."

"Well, glory be. I missed my guess. I had given up, figured you were an untouchable."

"I am."

"Now, sure. I can understand that. You're in pain and probably worse because you were considering someone besides your wife for a while. But does that mean I can't even fly with you, talk to you, have a drink with you? We could go back to the way things used to be, and except for what's in your mind there still wouldn't be anything wrong with it."

"It doesn't mean you can't talk with me or work with me when our schedules coincide. If I didn't want to have anything to do with you, I wouldn't have invited you over."

"I can see what that's all about, Rayford. You can't tell me I wasn't going to get the 'let's be friends' routine."

"Maybe that and a little more."

"Like what?"

"Just something I want to tell you about."

"What if I told you I'm not interested in that kind of socializing? I don't expect you to run to me now that your wife is gone, but I didn't expect to be ignored either."

"How is having you over for dinner ignoring you?"

"Why did you never have me over before?"

Rayford was silent.

"Well?"

"It would have been inappropriate," he muttered.

"And now it's inappropriate to meet any other way?"

"Frankly, yes. But I do want to talk to you, and it isn't about brushing you off."

"Is my curiosity supposed to force me to come now, Rayford? Because, I'll tell you what, I have to decline. I'm going to be busy. Accept my regrets. Something came up, unavoidable, you understand."

"Please. Hattie. We really want you to come. I want you to."

"Rayford, don't bother. There are plenty of flights to New York. I won't go through any gymnastics to get on yours. In fact, I'll make sure I stay away from them."

"You don't have to do that."

"Of course I do. No hard feelings. I would have liked to have met Chloe, but you probably would have felt obligated to tell her you once nearly fell for me."

"Hattie, will you listen to me for a second? Please."

"No."

"I want you to come over Thursday night, and I really have something important to talk to you about."

"Tell me what it is."

"Not on the phone."

"Then I'm not coming."

"If I tell you generally, will you?"

"Depends."

"Well, I know what the disappearances were all about, all right? I know what they meant, and I want to help you find the truth."

Hattie was dead silent for a long moment. "You haven't become some kind of a fanatic, have you?"

Rayford had to think about that one. The answer was yes, he most certainly had, but he wasn't going to say that. "You know me better than that."

"I thought I did."

"Trust me, this is worth your time."

"Give me the basics, and I'll tell you if I want to hear it."

"Absolutely not," Rayford said, surprising himself with his resolve. "That I will not do, except in person."

"Then I'm not coming."

"Hattie!"

"Good-bye, Rayford."

"Hat—"

She hung up.

SIXTEEN

"I WOULDN'T do this for just anybody," Steve Plank said after he and Buck had thanked Marge and headed to separate cabs. "I don't know how long I can hold them off and convince them I'm you pretending to be someone else, so don't be far behind."

"Don't worry."

Steve took the first cab, Buck's George Oreskovich press credentials on his chest. He was to go directly to the Plaza Hotel, where he would ask for his appointment with Carpathia. Buck's hope was that Steve would be immediately intercepted, arrested as Buck, and clear the way for Buck to get in. If Buck was accosted by authorities, he would show his identity as Steve Plank. Both knew the plan was flimsy, but Buck was willing to try anything to keep from being extradited and framed for Alan Tompkins's murder, and possibly even Dirk Burton's.

Buck asked his cabbie to wait about a minute after Steve had left for the Plaza. He arrived at the hotel in the midst of flashing police lights, a paddy wagon, and several unmarked cars. As he threaded his way through onlookers, the police hustled Steve, hands cuffed behind his back, out the door and down the steps.

"I'm telling you," Steve said. "The name's Oreskovich!"

"We know who you are, Williams. Save your breath."

"That's not Cam Williams!" another reporter said, pointing and laughing. "You idiots! That's Steve Plank."

"Yeah, that's it," Plank joined in. "I'm Williams's boss from the *Weekly!*"

"Sure you are," a plainclothesman said, stuffing him into an unmarked car.

Buck ducked the reporter who had recognized Plank, but when he got inside and picked up a courtesy phone to call Rosenzweig's room, another press colleague, Eric Miller, whirled around and covered his own phone, whispering, "Williams, what's going on? The cops just shuttled your boss out of here, claiming he was you!"

"Do me a favor," Buck said. "Sit on this for at least half an hour. You owe me that."

"I owe you nothing, Williams," Miller said. "But you look scared enough. Give me your word you'll tell me first what's going on."

"All right. You'll be the first press guy I tell anyway. Can't promise I won't tell someone else."

"Who?"

"Nice try."

"If you're trying to call Carpathia, Cameron, you can

forget it. We've been trying all night. He's not giving any more interviews tonight."

"Is he back?"

"He's back, but he's incommunicado."

Rosenzweig answered Buck's call. "Chaim, it's Cameron Williams. May I come up?"

Eric Miller slammed his phone down and moved close.

"Cameron!" Rosenzweig said. "I can't keep up with you. First you're dead, then you're alive. We just got a call that you had been arrested in the lobby and would be questioned about a murder in London."

Buck didn't want Miller to detect anything. "Chaim, I have to move quickly. I'll be using the name Plank, all right?"

"I'll arrange it with Nicolae and get him to my room somehow. You come." He told Buck the number.

Buck put a finger to his lips so Miller wouldn't ask, but he couldn't shake him. He jogged to the elevator, but Eric stepped on with him. A couple tried to join them. "I'm sorry, folks," Buck said. "This car is malfunctioning." The couple left but Miller stayed. Buck didn't want him to see what floor he was going to, so he waited till the doors shut, then turned the car off. He grabbed Miller's shirt at the neck and pressed him against the wall.

"Listen, Eric, I told you I'd call you first with what's shakin' here, but if you try to horn in on this or follow me, I'm gonna leave you dry."

Miller shook loose and straightened his clothes. "All right, Williams! Geez! Lighten up!"

"Yeah, I lighten up and you come snooping around."

"That's my job, man. Don't forget that."

"Mine too, Eric, but I don't follow other people's leads. I make my own."

"You interviewing Carpathia? Just tell me that."

"No, I'm risking my life to see if a movie star's in the house."

"So it's Carpathia then, really?"

"I didn't say that."

"C'mon, man, let me in on it! I'll give you anything!"

"You said Carpathia wasn't giving any more interviews tonight," Buck said.

"And he's not giving any more to anybody except the networks and national outlets, so I'll never get to him."

"That's your problem."

"Williams!"

Buck reached for Miller's throat again. "I'm going!" Eric said.

When Buck emerged at the VIP floor, he was astounded to see that Miller had somehow beat him there and was hurriedly introducing himself to a uniformed guard as Steve Plank. "Mr. Rosenzweig is waiting for you, sir," the guard said.

"Wait a minute!" Buck shouted, showing Steve's press credentials. "I'm Plank. Run this impostor off."

The guard put a hand on each man. "You'll both have to wait here while I call the house detective."

Buck said, "Just call Rosenzweig and have him come out here."

The guard shrugged and punched in the room number on a portable phone. Miller leaned in, saw the number, and sprinted toward the room. Buck took off after him, the unarmed guard yelling and still trying to reach someone on the phone.

Buck, younger and in better shape, overtook Miller and tackled him in the hallway, causing doors up and down the corridor to open. "Take your brawl somewhere else," a woman shouted.

Buck yanked Miller to his feet and put him in a headlock. "You are a clown, Eric. You really think Rosenzweig would let a stranger into his room?"

"I can sweet-talk my way into anywhere, Buck, and you know you would do the same thing."

"Problem is, I already did. Now beat it."

The guard caught up with them. "Dr. Rosenzweig will be out in a minute."

"I have just one question for him," Miller said.

"No, you don't," Buck said. He turned to the guard. "He doesn't."

"Let the old man decide," the guard said, then just as suddenly stepped aside, pulling Buck and Miller with him to clear the hall. There, sweeping past them, were four men in dark suits, surrounding the unmistakable Nicolae Carpathia.

"Excuse me, gentlemen," Carpathia said. "Pardon me."

"Oh, Mr. Carpathia, sir. I mean President Carpathia," Miller called out.

"Sir?" Carpathia said, turning to face him. The bodyguards glowered. "Oh, hello, Mr. Williams," Carpathia said, noticing Buck. "Or should I say Mr. Oreskovich? Or should I say Mr. Plank?"

The interloper stepped forward. "Eric Miller from *Seaboard Monthly.*"

"I know it well, Mr. Miller," Carpathia said, "but I am late for an appointment. If you will call me tomorrow, I will talk to you by phone. Fair enough?"

Miller looked overwhelmed. He nodded and backed away. "I thought you said your name was Plank!" the guard said, causing everyone but Miller to smile.

"Come on in, Buck," Carpathia said, motioning him to follow. Buck was silent. "That is what they call you, is it not?"

"Yes, sir," Buck said, certain that not even Rosenzweig knew that.

Rayford felt terrible about Hattie Durham. Things couldn't have gone worse. Why hadn't he just let her work his flight? She'd have been none the wiser and he could have eased into his real reason for inviting her to dinner Thursday night. Now he had spoiled everything.

How would he get to Chloe now? His real motive, even for talking with Hattie, was to communicate to Chloe. Hadn't she seen enough yet? Shouldn't he be more encouraged by her insistence on replacing the stolen videotape? He asked if she wanted to go to New York with him for the overnight trip. She said she'd rather stay home and start looking into taking classes locally. He wanted to push, but he didn't dare.

After she had gone to bed, he called Bruce Barnes and told him his frustrations.

"You're trying too hard, Rayford," the younger man said. "I should think telling other people about our faith would be easier than ever now, but I've run into the same kind of resistance."

"It's really hard when it's your own daughter."

"I can imagine," Bruce said.

"No, you can't," Rayford said. "But it's all right."

Chaim Rosenzweig was in a beautiful suite of rooms. The bodyguards were posted out front, while Carpathia invited Rosenzweig and Buck into a private parlor for a meeting of just the three of them. Carpathia shed his coat and laid it carefully across the back of a couch. "Make yourselves comfortable, gentlemen," he said.

"I do not need to be here, Nicolae," Rosenzweig whispered.

"Oh, nonsense, Doctor!" Carpathia said. "You do not mind, do you, Buck?"

"Not at all."

"You do not mind my calling you Buck, do you?"

"No, sir, but usually it's just people at—"

"Your magazine, yes, I know. They call you that because you buck the traditions and the trends and the conventions, am I right?"

"Yes, but how—"

"Buck, this has been the most incredible day of my

life. I have felt so welcome here. And the people have seemed so receptive to my proposals. I am overwhelmed. I shall go back to my country a happy and satisfied man. But not soon. I have been asked to stay longer. Did you know that?"

"I heard."

"It is amazing, is it not, that all those different international meetings right here in New York over the next few weeks are all about the worldwide cooperation in which I am interested?"

"It is," Buck said. "And I've been assigned to cover them."

"Then we will be getting to know each other better."

"I look forward to that, sir. I was most moved at the U.N. today."

"Thank you."

"And Dr. Rosenzweig has told me so much about you."

"As he has told me much about you."

There was a knock at the door. Carpathia looked pained. "I had hoped we would not be disturbed." Rosenzweig rose slowly and shuffled to the door and a subdued conversation.

He slipped back to Buck. "We'll have to give him a couple of minutes, Cameron," he whispered, "for an important phone call."

"Oh, no," Carpathia said. "I will take it later. This meeting is a priority for me—"

"Sir," Rosenzweig said, "begging your pardon . . . it is the president."

"The president?"

"Of the United States."

Buck rose quickly to leave with Rosenzweig, but Carpathia insisted they stay. "I am not such a dignitary that I would not share this honor with my old friend and my new friend. Sit down!"

They sat and he pushed the speaker button on the phone. "This is Nicolae Carpathia speaking."

"Mr. Carpathia, this is Fitz. Gerald Fitzhugh."

"Mr. President, I am honored to hear from you."

"Well, hey, it's good to have you here!"

"I appreciated your note of congratulations on my presidency, sir, and your immediate recognition of my administration."

"Boy, that was a heckuva thing, how you took over there. I wasn't sure what had happened at first, but I don't suppose you were either."

"That is exactly right. I am still getting used to it."

"Well, take it from a guy who's been in the saddle for six years. You don't ever get used to it. You just develop calluses in the right places, if you know what I mean."

"Yes, sir."

"Listen, the reason I called is this. I know you're gonna be here a little longer than you expected, so I want you to spend a night or two here with me and Wilma. Can you do that?"

"In Washington?"

"Right here at the White House."

"That would be such a privilege."

"We'll have somebody talk to your people about the

right time, but it's got to be soon 'cause Congress is in session, and I know they'll want to hear from you."

Carpathia shook his head and Buck thought he seemed overcome emotionally. "I would be more than honored, sir."

"Speaking of something that was a heckuva thing, your speech today and your interview tonight—well, that was something. Look forward to meetin' ya."

"The feeling is mutual, sir."

Buck was only a little less overcome than Carpathia and Rosenzweig. He had long since lost his awe of U.S. presidents, especially this one, who insisted on being called Fitz. He had done a Newsmaker of the Year piece on Fitzhugh—Buck's first, Fitz's second. On the other hand, it wasn't every day that the president called the room in which you sat.

The glow of the call seemed to stay with Carpathia, but he quickly changed the subject. "Buck, I want to answer all your questions and give you whatever you need. You have been so good to Chaim, and I am prepared to give you a bit of a secret—you would call it a scoop. But first, you are in deep trouble, my friend. And I want to help you if I can."

Buck had no idea how Carpathia knew he was in trouble. So he wouldn't even have to bring him up to speed and ask for his help? This was too good to be true. The question was, what did Carpathia know, and what did he need to know?

The Romanian sat forward and looked directly into Buck's eyes. That gave Buck such a feeling of peace and security that he felt free to tell him everything. Everything. Even that his friend Dirk had tipped him off about someone meeting with Stonagal and Todd-Cothran, and Buck's assuming it was Carpathia.

"It *was* I," Carpathia said. "But let me make this very clear. I know nothing of any conspiracy. I have never even heard of such a thing. Mr. Stonagal felt it would be good for me to meet some of his colleagues and men of international influence. I formed no opinions about any of them, neither am I beholden to any of them.

"I will tell you something, Mr. Williams. I believe your story. I do not know you except by your work and your reputation with people I respect, such as Dr. Rosenzweig. But your account has the ring of truth. I have been told that you are wanted in London for the murder of the Scotland Yard agent and that they have several witnesses who will swear they saw you distract Tompkins, plant the device, and activate it from within the pub."

"That's crazy."

"Well, of course it is if you were mourning the mysterious death of your mutual friend."

"That's exactly what we were doing, Mr. Carpathia. That and trying to get to the bottom of it."

Rosenzweig was called to the door again, then he whispered in Carpathia's ear. "Buck, come here," Carpathia said, rising and leading Buck toward a window, away from Rosenzweig. "Your plan to get in here while being pursued was most ingenious, but your boss has been identified and now they know you are here.

They would like to take you into custody and extradite you to England."

"If that happens and Tompkins's theory is right," Buck said, "I'm a dead man."

"You believe they will kill you?"

"They killed Burton and they killed Tompkins. I'm much more dangerous to them with my potential readership."

"If this plot is as you and your friends say it is, Cameron, writing about these people, exposing them, will not protect you."

"I know. Maybe I should do it anyway. I don't see any way out."

"I can make this go away for you."

Buck's mind was suddenly reeling. This was what he had wanted, but he had feared Carpathia could do nothing quickly enough to keep him from getting into Todd-Cothran's and Sullivan's hands. Was it possible Carpathia was in deeper with these people than he had let on?

"Sir, I need your help. But I am a journalist first. I can't be bought or bargained with."

"Oh, of course not. I would never ask such a thing. Let me tell you what I can do for you. I will arrange to have the London tragedies revisited and reevaluated, exonerating you."

"How will you do that?"

"Does it matter, if it is the truth?"

Buck thought a moment. "It *is* the truth."

"Of course."

"But how will you do that? You have maintained this

innocence, Mr. Carpathia, this man-from-nowhere persona. How can you affect what has happened in London?"

Carpathia sighed. "Buck, I told you your friend Dirk was wrong about a conspiracy. That is true. I am not in bed with Todd-Cothran or Stonagal or any of the other international leaders I have been honored to meet recently. However, there are important decisions and actions coming up that will affect them, and it is my privilege to have a say in those developments."

Buck asked Carpathia if he minded if they sat down again. Carpathia signaled to Rosenzweig to leave them for a few minutes. "Look," Buck said when they were seated, "I'm a young man, but I've been around the block. It feels to me as if I'm about to find out just how deep into this—well, if it's not a conspiracy, it's something organized—how deep into this thing you are. I can play along and save my life, or I can refuse and you let me take my chances in London."

Carpathia held up a hand and shook his head. "Buck, let me reiterate that we are talking politics and diplomacy, not skullduggery or crime."

"I'm listening."

"First," Carpathia said, "a little background. I believe in the power of money. Do you?"

"No."

"You will. I was a better-than-average businessman in Romania while still in secondary school. I studied at night, many languages, the ones I needed to succeed. During the day I ran my own import-and-export businesses and made myself wealthy. But what I thought was wealth was paltry compared to what was possible. I needed to learn that. I learned it the hard way. I borrowed millions from a European bank, then found that someone in that bank informed my major competitor what I was doing. I was defeated at my own game, defaulted on my loan, and was struggling. Then that same bank bailed me out and ruined my rival. I didn't mean to or want to hurt the rival. He was used by the bank to lock me into a relationship."

"Was that bank owned by an influential American?"

Carpathia ignored the question. "What I had to learn, in just over a decade, is how much money is out there."

"Out there?"

"In the banks of the world."

"Especially those owned by Jonathan Stonagal," Buck suggested.

Carpathia still wasn't biting. "That kind of capital is power."

"This is the kind of thing I write against."

"It is about to save your life."

"I'm still listening."

"That kind of money gets a man's attention. He becomes willing to make concessions for it. He begins to see the wisdom of letting someone else, a younger man, someone with more enthusiasm and vigor and fresh vision take over."

"That's what happened in Romania?"

"Buck, do not insult me. The former president of Romania asked me of his own free will to replace him, and the support for that move was unanimous within the government and almost totally favorable among the masses. Everyone is better off."

"The former president is out of power."

"He lives in luxury."

Buck could not breathe. What was Carpathia implying? Buck stared at him, unable to move, unable to respond. Carpathia continued. "Secretary-General Ngumo presides over a country that is starving. The world is ripe for my plan of ten members of the Security Council. These things will work together. The secretary-general must devote his time to the problems within Botswana. With the right incentive, he will do that. He will be a happy, prosperous man, with a happy and prosperous people. But first he will endorse my plan for the Security Council. The representatives from each of the ten will be an interesting mix, some current ambassadors, but mostly new people with good financial backgrounds and progressive ideas."

"Are you telling me you will become secretary-general of the U.N.?"

"I would never seek such a position, but how could I refuse such an honor? Who could turn his back on such an enormous responsibility?"

"How much say will you have about who represents each of the ten permanent members of the Security Council?"

"I will merely be there to provide servant leadership. Are you aware of that concept? One leads by serving, not by dictating."

"Let me take a wild guess," Buck said. "Todd-Cothran is in line for a role on your new Security Council."

Carpathia sat back, as if learning something. "Would that not be interesting?" he said. "A nonpolitician, a brilliant financial mind, one who was wise enough and kind enough and globally minded enough to allow the world to go to a three-currency system that did not include his own pounds sterling? He brings no baggage to such a role. The world would have a certain level of comfort with him, would they not?"

"I suppose they would," Buck said, his mind black with depression as if he was losing his soul before his very eyes. "Unless, that is, Todd-Cothran were in the middle of a mysterious suicide, a car bombing, that sort of a thing."

Carpathia smiled. "I should think a man in a position of international potential like that would want a very clean house just now."

"And you could effect that?"

"Buck, you overestimate me. I am just saying that if you are right, I might try to stop what is clearly an unethical and illegal action against an innocent man— you. I cannot see how there is anything wrong with that."

Rayford Steele could not sleep. For some reason he was overcome anew with grief and remorse over the loss of his wife and son. He slid out of bed and onto his knees, burying his face in the sheet on the side where his wife used to sleep. He had been so tired, so tense, so worried about Chloe that he had pushed from his heart and mind and soul his terrible loss. He believed totally that his wife and son were in heaven, and he knew they were better off than they had ever been.

Rayford knew he had been forgiven for mocking his wife, for never really listening, for having ignored God for so many years. He was grateful he had been given a second chance and that he now had new friends and a place to learn the Bible. But that didn't stop the aching emptiness in his heart, the longing to hold his wife and son, to kiss them and tell them how much he loved them. He prayed for the grief to lessen, but part of him wanted it, needed it, to remain.

In a way he felt he deserved this pain, though he knew better. He was beginning to understand the forgiveness of God, and Bruce had told him that he needn't continue to feel shame over sin that had been dealt with.

As Rayford knelt praying and weeping, a new anguish flooded over him. He felt hopeless about Chloe. Everything he had tried had failed. He knew it had been only days since the disappearance of her mother and brother, and even less time since his own conversion. What more could he say or do? Bruce had encouraged him just to pray, but he was not made that way. He would pray, of course, but he had always been a man of action.

Now, every action seemed to push her farther away. He felt that if he said or did anything more, he would be responsible for her deciding against Christ once and for all. Rayford had never felt more powerless and desperate. How he longed to have Irene and Raymie with him right then. And how he despaired over Chloe.

He had been praying silently, but the torment welled up within him, and despite himself he heard his own muffled cries, "Chloe! Oh, Chloe! Chloe!"

He wept bitterly in the darkness, suddenly jarred by a creak and footsteps. He turned quickly to see Chloe, the dim light from her room silhouetting her robed form in the doorway. He didn't know what she had heard.

"Are you all right, Dad?" she asked quietly.

"Yeah."

"Nightmare?"

"No. I'm sorry to disturb you."

"I miss them, too," she said, her voice quavery. Rayford turned and sat with his back to the bed. He held his arms open to her. She came and sat next to him, letting him hold her.

"I believe I'll see them again someday," he said.

"I know you do," she said, no disrespect in her voice. "I know you do."

SEVENTEEN

AFTER a few minutes, Chloe gave Rayford evidence that she had heard his cry. "Don't worry about me, Daddy, OK? I'm getting there."

Getting where? Did she mean that her decision was just a matter of time or simply that she was getting over her grief? He wanted so badly to tell her he was worried, but she knew that. Her very presence brought him comfort, but when she padded back to her room he felt desperately alone again.

He could not sleep. He tiptoed downstairs and turned on the new TV, tuning in CNN. From Israel came the strangest report. The screen showed a mob in front of the famous Wailing Wall, surrounding two men who seemed to be shouting.

"No one knows the two men," said the CNN reporter on the scene, "who refer to each other as Eli and Moishe.

They have stood here before the Wailing Wall since just before dawn, preaching in a style frankly reminiscent of the old American evangelists. Of course the Orthodox Jews here are in an uproar, charging the two with desecrating this holy place by proclaiming that Jesus Christ of the New Testament is the fulfillment of the Torah's prophecy of a messiah.

"Thus far there has been no violence, though tempers are flaring, and authorities keep a watchful eye. Israeli police and military personnel have always been loath to enter this area, leaving religious zealots here to handle their own problems. This is the most explosive situation in the Holy Land since the destruction of the Russian air force, and this newly prosperous nation has been concerned almost primarily with outside threats.

"For CNN, this is Dan Bennett in Jerusalem."

Had it not been so late, Rayford would have called Bruce Barnes. He sat there, feeling a part of the family of believers to which the two men in Jerusalem apparently belonged. This was exactly what he had been learning, that Jesus was the Messiah of the Old Testament. Bruce had told him and the rest of the core group at New Hope that there would soon spring up 144,000 Jews who would believe in Christ and begin to evangelize around the world. Were these the first two?

The CNN anchorwoman turned to national news. "New York is still abuzz following several appearances today by new Romanian president Nicolae Carpathia. The thirty-three-year-old leader wowed the media at a small press conference this morning, followed by a masterful speech to the United Nations General Assembly in which he had the entire crowd standing and cheering, including the press. He reportedly sat for a cover photo session with *People* magazine and will be their first ever Sexiest Man Alive to appear less than a year after the previous designate.

"Associates of Carpathia have announced that he has already extended his schedule to include addresses to several international meetings in New York over the next two weeks and that he has been invited by President Fitzhugh to speak to a joint session of Congress and spend a night at the White House.

"At a press conference this afternoon the president voiced support for the new leader."

The president's image filled the screen. "At this difficult hour in world history, it's crucial that lovers of peace and unity step forward to remind us that we're part of a global community. Any friend of peace is a friend of the United States, and Mr. Carpathia is a friend of peace."

CNN broadcast a question asked of the president. "Sir, what do you think of Carpathia's ideas for the U.N.?"

"Let me just say this: I don't believe I've ever heard anybody, inside or outside the U.N., show such a total grasp of the history and organization and direction of the place. He's done his homework, and he has a plan. I was listening. I hope the respective ambassadors and Secretary-General Ngumo were, too. No one should see a fresh vision as a threat. I'm sure every leader in the world shares my view that we need all the help we can get at this hour."

The anchorwoman continued: "Out of New York late this evening comes a report that a *Global Weekly* writer has been cleared of all charges and suspicion in the death of a Scotland Yard investigator. Cameron Williams, award-winning senior writer at the *Weekly,* had been feared dead in a car bombing that took the life of the investigator Alan Tompkins, who was also an acquaintance of Williams.

"Tompkins's remains had been identified and Williams's passport and ID were found among the rubble after the explosion. Williams's assumed death was reported in newspapers across the country, but he reappeared in New York late this afternoon and was seen at the United Nations press conference following Nicolae Carpathia's speech.

"Earlier this evening, Williams was considered an international fugitive, wanted by both Scotland Yard and Interpol for questioning in connection with the bombing death. Both agencies have since announced he has been cleared of all charges and is considered lucky to have escaped unharmed.

"In sports news, Major League Baseball teams in spring training face the daunting task of replacing the dozens of players lost in the cosmic disappearances. . . ."

Rayford still was not sleepy. He made himself coffee, then phoned the twenty-four-hour line that kept track of flight and crew assignments. He had an idea. "Can you tell me whether I can still get Hattie Durham assigned to my JFK run Wednesday?" he asked.

"I'll see what I can do," came the response. "Whoops,

no. I guess you can't. She's going to New York already. Yours is the 10 A.M. flight. Hers is the 8 A.M."

———————

Buck Williams had returned to his apartment after midnight, assured by Nicolae Carpathia that his worries were over. Carpathia had phoned Jonathan Stonagal, put him on speakerphone, and Stonagal had done the same as he made the middle-of-the-night phone call to London that cleared Williams. Buck heard Todd-Cothran's husky-voiced agreement to call off the Yard and Interpol. "But my package is secure?" Todd-Cothran asked.

"Guaranteed," Stonagal had said.

Most alarming to Buck was that Stonagal did his own dirty work, at least in this instance. Buck had looked accusingly at Carpathia, despite his relief and gratitude.

"Mr. Williams," Carpathia said, "I was confident Jonathan could handle this, but I am just as ignorant of the details as you are."

"But this just proves Dirk was right! Stonagal *is* conspiring with Todd-Cothran, and you knew it! And Stonagal promised him his package was secure, whatever that means."

"I assure you I knew nothing until you told me, Buck. I had no prior knowledge."

"But now you know. Can you still in good conscience allow Stonagal to help promote you in international politics?"

"Trust me, I will deal with them both."

"But there have to be many more! What about all the other so-called dignitaries you met?"

"Buck, just be assured there is no place around me for insincerity or injustice. I will deal with them in due time."

"And meanwhile?"

"What would you advise? It seems to me that I am in no position to do anything right now. They seem intent on elevating me, but until they do I can do nothing but what your media calls whistle-blowing. How far would I get with that, before I know how far their tentacles reach? Before recently, would you not have thought Scotland Yard would be a trustworthy place to start?"

Buck nodded miserably. "I know what you mean, but I hate this. They know that you know."

"That may work to my advantage. They may think I am with them, that this makes me even more dependent upon them."

"Doesn't it?"

"Only temporarily. You have my word. I *will* deal with this. For now I am glad to have extricated you from a most delicate situation."

"I'm glad, too, Mr. Carpathia. Is there anything I can do for you?"

The Romanian smiled. "Well, I need a press secretary."

"I was afraid you were going to say that. I'm not your man."

"Of course not. I would not have dreamed of asking."

As a joke, Buck suggested, "What about the man you met in the hall?"

Carpathia displayed his prodigious memory once more. "That Eric Miller fellow?"

"He's the one. You'd love him."

"And I already told him to call me tomorrow. May I say you recommended him?"

Buck shook his head. "I was kidding." He told Carpathia what had happened in the lobby, on the elevator, and in the hall before Miller introduced himself. Nicolae was not amused. "I'll rack my brain and see if I can think of another candidate for you," Buck said. "Now you promised me a scoop tonight, too."

"True. It is new information, but it must not be announced until I have the ability to effect it."

"I'm listening."

"Israel is particularly vulnerable, as they were before Russia tried to invade them. They were lucky that time, but the rest of the world resents their prosperity. They need protection. The U.N. can give it to them. In exchange for the chemical formula that makes the desert bloom, the world will be content to grant them peace. If the other nations disarm and surrender a tenth of their weapons to the U.N., only the U.N. will have to sign a peace accord with Israel. Their prime minister has given Dr. Rosenzweig the freedom to negotiate such an agreement because he is the true owner of the formula. They are, of course, insisting on guarantees of protection for no less than seven years."

Buck sat shaking his head. "You're going to get the Nobel Peace prize, *Time*'s Man of the Year, and our Newsmaker of the Year."

"Those certainly are not my goals."

Buck left Carpathia believing that as deeply as he had ever believed anything. Here was a man unaffected by the money that could buy lesser men.

At his apartment Buck discovered yet another phone message from Hattie Durham. He had to call that girl.

———

Bruce Barnes called the core group together for an emergency meeting at New Hope Village Church Tuesday afternoon. Rayford drove over, hoping it would be worth his time and that Chloe wouldn't mind being home alone for a while. They had both been edgy since the break-in.

Bruce gathered everyone around his desk in the office. He began by praying that he would be lucid and instructive in spite of his excitement and then had everyone turn to the book of Revelation.

Bruce's eyes were bright and his voice carried the same passion and emotion as when he had called. Rayford wondered what had him so excited. He had asked Bruce on the phone, but Bruce insisted on telling everyone in person.

"I don't want to keep you long," he said, "but I'm onto something deep here and wanted to share it. In a way, I want you all to be wary, to be wise as serpents and harmless as doves, as the Bible says.

"As you know, I've been studying Revelation and several commentaries about end-times events. Well, today in the pastor's files I ran across one of his sermons on the subject. I've been reading the Bible and the books on the subject, and here's what I've found."

Bruce pulled up the first blank sheet on a flip chart and showed a time line he had drawn. "I'll take the time to carefully teach you this over the next several weeks, but it looks to me, and to many of the experts who came before us, that this period of history we're in right now will last for seven years. The first twenty-one months encompass what the Bible calls the seven Seal Judgments, or the Judgments of the Seven-Sealed Scroll. Then comes another twenty-one-month period in which we will see the seven Trumpet Judgments. In the last forty-two months of this seven years of tribulation, if we have sur-vived, we will endure the most severe tests, the seven Vial Judgments. That last half of the seven years is called the Great Tribulation, and if we are alive at the end of it, we will be rewarded by seeing the Glorious Appearing of Christ."

Loretta raised her hand. "Why do you keep saying 'if we survive'? What are these judgments?"

"They get progressively worse, and if I'm reading this right, they will be harder and harder to survive. If we die, we will be in heaven with Christ and our loved ones. But we may suffer horrible deaths. If we somehow make it through the seven terrible years, especially the last half, the Glorious Appearing will be all that more glorious. Christ will come back to set up his thousand-year reign on earth."

"The Millennium."

"Exactly. Now, that's a long time off, and of course we may be only days from the beginning of the first twenty-one-month period. Again, if I'm reading it right, the Antichrist will soon come to power, promising peace and trying to unite the world."

"What's wrong with uniting the world?" someone asked. "At a time like this it seems we need to come together."

"There might be nothing wrong with that, except that the Antichrist will be a great deceiver, and when his true goals are revealed, he will be opposed. This will result in a great war, probably World War III."

"How soon?"

"I fear it will be very soon. We need to watch for the new world leader."

"What about the young man from Europe who is so popular with the United Nations?"

"I'm impressed with him," Bruce said. "I will have to be careful and study what he says and does. He seems too humble and self-effacing to fit the description of this one who would take over the world."

"But we're ripe for someone to do just that," one of the older men said. "I found myself wishing that guy was our president." Several others agreed.

"We need to keep an eye on him," Bruce said. "But for now, let me just briefly outline the Seven-Sealed Scroll from Revelation five, and then I'll let you go. On the one hand, I don't want to give you a spirit of fear, but we all know we're still here because we neglected salvation before the Rapture. I know we're all grateful for the second chance, but we cannot expect to escape the trials that are coming."

Bruce explained that the first four seals in the scroll were described as men on four horses: a white horse, a red horse, a black horse, and a pale horse. "The white horseman apparently is the Antichrist, who ushers in one to three months of diplomacy while getting organized and promising peace.

"The red horse signifies war. The Antichrist will be opposed by three rulers from the south, and millions will be killed."

"In World War III?"

"That's my assumption."

"That would mean within the next six months."

"I'm afraid so. And immediately following that, which will take only three to six months because of the nuclear weaponry available, the Bible predicts inflation and famine—the black horse. As the rich get richer, the poor starve to death. More millions will die that way."

"So if we survive the war, we need to stockpile food?"

Bruce nodded. "I would."

"We should work together."

"Good idea, because it gets worse. That killer famine could be as short as two or three months before the arrival of the fourth Seal Judgment, the fourth horseman on the pale horse—the symbol of death. Besides the postwar famine, a plague will sweep the entire world. Before the fifth Seal Judgment, a quarter of the world's current population will be dead."

"What's the fifth Seal Judgment?"

"Well," Bruce said, "you're going to recognize this one because we've talked about it before. Remember my telling you about the 144,000 Jewish witnesses who try to evangelize the world for Christ? Many of their converts, perhaps millions, will be martyred by the world leader and the harlot, which is the name for the one world religion that denies Christ."

Rayford was furiously taking notes. He wondered what he would have thought about such crazy talk just three weeks earlier. How could he have missed this? God had tried to warn his people by putting his Word in written form centuries before. For all Rayford's education and intelligence, he felt he had been a fool. Now he couldn't get enough of this information, though it was becoming clear that the odds were against a person living until the Glorious Appearing of Christ.

"The sixth Seal Judgment," Bruce continued, "is God pouring out his wrath against the killing of his saints. This will come in the form of a worldwide earthquake so devastating that no instruments would be able to measure it. It will be so bad that people will cry out for rocks to fall on them and put them out of their misery." Several in the room began to weep. "The seventh seal introduces the seven Trumpet Judgments, which will take place in the second quarter of this seven-year period."

"The second twenty-one months," Rayford clarified.

"Right. I don't want to get into those tonight, but I warn you they are progressively worse. I want to leave you with a little encouragement. You remember we talked briefly about the two witnesses, and I said I would study that more carefully? Revelation 11:3-14 makes it clear that God's two special witnesses, with supernatural power to work miracles, will prophesy one thousand two hundred and sixty days, clothed in sackcloth. Anyone who tries to harm them will be devoured. No rain will fall during the time that they prophesy. They will be able to turn water to blood and to strike the earth with plagues whenever they want.

"Satan will kill them at the end of three and a half years, and their bodies will lie in the street of the city where Christ was crucified. The people they have tormented will celebrate their deaths, not allowing their bodies to be buried. But after three and a half days, they will rise from the dead and ascend to heaven in a cloud while their enemies watch. God will send another great earthquake, a tenth of the city will fall, and seven thousand people will die. The rest will be terrified and give glory to God."

Rayford glanced around the office as people murmured among themselves. They had all seen it, the report of the two crazy men preaching about Jesus at the Wailing Wall in Jerusalem.

"Is that them?" someone asked.

"Who else could it be?" Bruce said. "It has not rained in Jerusalem since the disappearances. These men came out of nowhere. They have the miraculous power of saints like Elijah and Moses, and they call each other Eli and Moishe. At this moment, the men are still preaching."

"The witnesses."

"Yes, the witnesses. If any one of us still harbored any doubts or fears, not sure what has been going on, these witnesses should allay them all. I believe these witnesses will see hundreds of thousands of converts, the 144,000, who will preach Christ to the world. We're on their side. We have to do our parts."

Buck reached Hattie Durham at her home number Tuesday night. "So, you're coming through New York?" he said.

"Yes," she said, "and I'd love to see you and maybe get to meet a VIP."

"You mean other than me?"

"Cute," she said. "Have you met Nicolae Carpathia yet?"

"Of course."

"I knew it! I was just telling someone the other day that I'd love to meet that man."

"No promises, but I'll see what I can do. Where should we meet?"

"My flight gets in there about eleven and I have a one o'clock appointment in the Pan-Con Club. But if we don't get back in time for that, it's OK. I don't fly out till morning, and I didn't even tell the guy I would meet him at one."

"Another guy?" Buck said. "You've got some weekend planned."

"It's nothing like that," she said. "It's a pilot who wants to talk to me about something, and I'm not sure I even want to listen. If I'm back and have time, fine. But I haven't committed to it. Why don't we meet at the club and see where we want to go from there?"

"I'll try to arrange the meeting with Mr. Carpathia, probably at his hotel."

———————

It was late Tuesday night when Chloe changed her mind and agreed to go to New York with her father. "I can see you're not ready to be out without me," she said, embracing him and smiling. "It's nice to be needed."

"To tell you the truth," he said, "I'm going to insist on a meeting with Hattie, and I want you there."

"For her protection or yours?"

"Not funny. I've left her a message insisting that she see me in the Pan-Con Club at JFK at one in the afternoon. Whether she will or not, I don't know. Either way, you and I will get some time together."

"Daddy, time together is all we've had. I'd think you'd be tired of me by now."

"That'll never happen, Chloe."

———————

Early Wednesday morning Buck was summoned to the office of Stanton Bailey, publisher of *Global Weekly*. In all his years of award-winning work, he had been in there only twice, once to celebrate his Hemingway war correspondence award and once on a Christmas tour of what the employees enviously called Mahogany Row.

Buck ducked in to see Steve first, only to be told by Marge that he was in with the publisher already. Her eyes were red and puffy. "What's happening?" he said.

"You know I can't say anything," she said. "Just get in there."

Buck's imagination ran wild as he entered the suite of offices inhabited by the brass. He hadn't known Plank had been summoned, too. What could it mean? Were they in trouble for the shenanigans they had pulled Monday night? Had Mr. Bailey somehow found out the details of the London business and how Buck had escaped? And he certainly hoped this meeting would be over in time for his appointment with Hattie Durham.

Bailey's receptionist pointed him to the publisher's outer office, where his secretary raised one brow and waved him in. "You're not going to announce me?" he joked. She smirked and returned to her work.

Buck knocked quietly and carefully pushed open the door. Plank sat with his back to Buck and didn't turn. Bailey didn't rise but beckoned him in. "Sit right there next to your boss," Bailey said, which Buck thought an interesting choice of words. Of course, it was true, but that was not how Steve was usually addressed.

Buck sat and said, "Steve."

Steve nodded but kept looking at Bailey.

"Couple of things, Williams," Bailey began, "before I

get down to business. You're cleared of everything over-seas, right?"

Buck nodded. "Yes, sir. There should never have been any doubt."

"Well, 'course there shouldn't, but you were lucky. I guess it was smart to make it look like whoever was after you got you, but you made us think that for a while too, you know."

"Sorry. I'm afraid that was unavoidable."

"And you wound up giving them ammunition to use against you if they wanted to bust you for some reason."

"I know. That surprised me."

"But you got it taken care of."

"Right."

"How?"

"Sir?"

"What part of 'how' don't you understand? How did you extricate yourself? We got word there were witnesses who say you did it."

"There must have been enough others who knew the truth. Tompkins was a friend of mine. I had no reason to kill him, and I sure didn't have the means. I wouldn't have the slightest idea how to make a bomb or transport it or detonate it."

"You could have paid to have it done."

"But I didn't. I don't run in those circles, and if I did, I wouldn't have had Alan killed."

"Well, the news coverage is all vague enough that none of us look bad. Just looks like a misunderstanding."

"Which it was."

"Of course it was. Cameron, I asked to see you this morning because I have just accepted one of the least welcome resignations I have ever received."

Buck sat silent, his head spinning.

"Steve here tells me this will be news to you, so let me just drop it on you. He is resigning immediately to accept the position of international press secretary to Nicolae Carpathia. He's received an offer we can't come close to, and while I don't think it's wise or a good fit, he does, and it's his life. What do you think about that?"

Buck couldn't contain himself. "I think it stinks. Steve, what are you thinking of? You're going to move to Romania?"

"I'll be headquartered here, Buck. At the Plaza."

"Nice."

"I'll say."

"Steve, this isn't you. You're not a PR guy."

"Carpathia is no ordinary political leader. Tell me you weren't on your feet cheering Monday."

"I was, but—"

"But nothing. This is the opportunity of a lifetime. Nothing else would have lured me from this job."

Buck shook his head. "I can't believe it. I knew Carpathia was looking for somebody, but—"

Steve laughed. "Tell the truth, Buck. He offered it to you first, didn't he?"

"No."

"He as much as told me he did."

"Well, he didn't. Matter of fact, I recommended Miller from *Seaboard*."

Plank recoiled and shot a glance at Bailey. "Really?"

"Yeah, why not? He's more the type."

"Buck," Steve said, "Eric Miller's body washed up on Staten Island last night. He fell off the ferry and drowned."

"Well," Bailey said summarily, "enough of that ugly business. Steve has recommended you to replace him."

Buck was still reeling from the news about Miller, but he heard the offer. "Oh, please," he said, "you're not serious."

"You wouldn't want the job?" Bailey asked. "Shape the magazine, determine the coverage, still write the top stories yourself? Sure you would. By policy it would almost double your salary, and if that's what it took to get you to agree, I'd guarantee it."

"That's not it," Buck said. "I'm too young for the job I've got now."

"You don't believe that or you wouldn't be as good at it as you are."

"Yeah, but that's the sentiment of the staff."

"What else is new?" Bailey roared. "They think I'm too old. They thought Steve was too laid-back. Others thought he was too pushy. They'd complain if we brought in the pope himself."

"I thought he was missing."

"You know what I mean. Now how about it?"

"I could never replace, Steve, sir. I'm sorry. People may have complained, but they knew he was fair and in their corner."

"And so would you be."

"But they'd never give me the benefit of the doubt. They'd be in here undermining me and complaining from day one."

"I wouldn't allow it. Now, Buck, this offer isn't going to sit on the table indefinitely. I want you to take it, and I want to be able to announce it immediately."

Buck shrugged and looked at the floor. "Can I have a day to think about it?"

"Twenty-four hours. Meantime, don't say a word to anybody. Plank, anybody else know about you?"

"Only Marge."

"We can trust her. She'll never tell a soul. I had a three-year affair with her and never worried about anybody finding out."

Steve and Buck flinched.

"Well," Bailey said, "you never knew, did you?"

"No," they said in unison.

"See how tight-lipped she is?" He waited a beat. "I'm kidding, boys. I'm kidding!"

He was still laughing as they left the office.

EIGHTEEN

Buck followed Steve to his office. "Did you hear about those kooks at the Wailing Wall?" Steve said.

"Like I'm interested in that right now," Buck said. "Yeah, I saw them, and no, I don't want to cover that story. Now what is this?"

"This will be your office, Buck. Marge will be your secretary."

"You can't possibly think I would want your job. First off, we can't afford to lose you. You're the only sane person here."

"Including you?"

"Especially including me. You must have really run interference for me with Bailey if he thinks I would be anything but a powder keg in your job."

"*Your* job."

"You think I should take it."

"You bet I do. I suggested no one else and Bailey had no other candidates."

"He'd have all the candidates he wanted if he just announced the opening. Who wouldn't want this job, besides me?"

"If it's such a plum, why *don't* you want it?"

"I'd feel as if I were sitting in your chair."

"So order your own chair."

"You know what I mean, Steve. It won't be the same without you. This job isn't me."

"Look at it this way, Buck. If you don't take it, you have no say in who becomes your new boss. Anybody on this staff you want to work for?"

"Yeah, you."

"Too late. I'm gone tomorrow. Now seriously, you want to work for Juan?"

"You wouldn't recommend him."

"I'm not going to recommend anybody but you. You don't take it, you're on your own. You take your chances you'll wind up working for a colleague who already resents you. How many hot assignments you think you'll get then?"

"If I got dumped on, I'd threaten to go to *Time* or somewhere. Bailey wouldn't let that happen."

"You turn down a promotion, he might make it happen. Rejecting advancement is not a good career move."

"I just want to write."

"Tell me you haven't thought you could run this editorial department better than I do at times."

"A lot of times."

"Here's your chance."

"Bailey would never stand for my assigning myself all the best stuff."

"Make that a condition of your acceptance. If he doesn't like it, it's his decision, not yours."

For the first time, Buck allowed a sliver of light to enter his head about the possibility of taking the executive editor job. "I still can't believe you'd leave to become a press secretary, Steve. Even for Nicolae Carpathia."

"Do you know what's in store for him, Buck?"

"A little."

"There's a sea of power and influence and money behind him that will propel him to world prominence so quick it'll make everyone's head spin."

"Listen to yourself. You're supposed to be a journalist."

"I hear myself, Buck. I wouldn't feel this way about anybody else. No U.S. president could turn my head like this, no U.N. secretary-general."

"You think he'll be bigger than that."

"The world is ready for Carpathia, Buck. You were there Monday. You saw it. You heard it. Have you ever met anyone like him?"

"No."

"You never will again, either. If you ask me, Romania is too small for him. Europe is too small for him. The U.N. is too small for him."

"What's he gonna be, Steve, king of the world?"

Steve laughed. "That won't be the title, but don't put it past him. The best part is, he's not even aware of his own presence. He doesn't seek these roles. They are thrust upon him because of his intellect, his power, his passion."

"You know, of course, that Stonagal is behind him."

"Of course. But he'll soon supersede Stonagal in influence because of his charisma. Stonagal can't be too visible, and so he will never have the masses behind him. When Nicolae comes to power, he'll in essence have jurisdiction over Stonagal."

"Wouldn't that be something?"

"I say it'll happen sooner than any of us can imagine, Buck."

"Except you, of course."

"That's exactly how I feel. You know I've always had good instincts. I'm sure I'm sitting on one of the greatest rises to power of anyone in history. Maybe *the* greatest. And I'll be right there helping it happen."

"What do you think of *my* instincts, Steve?"

Steve pressed his lips together. "Other than your writing and reporting, your instincts are the things I most envy."

"Then rest easy. My gut feeling is the same as yours. And except that I could never be anybody's press secretary, I almost envy you. You *are* uniquely positioned to enjoy the ride of your life."

Steve smiled. "We'll keep in touch. You'll always have access, to me and to Nicolae."

"I can't ask for more than that."

Marge interrupted on the intercom without signaling first. "Hit your TV, Steve, or whoever's TV it is now."

Steve smiled at Buck and switched it on. CNN was broadcasting live from Jerusalem, where two men had tried to attack the preachers at the Wailing Wall. Dan Bennett was on the scene for CNN.

"It was an ugly and dangerous confrontation for what many here are calling the two heretical prophets, known only as Moishe and Eli," Bennett said. "We know these names only because they have referred to each other thus, but we have been unable to locate anyone who knows any more about them. We know of no last names, no cities of origin, no families or friends. They have been taking turns speaking—preaching, if you will—for hours and continuing to claim that Jesus Christ is the Messiah. They have proclaimed over and over that the great worldwide disappearances last week, including many here in Israel, evidenced Christ's rapture of his church.

"A heckler asked why they had not disappeared, if they knew so much. The one called Moishe answered, and I quote, 'Where we come from and where we go, you cannot know.' His companion, Eli, was quoted, 'In my Father's house are many mansions,' apparently a New Testament quotation attributed to Christ."

Steve and Buck exchanged glances.

"Surrounded by zealots most of the day, the preachers were finally attacked just moments ago by two men in their midtwenties. Watch the tape as our cameras caught the action. You can see the two at the back of the crowd, working their way to the front. Both are wearing long, hooded robes and are bearded. You can see that they produce weapons as they emerge from the crowd.

"One has an Uzi automatic weapon and the other a bayonet-type knife that appears to have come from an Israeli-issue military rifle. The one wielding the knife surges forward first, displaying his weapon to Moishe, who had been speaking. Eli, behind him, immediately falls to his knees, his face toward the sky. Moishe stops speaking and merely looks at the man, who appears to trip. He sprawls while the man with the Uzi points the weapon at the preachers and appears to pull the trigger.

"There is no sound of gunfire as the Uzi apparently jams, and the attacker seems to trip over his partner and both wind up on the ground. The group of onlookers has backed away and run for cover, but watch again closely as we rerun this. The one with the gun seems to fall of his own accord.

"As we speak, both attackers lie at the feet of the preachers, who continue to preach. Angry onlookers demand help for the attackers, and Moishe is speaking in Hebrew. Let's listen and we'll translate as we go.

"He's saying, 'Men of Zion, pick up your dead! Remove from before us these jackals who have no power over us!'

"A few from the crowd approach tentatively while Israeli soldiers gather at the entrance to the Wall. The zealots are waving them off. Eli is speaking.

"'You who aid the fallen are not in danger unless you come against the anointed ones of the Most High,' apparently referring to himself and his partner. The fallen attackers are being rolled onto their backs, and those attending them are weeping and shouting and backing away. 'Dead! Both dead!' they are saying, and now the crowd seems to want the soldiers to enter. They are clearing the way. The soldiers are, of course, heavily armed. Whether they will try to arrest the strangers, we don't know, but from what we saw, the two preachers neither attacked nor defended themselves against the men now on the ground.

"Moishe is speaking again: 'Carry off your dead, but do not come nigh to us, says the Lord God of Hosts!' This he has said with such volume and authority that the soldiers quickly have checked pulses and carried off the men. We will report any word we receive on the two who attempted to attack the preachers here at the Wailing Wall in Jerusalem. At this moment, the preachers have continued their shouting, proclaiming, 'Jesus of Nazareth, born in Bethlehem, King of the Jews, the chosen one, ruler of all nations.'

"In Israel, Dan Bennett for CNN."

Marge and a few others on the staff had drifted into Steve's office during the telecast. "If that doesn't beat all," one said. "What a couple of kooks."

"Which two?" Buck said. "You can't say the preachers, whoever they are, didn't warn 'em."

"What's going on over there?" someone else asked.

"All I know," Buck said, "is that things happen there that no one can explain."

Steve raised his eyebrows. "If you believe in the Virgin Birth, that's been true for centuries."

Buck rose. "I've got to get to JFK," he said.

"What are you gonna do about the job?"

LEFT BEHIND

"I've got twenty-four hours, remember?"

"Don't use them all. Answer too quick, you look eager; too slow, you look indecisive."

Buck knew Steve was right. He was going to have to accept the promotion just to protect himself from other pretenders. He didn't want to be obsessed with it all day. Buck was glad for the diversion of seeing Hattie Durham. His only question now was whether he would recognize her. They had met under most traumatic circumstances.

———————

Rayford and Chloe arrived in New York just after noon on Wednesday and went directly to the Pan-Con Club to wait for Hattie Durham. "I'm guessing she won't show," Chloe said.

"Why?"

"Because I wouldn't if I were her."

"You're not her, thank God."

"Oh, don't put her down, Dad. What makes you any better?"

Rayford felt awful. Chloe was right. Why should he think less of Hattie just because she seemed dim at times? That hadn't bothered him when he had seen her only as a physical diversion. And now, just because she had been nasty with him on the phone and never acknowledged his last invitation to meet today, he had categorized her as less desirable or less deserving.

"I *am* no better," he conceded. "But why wouldn't you show up if you were her?"

328

"Because I'd have an idea of what you'd have in mind. You're going to tell her you no longer have feelings for her, but that now you care about her eternal soul."

"You make that sound cheap."

"Why should it impress her that you care about her soul when she thinks you used to be interested in her as a person?"

"That's just it, Chloe. I wasn't ever interested in her as a person."

"She doesn't know that. Because you were so circumspect and so careful, she thought you were better than most men, who would just come right out and hit on her. I'm sure she feels bad about Mom, and she probably understands that you're not in any state of mind to start a new relationship. But it can't make her day to be sent away like it was just as much her fault."

"It *was*, though."

"No, it wasn't, Dad. She was available. You shouldn't have been, but you were giving signals like you were. In this day and age, that made you fair game."

He shook his head. "Maybe that was why I was never good at that game."

"I'm glad, for Mom's sake, that you weren't."

"So, you think I shouldn't what, let her down easy or tell her about God?"

"You've already let her down, Daddy. She guessed what you were going to say and you confirmed it. That's why I say she won't come. She's still hurt. Probably mad."

"Oh, she was mad, all right."

"Then what makes you think she's going to be receptive to your heaven pitch?"

"It's not a pitch! Anyway, doesn't it prove I care about her in a genuine way now?"

Chloe went and got a soft drink. When she returned and sat next to her father, she put a hand on his shoulder. "I don't want to sound like a know-it-all," she said. "I know you're more than twice my age, but let me give you an idea how a woman thinks, especially someone like Hattie. OK?"

"I'm all ears."

"Does she have any religious background?"

"I don't think so."

"You never asked? She never said?"

"Neither of us ever gave it much thought."

"You never complained to her about Mom's obsession, like you sometimes did with me?"

"Come to think of it, I did. Of course, I was trying to use that to prove that your mother and I were not communicating."

"But Hattie didn't say anything about her own thoughts about God?"

Rayford tried to remember. "You know, I think she did say something supportive, or maybe sympathetic, about your mom."

"That makes sense. Even if she had wanted to come between you, she might have wanted to be sure you were the one putting the wedge between yourself and Mom, not her."

"I'm not following."

"That's not my point anyway. What I'm getting at is that you can't expect someone who is not even a church person to give a rip about heaven and God and all that. I'm having trouble dealing with it, and I love you and know it's become the most important thing in your life. You can't assume she has any interest, especially if it comes to her as a sort of a consolation prize."

"For?"

"For losing your attention."

"But my attention is purer now, more genuine!"

"To you, maybe. To her this is going to be much less attractive than the possibility of having someone who might love her and be there for her."

"That's what God will do for her."

"Which sounds real good to you. I'm just telling you, Dad, it's not going to be something she wants to hear right now."

"So, what if she does show up? Should I not talk to her about it?"

"I don't know. If she shows, that might mean she's still hoping there's a chance with you. Is there?"

"No!"

"Then you owe it to her to make that clear. But don't be so emphatic, and don't choose that time to try to sell her on—"

"Stop talking about my faith as something I'm trying to sell or pitch."

"Sorry. I'm just trying to reflect how it's going to sound to her."

Rayford had no idea what to say or do about Hattie

now. He feared his daughter was right, and that gave him a glimpse of where her mind was, too. Bruce Barnes had told him that most people are blind and deaf to the truth until they find it; then it makes all the sense in the world. How could he argue? That's what had happened to him.

Hattie had rushed up to Buck when he arrived at the club around eleven. His anticipation of any possibilities dissipated when the first thing out of her mouth was, "So, am I gonna get to meet Nicolae Carpathia?"

When Buck had originally promised to try to introduce her to Nicolae, he hadn't thought it through. Now, after hearing Steve rhapsodize about the prominence of Carpathia, he felt trivial calling to ask if he could introduce a friend, a fan. He called Dr. Rosenzweig. "Doc, I feel kinda stupid about this, and maybe you should just say no, that he's too busy. I know he's got a lot on his plate and this girl is no one he needs to meet."

"It's a girl?"

"Well, a young woman. She's a flight attendant."

"You want him to meet a flight attendant?"

Buck didn't know what to say. That reaction was exactly what he had feared. When he hesitated, he heard Rosenzweig cover the phone and call out for Carpathia. "Doc, no! Don't ask him!"

But he did. Rosenzweig came back on and said, "Nicolae says that any friend of yours is a friend of his. He has a few moments, but only a few moments, right now."

Buck and Hattie rushed to the Plaza in a cab. Buck realized immediately how awkward he felt and how much worse he was about to feel. Whatever reputation he enjoyed with Rosenzweig and Carpathia as an international journalist would forever be marred. He would be known as the hanger-on who dragged a groupie up to shake hands with Nicolae.

Buck couldn't hide his discomfort, and on the elevator he blurted, "He really has only a second, so we shouldn't stay long."

Hattie stared at him. "I know how to treat VIPs, you know," she said. "I often serve them on flights."

"Of course you do."

"I mean, if you're embarrassed by me or—"

"It's not that at all, Hattie."

"If you think I won't know how to act—"

"I'm sorry. I'm just thinking of his schedule."

"Well, right now we're on his schedule, aren't we?"

He sighed. "I guess we are."

Why, oh, why, do I get myself into these things?

In the hallway Hattie stopped by a mirror and checked her face. A bodyguard opened the door, nodded at Buck, and looked Hattie over from head to toe. She ignored him, craning her neck to find Carpathia. Dr. Rosenzweig emerged from the parlor. "Cameron," he said, "a moment please."

Buck excused himself from Hattie, who looked none too pleased. Rosenzweig pulled him aside and whispered, "He wonders if you could join him alone first?"

Here it comes, Buck thought, flashing Hattie an apologetic look and holding up a finger to indicate he would not be long. *Carpathia's gonna have my neck for wasting his time.*

He found Nicolae standing a few feet in front of the TV, watching CNN. His arms were crossed, his chin in his hand. He glanced Buck's way and waved him in. Buck shut the door behind him, feeling as if he had been sent to the principal's office. But Nicolae did not mention Hattie.

"Have you seen this business in Jerusalem?" he said. Buck said he had. "Strangest thing I have ever seen."

"Not me," Buck said.

"No?"

"I was in Tel Aviv when Russia attacked."

Carpathia kept his eyes on the screen as CNN played over and over the attack on the preachers and the collapsing of the would-be assassins. "Yes," he mumbled. "That would have been something akin to this. Something unexplainable. Heart attacks, they say."

"Pardon?"

"The attackers are dead of heart attacks."

"I hadn't heard that."

"Yes. And the Uzi did not jam. It is in perfect working order."

Nicolae seemed transfixed by the images. He continued to watch as he talked. "I wondered what you thought of my choice for press secretary."

"I was stunned."

"I thought you might be. Look at this. The preachers

never touched either of them. What are the odds? Were they scared to death, was that it?"

The question was rhetorical. Buck didn't answer.

"Hm, hm, hm," Carpathia exclaimed, the least articulate Buck had ever heard him. "Strange indeed. There is no question Plank can do the job though, do you agree?"

"Of course. I hope you know you've crippled the *Weekly.*"

"Ah! I have strengthened it. What better way to have the person I want at the top?"

Buck shuddered, relieved when Carpathia looked away from the TV at last. "This makes me feel just like Jonathan Stonagal, maneuvering people into positions." He laughed, and Buck was pleased to see that he was kidding.

"Did you hear what happened to Eric Miller?" Buck asked.

"Your friend from *Seaboard Monthly?* No. What?"

"Drowned last night."

Carpathia looked shocked. "You do not say! Dreadful!"

"Listen, Mr. Carpathia—"

"Buck, please! Call me Nicolae."

"I'm not sure I'll be comfortable doing that. I just wanted to apologize for bringing this girl up to meet you. She's just a flight attendant, and—"

"Nobody is just anything," he said, taking Buck's arm. "Everyone is of equal value, regardless of their station."

Carpathia led Buck to the door, insisting he be introduced. Hattie was appropriate and reserved, though she giggled when Carpathia kissed her on each cheek. He asked her about herself, her family, her job. Buck wondered if he had ever taken a Carnegie course on how to win friends and influence people.

"Cameron," Dr. Rosenzweig whispered. "Telephone."

Buck took it in the other room. It was Marge. "I hoped you'd be there," she said. "You just got a call from Carolyn Miller, Eric's wife. She's pretty shook up and really wants to talk to you."

"I can't call her from here, Marge."

"Well, get back to her as soon as you get a minute."

"What's it about?"

"I have no idea, but she sounded desperate. Here's her number."

When Buck reemerged, Carpathia was shaking hands with Hattie and then kissed her hand. "I am charmed," he said. "Thank you, Mr. Williams. And Miss Durham, it shall be my pleasure should our paths cross again."

Buck ushered her out and found her nearly overcome. "Some guy, huh?" he said.

"He gave me his number!" she said, nearly squealing.

"His number?"

Hattie showed Buck the business card Nicolae had handed her. It showed his title as president of the Republic of Romania, but his address was not Bucharest as one would expect. It was the Plaza Hotel, his suite number, phone number, and all. Buck was speechless. Carpathia had penciled in another phone number, not at the Plaza, but also in New York. Buck memorized it.

"We can eat at the Pan-Con Club," Hattie said. "I

don't really want to see this pilot at one, but I think I will, just to brag about meeting Nicolae."

"Oh, now it's Nicolae, is it?" Buck managed, still shaken by Carpathia's business card. "Trying to make someone jealous?"

"Something like that," she said.

"Would you excuse me a second?" he said. "I need to make a call before we head back."

Hattie waited in the lobby while Buck ducked around the corner and dialed Carolyn Miller. She sounded horrible, as if she had been crying for hours and hadn't slept, which was no doubt true.

"Oh, Mr. Williams, I appreciate your calling."

"Of course, ma'am, and I am so sorry about your loss. I—"

"You remember that we've met?"

"I'm sorry, Mrs. Miller. Refresh me."

"On the presidential yacht two summers ago."

"Certainly! Forgive me."

"I just didn't want you to think we'd never met. Mr. Williams, my husband called me last night before heading for the ferry. He said he was tracking a big story at the Plaza and had run into you."

"True."

"He told me a crazy story about how you two had a wrestling match or something over an interview with this Romanian guy who spoke at—"

"Also true. It wasn't anything serious, ma'am. Just a disagreement. No hard feelings."

"That's how I took it. But that was the last conversation I'll ever have with him, and it's driving me crazy. Do you know how cold it was last night?"

"Nippy, as I recall," Buck said, puzzled at her abrupt change of subject.

"Cold, sir. Too cold to be standing outside on the ferry, wouldn't you say?"

"Yes, ma'am."

"And even if he was, he's a good swimmer. He was a champion in high school."

"All due respect, ma'am, but that had to be—what, thirty years ago?"

"But he's still a strong swimmer. Trust me. I know."

"What are you saying, Mrs. Miller?"

"I don't know!" she shouted, crying. "I just wondered if you could shed any light. I mean, he fell off the ferry and drowned? It doesn't make any sense!"

"It doesn't to me either, ma'am, and I wish I could help. But I can't."

"I know," she said. "I was just hoping."

"Ma'am, is someone with you, watching out for you?"

"Yes, I'm OK. I have family here."

"I'll be thinking of you."

"Thank you."

Buck could see Hattie in a reflection. She seemed patient enough. He called a friend at the telephone company. "Alex! Do me a favor. Can you still tell me who's listed if I give you a number?"

"Long as you don't tell anybody I'm doin' it."

"You know me, man."

"Go ahead."

Buck recited the number he had memorized from the card Carpathia had given Hattie. Alex was back to him in seconds, reading off the information as it scrolled onto his computer screen. "New York, U.N., administrative offices, secretary-general's office, unlisted private line, bypasses switchboard, bypasses secretary. OK?"

"OK, Alex. I owe you."

Buck was lost. He couldn't make any of this compute. He jogged out to Hattie. "I'm gonna be another minute," he said. "Do you mind?"

"No. As long as we can get back by one. No telling how long that pilot will wait. He's got his daughter with him."

Buck turned back to the phones, glad he had no interest in competing with Carpathia or this pilot for Hattie Durham's affection. He called Steve. Marge answered and he was short with her. "Hey, it's me. I need Plank right away."

"Well, have a nice day yourself," she said and rang him through.

"Steve," he said quickly, "your boy just made his first mistake."

"What're you talking about, Buck?"

"Is your first job going to be announcing Carpathia as the new secretary-general?"

Silence.

"Steve? What's next?"

"You're a good reporter, Buck. The best. How did this get out?"

Buck told him about the business card.

"Whew! That doesn't sound like Nicolae. I can't imagine it was an oversight. Must have been on purpose."

"Maybe he's assuming this Durham woman is too ditzy to figure it out," Buck said, "or that she wouldn't show me. But how does he know she won't call the number too soon and ask for him there?"

"As long as she waits until tomorrow, Buck, he'll be all right."

"Tomorrow?"

"You can't use this, all right? Are we off the record?"

"Steve! Who do you think you're talking to? Are you working for Carpathia already? You're still my boss. You don't want me to run with something, you just tell me. Remember?"

"Well, I'm telling you. The Kalahari Desert makes up much of Botswana where Secretary-General Ngumo is from. He returns there tomorrow a hero, having become the first leader to gain access to the Israeli fertilizer formula."

"And how did he do that?"

"By his stellar diplomacy, of course."

"And he cannot be expected to handle the duties of both the U.N. and Botswana during this strategic moment in Botswana history, right, Steve?"

"And why should he, when someone is so perfectly suited to step right in? We were there Monday, Buck. Who's going to oppose this?"

"Don't you?"

"I think it's brilliant."

"You're going to be a perfect press secretary, Steve. And I've decided to accept your old job."

"Good for you! Now you'll sit on this till tomorrow, you got it?"

"Promise. But will you tell me one more thing?"

"If I can, Buck."

"What did Eric Miller get too close to? What lead was he tracking?"

Steve's voice became hollow, his tone flat. "All I know about Eric Miller," he said, "is that he got too close to the railing on the Staten Island Ferry."

NINETEEN

RAYFORD watched Chloe as she wandered around the Pan-Con Club, then stared out the window. He felt like a wimp. For days he had told himself not to push, not to badger her. He knew her. She was like him. She would run the other way if he pushed too hard. She had even talked him into backing off of Hattie Durham, should Hattie show up.

What was the matter with him? Nothing was as it was before or would ever be again. If Bruce Barnes was right, the disappearance of God's people was only the beginning of the most cataclysmic period in the history of the world. *And here I am,* Rayford thought, *worried about offending people. I'm liable to "not offend" my own daughter right into hell.*

Rayford also felt bad about his approach to Hattie. He had dealt with his own wrong in having pursued her,

and he regretted having led her on. But he could no
longer treat her with kid gloves, either. What scared him
most was that it seemed, from what Bruce was teaching,
that many people would be deceived during these days.
Whoever came forward with proclamations of peace and
unity had to be suspect. There would be no peace. There
would be no unity. This was the beginning of the end,
and all would be chaos from now on.

The chaos would make peacemakers and smooth talk-
ers only more attractive. And to people who didn't want
to admit that God had been behind the disappearances,
any other explanation would salve their consciences.
There was no more time for polite conversation, for gentle persuasion. Rayford had to direct people to the Bible,
to the prophetic portions. He felt so limited in his understanding. He had always been an erudite reader, but this
stuff from Revelation and Daniel and Ezekiel was new
and strange to him. Frighteningly, it made sense. He had
begun taking Irene's Bible with him everywhere he went,
reading it whenever possible. While the first officer read
magazines during his downtime, Rayford would pull out
the Bible.

"What in the world?" he was asked more than once.

Unashamed, he said he was finding answers and direction he had never seen before. But with his own daughter
and his friend? He had been too polite.

Rayford looked at his watch. Still a few minutes before
one o'clock. He caught Chloe's eye and signaled that he
was going to make a phone call. He dialed Bruce Barnes
and told him what he had been thinking.

"You're right, Rayford. I went through a few days of that, worried what people would think of me, not wanting to turn anybody off. It just doesn't make sense anymore, does it?"

"No, it doesn't. Bruce, I need support. I'm going to start becoming obnoxious, I'm afraid. If Chloe wants to laugh or run the other way, I'm going to force her to make a decision. She'll have to know exactly what she's doing. She'll have to face what we've found in the Bible and deal with it. I mean, the two preachers in Israel alone are enough to give me the confidence that things are happening exactly the way the Bible said they would."

"Have you been watching this morning?"

"From a distance here in the terminal. They keep rerunning the attack."

"Rayford, get to a TV right now."

"What?"

"I'm hanging up, Ray. See what happened to the attackers and see if that doesn't confirm everything we read about the two witnesses."

"Bruce—"

"Go, Rayford. And start witnessing yourself, with total confidence."

Bruce hung up on him. Rayford knew him well enough, despite their brief relationship, to be more intrigued than offended. He hurried to a TV monitor where he was stunned to hear the report of the deaths of the attackers. He dug out Irene's Bible and read the passage from Revelation Bruce had spoken from. The men in Jerusalem were the two witnesses, preaching Christ. They had been attacked, and they didn't even have to respond. The attackers had fallen dead and no harm had been done to the witnesses.

Now, on CNN, Rayford watched as crowds surged into the area in front of the Wailing Wall to listen to the witnesses. People knelt, weeping, some with their faces on the ground. These were people who had felt the preachers were desecrating the holy place. Now it appeared they were believing what the witnesses said. Or was it merely fear?

Rayford knew better. He knew that the first of the 144,000 Jewish evangelists were being converted to Christ before his eyes. Without taking his gaze from the screen, he prayed silently, *God, fill me with courage, with power, with whatever I need to be a witness. I don't want to be afraid anymore. I don't want to wait any longer. I don't want to worry about offending. Give me a persuasiveness rooted in the truth of your Word. I know it is your Spirit that draws people, but use me. I want to reach Chloe. I want to reach Hattie. Please, Lord. Help me.*

Buck Williams felt naked without his equipment bag. He would feel ready to work only when he had his cellular phone, his tape recorder, and his new laptop. He asked the cabbie to stop by the *Global Weekly* office so he could pick up the bag. Hattie waited in the cab, but she told him she was not going to be happy if she missed her appointment. Buck stood by the window of the cab. "I'll just be a minute," he said. "I thought you weren't sure whether you wanted to see this guy."

"Well, now I do, OK? Call it revenge or rubbing it in or whatever you want, but it's not often you get to tell a captain you've met someone he hasn't."

"You talking about Nicolae Carpathia or me?"

"Very funny. Anyway, he has met you."

"This is the captain from that flight where you and I met?"

"Yes—now hurry!"

"I might want to meet him."

"Go!"

Buck called Marge from the lobby. "Could you meet me at the elevator with my equipment bag? I've got a cab waiting here."

"I would," she said, "but both Steve and the old man are asking for you."

What now? he wondered. Buck checked his watch, wishing the elevator was faster. Such was life in the sky-scrapers.

He grabbed his bag from Marge, breezed into Steve's office, and said, "What's up? I'm on the run."

"Boss wants to see us."

"What's it about?" Buck said as they headed down the hall.

"Eric Miller, I think. Maybe more. You know Bailey wasn't thrilled at my short notice. He only agreed to it thinking that you'd jump at the promotion, because you know where everything is and what's planned for the next couple of weeks."

In Bailey's office the boss got right to the point. "I'm gonna ask you two some pointed questions, and I want some quick and straight answers. A whole bunch of stuff is coming down right now, and we're gonna be on top of every bit of it. First off, Plank, rumors are flying that Mwangati Ngumo is calling a press conference for late this afternoon, and everybody thinks he's stepping down as secretary-general."

"Really?" Plank said.

"Don't play dumb with me," Bailey growled. "It doesn't take a genius to figure what's happening here. If he's stepping down, your guy knows about it. You forget I was in charge of the African bureau when Botswana became an associate member of the European Common Market. Jonathan Stonagal had his fingers all over that, and everybody knows he's one of this Carpathia guy's angels. What's the connection?"

Buck saw Steve pale. Bailey knew more than either of them expected. For the first time in years, Steve sounded nervous, almost panicky. "I'll tell you what I know," he said, but Buck guessed there was more he didn't say. "My first assignment tomorrow morning is to deny Carpathia's interest in the job. He's going to say he has too many revolutionary ideas and that he would insist on almost unanimous approval on the parts of the current members. They would have to agree to his ideas for reorganization, a change of emphasis, and a few other things."

"Like what?"

"I'm not at liberty to—"

Bailey rose, his face red. "Let me tell you something, Plank. I like you. You've been a superstar for me. I sold you to the rest of the brass when nobody else recognized you had what it takes. You sold me on this punk here, and he's made us all look good. But I paid you six figures long before you deserved it because I knew someday it would pay off. And it did. Now, I'm telling you that nothing you say here is gonna go past these walls, so I don't want you holdin' out on me.

"You brats think that because I'm two or three years from the pasture, I don't still have contacts, don't have my ear to the ground. Well, let me tell you, my phone's been ringing off the hook since you left here this morning, and I've got a gut feeling something big is coming down. Now what is it?"

"Who's been calling you, sir?" Plank said.

"Well, first off, I get a call from a guy who knows the vice president of Romania. Word over there is the guy has been asked to be prepared to run the day-to-day stuff indefinitely. He's not going to become the new president because they just got one, but that tells me Carpathia expects to be here a while.

"Then, people I know in Africa tell me Ngumo has some inside track on the Israeli formula but that he's quietly not happy about the deal requiring him to step down from the U.N. He's going to do it, but there's going to be trouble if everything doesn't go as promised.

"Then, of all things, I get a call from the publisher at

Seaboard Monthly wanting to talk to me about how you, Cameron, and his guy that drowned last night were working the same angle on Carpathia, and whether I think you're going to mysteriously get dead, too. I told him that as far as I knew, you were working on a general cover story about the guy and that we were going to be positive. He said his guy had intended to take a slightly different approach—you know, zig when everybody else is zagging. Miller was doing a story on the meaning behind the disappearances, which I know you were planning for an issue or two from now. How that ties in with Carpathia, and why it might paint him in a dark light, I don't know. Do you?"

Buck shook his head. "I see them as two totally different pieces. I asked Carpathia what he made of what happened, and everybody has heard that answer. I didn't know that's what Miller was working on, and I sure wouldn't have thought he would somehow link Carpathia with the disappearances."

Bailey sat back down. "To tell you the truth, when I first took the call from the guy at *Seaboard,* I thought he was calling for a reference on you, Cameron. I was thinking, if I lose both these turkeys the same week, I'm taking early retirement. Can we get that stuff out of the way, before I make Plank tell me what else he knows?"

"What stuff?" Buck said.

"You looking to leave?"

"I'm not."

"You taking the promotion?"

"I am."

"Good! Now, Steve. What else is Carpathia gonna push for before he accepts the U.N. job?" Plank hesitated and looked as if he were considering whether he should tell what he knew. "I'm telling you, you owe me," Bailey said. "Now I don't intend to use this. I just want to know. Cameron and I have to decide which story we're going to push first. I want to get him onto the one that interests me most, the one about what was behind the disappearances. Sometimes I think we get too snooty as a newsmagazine and we forget that everyday people out there are scared to death, wanting to make some sense of all this. Now, Steve, you can trust me. I already told you I won't tell anyone or compromise you. Just run it down for me. What does Carpathia want, and is he going to take this job?"

Steve pursed his lips and began reluctantly. "He wants a new Security Council setup, which will include some of his own ideas for ambassadors."

"Like Todd-Cothran from England?" Buck said.

"Probably temporarily. He's not entirely pleased with that relationship, as you may know."

Buck suddenly realized that Steve knew everything.

"And?" Bailey pressed.

"He wants Ngumo personally to insist on him as his replacement, a large majority vote of the representatives, and two other things that, frankly, I don't think he'll get. Militarily, he wants a commitment to disarmament from member nations, the destruction of ninety percent of their weapons, and the donation of the other ten percent to the U.N."

"For peacekeeping purposes," Bailey said. "Naive, but logical sounding. You're right, he probably won't get that. What else?"

"Probably the most controversial and least likely. The logistics alone are incredible, the cost, the . . . everything."

"What?"

"He wants to move the U.N."

"Move it?"

Steve nodded.

"Where?"

"It sounds stupid."

"Everything sounds stupid these days," Bailey said.

"He wants to move it to Babylon."

"You're not serious."

"*He* is."

"I hear they've been renovating that city for years. Millions of dollars invested in making it, what, New Babylon?"

"Billions."

"Think anyone will agree to that?"

"Depends how bad they want him." Steve chuckled. "He's on *The Tonight Show* tonight."

"He'll be more popular than ever!"

"He's meeting right now with the heads of all these international groups that are in town for unity meetings."

"What does he want with them?"

"We're still confidential here, right?" Steve asked.

"Of course."

"He's asking for resolutions supporting some of the things he wants to do. The seven-year peace treaty with Israel, in exchange for his ability to broker the desert-fertilizer formula. The move to New Babylon. The establishment of one religion for the world, probably headquartered in Italy."

"He's not going to get far with the Jews on that one."

"They're an exception. He's going to help them rebuild their temple during the years of the peace treaty. He believes they deserve special treatment."

"And they do," Bailey said. "The man is brilliant. Not only have I never seen someone with such revolutionary ideas, but I've also never seen anyone who moves so quickly."

"Aren't either of you the least bit shaky about this guy?" Buck said. "It looks to me like people who get too close wind up eliminated."

"Shaky?" Bailey said. "Well, I think he's a little naive, and I'll be very surprised if he gets everything he's asking for. But then he's a politician. He won't couch these as ultimatums, and he can still accept the position even if he doesn't get them. It sounds like he may have run rough-shod over Ngumo, but I think he had Botswana's best interest in mind. Carpathia will be a better U.N. chief. And he's right. If what happened in Israel happens in Botswana, Ngumo needs to stay close to home and manage the prosperity. Shaky? No. I'm as impressed with the guy as you two are. He's what we need right now. Nothing wrong with unity and togetherness at a time of crisis."

"What about Eric Miller?"

"I think people are making too much of that. We don't know that his death wasn't just what it appeared and was only coincidental with his run-in with you and Carpathia. Anyway, Carpathia didn't know what Miller was after, did he?"

"Not that I know of," Buck said, but he noticed that Steve said nothing.

Marge buzzed in on the intercom. "Cameron has an urgent message from a Hattie Durham. Says she can't wait any longer."

"Oh, no," Buck said. "Marge, apologize all over the place for me. Tell her it was unavoidable and that I'll either call her or catch up with her later."

Bailey looked disgusted. "Is this what I can expect from you on work time, Cameron?"

"Actually, I introduced her to Carpathia this morning, and I want her to introduce me to an airline captain in town today for part of that story on what people think happened last week."

"I'll make no bones about it, Cameron," Bailey said. "Let's do the big Carpathia story next issue, then follow up with the theories behind the vanishings after that. If you ask me, that could be the most talked about story we've ever done. I thought we beat *Time* and everybody else on our coverage of the event itself. I liked your stuff, by the way. I don't know that we'll have anything terribly fresh or different about Carpathia, but we have to give it all we've got. Frankly, I love the idea of you running the point on this coverage of all the theories. You must have one of your own."

"I wish I did," Buck said. "I'm as in the dark as anybody. What I'm finding, though, is that the people who have a theory believe in it totally."

"Well, I've got mine," Bailey said. "And it's almost eerie how close it matches Carpathia's, or Rosenzweig's, or whoever. I've got relatives who believe the space alien stuff. I've got an uncle who thinks it was Jesus, but he also thinks Jesus forgot *him*. Ha! I think it was natural, some kind of a phenomenon where all our high-tech stuff interacted with the forces of nature and we really did a number on ourselves. Now come on, Cameron. Where are you on this?"

"I'm in the perfect position for my assignment," he said. "I haven't the foggiest."

"What are people saying?"

"The usual. A doctor at O'Hare told me he was sure it was the Rapture. Other people have said the same. You know our Chicago bureau chief—"

"Lucinda Washington? It's going to be your job to find a replacement for her, you know. You'll have to go there, get the lay of the land, get acquainted. But you were saying?"

"Her son believes she and the rest of the family were taken to heaven."

"So, how'd *he* get left behind?"

"I'm not sure what the deal is on that," Buck said. "Some Christians are better than others or something. That's one thing I'm going to find out before I finish this piece. This flight attendant who just called, I'm not sure what she thinks, but she said the captain she's meeting today thinks he has an idea."

"An airline captain," Bailey repeated. "That would be interesting. Unless his idea is the same as the other scientific types. Well, carry on. Steve, we're gonna announce this today. Good luck, and don't worry about anything you've said here finding its way into the magazine, unless we get it through other sources. We're agreed on that, aren't we, Williams?"

"Yes, sir," Buck said.

Steve didn't look so sure.

Buck ran to the elevator and called information for the number of the Pan-Con Club. He asked them to page Hattie, but when they couldn't locate her, he assumed she hadn't arrived yet or had gone out with her pilot friend. He left a message to have her call him on his cellular phone, then headed that way in a cab just in case.

His mind was whirring. He agreed with Stanton Bailey that the big story was what had been behind the disappearances, but he was also becoming suspicious of Nicolae Carpathia. Maybe he shouldn't be. Maybe he should focus on Jonathan Stonagal. Carpathia should be smart enough to see that his elevation could help Stonagal in ways that would be unfair to his competitors. But Carpathia had pledged that he would "deal with" both Stonagal and Todd-Cothran, knowing full well they were behind illegal deeds.

Did that make Carpathia innocent? Buck certainly hoped so. He had never in his life wanted to believe more in a person. In the days since the disappearances, he'd hardly had a second to think for himself. The loss of his sister-in-law and niece and nephew tugged at his heart almost constantly, and something made him wonder if there wasn't something to this Rapture thing. If anybody in his orbit would be taken to heaven, it would have been them.

But he knew better than that, didn't he? He was Ivy League educated. He had left the church when he left the claustrophobic family situation that threatened to drive him crazy as a young man. He had never considered himself religious, despite a prayer for help and deliverance once in a while. He had built his life around achievement, excitement, and—he couldn't deny it—attention. He loved the status that came with having his byline, his writing, his thinking in a national magazine. And yet there was a certain loneliness in his existence, especially now with Steve moving on. Buck had dated and had considered escalating a couple of serious relationships, but he had always been considered too mobile for a woman who wanted stability.

Since the clearly supernatural event he had witnessed in Israel with the destruction of the Russian air force, he had known the world was changing. Things would never again be as they had been. He wasn't buying the space alien theory of the disappearances, and while it very well could be attributed to some incredible cosmic energy reaction, who or what was behind that? The incident at the Wailing Wall was another unexplainable bit of the supernatural.

Buck found himself more intrigued by the "whys and wherefores" story, as he liked to think of it, than even the rise of Nicolae Carpathia. As taken as he was with the man, Buck hoped against hope that he wasn't just another slick politician. He was the best Buck had ever seen, but was it possible that Dirk's death, Alan's death, Eric's death, and Buck's predicament were totally independent of Carpathia?

He hoped so. He wanted to believe a person could come along once in a generation who could capture the imagination of the world. Could Carpathia be another Lincoln, a Roosevelt, or the embodiment of Camelot that Kennedy had appeared to some?

On impulse, as the cab crawled into the impossible traffic at JFK, Buck plugged his laptop modem into his cellular phone and brought up a news service on his screen. He quickly called up Eric Miller's major pieces for the last two years and was stunned to find he had written about the rebuilding and improvement in Babylon. The title of Miller's series was "New Babylon, Stonagal's Latest Dream." A quick scan of the article showed that the bulk of the financing came from Stonagal banks throughout the world. And of course there was a quote attributed to Stonagal: "Just coincidence. I have no idea the particulars of the financing undertaken by our various institutions."

Buck knew that the bottom line with Nicolae Carpathia would have nothing to do with Mwangati Ngumo or Israel or even the new Security Council. To Buck, the litmus test for Carpathia was what he did about Jonathan Stonagal once Carpathia was installed as secretary-general of the United Nations.

Because if the rest of the U.N. went along with

Nicolae's conditions, he would become the most powerful leader in the world overnight. He would have the
ability to enforce his wishes militarily if every member
were disarmed and U.N. might were increased. The
world would have to be desperate for a leader they
trusted implicitly to agree to such an arrangement. And
the only leader worth the mantle would be one with zero
tolerance for a murderous, behind-the-scenes schemer
like Jonathan Stonagal.

TWENTY

RAYFORD and Chloe Steele waited until one-thirty in the afternoon, then decided to head for their hotel. On their way out of the Pan-Con Club, Rayford stopped to leave a message for Hattie, in case she came in. "We just got another message for her," the girl at the counter said. "A secretary for a Cameron Williams said Mr. Williams would catch up with her here if she would call him when she got in."

"When did that message come?" Rayford asked.

"Just after one."

"Maybe we'll wait a few more minutes."

Rayford and Chloe were sitting near the entrance when Hattie rushed in. Rayford smiled at her, but she immediately seemed to slow, as if she had just happened to run into them. "Oh, hi," she said, showing her identification at the counter and taking her message. Rayford let her play her game. He deserved it.

"I really shouldn't have come to see you," she said, after being introduced to Chloe. "And now that I'm here, I should return this call. It's from the writer I told you about. He introduced me to Nicolae Carpathia this morning."

"You don't say."

Hattie nodded, smiling. "And Mr. Carpathia gave me his card. Did you know he's going to be named *People* magazine's Sexiest Man Alive?"

"I had heard that, yes. Well, I'm impressed. Quite a morning for you, wasn't it? And how is Mr. Williams?"

"Very nice, but very busy. I'd better call him. Excuse me."

———

Buck was on an escalator inside the terminal when his phone rang. "Well, hello yourself," Hattie said.

"I am so sorry, Miss Durham."

"Oh, please," she said. "Anybody who leaves me in midtown Manhattan in an expensive cab can call me by my first name. I insist."

"And I insist on paying for that cab."

"I'm just kidding, Buck. I'm going to meet with this captain and his daughter, so don't feel obligated to come over."

"Well, I'm already here," he said.

"Oh."

"But that's all right. I've got plenty to do. It was good to see you again, and next time you come through New York—"

"Buck, I don't want you to feel obligated to entertain me."

"I don't."

"Sure you do. You're a nice guy, but it's obvious we're not kindred spirits. Thanks for seeing me and especially for introducing me to Mr. Carpathia."

"Hattie, I could use a favor. Would it be possible to introduce me to this captain? I'd like to interview him. Is he staying overnight?"

"I'll ask him. You should meet his daughter anyway. She's a doll."

"Maybe I'll interview her, too."

"Yeah, good approach."

"Just ask him, Hattie, please."

Rayford wondered if Hattie had a date with Buck Williams that evening. The right thing to do would be to invite her to dinner at his and Chloe's hotel. Now she was waving him over to the pay phone.

"Rayford, Buck Williams wants to meet you. He's doing a story and wants to interview you."

"Really? Me?" he said. "About what?"

"I don't know. I didn't ask. I suppose about flying or the disappearances. You *were* in the air when it happened."

"Tell him sure, I'll see him. In fact, why don't you ask him to join the three of us for dinner tonight, if you're free." Hattie stared at Rayford as if she had been tricked into something. "Come on, Hattie. You and I will talk this afternoon, then we'll all get together for dinner at six at the Carlisle."

She turned back to the phone and told Buck. "Where are you now?" she asked. She paused. "You're not!" Hattie peeked around the corner, laughed, and waved. Covering the mouthpiece, she turned to Rayford. "That's him, right there on the portable phone!"

"Well, why don't you both hang up and you can make the introductions," Rayford said. Hattie and Buck hung up, and Buck tucked his phone away as he entered.

"He's with us," Rayford told the woman at the desk. He shook Buck's hand. "So you're the writer for *Global Weekly* who was on my plane."

"That's me," Buck said.

"What do you want to interview me about?"

"Your take on the disappearances. I'm doing a cover story on the theories behind what happened, and it would be good to get your perspective as a professional and as someone who was right in the middle of the turmoil when it happened."

What an opportunity! Rayford thought. "Happy to," he said. "You can join us for dinner then?"

"You bet," Buck said. "And this is your daughter?"

———————

Buck was stunned. He loved Chloe's name, her eyes, her smile. She looked directly at him and gave a firm handshake, something he liked in a woman. So many women felt it was feminine to offer a limp hand. *What a beautiful girl!* he thought. He had been tempted to tell Captain Steele that, as of the next day, he would no longer be just a writer but would become executive editor. But he feared that would sound like bragging, not complaining, so he had said nothing.

"Look," Hattie said, "the captain and I need a few minutes, so why don't you two get acquainted and we'll all get back together later. Do you have time, Buck?"

I do now, he thought. "Sure," he said, looking at Chloe and her father. "Is that all right with you two?"

The captain seemed to hesitate, but his daughter looked at him expectantly. She was clearly old enough to make her own decisions, but apparently she didn't want to make things awkward for her dad.

"It's OK," Captain Steele said hesitantly. "We'll be in here."

"I'll stash my bag, and we'll just take a walk in the terminal," Buck said. "If you want to, Chloe."

She smiled and nodded.

It had been a long time since Buck had felt awkward and shy around a girl. As he and Chloe strolled and talked, he didn't know where to look and was self-conscious about where to put his hands. Should he keep them in his pockets or let them hang free? Let them swing? Would she rather sit down or people watch or window-shop?

He asked her about herself and where she went to college, what she was interested in. She told him about her mother and her brother, and he sympathized. Buck was impressed at how smart and articulate and mature she seemed. This was a girl he could be interested in, but she had to be at least ten years younger than he was.

She wanted to know about his life and career. He told her anything she asked but little more. Only when she asked if he had lost anybody in the vanishings did he tell her about his family in Tucson and his friends in England. Naturally, he said nothing about the Stonagal or Todd-Cothran connections.

When the conversation lulled, Chloe caught him gazing at her, and he looked away. When he looked back, she was looking at him. They smiled shyly. *This is crazy,* he thought. He was dying to know if she had a boyfriend, but he wasn't about to ask.

Her questions were more along the lines of a young person asking a veteran professional about his career. She envied his travel and experience. He pooh-poohed it, assuring her she would tire of that kind of a life.

"Ever been married?" she asked.

He was glad she had asked. He was happy to tell her no, that he had never really been serious enough with anyone to be engaged. "How about you?" he asked, feeling the discussion was now fair game. "How many times have you been married?"

She laughed. "Only had one steady. When I was a freshman in college, he was a senior. I thought it was love, but when he graduated, I never heard from him again."

"Literally?"

"He went on some kind of an overseas trip, sent me a

cheap souvenir, and that was the end of it. He's married now."

"His loss."

"Thank you."

Buck felt bolder. "What was he, blind?" She didn't respond. Buck mentally kicked himself and tried to recover. "I mean, some guys don't know what they have."

She was still silent, and he felt like an idiot. *How can I be so successful at some things and such a klutz at others?* he wondered.

She stopped in front of a gourmet bakery shop. "You feel like a cookie?" she asked.

"Why? Do I look like one?"

"How did I know that was coming?" she said. "Buy me a cookie and I'll let that groaner die a natural death."

"Of old age, you mean," he said.

"Now *that* was funny."

———

Rayford was as earnest, honest, and forthright with Hattie as he had ever been. They sat across from each other in overstuffed chairs in the corner of a large, noisy room where they could not be heard by anyone else.

"Hattie," he said, "I'm not here to argue with you or even to have a conversation. There are things I must tell you, and I want you just to listen."

"I don't get to say anything? Because there may be things I'll want you to know, too."

"Of course I'll let you tell me anything you want, but this first part, my part, I don't want to be a dialogue. I have to get some things off my chest, and I want you to get the whole picture before you respond, OK?"

She shrugged. "I don't see how I have a choice."

"You had a choice, Hattie. You didn't have to come."

"I didn't really want to come. I told you that and you left that guilt-trip message, begging me to meet you here."

Rayford was frustrated. "You see what I didn't want to get into?" he said. "How can I apologize when all you want to do is argue about why you're here?"

"You want to apologize, Rayford? I would never stand in the way of that."

She was being sarcastic, but he had gotten her attention. "Yes, I do. Now will you let me?" She nodded. "Because I want to get through this, to set the record straight, to take all the blame I should, and then I want to tell you what I hinted at on the phone the other night."

"About how you've discovered what the vanishings are all about."

He held up a hand. "Don't get ahead of me."

"Sorry," she said, putting her hand over her mouth. "But why don't you just let me hear it when you answer Buck's questions tonight?" Rayford rolled his eyes. "I was just wondering," she said. "Just a suggestion so you don't have to repeat yourself."

"Thank you," he said, "but I'll tell you why. This is so important and so personal that I need to tell you privately. And I don't mind telling it over and over, and if my guess is right, you won't mind hearing it again and again."

Hattie raised her eyebrows as if to say she would be surprised, but she said, "You have the floor. I won't interrupt again."

Rayford leaned forward and rested his elbows on his knees, gesturing as he spoke. "Hattie, I owe you a huge apology, and I want your forgiveness. We were friends. We enjoyed each other's company. I loved being with you and spending time with you. I found you beautiful and exciting, and I think you know I was interested in a relationship with you."

She looked surprised, but Rayford assumed that, had it not been for her pledge of silence, she would have told him he had a pretty laid-back way of showing interest. He continued.

"Probably the only reason I never pursued anything further with you was because I didn't have any experience in such things. But it was only a matter of time. If I had found you willing, I'd have eventually done something wrong." She furrowed her brow and looked offended.

"Yes," he said, "it would have been wrong. I was married, not happily and not successfully, but that was my fault. Still, I had made a vow, a commitment, and no matter how I justified my interest in you, it would have been wrong."

He could tell from her look that she disagreed. "Anyway, I led you on. I wasn't totally honest. But now I have to tell you how grateful I am that I didn't do something—well, stupid. It would not have been right for you either. I know I'm not your judge and jury, and your morals are your own decision. But there would have been no future for us.

"It isn't just that we're so far apart in age, but the fact is that the only real interest I had in you was physical. You have a right to hate me for that, and I'm not proud of it. I did not love you. You have to agree, that would have been no kind of a life for you."

She nodded, appearing to cloud up. He smiled. "I'll let you break your silence temporarily," he said. "I need to know that you at least forgive me."

"Sometimes I wonder if honesty is always the best policy," she said. "I might have been able to accept this if you had just said your wife's disappearance made you feel guilty about what we had going. I know we didn't really have anything going yet, but that would have been a kinder way to put it."

"Kinder but dishonest. Hattie, I'm through being dishonest. Everything in me would rather be kind and gentle and keep you from resenting me, but I just can't be phony anymore. I was not genuine for years."

"And now you are?"

"To the point where it's unattractive to you," he said. She nodded again. "Why would I want to do that? Everybody likes to be liked. I could have blamed this on something else, on my wife, whatever. But I want to be able to live with myself. I want to be able to convince you, when I talk about even more important things, that I have no ulterior motives."

Hattie's lips quivered. She pressed them together and looked down, a tear rolling down her cheek. It was all Rayford could do to keep from embracing her. There would be nothing sensual about it, but he couldn't afford to give a wrong signal. "Hattie," he said. "I'm so sorry. Forgive me."

She nodded, unable to speak. She tried to say something but couldn't regain her composure.

"Now, after all that," Rayford said, "I somehow have to convince you that I do care for you as a friend and as a person."

Hattie held up both hands, fighting not to cry. She shook her head, as if not ready for this. "Don't," she managed. "Not right now."

"Hattie, I've got to."

"Please, give me a minute."

"Take your time, but don't run from me now," he said. "I would be no friend if I didn't tell you what I've found, what I've learned, what I'm discovering more of each day."

Hattie buried her face in her hands and cried. "I wasn't going to do this," she said. "I wasn't going to give you the satisfaction."

Rayford spoke as tenderly as he could. "Now you're going to offend *me*," he said. "If you take nothing else from this conversation, you must know that your tears give me no satisfaction. Every one of them is a dagger to me. I'm responsible. I was wrong."

"Give me a minute," she said, hurrying off.

Rayford dug out Irene's Bible and quickly scanned

some passages. He had decided not to sit talking to Hattie with the Bible open. He didn't want to embarrass or intimidate her, despite his newfound courage and determination.

———————

"You're gonna find my dad's theory of the disappearings very interesting," Chloe said.

"Am I?" Buck said. She nodded and he noticed a dab of chocolate at the corner of her mouth. He said, "May I?" extending his hand. She raised her chin and he transferred the chocolate to his thumb. Now what should he do? Wipe it on a napkin? Impulsively he put his thumb to his lips.

"Gross!" she said. "How embarrassing! What if I have the creeping crud or something?"

"Then now we've both got it," he said, and they laughed. Buck realized he was blushing, something he hadn't done for years, and so he changed the subject. "You say your dad's theory, as if maybe it's not yours, too. Do you two disagree?"

"He thinks we do, because I argue with him and give him a hard time about it. I just don't want to be too easy to convince, but if I had to be honest, I'd have to say we're pretty close. See, he thinks that—"

Buck held up a hand. "Oh, I'm sorry, don't tell me. I want to get it fresh from him, on tape."

"Oh. Excuse me."

"No, it's OK. I didn't mean to embarrass you, but

that's just how I like to work. I'd love to hear your theory, too. We're going to get some college kids' ideas, but it would be unlikely we would use two people from the same family. Of course, you just told me that you pretty much agree with your father, so I'd better wait and hear them both at the same time."

She had fallen silent and looked serious. "I'm sorry, Chloe, I didn't mean to imply I'm not interested in *your* theory."

"It's not that," she said. "But you just kind of categorized me there."

"Categorized you?"

"As a college kid."

"Ooh, I did, didn't I? My fault. I know better. Collegians aren't kids. I don't see you as a kid, although you are a lot younger than I am."

"Collegians? I haven't heard that term in a while."

"I *am* showing my age, aren't I?"

"How old *are* you, Buck?"

"Thirty and a half, going on thirty-one," he said with a twinkle.

"I say, how old are you?" she shouted, as if talking to a deaf old man. Buck roared.

"I'd buy you another cookie, little girl, but I don't want to spoil your appetite."

"You'd better not. My dad loves good food, and he's buying tonight. Save room."

"I will, Chloe."

"Can I tell you something, without you thinking I'm weird?" she said.

"Too late," he said.

She frowned and punched him. "I was just going to say that I like the way you say my name."

"I didn't know there was any other way to say it," he said.

"Oh, there is. Even my friends slip into making it one syllable, like Cloy."

"Chloe," he repeated.

"Yeah," she said. "Like that. Two syllables, long *O*, long *E*."

"I like your name." He slipped into an old man's husky voice. "It's a young person's name. How old are you, kid?"

"Twenty and a half, going on twenty-one."

"Oh, my goodness," he said, still in character, "I'm consortin' with a minor!"

As they headed back toward the Pan-Con Club, Chloe said, "If you promise not to make a big deal of my youth, I won't make a big deal of your age."

"Deal," he said, a smile playing at his lips. "You play a lot older."

"I'll take that as a compliment," she said, smiling self-consciously as if she wasn't sure he was serious.

"Oh, do," he said. "Few people your age are as well-read and articulate as you are."

"That was definitely a compliment," she said.

"You catch on quick."

"Did you really interview Nicolae Carpathia?"

He nodded. "We're almost buddies."

"No kidding?"

"Well, not really. But we hit it off."

"Tell me about him."

And so Buck did.

Hattie returned slightly refreshed but still puffy eyed and sat again as if ready for more punishment. Rayford reiterated that he was sincere about his apology, and she said, "Let's just put that behind us, shall we?"

"I need to know you forgive me," he said.

"You seem really hung up on that, Rayford. Would that let you off the hook, ease your conscience?"

"I guess maybe it would," he said. "Mostly it would tell me you believe I'm sincere."

"I believe it," she said. "It doesn't make it any more pleasant or easier to take, but if it makes you feel better, I do believe you mean it. And I don't hold grudges, so I guess that's forgiveness."

"I'll take what I can get," he said. "Now I want to be very honest with you."

"Uh-oh, there's more? Or is this where you educate me about what happened last week?"

"Yeah, this is it, but I need to tell you that Chloe advised against getting into this right now."

"In the same conversation as the, uh, other, you mean."

"Right."

"Smart girl," she said. "We must understand each other."

"Well, you're not that far apart in age."

"Wrong thing to say, Rayford. If you were going to

use that you're-young-enough-to-be-my-daughter approach, you should have brought it up earlier."

"Not unless I fathered you when I was fifteen," Rayford said. "Anyway, Chloe is convinced you're not going to be in the mood for this just now."

"Why? Does this require some reaction? Do I have to buy into your idea or something?"

"That's my hope, but no. If it's something you can't handle right now, I'll understand. But I think you'll see the urgency of it."

Rayford felt much like Bruce Barnes had sounded the day they met. He was full of passion and persuasion, and he felt his prayers for courage and coherence were answered as he spoke. He told Hattie of his history with God, having been raised in a churchgoing home and how he and Irene had attended various churches throughout their marriage. He even told her that Irene's preoccupation with end-time events had been one thing that made him consider looking elsewhere for companionship.

Rayford could tell by Hattie's look that she knew where he was going, that he had now come to agree with Irene and had bought the whole package. Hattie sat motionless as he told the story of knowing what he would find at home that morning after they had landed at O'Hare.

He told her of calling the church, meeting Bruce, Bruce's story, the videotape, their studies, the prophecies from the Bible, the preachers in Israel that clearly paralleled the two witnesses spoken of in Revelation.

Rayford told her how he had prayed the prayer with the pastor as the videotape rolled and how he now felt so responsible for Chloe and wanted her to find God, too. Hattie stared at him. Nothing in her body language or expression encouraged him, but he kept going. He didn't ask her to pray with him. He simply told her he would no longer apologize for what he believed.

"You can see, at least, how if a person truly accepts this, he must tell other people. He would be no friend if he didn't." Hattie wouldn't even give him the satisfaction of a nod to concede that point.

After nearly half an hour, he exhausted his new knowledge, and he concluded, "Hattie, I want you to think about it, consider it, watch the tape, talk to Bruce if you want to. I can't make you believe. All I can do is make you aware of what I have come to accept as the truth. I care about you and wouldn't want you to miss out simply because no one ever told you."

Finally, Hattie sat back and sighed. "Well, that's sweet, Rayford. It really is. I appreciate your telling me all that. It hits me real strange and different, because I never knew that stuff was in the Bible. My family went to church when I was a kid, mostly on holidays or if we got invited, but I never heard anything like that. I *will* think about it. I sort of have to. Once you hear something like this, it's hard to put it out of your mind for a while. Is this what you're going to tell Buck Williams at dinner?"

"Word for word."

She chuckled. "Wonder if any of it will find its way into his magazine."

"Probably along with space aliens, germ gas, and death rays," Rayford said.

TWENTY-ONE

WHEN Buck and Chloe reconnected with Hattie and Chloe's father, it was clear Hattie had been crying. Buck didn't feel close enough to ask what was wrong, and she never offered.

Buck was glad for the opportunity to interview Rayford Steele, but his emotions were mixed. The reactions of the captain who had piloted the plane on which he had been a passenger when the disappearances occurred would add drama to his story. But even more, he wanted to spend time with Chloe. Buck would run back to the office, then home to change, and meet them later at the Carlisle. At the office he took a call from Stanton Bailey, asking how soon he could go to Chicago to get Lucinda Washington replaced. "Soon, but I don't want to miss developments at the U.N."

"Everything happening there tomorrow morning you

already know about from Plank," Bailey said. "Word I get is it's already starting to come down. Plank assumes his new position in the morning, denies Carpathia's interest, reiterates what it would take, and we all wait and see if anybody bites. I don't think they will."

"I wish they would," Buck said, still hoping he could trust Carpathia and eager to see what the man would do about Stonagal and Todd-Cothran.

"I do, too," Bailey said, "but what are the odds? He's a man for this time, but his global disarmament and his reorganization plans are too ambitious. It'll never happen."

"I know, but if you were deciding, wouldn't you go along with it?"

"Yeah," Bailey said, sighing. "I probably would. I'm so tired of war and violence. I'd probably even go for moving the place to this New Babylon."

"Maybe the U.N. delegates will be smart enough to know the world is ready for Carpathia," Buck said.

"Wouldn't that be too good to be true?" Bailey said. "Don't bet the farm or hold your breath or whatever it is you're not supposed to do when the odds are against you."

Buck told his new boss he would fly to Chicago the next morning and get back to New York by Sunday night. "I'll get the lay of the land, find out who's solid in Chicago and whether we need to look at outside applicants."

"I'd prefer staying inside," Bailey said. "But it's my style to let you make those decisions."

Buck phoned Pan-Con Airlines, knowing Rayford Steele's flight left at eight the next morning. He told the reservation clerk his traveling companion was Chloe Steele. "Yes," she said, "Ms. Steele is flying complimentary in first class. There is a seat open next to her. Will you be a guest of the crew as well?"

"No."

He booked a cheap seat and charged it to the magazine, then upgraded to the seat next to Chloe. He would say nothing that night about going to Chicago.

It had been ages since Buck had worn a tie, but this was, after all, the Carlisle Hotel dining room. He wouldn't have gotten in without one. Fortunately they were directed to a private table in a little alcove where he could stash his bag without appearing gauche. His tablemates assumed he needed the bag for his equipment, not aware he had packed a change of clothes, too.

Chloe was radiant, looking five years older in a classy evening dress. It was clear she and Hattie had spent the late afternoon in a beauty salon.

Rayford thought his daughter looked stunning that evening, and he wondered what the magazine writer thought of her. Clearly this Williams guy was too old for her.

Rayford had spent his free hours before dinner napping and then praying that he would have the same courage and clarity he'd had with Hattie. He had no idea what she thought except that he was "sweet" for telling her everything. He wasn't sure whether that was sarcasm or condescension. He could only hope he had gotten through. That she had spent time alone with Chloe might have been good. Rayford hoped Chloe wasn't so antagonistic and closed minded that she had become an ally against him with Hattie.

At the restaurant Williams seemed to gaze at Chloe and ignore Hattie. Rayford considered this insensitive, but it didn't seem to bother Hattie. Maybe Hattie was matchmaking behind his back. Rayford himself had said nothing about Hattie's new look for the evening, but that was by design. She was striking and always had been, but he was not going down that path again.

During dinner Rayford kept the conversation light. Buck said to let him know when he was ready to be interviewed. After dessert Rayford spoke to the waiter privately. "We'd like to spend another hour or so here, if it's all right."

"Sir, we do have an extensive reservation list—"

"I wouldn't want this table to be less than profitable for you," Rayford said, pressing a large bill into the waiter's palm, "so boot us out whenever it becomes necessary."

The waiter peeked at the bill and slipped it into his pocket. "I'm sure you will not be disturbed," he said. And the water glasses were always full.

Rayford enjoyed answering Williams's initial questions about his job, his training, his background and upbringing, but he was eager to get on with his new mission in life. And finally the question came.

———————

Buck tried to concentrate on the captain's answers but felt himself trying to impress Chloe, too. Everyone in the business knew he was one of the best in the world at interviewing. That and his ability to quickly sift through the stuff and make a readable, engaging article of it had made him who he was.

Buck had breezed through the preliminaries, and he liked this guy. Steele seemed honest and sincere, smart and articulate. He realized he had seen a lot of Rayford in Chloe. "I'm ready," he said, "to ask your idea of what happened on that fateful flight to London. Do you have a theory?"

The captain hesitated and smiled as if gathering himself. "I have more than a theory," he said. "You may think this sounds crazy coming from a technically minded person like me, but I believe I have found the truth and know exactly what happened."

Buck knew this would play well in the magazine. "Gotta appreciate a man who knows his mind," he said. "Here's your chance to tell the world."

Chloe chose that moment to gently touch Buck's arm and ask if he minded if she excused herself for a moment.

"I'll join you," Hattie said.

Buck smiled, watching them go. "What was that?" he said. "A conspiracy? Were they supposed to leave me alone with you, or have they heard this before and don't want to rehash it?"

Rayford was privately frustrated, almost to the point of anger. That was the second time in a few hours that Chloe had somehow been spirited away at a crucial time. "I assure you that is not the case," he said, forcing himself to smile. He couldn't slow down and wait for their return. The question had been asked, he felt ready, and so he stepped off the edge of a social cliff, saying things he knew could get him categorized as a kook. As he had done with Hattie, he outlined his own spotty spiritual history and brought Williams up to the present in a little over half an hour, covering every detail he felt was relevant. At some point the women returned.

Buck sat without interrupting as this most lucid and earnest professional calmly propounded a theory that only three weeks before Buck would have found absurd. It sounded like things he had heard in church and from friends, but this guy had chapter and verse from the Bible to back it up. And this business of the two preachers in Jerusalem representing two witnesses predicted in the book of Revelation? Buck was aghast. He finally broke in.

"That's interesting," he said. "Have you heard the latest?" Buck told him what he had seen on CNN during his few brief minutes at his apartment. "Apparently thousands are making some sort of a pilgrimage to the Wailing Wall. They're lined up for miles, trying to get in and hear the preaching. Many are converting and going out themselves to preach. The authorities seem powerless to keep them out, despite the opposition of the Orthodox Jews. Anyone who comes against the preachers is struck dumb or paralyzed, and many of the old orthodox guard are joining forces with the preachers."

"Amazing," the pilot responded. "But even more amazing, it was all predicted in the Bible."

Buck was desperate to maintain his composure. He wasn't sure what he was hearing, but Steele was impressive. Maybe the man was reaching to link Bible prophecy with what was happening in Israel, but no one else had an explanation. What Steele had read to Buck from Revelation appeared clear. Maybe it was wrong. Maybe it was mumbo jumbo. But it was the only theory that tied the incidents so closely to any sort of explanation. What else would give Buck this constant case of the chills?

Buck focused on Captain Steele, his pulse racing, looking neither right nor left. He could not move. He was certain the women could hear his crashing heart. Was all this possible? Could it be true? Had he been exposed to a clear work of God in the destruction of the Russian air corps just to set him up for a moment like this? Could he shake his head and make it all go away? Could he sleep on it and come to his senses in the morning? Would a conversation with Bailey or Plank set him straight, snap him out of this silliness?

He sensed not. Something about this demanded attention. He wanted to believe something that tied everything together and made it make sense. But Buck also wanted to believe in Nicolae Carpathia. Maybe Buck was going through a scary time where he was vulnerable to impressive people. That wasn't like him, but then, who *was* himself these days? Who could be expected to be himself during times like these?

Buck didn't want to rationalize this away, to talk himself out of it. He wanted to ask Rayford Steele about his own sister-in-law and niece and nephew. But that would be personal, that would not relate to the story he was working on. This had not begun as a personal quest, a search for truth. This was merely a fact-finding mission, an element in a bigger story.

In no way did Buck even begin to think he was going to pick a favorite theory and espouse it as *Global Weekly*'s position. He was supposed to round up all the theories, from the plausible to the bizarre. Readers would add their own in the Letters column, or they would make a decision based on the credibility of the sources. This airline pilot, unless Buck made him look like a lunatic, would come off profound and convincing.

For the first time in his memory Buck Williams was speechless.

Rayford was certain he was not getting through. He only hoped this writer was astute enough to understand, to quote him correctly, and to represent his views in such a way that readers might look into Christianity. It was clear that Williams wasn't buying it personally. If Rayford had to guess, he'd say Williams was trying to hide a smirk—or else he was so amused, or amazed, that he couldn't frame a response.

Rayford had to remind himself that his purpose was to get through to Chloe first and then maybe to influence the reading public, if the thing found its way into print. If Cameron Williams thought Rayford was totally out to lunch, he might just leave him out, along with all his cockamamie views.

———————

Buck did not trust himself to respond with coherence. He still had chills, yet he felt sticky with sweat. What was happening to him? He managed a whisper. "I want to thank you for your time, and for dinner," he said. "I will get back to you before using any of your quotes." That was nonsense, of course. He had said it only to give himself a reason to reconnect with the pilot. He might have a lot of personal questions about this, but he never allowed people he interviewed to see their quotes in advance. He trusted his tape recorder and his memory, and he had never been accused of misquoting.

Buck looked back up at the captain and saw a strange look cross his face. He looked—what? Disappointed? Yes, then resigned.

Suddenly Buck remembered who he was dealing with.

This was an intelligent, educated man. Surely he knew that reporters never checked back with their sources. He probably thought he was getting a journalistic brush-off.

A rookie mistake, Buck, he reprimanded himself. *You just underestimated your own source.*

Buck was putting his equipment away when he noticed Chloe was crying, tears streaming down her face. What was it with these women? Hattie Durham had been weeping when she and the captain had finished talking that afternoon. Now Chloe.

Buck could identify, at least with Chloe. If she was crying because she had been moved by her father's sincerity and earnestness, it was no surprise. Buck had a lump in his throat, and for the first time since he had lain facedown in fear in Israel during the Russian attack, he wished he had a private place to cry.

"Could I ask you one more thing, off the record?" he said. "May I ask what you and Hattie were talking about this afternoon in the club?"

"Buck!" Hattie scolded. "That's none of your—"

"If you don't want to say, I'll understand," Buck said. "I was just curious."

"Well, much of it was personal," the captain said.

"Fair enough."

"But, Hattie, I don't see any harm in telling him that the rest of it was what we just went over. Do you?"

She shrugged.

"Still off the record, Hattie," Buck said, "do you mind if I ask your reaction to all this?"

"Why off the record?" Hattie snapped. "The opinions

of a pilot are important but the opinions of a flight attendant aren't?"

"I'll put you on the machine if you want," he said. "I didn't know you wanted to be on the record."

"I don't," she said. "I just wanted to be asked. It's too late now."

"And you don't care to say what you think—"

"No, I'll tell you. I think Rayford is sincere and thoughtful. Whether he's right, I have no idea. That's all beyond me and very foreign. But I am convinced he believes it. Whether he should or not, with his background and all that, I don't know. Maybe he's susceptible to it because of losing his family."

Buck nodded, realizing he was closer to buying Rayford's theory than Hattie was. He glanced at Chloe, hoping she had composed herself and that he could draw her out. She still had a tissue pressed under her eyes.

"Please don't ask me right now," she said.

———

Rayford was not surprised at Hattie's response, but he was profoundly disappointed with Chloe's. He was convinced she didn't want to embarrass him by saying how off the wall he sounded. He should have been grateful, he guessed. At least she was still sensitive to his feelings. Maybe he should have been more sensitive to hers, but he had decided he couldn't let those gentilities remain priorities anymore. He was going to contend for the faith with her until she made a decision. For tonight, however, it was clear she had heard enough. He wouldn't be pushing her anymore. He only hoped he could sleep despite his remorse over her condition. He loved her so much.

"Mr. Williams," he said, standing and thrusting out his hand, "it's been a pleasure. The pastor I told you about in Illinois really has a handle on this stuff and knows much more than I do about the Antichrist and all. It might be worth a call if you want to know any more. Bruce Barnes, New Hope Village Church, Mount Prospect."

"I'll keep that in mind," Buck said.

Rayford was convinced Williams was merely being polite.

Talking to this Barnes was a great idea, Buck thought. Maybe he'd find the time the next day in Chicago. That way he could pursue this for himself and not confuse the professional angle with his own interest.

The foursome moseyed to the lobby. "I'm going to say my good-nights," Hattie said. "I've got the earlier flight tomorrow." She thanked Rayford for dinner, whispered something to Chloe—which seemed to get no response— and thanked Buck for his hospitality that morning. "I may just call Mr. Carpathia one of these days," she said. Buck resisted the urge to tell her what he knew about Carpathia's immediate future. He doubted the man would have time for her.

Chloe looked as if she wanted to follow Hattie to the elevators and yet wanted to say something to Buck as well. He was shocked when she said, "Give us a minute, will you, Daddy? I'll be right up."

Buck found himself flattered that Chloe had hung back to say good-bye personally, but she was still emotional. Her voice was quavery as she formally told him what a good time she had had that day. He tried to prolong the conversation.

"Your dad is a pretty impressive guy," he said.

"I know," she said. "Especially lately."

"I can see why you might agree with him on a lot of that stuff."

"You can?"

"Sure! I have a lot of thinking to do myself. You give him a hard time about it though, huh?"

"I used to. Not anymore."

"Why not?"

"You can see how much it means to him."

Buck nodded. She seemed on the edge emotionally again. He reached to take her hand. "It's been wonderful spending time with you," he said.

She chuckled, as if embarrassed about what she was thinking.

"What?" he pressed.

"Oh, nothing. It's silly."

"C'mon, what? We've both been silly today."

"Well, I feel stupid," she said. "I just met you and I'm really gonna miss you. If you get through Chicago, you have to call."

"It's a promise," Buck said. "I can't say when, but let's just say sooner than you think."

TWENTY-TWO

BUCK did not sleep well. Partly he was excited about his morning surprise. He could only hope Chloe would be happy about it. The larger part of his mind reeled with wonder. If this was true, all that Rayford Steele had postulated—and Buck knew instinctively that if any of it was true, all of it was true—why had it taken Buck a lifetime to come to it? Could he have been searching for this all the time, hardly knowing he was looking?

Yet even Captain Steele—an organized, analytical airline pilot—had missed it, and Steele claimed to have had a proponent, a devotee, almost a fanatic living under his own roof. Buck was so restless he had to leave his bed and pace. Strangely, somehow, he was not upset, not miserable. He was simply overwhelmed. None of this would have made a bit of sense to him just days before, and now, for the first time since Israel, he was unable to separate himself from his story.

The Holy Land attack had been a watershed event in his life. He had stared his own mortality in the face and had to acknowledge that something otherworldly—yes, supernatural, something directly from God almighty—had been thrust upon those dusty hills in the form of a fire in the sky. And he had known beyond a doubt for the first time in his life that unexplainable things out there could not be dissected and evaluated scientifically from a detached Ivy League perspective.

Buck had always prided himself on standing apart from the pack, for including the human, the everyday, the everyman element in his stories when others resisted such vulnerability. This skill allowed readers to identify with him, to taste and feel and smell those things most important to them. But he had still been able, even after his closest brush with death, to let the reader live it without revealing Buck's own deep angst about the very existence of God. Now, that separation seemed impossible. How could he cover this most important story of his life, one that had already probed closest to his soul, without subconsciously revealing his private turmoil?

He was, he knew by the wee hours, leaning over the line. He wasn't ready to pray yet, to try to talk to a God he had ignored for so long. He hadn't even prayed when he became convinced of God's existence that night in Israel. What had been the matter with him? Everyone in the world, at least those intellectually honest with themselves, had to admit there was a God after that night.

Amazing coincidences had occurred before, but that had defied all logic.

To win against the mighty Russians was an upset, of course. But Israel's history was replete with such legends. Yet to not defend yourself and suffer no casualties? That was beyond all comprehension—apart from the direct intervention of God.

Why, Buck wondered, hadn't that made more of an impact on his own introspective inventory? In the lonely darkness he came to the painful realization that he had long ago compartmentalized this most basic of human needs and had rendered it a nonissue. What did it say about him, what despicable kind of a subhuman creature had he become, that even the stark evidence of the Israel miracle—for it could be called nothing less—had not thawed his spirit's receptiveness to God?

Not that many months later came the great disappearance of millions around the world. Dozens had vanished from the plane in which he was a passenger. What more did he need? It already seemed as if he were living in a science fiction thriller. Without question he had lived through the most cataclysmic event in history. Buck realized he'd not had a second to think in the last two weeks. Had it not been for the personal tragedies he had witnessed, he might have been more private in his approach to what appeared to be a universe out of control.

He wanted to meet this Bruce Barnes, not even pretending to be interviewing him for an article. Buck was on a personal quest now, looking to satisfy deep needs. For so many years he had rejected the idea of a personal

God or that he had need of God—if there was one. The idea would take some getting used to. Captain Steele had talked about everyone being a sinner. Buck was not unrealistic about that. He knew his life would never stand up to the standards of a Sunday school teacher. But he had always hoped that if he faced God someday, his good would outweigh his bad and that relatively speaking, he was as good or better than the next guy. That would have to do.

Now, if Rayford Steele and all his Bible verses could be believed, it didn't make any difference how good Buck was or where he stood in relation to anybody else. One archaic phrase had struck him and rolled around in his head. *There is none righteous, no, not one.* Well, he had never considered himself righteous. Could he go the next level and admit his need for God, for forgiveness, for Christ?

Was it possible? Could he be on the cusp of becoming a born-again Christian? He had been almost relieved when Rayford Steele had used that term. Buck had read and even written about "those kinds" of people, but even at his level of worldly wisdom he had never quite understood the phrase. He had always considered the "born-again" label akin to "ultraright-winger" or "fundamentalist." Now, if he chose to take a step he had never dreamed of taking, if he could not somehow talk himself out of this truth he could no longer intellectually ignore, he would also take upon himself a task: educating the world on what that confusing little term really meant.

Buck finally dozed on the couch in his living room, despite a lamp shining close to his face. He slept soundly for a couple of hours but awoke in time to get to the airport. The prospect of surprising Chloe and traveling with her gave him a rush that helped overcome his fatigue. But even more exciting was the possibility that another answer man awaited him in Chicago, a man he trusted simply on the recommendation of a pilot who had seemed to speak the truth with authority. It would be fun someday to tell Rayford Steele how much that otherwise innocuous interview had meant to him. But Buck assumed Steele had already figured that out. That was probably why Steele had seemed so passionate.

If this signaled the soon beginning of the tribulation period predicted in the Bible, and Rayford had no doubt that it did, he wondered if there would be any joy in it. Bruce didn't seem to think there would be, aside from the few converts they might be privileged to win. So far Rayford felt he was a failure. While he was certain God had given him the words and the courage to say them, he felt he had done something wrong in communicating to Hattie. Maybe she was right. Maybe he had been self-serving. It had to appear to her that he was merely getting out from under his own load of guilt. But he knew better. Before God he believed his motives pure. Yet clearly he had not persuaded Hattie of more than that he was sincere and that he believed. What good was that? If he believed and she didn't, she had to assume he believed something bogus, or she would have to admit she was ignoring the truth. What he had told her carried no other option.

And his performance during the interview with Cameron Williams! At the time, Rayford had felt good about it, articulate, calm, rational. He knew he was discussing revolutionary, jarring stuff, but he felt God had enabled him to be lucid. Yet if he couldn't get any more reaction out of the reporter than polite deference, what kind of a witness could he be? From the depths of his soul Rayford wanted to be more productive. He believed he had wasted his life before this, and he had only a short period to make up for lost time. He was eternally grateful for his own salvation, but now he wanted to share it, to bring more people to Christ. The magazine interview had been an incredible opportunity, but in his gut he felt it had not come off well. Was it even worth the effort to pray for another chance? Rayford believed he had seen the last of Cameron Williams. He wouldn't be calling Bruce Barnes, and Rayford's quotes would never see the pages of *Global Weekly*.

As Rayford shaved and showered and dressed, he heard Chloe packing. She had obviously been embarrassed by him last night, probably even apologized to Mr. Williams for her father's absurd ramblings. At least she had tapped on his door and said good night when she came in. That was *something*, wasn't it?

Every time Rayford thought of Chloe, he felt a tightness in his chest, a great emptiness and grief. He could live with his other failures if he must, but his knees

Tim LaHaye & Jerry B. Jenkins

nearly buckled as he prayed silently for Chloe. *I cannot lose her,* he thought, and he believed he would trade his own salvation for hers if that was what it took.

With that commitment, he sensed God speaking to him, impressing upon him that that was precisely the burden required for winning people, for leading them to Christ. That was the attitude of Jesus himself, being willing to take on himself the punishment of men and women so they could live.

Rayford was emboldened anew as he prayed for Chloe, still fighting the nagging fear of failure. "God, I need encouragement," he breathed. "I need to know I haven't turned her off forever." She had said good night, but he had also heard her crying in bed.

He emerged in uniform and smiled at her as she stood by the door, dressed casually for travel. "Ready, sweetie?" he said tentatively.

She nodded and seemed to work up a smile, then embraced him tight and long, pressing her cheek against his chest. *Thank you,* he prayed silently, wondering if he should say anything. Was this the time? Dare he press now?

Again he felt deeply impressed of God, as if the Lord were speaking directly to his spirit, *Patience. Let her be. Let her be.* Keeping silent seemed as hard as anything he had ever done. Chloe said nothing either. They grabbed a light breakfast and headed to JFK.

Chloe was the first passenger on the plane. "I'll try to get back and see you," Rayford told her before heading to the cockpit.

"Don't worry if you can't," she said. "I'll understand."

Buck waited until everyone else had boarded. As he approached his seat next to Chloe, her body was turned toward the window, arms crossed, chin in her hand. Whether she even had her eyes open, Buck couldn't tell. He assumed she would turn to glance as he sat next to her, and he couldn't suppress a smile, anticipating her reaction and only slightly worried that she would be less positive than he hoped.

He sat and waited, but she did not turn. Was she sleeping? Staring? Meditating? Praying? Was it possible she was crying? Buck hoped not. He already cared for her enough to be bothered when she seemed in pain.

And now he had a problem. As he warily watched for the change in position that would allow Chloe to see him in her peripheral vision, he was suddenly awash in fatigue. His muscles and joints ached, his eyes burned. His head felt like lead. No way was he going to fall asleep and have her discover him dozing next to her.

Buck gestured to get the attendant's attention. "Coke, please," he whispered. The temporary caffeine rush would allow him to stay awake a little longer.

When Chloe didn't move even to watch the safety instructions, Buck grew impatient. Still, he didn't want to reveal himself. He wanted to be discovered. And so he waited.

She must have grown weary of her position, because she stretched and used her feet to push her carry-on bag under the seat in front of her. She took a last sip of her juice and set it on the small tray between them. She stared at Buck's glove-leather boots, the ones he had worn the day before. Chloe's eyes traveled up to his smiling, expectant face.

Her reaction was more than worth the wait. She folded her hands and drew them to her mouth, her eyes filling. Then she took his hand in both of hers. "Oh, Buck," she whispered. "Oh, Buck."

"It's nice to see you, too," he said.

Chloe quickly let go of his hand as if catching herself. "I don't mean to act like a schoolgirl," she said, "but have you ever received a direct answer to prayer?"

Buck shot her a double take. "I thought your dad was the praying member of your family."

"He is," she said. "But I just tried out my first one in years, and God answered it."

"You prayed I would sit next to you?"

"Oh, no, I never would have dreamed of anything that impossible. How did you do it, Buck?"

He told her. "It wasn't hard once I knew your flight time, and I said I was traveling with you to get next to you."

"But why? Where are you going?"

"You don't know where this plane's going? San José, I hope."

She laughed.

"But come on now, Chloe. Finish your story. I've never been an answer to prayer before."

"It's kind of a long story."

"I think we've got time."

She took his hand again. "Buck, this is too special. This is the nicest thing anyone's done for me in a long time."

"You said you were going to miss me, but I didn't do it only for you. I've got business in Chicago."

She giggled and let go again. "I wasn't talking about you, Buck, though this is sweet. I was talking about God doing the nice thing for me."

Buck couldn't hide his embarrassment. "I knew that," he said.

And she told him her story. "You might have noticed I was pretty upset last night. I was so moved by my dad's story. I mean, I had heard it before. But all of a sudden he seemed so loving, so interested in people. Could you tell how important it was to him and how serious he was about it?"

"Who couldn't?"

"If I didn't know better, Buck, I would have thought he was trying to convince you personally rather than just answering your questions."

"I'm not so sure he wasn't."

"Did it offend you?"

"Not at all, Chloe. To tell you the truth, he was getting to me."

Chloe fell silent and shook her head. When she finally spoke she was nearly whispering, and Buck had to lean toward her to hear. He loved the sound of her voice. "Buck," she said, "he was getting to me, too, and I don't mean my dad."

"Too bizarre," he said. "I was up half the night thinking about this."

"It won't be long for either of us, will it?" she said. Buck didn't respond, but he knew what she meant.

"When do I get to be the answer to prayer?" he prodded.

"Oh, right. I was sitting there at dinner with my dad pouring his guts out to you, and I suddenly realized why he wanted me to be there when he said the same things to Hattie. I gave him such a hard time at first that he backed off on me, and now that he had the knowledge and the real need to convince me, he was afraid to come right at me. He wanted me to get it indirectly. And I did. I didn't hear how he started because Hattie and I were in the ladies' room, but I had probably heard that before. When I got back, I was transfixed.

"It wasn't that I was hearing anything new. It was new to me when I heard it from Bruce Barnes and saw that videotape, but my dad showed such urgency and confidence. Buck, there's no other explanation for those two guys in Jerusalem, is there, except that they have to be the two witnesses talked about in the Bible?"

Buck nodded.

"So, Dad and God were getting to me, but I wasn't ready yet. I was crying because I love him so much and because it's true. It's all true, Buck, do you know that?"

"I think I do, Chloe."

"But still I couldn't talk to my dad about it. I didn't know what was in my way. I've always been so blasted independent. I knew he was frustrated with me, maybe disappointed, and all I could do was cry. I had to think, to try to pray, to sort it out. Hattie was no help. She doesn't get it and maybe never will. All she cared about was trivial stuff, like trying to matchmake you and me."

Buck smiled and tried to look insulted. "That's trivial?"

"Well, compared to what we're talking about right now, I'd have to say so."

"Gotta give you that one," Buck said.

She laughed. "So I knew something was wrong with Dad because I talked to you for only, what, three minutes or so before I went up?"

"Less than that, probably."

"By the time I got to our suite, he was already in bed. So I told him good night, just to make sure he was still talking to me. He was. And then I tossed and turned, not ready to take the last step, crying about my dad's worrying so much about me and loving me so much."

"That's while I was up, probably," Buck said.

"But," Chloe said, "this is so out of character for me. Even though I'm there, I mean, I'm right there. You follow me?"

Buck nodded. "I've been going through the same thing."

"I've been convinced," she said, "but I'm still fighting. I'm supposed to be an intellectual. I have critical friends to answer to. Who's going to believe this? Who's going to think I haven't lost my mind?"

"Believe me, I understand," Buck said, amazed at the similarities between their journeys.

"So, I was stuck," she said. "I wasn't getting anywhere. I tried to encourage my dad by not being so distant, but I could tell he saw me suffering, but I don't think he had any idea how close I was. I got on this plane, desperate for some closure, pardon the psycho-babble, and I started wondering if God answers your prayers before you're . . . um, you know, before you're actually a . . ."

"Born-again Christian," Buck offered.

"Exactly. I don't know why that's so hard for me to say. Maybe somebody who knows better can tell me for sure, but I prayed and I think God answered. Tell me this, Buck, just with your cognitive-reasoning skills. If there is a God and if this is all true, wouldn't he want us to know? I mean, God wouldn't make it hard to learn and he wouldn't, or I should say he *couldn't,* ignore a desperate prayer, could he?"

"I don't see how he could, no."

"Well, that's what I think. So I think it was a good test, a reasonable one, and that I wasn't out of line. I'm convinced God answered."

"And I was the answer."

"And you were the answer."

"Chloe, what exactly did you pray for?"

"Oh, well, the prayer itself wasn't that big of a deal, until it was answered. I just told God I needed a little more. I felt bad that all the stuff I'd heard and all that I knew from my dad wasn't enough. I just prayed really sincerely and said I would appreciate it if God could show me personally that he cared, that he knew what I was going through, and that he wanted me to know he was there."

Buck felt a strange emotion—that if he tried to speak, his voice would be husky and he might be unable to finish a sentence. He pressed his hand over his mouth to compose himself. Chloe stared at him. "And you feel I was the answer to that prayer?" he said at last.

"No doubt in my mind. See, like I said, I wouldn't even have conceived of praying that you would wind up next to me on the biggest day of my life. I wasn't even sure I'd ever see you again. But it's as if God knew better than I did that there was no one I would rather see today than you."

Buck was touched, moved beyond expression. He had wanted to see her, too. Otherwise, he could have flown on Hattie's flight or any one of a dozen that would have gotten him to Chicago that morning. Buck just looked at her. "So, what are you going to do now, Chloe? It seems to me that God has called your bluff. It wasn't a bluff, exactly, but you asked and he delivered. Sounds like you're obligated."

"I have no choice," she agreed. "Not that I want one. From what I've gathered from Bruce Barnes and the tape and Dad, you don't have to have somebody lead you through this, and you don't have to be in a church or anything. Just like I prayed for a clearer sign, I can pray about this."

"Your dad made that clear last night."

"You want to join me?" she asked.

Buck hesitated. "Don't take this personally, Chloe, but I'm not ready."

"What more do you need? . . . Oh, I'm sorry, Buck.

I'm doing just what my dad did the day he became a Christian. He could hardly help himself, and I was so awful to him. But if you're not ready, you're not ready."

"I won't need to be forced," Buck said. "Like you, I feel like I'm right on the doorstep. But I'm pretty careful, and I want to talk to this Barnes guy today. I have to tell you, though, my remaining doubts can hardly stand up to what's happening to you."

"You know, Buck," Chloe said, "I promise this will be the last thing I say about it, but I'm thinking the same way my dad did. I have this urge to tell you not to wait too long because you never know what might happen."

"I hear you," he said. "I'm going to have to take my chances this plane won't go down because I still feel I need to talk to Barnes, but you have a point."

Chloe turned and looked over her shoulder. "There are two vacant seats right there," she said. She stopped a passing attendant. "Can I give you a message for my dad?"

"Sure. Is he captain or first officer?"

"Captain. Please just tell him his daughter has extremely good news for him."

"Extremely good news," the attendant repeated.

———

Rayford was manually flying the plane as a diversion when his senior flight attendant gave him the message. He had no idea what it meant, but it was so unlike Chloe to initiate communication lately, he was intrigued.

He asked his first officer to take over. Rayford unstrapped himself and made his way out, surprised to see Cameron Williams. He hoped Williams wasn't the extent of Chloe's good news. Pleasant as it was to think the man might already be making good on his promise to look up Bruce Barnes, Rayford also hoped that Chloe wasn't about to announce some ill-advised whirlwind romance in the bud.

He shook hands with the writer and expressed his pleasant, but wary, surprise. Chloe reached for his neck with both hands and gently pulled him down to where she could whisper to him. "Daddy, could you and I sit back there for a couple of minutes so I can talk to you?"

Buck sensed disappointment in Captain Steele's eyes at first. He looked forward to telling the pilot why he was glad to be flying to Chicago. Sitting next to Chloe had been only a bonus. He peeked back at Steele with his daughter, engaged in intense conversation and then praying together. Buck wondered if there was any airline regulation against that. He knew Rayford couldn't fraternize for long.

In a few minutes Chloe stepped into the aisle, and Rayford stood and embraced her. They both appeared overcome with emotion. A middle-aged couple across the aisle leaned out and stared, brows raised. The captain noticed, straightened, and headed toward the cockpit.

"My daughter," he said awkwardly, pointing at Chloe who smiled through her tears. "She's my daughter."

The couple looked at each other and the woman spoke. "Right. And I'm the queen of England," she said, and Buck laughed out loud.

TWENTY-THREE

Buck called New Hope Village Church to set up an early evening meeting with Bruce Barnes, then spent most of the afternoon at the Chicago bureau of *Global Weekly*. News of his becoming their boss had swept the place, and he was greeted with coolness by Lucinda Washington's former assistant, a young woman in sensible shoes. She told him in no uncertain terms, "Plank did nothing about replacing Lucinda, so I assumed I would move into her slot."

Her attitude and presumption alone made Buck say, "That's unlikely, but you'll be the first to know. I wouldn't be moving offices just yet."

The rest of the staff still grieved over Lucinda's disappearance and seemed grateful for Buck's visit. Steve Plank had hardly ever come to Chicago and had not been there since Lucinda had vanished.

Buck camped out in Lucinda's old office, interviewing key people at twenty-minute intervals. He also told each about his writing assignment and asked their personal theories of what had happened. His final question to each was, "Where do you think Lucinda Washington is right now?" More than half said they didn't want to be quoted but expressed variations of, "If there's a heaven, that's where she is."

Near the end of the day, Buck was told that CNN was live at the U.N. with big news. He invited the staff into the office and they watched together. "In the most dramatic and far-reaching overhaul of an international organization anyone can remember," came the report, "Romanian president Nicolae Carpathia was catapulted into reluctant leadership of the United Nations by a nearly unanimous vote. Carpathia, who insisted on sweeping changes in direction and jurisdiction of the United Nations, in what appeared an effort to gracefully decline the position, became secretary-general here just moments ago.

"As late as this morning his press secretary and spokesman, Steven Plank, former executive editor of the *Global Weekly,* had denied Carpathia's interest in the job and outlined myriad demands the Romanian would insist upon before even considering the position. Plank said the request for Carpathia's elevation came from outgoing Secretary-General Mwangati Ngumo of Botswana. We asked Ngumo why he was stepping down."

Ngumo's face filled the screen, eyes downcast, his expression carefully masked. "I have long been aware that divided loyalties between my country and the United Nations have made me less effective in each role. I had to choose, and I am first and foremost a Botswanian. We have the opportunity now to become prosperous, due to the generosity of our friends in Israel. The time is right, and the new man is more than right. I will cooperate with him to the fullest."

"Would you, sir, have stepped down had Mr. Carpathia declined the position?"

Ngumo hesitated. "Yes," he said, "I would have. Perhaps not today, and not with as much confidence in the future of the United Nations, but yes, eventually."

The CNN reporter continued, "In only a matter of hours, every request Carpathia had outlined in an early morning press conference was moved as official business, voted upon, and ratified by the body. Within a year the United Nations headquarters will move to New Babylon. The makeup of the Security Council will change to ten permanent members within the month, and a press conference is expected Monday morning in which Carpathia will introduce several of his personal choices for delegates to that body.

"There is no guarantee, of course, that even member nations will unanimously go along with the move to destroy ninety percent of their military strength and turn over the remaining ten percent to the U.N. But several ambassadors expressed their confidence 'in equipping and arming an international peacekeeping body with a thoroughgoing pacifist and committed disarmament activist as its head.' Carpathia himself was quoted as saying, 'The U.N. will not need its military might if no one else has any, and I look forward to the day when even the U.N. disarms.'

"Also coming out of today's meetings was the announcement of a seven-year pact between U.N. members and Israel, guaranteeing its borders and promising peace. In exchange, Israel will allow the U.N. to selectively franchise the use of the fertilizer formula, developed by Nobel prizewinner Dr. Chaim Rosenzweig, which makes desert sands tillable and has made Israel a top exporter."

Buck stared as CNN broadcast Rosenzweig's excitement and unequivocal endorsement of Carpathia. The news also carried a report that Carpathia had asked several international groups already in New York for upcoming meetings to get together this weekend to hammer out proposals, resolutions, and accords. "I urge them to move quickly toward anything that contributes to world peace and a sense of global unity."

A reporter asked Carpathia if that included plans for one world religion and eventually one world government. His response: "I can think of little, more encouraging than the religions of the world finally cooperating. Some of the worst examples of discord and infighting have been between groups whose overall mission is love among people. Every devotee of pure religion should welcome this potential. The day of hatred is past. Lovers of humankind are uniting."

The CNN anchor continued, "Among other developments today, there are rumors of the organization of groups espousing one world government. Carpathia was asked if he aspired to a position of leadership in such an organization."

Carpathia looked directly into the network pool camera and with moist eyes and thick voice said, "I am overwhelmed to have been asked to serve as secretary-general of the United Nations. I aspire to nothing else. While the idea of one world government resonates deep within me, I can say only that there are many more qualified candidates to lead such a venture. It would be my privilege to serve in any way I am asked, and while I do not see myself in the leadership role, I will commit the resources of the United Nations to such an effort, if asked."

Smooth, Buck thought, his mind reeling. As commentators and world leaders endorsed one world currency, one language, and even the largesse of Carpathia expressing his support for the rebuilding of the temple in Israel, the staff of *Global Weekly*'s Chicago bureau seemed in a mood to party. "This is the first time in years I've felt optimistic about society," one reporter said.

Another added, "This has to be the first time I've smiled since the disappearances. We're supposed to be objective and cynical, but how can you not like this? It'll take years to effect all this stuff, but someday, somewhere down the line, we're going to see world peace. No more weapons, no more wars, no more border disputes or bigotry based on language or religion. Whew! Who'd have believed it would come to this?"

Buck took a call from Steve Plank. "You been watching what's going on?" Plank said.

"Who hasn't?"

"Pretty exciting, isn't it?"

"Mind boggling."

"Listen, Carpathia wants you here Monday morning."

"What for?"

"He likes you, man. Don't knock it. Before the press conference he's going to have a meeting with his top people and the ten delegates to the permanent Security Council."

"And he wants me there?"

"Yup. And you can guess who some of his top people are."

"Tell me."

"Well, one's obvious."

"Stonagal."

"Of course."

"And Todd-Cothran. I assume he'll move in as new ambassador from the U.K."

"Maybe not," Steve said. "Another Brit is there. I don't know his name, but he's also with this international finance group Stonagal runs."

"You think Carpathia told Stonagal to have someone else in the wings, in case Carpathia wants to squeeze Todd-Cothran out?"

"Could be, but nobody tells Stonagal anything."

"Not even Carpathia?"

"Especially not Carpathia. He knows who made him. But he's honest and sincere, Buck. Nicolae will not do anything illegal or underhanded or even too political. He's pure, man. Pure as the driven snow. So, can you make it?"

"Guess I'd better. How many press will be there?"

"You ready for this? Only you."

"You're kidding."

"I'm serious. He likes you, Buck."

"What's the catch?"

"No catch. He didn't ask for a thing, not even favorable coverage. He knows you have to be objective and fair. The media will get the whole scoop at the press conference afterward."

"Obviously I can't pass this up," Buck said, aware his voice sounded flat.

"What's the matter, Buck? This is history! This is the world the way we've always wanted it and hoped it would be."

"I hope you're right."

"I'm right. There's something else Carpathia wants."

"So there *is* a catch."

"No, nothing hinges on this. If you can't do it, you can't do it. You're still welcome Monday morning. But he wants to see that stewardess friend of yours again."

"Steve, no one calls them stews anymore. They're flight attendants."

"Whatever. Bring her with you if you can."

"Why doesn't he ask her himself? What am I now, a pimp?"

"C'mon, Buck. It's not like that. Lonely guy in a position like this? He can't be out hustling up dates. You introduced them, remember? He trusts you."

He must, Buck thought, *if he's inviting me to his big pre-press-conference meeting.* "I'll ask her," he said. "No promises."

"Don't let me down, buddy."

Rayford Steele was as happy as he had been since his own decision to receive Christ. To see Chloe smiling, to see her hungry to read Irene's Bible, to be able to pray with her and talk about everything together was more than he had dreamed of. "One thing we need to do," he said, "is to get you your own Bible. You're going to wear that one out."

"I want to join that core group of yours," she said. "I want to get all the stuff from Bruce firsthand. The only part that bothers me is that it sounds like things are going to get worse."

Late in the afternoon they dropped in on Bruce, who confirmed Chloe's view. "I'm thrilled to welcome you into the family," he said, "but you're right. God's people are in for dark days. Everybody is. I've been thinking and praying about what we're supposed to do as a church between now and the Glorious Appearing."

Chloe wanted to know all about that, so Bruce showed her from the Bible why he believed Christ would appear in seven years, at the end of the Tribulation. "Most Christians will be martyred or die from war, famine, plagues, or earthquakes," he said.

Chloe smiled. "This isn't funny," she said, "but maybe I should have thought of that before I signed on. You're going to have trouble convincing people to join the cause with that in your sign-up brochure."

Bruce grimaced. "Yes, but the alternative is worse. We all missed out the first time around. We could be in heaven right now if we'd listened to our loved ones. Dying a horrible death during this period is not my preference, but I'd sure rather do it this way than while I was still lost. Everyone else is in danger of death, too. The only difference is, we have one more way to die than they do."

"As martyrs."

"Right."

Rayford sat listening, aware how his world had changed in such a short time. It had not been that long ago that he had been a respected pilot at the top of his profession, living a phony life, a shell of a man. Now here he was, talking secretly in the office of a local church with his daughter and a young pastor, trying to determine how they would survive seven years of tribulation following the Rapture of the church.

"We have our core group," Bruce said, "and Chloe, you're welcome to join us if you're serious about total commitment."

"What's the option?" she said. "If what you're saying is true, there's no room for dabbling."

"You're right. But I've also been thinking about a smaller group within the core. I'm looking for people of unusual intelligence and courage. I don't mean to disparage the sincerity of others in the church, especially those on the leadership team. But some of them are timid, some old, many infirm. I've been praying about sort of an inner circle of people who want to do more than just survive."

"What are you getting at?" Rayford asked. "Going on the offensive?"

"Something like that. It's one thing to hide in here,

studying, figuring out what's going on so we can keep from being deceived. It's great to pray for the witnesses springing up out of Israel, and it's nice to know there are other pockets of believers all over the world. But doesn't part of you want to jump into the battle?"

Rayford was intrigued but not sure. Chloe was more eager. "A cause," she said. "Something not just to die for but to live for."

"Yes!"

"A group, a team, a force," Chloe said.

"You've got it. A force."

Chloe's eyes were bright with interest. Rayford loved her youth and her eagerness to commit to a cause that to her was only hours old. "And what is it you call this period?" she asked.

"The Tribulation," Bruce said.

"So your little group inside the group, a sort of Green Berets, would be your Tribulation force."

"Tribulation Force," Bruce said, looking at Rayford and rising to scribble it on his flip chart. "I like it. Make no mistake, it won't be fun. It would be the most danger-ous cause a person could ever join. We would study, pre-pare, and speak out. When it becomes obvious who the Antichrist is, the false prophet, the evil, counterfeit reli-gion, we'll have to oppose them, speak out against them. We would be targeted. Christians content to hide in basements with their Bibles might escape everything but earthquakes and wars, but we will be vulnerable to everything.

"There will come a time, Chloe, that followers of

Antichrist will be required to bear the sign of the beast.
There are all kinds of theories on what form that might
take, from a tattoo to a stamp on the forehead that
might be detected only under infrared light. But obviously we would refuse to bear that mark. That very act
of defiance will be a mark in itself. We will be the naked
ones, the ones devoid of the protection of belonging to
the majority. You still want to be part of the Tribulation
Force?"

Rayford nodded and smiled at his daughter's firm
reply. "I wouldn't miss it."

Two hours after the Steeles had left, Buck Williams
parked his rental car in front of New Hope Village
Church in Mount Prospect, Illinois. He had a sense of
destiny tinged with fear. Who would this Bruce Barnes
be? What would he look like? And would he be able to
detect a non-Christian at a glance?

Buck sat in the car, his head in his hands. He was too
analytical, he knew, to make a rash decision. Even his
leaving home years before to pursue an education and
become a journalist had been plotted for years. To his
family it came like a thunderbolt, but to young Cameron
Williams it was a logical next step, a part of his long-
range plan.

Where Buck sat now was not part of any plan. Nothing that had happened since that ill-fated flight to
Heathrow had fit into any predefined pattern for him.

He had always liked the serendipity of life, but he processed it through a grid of logic, attacked it from a perspective of order. The firestorm of Israel had jarred him, but even then he had been acting from a standpoint of order. He had a career, a position, a role. He had been in Israel on assignment, and though he hadn't expected to become a war correspondent overnight, he had been prepared by the way he had ordered his life.

But nothing had prepared him for the disappearances or for the violent deaths of his friends. While he should have been prepared for this promotion, that hadn't been part of his plan, either. Now his theory article was bringing him close to flames he had never known were burning in his soul. He felt alone, exposed, vulnerable, and yet this meeting with Bruce Barnes had been his idea. Sure, the airline pilot had suggested it, but Buck could have ignored him without remorse. This trip had not been about getting in a few extra hours with the beautiful Chloe, and the Chicago bureau could have waited. He was here, he knew, for this meeting. Buck felt a bone weariness as he headed for the church.

It was a pleasant surprise to find that Bruce Barnes was someone near Buck's own age. He seemed bright and earnest, having that same authority and passion Rayford Steele exhibited. It had been a long time since Buck had been in a church. This one seemed innocuous enough, fairly new and modern, neat and efficient. He and the young pastor met in a modest office.

"Your friends, the Steeles, told me you might call," Barnes said.

Buck was struck by his honesty. In the world in which Buck moved, he might have kept that information to himself, that edge. But he realized that the pastor had no interest in an edge. There was nothing to hide here. In essence, Buck was looking for information and Bruce was interested in providing it.

"I want to tell you right off," Bruce said, "that I am aware of your work and respect your talent. But to be frank, I no longer have time for the pleasantries and small talk that used to characterize my work. We live in perilous times. I have a message and an answer for people genuinely seeking. I tell everyone in advance that I have quit apologizing for what I'm going to say. If that's a ground rule you can live with, I have all the time you need."

"Well, sir," Buck said, nearly staggered by the emotion and humility he heard in his own voice, "I appreciate that. I don't know how long I'll need, because I'm not here on business. It might have made sense to get a pastor's view for my story, but people can guess what pastors think, especially based on the other people I'm quoting."

"Like Captain Steele."

Buck nodded. "I'm here for myself, and I have to tell you frankly, I don't know where I am on this. Not that long ago I would never have set foot in a place like this or dreamed anything intellectually worthwhile could come out of here. I know that wasn't exactly journalistically fair of me, but as long as you're being honest, I will be, too.

"I was impressed with Captain Steele. That's one smart guy, a good thinker, and he's into this. You seem like a bright person, and—I don't know. I'm listening, that's all I'll say."

Bruce began by telling Buck his life story, being raised in a Christian home, going to Bible college, marrying a Christian, becoming a pastor, the whole thing. He clarified that he knew the story of Christ and the way of forgiveness and a relationship with God. "I thought I had the best of both worlds. But the Scripture is clear that you can't serve two masters. You can't have it both ways. I discovered that truth in the severest way." And he told of losing his family and friends, everyone dear to him. He wept as he spoke. "The pain is every bit as great today as it was when it happened," he said.

Then Bruce outlined, as Rayford had done, the plan of salvation from beginning to end. Buck grew nervous, anxious. He wanted a break. He interrupted and asked if Bruce wanted to know a little more about him. "Sure," Bruce said.

Buck told of his own history, concentrating most on the Russia/Israel conflict and the roughly fourteen months since. "I can see," Bruce said at last, "that God is trying to get your attention."

"Well, he's got it," Buck said. "I just have to warn you, I'm not an easy sell. All this is interesting and sounds more plausible than ever, but it's just not me to jump into something."

"Nobody can force you or badger you into this, Mr. Williams, but I must also say again that we live in perilous times. We don't know how much pondering time we have."

"You sound like Chloe Steele."

"And she sounds like her father," Bruce said, smiling.

"And he, I guess, sounds like you. I can see why you all consider this so urgent, but like I say—"

"I understand," Bruce said. "If you have the time right now, let me take a different tack. I know you're a bright guy, so you might as well have all the information you need before you leave here."

Buck breathed easier. He had feared Bruce was about to pop the question, pushing him to pray the prayer both Rayford Steele and Chloe had talked about. He accepted that that would be part of it, that it would signal the transaction and start his relationship with God—someone he had never before really spoken to. But he wasn't ready. At least he didn't think he was. And he would not be pushed.

"I don't have to be back in New York until Monday morning," he said, "so I'll take as much time tonight as you'll give me."

"I don't mean to be morbid, Mr. Williams, but I have no family responsibilities anymore. I have a core group meeting tomorrow and church Sunday. You're welcome to attend. But I have enough energy to go to midnight if you do."

"I'm all yours."

Bruce spent the next several hours giving Buck a crash course in prophecy and the end times. Buck had heard much of the information about the Rapture and the two witnesses, and he had picked up snippets about the Antichrist. But when Bruce got to the parts about the great one-world religion that would spring up, the lying, so-called peacemaker who would bring bloodshed through war, the Antichrist who would divide the world into ten kingdoms, Buck's blood ran cold. He fell silent, no longer peppering Bruce with questions or comments. He scribbled notes as fast as he could.

Did he dare tell this unpretentious man that he believed Nicolae Carpathia could be the very man the Scriptures talked about? Could all this be coincidental? His fingers began to shake when Bruce told of the prediction of a seven-year pact between Antichrist and Israel, of the rebuilding of the temple, and even of Babylon becoming headquarters for a new world order.

Finally, as midnight came, Buck was overcome. He felt a terrible fear deep in his gut. Bruce Barnes could have had no knowledge whatever of the plans of Nicolae Carpathia before they had been announced on the news that afternoon. At one point he thought of accusing Bruce of having based everything he was saying on the CNN report he had heard and seen, but even if he had, here it was in black and white in the Bible.

"Did you see the news today?" Buck asked.

"Not today," Bruce said. "I've been in meetings since noon and grabbed a bite just before you got here."

Buck told him what had happened at the U.N. Bruce paled. "That's why we've been hearing all those clicking sounds on my answering machine," Bruce said. "I turned the ringer off on the phone, so the only way you can tell when a call comes in is by the clicking on the answering machine. People are calling to let me know. They do that a lot. We talk about what the Bible says may happen, and when it does, people check in."

"You think Carpathia is this Antichrist?"

"I don't see how I could come to any other conclusion."

"But I really believed in the guy."

"Why not? Most of us did. Self-effacing, interested in the welfare of the people, humble, not looking for power or leadership. But the Antichrist is a deceiver. And he has the power to control men's minds. He can make people see lies as truth."

Buck told Bruce of his invitation to the pre-press-conference meeting.

"You must not go," Bruce said.

"I can't *not* go," Buck said. "This is the opportunity of a lifetime."

"I'm sorry," Bruce said. "I have no authority over you, but let me plead with you, warn you, about what happens next. The Antichrist will solidify his power with a show of strength."

"He already has."

"Yes, but it appears that all these long-range agreements he has been conceded will take months or years to effect. Now he has to show some potency. What might he do to entrench himself so solidly that no one can oppose him?"

"I don't know."

"He undoubtedly has ulterior motives for wanting you there."

"I'm no good to him."

"You would be if he controlled you."

"But he doesn't."

"If he is the evil one the Bible speaks of, there is little he does not have the power to do. I warn you not to go there without protection."

"A bodyguard?"

"At least. But if Carpathia is the Antichrist, do you want to face him without God?"

Buck was taken aback. This conversation was bizarre enough without wondering if Bruce was using any means necessary to get him to convert. No doubt it had been a sincere and logical question, yet Buck felt pressured. "I see what you mean," he said slowly, "but I don't think I'm going to get hypnotized or anything."

"Mr. Williams, you have to do what you have to do, but I'm pleading with you. If you go into that meeting without God in your life, you will be in mortal and spiritual danger."

He told Buck about his conversation with the Steeles and how they had collectively come up with the idea of a Tribulation Force. "It's a band of serious-minded people who will boldly oppose the Antichrist. I just didn't expect that his identity would become so obvious so soon."

The Tribulation Force stirred something deep within Buck. It took him back to his earliest days as a writer, when he believed he had the power to change the world. He would stay up all hours of the night, plotting with his colleagues how they would have the courage and the audacity to stand up to oppression, to big government, to bigotry. He had lost that fire and verve over the years as he won accolades for his writing. He still wanted to do the right things, but he had lost the passion of the all-for-one and one-for-all philosophy as his talent and celebrity began to outstrip those same colleagues.

The idealist, the maverick in him, gravitated toward such ideas, but he caught himself before he talked himself into becoming a believer in Christ just because of an exciting little club he could join.

"Do you think I could sit in on your core group meeting tomorrow?" he asked.

"I'm afraid not," Bruce said. "I think you'd find it interesting and I personally believe it would help convince you, but it is limited to our leadership team. Truth is, I'll be going over with them tomorrow what you and I are talking about tonight, so it would be a rerun for you anyway."

"And church Sunday?"

"You're very welcome, but I must say, it's going to be the same theme I use every Sunday. You've heard it from Ray Steele and you've heard it from me. If hearing it one more time would help, then come on out and see how many seekers and finders there are. If it's anything like the last two Sundays, it will be standing room only."

Buck stood and stretched. He had kept Bruce long past midnight, and he apologized.

"No need," Bruce said. "This is what I do."

"Do you know where I can get a Bible?"

"I've got one you can have," Bruce said.

_____

The next day the core group enthusiastically and emotionally welcomed its newest member, Chloe Steele. They spent much of the day studying the news and trying to determine the likelihood of Nicolae Carpathia's being the Antichrist. No one could argue otherwise.

Bruce told the story of Buck Williams, without using his name or mentioning his connection with Rayford and Chloe. Chloe cried silently as the group prayed for his safety and for his soul.

TWENTY-FOUR

BUCK spent Saturday holed up in the otherwise empty Chicago bureau office, getting a head start on his article on the theory behind the disappearances. His mind continually swirled, forcing him to think about Carpathia and what he would say in that piece about how the man seemed to be a perfect parallel to biblical prophecy. Fortunately, he could wait on writing that until after the big day Monday.

Around lunchtime, Buck reached Steve Plank at the Plaza Hotel in New York. "I'll be there Monday morning," he said, "but I'm not inviting Hattie Durham."

"Why not? It's a small request, friend to friend."

"You to me?"

"Nick to you."

"So now it's Nick, is it? Well, he and I are not close enough for that familiarity, and I don't provide female companionship even to my friends."

"Not even for me?"

"If I knew you would treat her with respect, Steve, I'd set you up with Hattie."

"You're really not going to do this for Carpathia?"

"No. Am I uninvited?"

"I'm not going to tell him."

"How are you going to explain it when she doesn't show?"

"I'll ask her myself, Buck, you prude."

Buck didn't say he would warn Hattie not to go. He asked Steve if he could get one more exclusive with Carpathia before starting his cover story on him.

"I'll see what I can do, but you can't even do a small favor and you want another break?"

"He likes me, you said. You know I'm going to do the complete piece on the guy. He needs this."

"If you watched TV yesterday, you know he doesn't need anything. We need him."

"Do we? Have you run into any schools of thought that link him to end-times events in the Bible?"

Steve Plank did not respond.

"Steve?"

"I'm here."

"Well, have you? Anybody that thinks he might fill the bill for one of the villains of the book of Revelation?"

Steve said nothing.

"Hello, Steve."

"I'm still here."

"C'mon, old buddy. You're the press secretary. You know all. How's he going to respond if I hit him with that?"

Steve was still silent.

"Don't do this to me, Steve. I'm not saying that's where I am or that anybody who knows anything or who matters thinks that way. I'm doing the piece on what was behind the disappearances, and you know that takes me into all kinds of religious realms. Nobody any-where has drawn any parallels here?"

This time when Steve said nothing, Buck merely looked at his watch, determined to wait him out. About twenty seconds after a loud silence, Steve spoke softly. "Buck, I have a two-word answer for you. Are you ready?"

"I'm ready."

"Staten Island."

"Are you tellin' me that—?"

"Don't say the name, Buck! You never know who's listening."

"So you're threatening me with—"

"I'm not threatening. I'm warning. Let me say I'm cau-tioning you."

"And let me remind you, Steve, that I don't warn well. You remember that, don't you, from ages ago when we worked together and you thought I was the toughest bird dog you'd ever sent on a story?"

"Just don't go sniffing the wrong brier patch, Buck."

"Let me ask you this then, Steve."

"Careful, please."

"You want to talk to me on another line?"

"No, Buck, I just want you to be careful what you say so I can be, too."

Buck began scribbling furiously on a yellow pad. "Fair enough," he said, writing, *Carpathia or Stonagal resp. for Eric Miller?* "What I want to know is this: If you think I should stay off the ferry, is it because of the guy behind the wheel, or because of the guy who supplies his fuel?"

"The latter," Steve said without hesitation.

Buck circled *Stonagal.* "Then you don't think the guy behind the wheel is even aware of what the fuel distributor does in his behalf."

"Correct."

"So if someone got too close to the pilot, the pilot might be protected and not even know it."

"Correct."

"But if he found out about it?"

"He'd deal with it."

"That's what I expect to see soon."

"I can't comment on that."

"Can you tell me who you really work for?"

"I work for who it appears to you I work for."

What in the world did that mean? Carpathia or Stonagal? How could he get Steve to say on a phone from within the Plaza that might be bugged?

"You work for the Romanian businessman?"

"Of course."

Buck nearly kicked himself. That could be either Carpathia or Stonagal. "You do?" he said, hoping for more.

"My boss moves mountains, doesn't he?" Steve said.

"He sure does," Buck said, circling *Carpathia* this time. "You must be pleased with everything going on these days."

"I am."

Buck scribbled, *Carpathia. End times. Antichrist?*

"And you're telling me straight up that the other issue I raised is dangerous but also hogwash."

"Total roll in the muck."

"And I shouldn't even broach the subject with him, in spite of the fact that I'm a writer who covers all the bases and asks the tough questions?"

"If I thought you would consider mentioning it, I could not encourage the interview or the story."

"Boy, it didn't take long for you to become a company man."

After the core-group meeting, Rayford Steele talked privately with Bruce Barnes and was updated on the meeting with Buck. "I can't discuss the private matters," Bruce said, "but only one thing stands in the way of my being convinced that this Carpathia guy is the Antichrist. I can't make it compute geographically. Almost every end-times writer I respect believes the Antichrist will come out of Western Europe, maybe Greece or Italy or Turkey."

Rayford didn't know what to make of that. "You notice Carpathia doesn't look Romanian. Aren't they mostly dark?"

"Yeah. Let me call Mr. Williams. He gave me a number. I wonder how much more he knows about Carpathia." Bruce dialed and put Buck on the speakerphone. "Ray Steele is with me."

"Hey, Captain," Buck said.

"We're just doing some studying here," Bruce said, "and we've hit a snag." He told Buck what they had found and asked for more information.

"Well, he comes from a town, one of the larger university towns, called Cluj, and—"

"Oh, he does? I guess I thought he was from a mountainous region, you know, because of his name."

"His name?" Buck repeated, doodling it on his legal pad.

"You know, being named after the Carpathian Mountains and all. Or does that name mean something else over there?"

Buck sat up straight and it hit him! Steve had been trying to tell him he worked for Stonagal and *not* Carpathia. And of course all the new U.N. delegates would feel beholden to Stonagal because he had introduced them to Carpathia. Maybe *Stonagal* was the Antichrist! Where had *his* lineage begun?

"Well," Buck said, trying to concentrate, "maybe he was named after the mountains, but he was born in Cluj and his ancestry, way back, is Roman. That accounts for the blonde hair and blue eyes."

Bruce thanked him and asked if he would see Buck in church the next day. Rayford thought Buck sounded distracted and noncommittal. "I haven't ruled it out," Buck said.

Yes, Buck thought, hanging up. *I'll be there all right.* He wanted every last bit of input before he went to New

York to write a story that could cost him his career and maybe his life. He didn't know the truth, but he had never backed off from looking for it, and he wouldn't begin now. He phoned Hattie Durham.

"Hattie," he said, "you're going to get a call inviting you to New York."

"I already did."

"They wanted me to ask you, but I told them to do it themselves."

"They did."

"They want you to see Carpathia again, provide him some companionship next week if you're free."

"I know and I am and I will."

"I'm advising you not to do it."

She laughed. "Right, I'm going to turn down a date with the most powerful man in the world? I don't think so."

"That would be my advice."

"Whatever for?"

"Because you don't strike me as that kind of girl."

"First, I'm not a girl. I'm almost as old as you are, and I don't need a parent or legal guardian."

"I'm talking as a friend."

"You're not my friend, Buck. It was obvious you didn't even like me. I tried to shove you off onto Rayford Steele's little girl, and I'm not sure you even had the brains to pick up on that."

"Hattie, maybe I don't know you. But you don't seem the type who would allow herself to be taken advantage of by a stranger."

"You're pretty much a stranger, and you're trying to tell me what to do."

"Well, *are* you that kind of a person? By not passing along the invitation, was I protecting you from something you might enjoy?"

"You'd better believe it."

"I can't talk you out of it?"

"You can't even try," she said, and she hung up.

Buck shook his head and leaned back in his chair, holding the yellow pad in front of him. *My boss moves mountains, Steve had said. Carpathia is a mountain. Stonagal is the mover and shaker behind him. Steve thinks he's really wired in deep. He's not only press secretary to the man Hattie Durham correctly called the most powerful man on earth, but Steve is also actually in league with the man behind the man.*

Buck wondered what Rayford or Chloe would do if they knew Hattie had been invited to New York to be Carpathia's companion for a few days. In the end, he decided it was none of his, or their, business.

Rayford and Chloe watched for Buck until the last minute the next morning, but they could no longer save a seat for him when the sanctuary and the balcony filled. When Bruce began his message, Chloe nudged her father and pointed out the window, down onto the walk before the front door. There, in a small crowd listening to an external speaker, was Buck. Rayford raised a celebratory fist and whispered to Chloe, "Wonder what you're going to pray for this morning?"

Bruce played the former pastor's videotape, told his own story again, talked briefly about prophecy, invited people to receive Christ, and then opened the microphone for personal accounts. As had happened the previous two weeks, people streamed forward and stood in line until well after one in the afternoon, eager to tell how they had now, finally, trusted Christ.

Chloe told her father she had wanted to be first, as he had been, but by the time she made her way down from the last row of the balcony, she was one of the last. She told her story, including the sign she believed God had given her in the form of a friend who sat beside her on the flight home. Rayford knew she could not see Buck over the crowd, and Rayford couldn't either.

When the meeting was over, Rayford and Chloe went outside to find Buck, but he was gone. They went for lunch with Bruce, and when they got home, Chloe found a note from Buck on the front door.

It isn't that I didn't want to say good-bye. But I don't. I'll be back for bureau business and maybe just to see you, if you'll allow it. I've got a lot to think about right now, as you know, and frankly, I don't want my attraction to you to get in the way of that thinking. And it would. You are a lovely person, Chloe, and I was moved to tears by your story. You had told me before, but to hear it in that place and in that circumstance this morning was beautiful.

Would you do something I have never asked anyone to do for me ever before? Would you pray for me? I will call you or see you soon. I promise. Buck.

Buck felt more alone than ever on the flight home. He was in coach on a full plane, but he knew no one. He read several sections from the Bible Bruce had given him and had marked for him, prompting the woman next to him to ask questions. He answered in such a way that she could tell he was not in the mood for conversation. He didn't want to be rude, but neither did he want to mislead anyone with his limited knowledge.

Sleep was no easier for him that night, though he refused to allow himself to pace. He was going into a meeting in the morning that he had been warned to stay away from. Bruce Barnes had sounded convinced that if Nicolae Carpathia were the Antichrist, Buck ran the danger of being mentally overcome, brainwashed, hypnotized, or worse.

As he wearily showered and dressed in the morning, Buck concluded he had come a long way from thinking that the religious angle was on the fringe. He had gone from bemused puzzlement at people thinking their loved ones had flown to heaven to believing that much of what was happening had been foretold in the Bible. He was no longer wondering or doubting, he told himself. There was no other explanation for the two witnesses in Jerusalem. Nor for the disappearances.

And the furthest stretch of all, this business of an Antichrist who deceives so many . . . well, in Buck's mind it was no longer an issue of whether it was literal or true. He was long past that. He had already progressed to trying to decide who the Antichrist was: Carpathia or Stonagal. Buck still leaned toward Stonagal.

He slung his bag over his shoulder, tempted to take the gun from his bedside table but knowing he would never get it through the metal detectors. Anyway, he sensed, that was not the kind of protection he needed. What he needed was safekeeping for his mind and for his spirit.

All the way to the United Nations he agonized. *Do I pray?* he asked himself. *Do I "pray the prayer" as so many of those people said yesterday morning? Would I be doing it just to protect myself from the voodoo or the heebie-jeebies?* He decided that becoming a believer could not be for the purpose of having a good luck charm. That would cheapen it. Surely God didn't work that way. And if Bruce Barnes could be believed, there was no more protection for believers now, during this period, than there was for anyone else. Huge numbers of people were going to die in the next seven years, Christian or not. The question was, *then* where would they be?

There was only one reason to make the transaction, he decided—if he truly believed he could be forgiven and become one of God's people. God had become more than a force of nature or even a miracle worker to Buck, as God had been in the skies of Israel that night. It only made sense that if God made people, he would want to communicate with them, to connect with them.

Buck entered the U.N. through hordes of reporters already setting up for the press conference. Limousines disgorged VIPs and crowds waited behind police barriers. Buck saw Stanton Bailey in a crowd near the door. "What are you doing here?" Buck said, realizing that in five years at *Global* he had never seen Bailey outside the building.

"Just taking advantage of my position so I can be at this press conference. Proud you're going to be in the preliminary meeting. Be sure to remember everything. Thanks for transmitting your first draft of the theory piece. I know you've got a lot to do yet, but it's a terrific start. Gonna be a winner."

"Thanks," Buck said, and Bailey gave him a thumbs-up. Buck realized that if that had happened a month before, he would have had to stifle a laugh at the corny old guy and would have told his colleagues what an idiot he worked for. Now he was strangely grateful for the encouragement. Bailey could have no hint what Buck was going through.

Chloe Steele told her father of her plans to finally look into local college classes that Monday. "And I was thinking," she said, "about trying to get together with Hattie for lunch."

"I thought you didn't care for her," Rayford said.

"I don't, but that's no excuse. She doesn't even know what's happened to me. She's not answering her phone. Any idea what her schedule is?"

"No, but I have to check my own. I'll see if she's flying today."

Rayford was told that not only was Hattie not scheduled that day but also that she had requested a thirty-day leave of absence. "That's odd," he told Chloe. "Maybe she's got family troubles out West."

"Maybe she's just taking some time off," Chloe said. "I'll call her later when I'm out. What are you doing today?"

"I promised Bruce I'd come over and watch that Carpathia press conference later this morning."

"What time's that?"

"Ten our time, I think."

"Well, if Hattie's not around for lunch, maybe I'll come by there."

"Call us either way, hon, and we'll wait for you."

Buck's credentials were waiting for him at an information desk in the U.N. lobby. He was directed up to a private conference room off the suite of offices into which Nicolae Carpathia had already moved. Buck was at least twenty minutes early, but as he emerged from the elevator he felt alone in a crowd. He saw no one he recognized as he began the long walk down a corridor of glass and steel leading to the room where he was to join Steve, the ten designated ambassadors representing the permanent members of the new Security Council, several aides and advisers to the new secretary-general (including Rosenzweig, Stonagal, and various other members of his international brotherhood of financial wizards), and of course, Carpathia himself.

Buck had always been energetic and confident. Others had noticed his purposeful stride on assignment. Now his gait was slow and unsure, and with every step his dread increased. The lights seemed to grow dimmer, the walls close in. His pulse increased and he had a sense of foreboding.

The gripping fear reminded him of Israel, when he believed he was going to die. Was he about to die? He couldn't imagine physical danger, yet clearly people who got in Carpathia's way, or in the way of Stonagal's plans for Carpathia, were now dead. Would he be just another in a line that stretched from Carpathia's business rival in Romania years before, through Dirk Burton and Alan Tompkins, to Eric Miller?

No, what he feared, he knew, was not mortal danger. At least not now, not here. The closer he got to the conference room, the more he was repelled by a sense of evil, as if personified in that place. Almost without thinking, Buck found himself silently praying, *God, be with me. Protect me.*

He felt no sense of relief. If anything, his thoughts of God made his recognition of evil more intense. He stopped ten feet from the open door, and though he heard laughter and banter, he was nearly paralyzed by the atmosphere of blackness. He wanted to be anywhere but there, and yet he knew he could not retreat. This was the room in which the new leaders of the world congregated, and any sane person would have given anything to be there.

Buck realized that what he really wanted was to have been there. He wished it were over, that he had seen this welcoming of new people, this brief speech of commitment or whatever it was to be, and was already writing about it.

He tried to force himself toward the door, his thoughts deafening. Again he cried out to God, and he felt a coward—just like everyone else, praying in the foxhole. He had ignored God for most of his life, and now when he felt the darkest anguish of his soul, he was figuratively on his knees.

Yet he did not belong to God. Not yet. He knew that. God had answered Chloe's prayer for a sign before she had actually made the spiritual transaction. Why couldn't he have answered Buck's plea for calm and peace?

Buck could not move until Steve Plank noticed him. "Buck! We're almost ready to begin. Come on in."

But Buck felt terrible, panicky. "Steve, I need to run to the washroom. Do I have a minute?"

Steve glanced at his watch. "You've got five," he said. "And when you get back, you'll be right over there."

Steve pointed to a chair at one corner of a square block of tables. The journalist in Buck liked it. The perfect vantage point. His eyes darted to the name-

plates in front of each spot. He would face the main
table, where Carpathia had placed himself directly next
to Stonagal . . . or had Stonagal been in charge of the
seating? Next to Carpathia on the other side was a
hastily hand-lettered nameplate with "Personal Assistant" written on it. "Is that you?" Buck said.

"Nope." Steve pointed at the corner opposite Buck's
chair.

"Is Todd-Cothran here?" Buck said.

"Of course. Right there in the light gray."

The Brit looked insignificant enough. But just beyond
him were both Stonagal—in charcoal—and Carpathia,
looking perfect in a black suit, white shirt, electric-blue
tie, and a gold stickpin. Buck shuddered at the sight of
him, but Carpathia flashed a smile and waved him over.
Buck signaled that he would be a minute. "Now you've
got only four minutes," Steve said. "Get going."

Buck put his bag in a corner next to a heavyset,
white-haired security guard, waved at his old friend
Chaim Rosenzweig, and jogged to the washroom. He
placed a janitor's bucket outside and locked the door.
Buck backed up against the door, thrust his hands deep
into his pockets, and dropped his chin to his chest,
remembering Bruce's advice that he could talk to God
the same way he talked to a friend. "God," he said,
"I need you, and not just for this meeting."

And as he prayed he believed. This was no experiment,
no halfhearted attempt. He wasn't just hoping or trying
something out. Buck knew he was talking to God himself. He admitted he needed God, that he knew he was as

lost and as sinful as anyone. He didn't specifically pray the prayer he had heard others talk about, but when he finished he had covered the same territory and the deal was done. Buck was not the type to go into anything lightly. As well as he knew anything, he knew there would be no turning back.

Buck headed to the conference room, more quickly this time but strangely with no more confidence. He hadn't prayed for courage or peace this time. This prayer had been for his own soul. He hadn't known what he would feel, but he didn't expect this continued sense of dread.

He didn't hesitate, however. When he walked in, everyone was in place—Carpathia, Stonagal, Todd-Cothran, Rosenzweig, Steve, and the financial powers and ambassadors. And one person Buck never expected—Hattie Durham. He stared, dumbfounded, as she took her place as Nicolae Carpathia's personal assistant. She winked at him, but he did not acknowledge her. He hurried to his bag, nodded his thanks to the armed guard, and took only a notebook to his seat.

While no special feeling had come with Buck's decision, he had a heightened sensitivity that something was happening here. There wasn't a doubt in his mind that the Antichrist of the Bible was in this room. And despite all he knew about Stonagal and what the man had engineered in England and despite the ill feeling that came over him as he observed his smugness, Buck sensed the truest, deepest, darkest spirit of evil as he watched Carpathia take his place. Nicolae waited till everyone was seated, then rose with pseudodignity.

"Gentlemen . . . and lady," he began, "this is an important moment. In a few minutes we will greet the press and introduce those of you who shall be entrusted to lead the new world order into a golden era. The global village has become united, and we face the greatest task and the greatest opportunity ever bestowed upon humankind."

TWENTY-FIVE

NICOLAE Carpathia stepped out from his place at the table and went to each person individually. He greeted each by name, asking him to stand, shaking his hand, and kissing him on both cheeks. He skipped Hattie and started with the new British ambassador.

"Mr. Todd-Cothran," he said, "you shall be introduced as the ambassador of the Great States of Britain, which now include much of Western and Eastern Europe. I welcome you to the team and confer upon you all the rights and privileges that go with your new station. May you display to me and to those in your charge the consistency and wisdom that have brought you to this position."

"Thank you, sir," Todd-Cothran said, and sat down as Carpathia moved on. Todd-Cothran appeared shocked, as did several others, when Nicolae repeated

the same sentiment, including precisely the same title—
ambassador of the Great States of Britain—to the British
financier next to him. Todd-Cothran smiled tolerantly.
Obviously, Carpathia had merely misspoken and
should have referred to the man as one of his financial
advisers. Yet Buck had never seen Carpathia make such
a slip.

All around the four-sided table configuration
Carpathia went, one by one, saying exactly the same
words to every ambassador, but customizing the litany to
include the appropriate name and title. The recitation
changed only slightly for his personal aides and advisers.

When Carpathia got to Buck he seemed to hesitate.
Buck was slow on the draw, as if he wasn't sure he was
to be included in this. Carpathia's warm smile welcomed him to stand. Buck was slightly off balance, trying to hold pen and notebook while shaking hands with
the dramatic Carpathia. Nicolae's grip was firm and
strong, and he maintained it throughout his recitation.
He looked directly into Buck's eyes and spoke with
quiet authority.

"Mr. Williams," he said, "I welcome you to the team
and confer upon you all the rights and privileges that go
with your station. . . ."

What was this? It was not what Buck expected, but it
was so affirming, so flattering. He was not part of any
team, and no rights or privileges should be conferred
upon him! He shook his head slightly to signal that
Carpathia was again confused, that he had apparently
mistaken Buck for someone else. But Nicolae nodded

slightly and smiled all the more, looking more deeply into Buck's eyes. He knew what he was doing.

"May you display to me and to those in your charge the consistency and wisdom that have brought you to this position."

Buck wanted to stand taller, to thank his mentor, his leader, the bestower of this honor. But no! It wasn't right! He didn't work for Carpathia. He was an independent journalist, not a supporter, not a follower, and certainly not an employee. His spirit resisted the temptation to say, "Thank you, sir," as everyone else had. He sensed and read the evil of the man and it was all he could to do keep from pointing at him and calling him the Antichrist. He could almost hear himself screaming it at Carpathia.

Nicolae still stared, still smiled, still gripped his hand. After an awkward silence, Buck heard chuckles, and Carpathia said, "You are most welcome, my slightly overcome and tongue-tied friend." The others laughed and applauded as Carpathia kissed him, but Buck did not smile. Neither did he thank the secretary-general. Bile rose in his throat.

As Carpathia moved on, Buck realized what he had endured. Had he not belonged to God he would have been swept into the web of this man of deceit. He could see it in the others' faces. They were honored beyond measure to be elevated to this tier of power and confidence, even Chaim Rosenzweig. Hattie seemed to melt in Carpathia's presence.

Bruce Barnes had pleaded with Buck not to attend this

meeting, and now Buck knew why. Had he come in unprepared, had he not been prayed for by Bruce and Chloe and probably Captain Steele, who knows whether he would have made his decision and his commitment to Christ in time to have the power to resist the lure of acceptance and power?

Carpathia went through the ceremony with Steve, who gushed with pride. Nicolae eventually covered everyone in the room except the security guard, Hattie, and Jonathan Stonagal. He returned to his place and turned first to Hattie.

"Ms. Durham," he said, taking both her hands in his, "you shall be introduced as my personal assistant, having turned your back on a stellar career in the aviation industry. I welcome you to the team and confer upon you all the rights and privileges that go with your new station. May you display to me and to those in your charge the consistency and wisdom that have brought you to this position."

Buck tried to catch Hattie's eye and shake his head, but she was zeroed in on her new boss. Was this Buck's fault? He had introduced her to Carpathia in the first place. Was she still reachable? Would he have access? He glanced around the room. Everyone stared with beatific smiles as Hattie breathed her heartfelt thanks and sat down again.

Carpathia dramatically turned to Jonathan Stonagal. The latter smiled a knowing smile and stood regally. "Where do I begin, Jonathan, my friend?" Carpathia said. Stonagal dropped his head gratefully and others murmured their agreement that this indeed was the man among men in the room. Carpathia took Stonagal's hand and began formally, "Mr. Stonagal, you have meant more to me than anyone on earth." Stonagal looked up and smiled, locking eyes with Carpathia.

"I welcome you to the team," Carpathia said, "and confer upon you all the rights and privileges that go with your new station."

Stonagal flinched, clearly not interested in being considered a part of the team, to be welcomed by the very man he had maneuvered into the presidency of Romania and now the secretary-generalship of the United Nations. His smile froze, then disappeared as Carpathia continued, "May you display to me and to those in your charge the consistency and wisdom that have brought you to this position."

Rather than thanking Carpathia, Stonagal wrenched his hand away and glared at the younger man. Carpathia continued to gaze directly at him and spoke in quieter, warmer tones, "Mr. Stonagal, you may be seated."

"I will not!" Stonagal said.

"Sir, I have been having a bit of sport at your expense because I knew you would understand."

Stonagal reddened, clearly chagrined that he had over-reacted. "I beg your pardon, Nicolae," Stonagal said, forcing a smile but obviously insulted at having been pushed into this shocking display.

"Please, my friend," Carpathia said. "Please be seated. Gentlemen, and lady, we have only a few minutes before we meet the media."

Buck's eyes were still on Stonagal, who was seething.

"I would like to present to you all just a bit of an object lesson in leadership, followership, and may I say, chain of command. Mr. Scott M. Otterness, would you approach me, please?" The guard in the corner jerked in surprise and hurried to Carpathia. "One of my leadership techniques is my power of observation, combined with a prodigious memory," Carpathia said.

Buck couldn't take his eyes off Stonagal, who appeared to be considering revenge for having been embarrassed. He seemed ready to stand at any second and put Carpathia in his place.

"Mr. Otterness here was surprised because we had not been introduced, had we, sir?"

"No, sir, Mr. Carpathia, sir, we had not."

"And yet I knew your name."

The aging guard smiled and nodded.

"I can also tell you the make and model and caliber of the weapon you carry on your hip. I will not look as you remove it and display it to this group."

Buck watched in horror as Mr. Otterness unsnapped the leather strap holding the huge gun in his holster. He fumbled for it and held it with two hands so everyone but Carpathia, who had averted his eyes, could see it. Stonagal, still red-faced, appeared to be hyperventilating.

"I observed, sir, that you were issued a thirty-eight caliber police special with a four-inch barrel, loaded with high-velocity hollow-point shells."

"You are correct," Otterness said gleefully.

"May I hold it, please?"

"Certainly, sir."

"Thank you. You may return to your post, guarding Mr. Williams's bag, which contains a tape recorder, a cellular phone, and a computer. Am I correct, Cameron?"

Buck stared at him, refusing to answer. He heard Stonagal grumble about "some sort of a parlor trick." Carpathia continued to look at Buck. Neither spoke. "What is this?" Stonagal whispered. "You're acting like a child."

"I would like to tell you all what you are about to see," Carpathia said, and Buck felt anew the wash of evil in the room. He wanted more than anything to rub the gooseflesh from his arms and run for his life. But he was frozen where he sat. The others seemed transfixed but not troubled, as he and Stonagal were.

"I am going to ask Mr. Stonagal to rise once more," Carpathia said, the large ugly weapon safely at his side. "Jonathan, if you please."

Stonagal sat staring at him. Carpathia smiled. "Jonathan, you know you can trust me. I love you for all you have meant to me, and I humbly ask you to assist me in this demonstration. I see part of my role as a teacher. You have said that yourself, and you have been my teacher for years."

Stonagal stood, wary and rigid.

"And now I am going to ask that we switch places." Stonagal swore. "What is this?" he demanded.

"It will become clear quickly, and I will not need your help anymore."

To the others, Buck knew, it sounded as if Carpathia

meant he would no longer need Stonagal's help for whatever this demonstration was. Just as he had sent the guard back to the corner unarmed, they had to assume he would thank Stonagal and let him return to his seat.

Stonagal, with a disgusted frown, stepped out and traded places with Carpathia. That put Carpathia to Stonagal's right. On Stonagal's left sat Hattie, and beyond her, Mr. Todd-Cothran.

"And now I am going to ask you to kneel, Jonathan," Carpathia said, his smile and his light tone having disappeared. To Buck it seemed as if everyone in the room sucked in a breath and held it.

"That I will not do," Stonagal said.

"Yes, you will," Carpathia said quietly. "Do it now."

"No, sir, I will not," Stonagal said. "Have you lost your mind? I will not be humiliated. If you think you have risen to a position over me, you are mistaken."

Carpathia raised the .38, cocked it, and stuck the barrel into Stonagal's right ear. The older man at first jerked away, but Carpathia said, "Move again and you are dead."

Several others stood, including Rosenzweig, who cried plaintively, "Nicolae!"

"Everyone be seated, please," Carpathia said, calm again. "Jonathan, on your knees."

Painfully, the old man crouched, using Hattie's chair for support. He did not face Carpathia or look at him. The gun was still in his ear. Hattie sat pale and frozen.

"My dear," Carpathia said, leaning toward her over Stonagal's head, "you will want to slide your chair back about three feet so as not to soil your outfit."

She did not move.

Stonagal began to whimper. "Nicolae, why are you doing this? I am your friend! I am no threat!"

"Begging does not become you, Jonathan. Please be quiet. Hattie," he continued, looking directly into her eyes now, "stand and move your chair back and be seated. Hair, skin, skull tissue, and brain matter will mostly be absorbed by Mr. Todd-Cothran and the others next to him. I do not want anything to get on you."

Hattie moved her chair back, her fingers trembling.

Stonagal whined, "No, Nicolae, no!"

Carpathia was in no hurry. "I am going to kill Mr. Stonagal with a painless hollow-point round to the brain which he will neither hear nor feel. The rest of us will experience some ringing in our ears. This will be instructive for you all. You will understand cognitively that I am in charge, that I fear no man, and that no one can oppose me."

Mr. Otterness reached for his forehead, as if dizzy, and slumped to one knee. Buck considered a suicidal dive across the table for the gun, but he knew that others might die for his effort. He looked to Steve, who sat motionless as the others. Mr. Todd-Cothran shut his eyes and grimaced, as if expecting the report any second.

"When Mr. Stonagal is dead, I will tell you what you will remember. And lest anyone feel I have not been fair, let me not neglect to add that more than gore will wind up on Mr. Todd-Cothran's suit. A high-velocity bullet at this range will also kill him, which, as you know, Mr.

Williams, is something I promised you I would deal with in due time."

Todd-Cothran opened his eyes at that news, and Buck heard himself shouting, "No!" as Carpathia pulled the trigger. The blast rattled the windows and even the door. Stonagal's head crashed into the toppling Todd-Cothran, and both were plainly dead before their entwined bodies reached the floor.

Several chairs rolled back from the table as their occupants covered their heads in fear. Buck stared, mouth open, as Carpathia calmly placed the gun in Stonagal's limp right hand and twisted his finger around the trigger.

Hattie shivered in her seat and appeared to try to emit a scream that would not come. Carpathia took the floor again.

"What we have just witnessed here," he said kindly, as if speaking to children, "was a horrible, tragic end to two otherwise extravagantly productive lives. These men were two I respected and admired more than any others in the world. What compelled Mr. Stonagal to rush the guard, disarm him, take his own life and that of his British colleague, I do not know and may never fully understand."

Buck fought within himself to keep his sanity, to maintain a clear mind, to—as his boss had told him on the way in—"remember everything."

Carpathia continued, his eyes moist. "All I can tell you is that Jonathan Stonagal told me as recently as at breakfast this morning that he felt personally responsible for two recent violent deaths in England and that he could no longer live with the guilt. Honestly, I thought he was going to turn himself in to international authorities later today. And if he had not, I would have had to. How he conspired with Mr. Todd-Cothran, which led to the deaths in England, I do not know. But if he was responsible, then in a sad way, perhaps justice was meted out here today.

"We are all horrified and traumatized by having witnessed this. Who would not be? My first act as secretary-general will be to close the U.N. for the remainder of the day and to pronounce my regrettable benedictory obituary on the lives of two old friends. I trust you will all be able to deal with this unfortunate occurrence and that it will not forever hamper your ability to serve in your strategic roles.

"Thank you, gentlemen. While Ms. Durham phones security, I will be polling you for your version of what happened here."

Hattie ran to the phone and could barely make herself understood in her hysteria. "Come quick! There's been a suicide and two men are dead! It was awful! Hurry!"

"Mr. Plank?" Carpathia said.

"That was unbelievable," Steve said, and Buck knew he was dead serious. "When Mr. Stonagal grabbed the gun, I thought he was going to kill us all!"

Carpathia called on the United States ambassador.

"Why, I've known Jonathan for years," he said. "Who would have thought he could do something like this?"

"I'm just glad you're all right, Mr. Secretary-General," Chaim Rosenzweig said.

"Well, I am not all right," Carpathia said. "And I will not be all right for a long time. These were my friends."

And that's how it went, all around the room. Buck's body felt like lead, knowing Carpathia would eventually get to him and that he was the only one in the room not under Nicolae's hypnotic power. But what if Buck said so? Would he be killed next? Of course he would! He had to be. Could he lie? Should he?

He prayed desperately as Carpathia moved from man to man, making certain they had all seen what he wanted them to see and that they were sincerely convinced of it.

Silence, God seemed to impress upon Buck's heart. *Not a word!*

Buck was so grateful to feel the presence of God in the midst of this evil and mayhem that he was moved to tears. When Carpathia got to him Buck's cheeks were wet and he could not speak. He shook his head and held up a hand. "Awful, was it not, Cameron? The suicide that took Mr. Todd-Cothran with it?"

Buck could not speak and wouldn't have if he could. "You cared for and respected them both, Cameron, because you were unaware that they tried to have you killed in London." And Carpathia moved on to the guard.

"Why could you not keep him from taking your gun, Scott?"

The old man had risen. "It happened so fast! I knew who he was, an important rich man, and when he hurried over to me I didn't know what he wanted. He ripped that gun right out of my holster, and before I could react he had shot himself."

"Yes, yes," Carpathia said as security rushed into the room. Everyone talked at once as Carpathia retreated to a corner, sobbing over the loss of his friends.

A plainclothesman asked questions. Buck headed him off. "You have enough eyewitnesses here. Let me leave you my card and you can call if you need me, hm?" The cop traded cards with him and Buck was permitted to leave.

Buck grabbed his bag and sprinted for a cab, rushing back to the office. He shut and locked his office door and began furiously banging out every detail of the story. He had produced several pages when he received a call from Stanton Bailey. The old man could hardly catch his breath between his demanding questions, not allowing Buck to answer.

"Where have you been? Why weren't you at the press conference? Were you in there when Stonagal offed himself and took the Brit with him? You should have been here. There's prestige for us having you in there. How are you going to convince anybody you were in there when you didn't show up for the press conference? Cameron, what's the deal?"

"I hurried back here to get the story into the system."

"Don't you have an exclusive with Carpathia now?"

Buck had forgotten that, and Plank hadn't reconfirmed it. What was he supposed to do about that? He prayed but sensed no leading. How he needed to talk to Bruce or Chloe or even Captain Steele! "I'll call Steve and see," he said.

Buck knew he couldn't wait long to make the call, but

he was desperate to know what to do. Should he allow himself to be in a room alone with Carpathia? And if he did, should he pretend to be under his mind control as everyone else seemed to be? If he hadn't seen this for himself, he wouldn't have believed it. Would he always be able to resist the influence with God's help? He didn't know.

He dialed Steve's pager and the call was returned a couple of minutes later. "Really busy here, Buck. What's up?"

"I was wondering if I've still got that exclusive with Carpathia."

"You're kidding, right? You heard what happened here and you want an exclusive?"

"Heard? I was there, Steve."

"Well, if you were here, then you probably know what happened before the press conference."

"Steve! I saw it with my own eyes."

"You're not following me, Buck. I'm saying if you were here for the press conference, you heard about the Stonagal suicide in the preliminary meeting, the one you were supposed to come to."

Buck didn't know what to say. "You saw me there, Steve."

"I didn't even see you at the press conference."

"I wasn't *at* the press conference, Steve, but I was in the room when Stonagal and Todd-Cothran died."

"I don't have time for this, Buck. It's not funny. You were supposed to be there, you weren't there. I resent it, Carpathia is offended, and no, no exclusive."

"I have credentials! I got them downstairs!"

"Then why didn't you use them?"

"I did!"

Steve hung up on him. Marge buzzed and said the boss was on the line again. "What's the deal with you not even going to that meeting?" Bailey said.

"I was there! You saw me go in!"

"Yeah, I saw you. You were that close. What did you do, find something more important to do? You got some fast talking to do, Cameron!"

"I'm telling you I was there! I'll show you my credentials."

"I just checked the credential list, and you're not on it."

"Of course I'm on it. I'll show 'em to you."

"Your name's there, I'm saying, but it's not checked off."

"Mr. Bailey, I'm looking at my credentials right now. They're in my hand."

"Your credentials don't mean dirt if you didn't use 'em, Cameron. Now where were you?"

"Read my story," Buck said. "You'll know exactly where I was."

"I just talked to three, four people who *were* there, including a U.N. guard and Carpathia's personal assistant, not to mention Plank. None of them saw you; you weren't there."

"A cop saw me! We traded cards!"

"I'm coming back to the office, Williams. If you're not there when I get there, you're fired."

"I'll be here."

Buck dug out the cop's card and called the number. "Precinct station," a voice said.

Buck read off the card, "Detective Sergeant Billy Cenni, please."

"What's the name again?"

"Cenni, or maybe it's a hard *C*? Kenny?"

"Don't recognize it. You got the right precinct?"

Buck repeated the number from the card.

"That's our number, but that ain't our guy."

"How would I locate him?"

"I'm busy here, pal. Call midtown."

"It's important. Do you have a department directory?"

"Listen, we got thousands of cops."

"Just look up C-E-N-N-I for me, will ya?"

"Just a minute." Soon he was back on. "Nothing, OK?"

"Could he be new?"

"He could be your sister for all I know."

"Where do I call?"

He gave Buck the number for police headquarters. Buck ran through the whole conversation again, but this time he had reached a pleasant young woman. "Let me check one more thing for you," she said. "I'll get personnel on the line because they won't tell you anything unless you're a uniformed officer anyway."

He listened as she spelled the name for personnel. "Uh-huh, uh-huh," she said. "Thank you. I'll tell him." And she came back to Buck. "Sir? Personnel says there is nobody in the New York Police Department named

Cenni, and there never has been. If somebody's got a phony police business card dolled up, they'd like to see it."

All Buck could do now was try to convince Stanton Bailey.

Rayford Steele, Chloe, and Bruce Barnes watched the U.N. press conference, straining to see Buck. "Where is he?" Chloe said. "He has to be there somewhere. Everybody else from that meeting is there. Who's the girl?"

Rayford stood when he saw her and silently pointed at the screen. "Dad!" Chloe said. "You're not thinking what I'm thinking?"

"It sure looks like her," Rayford said.

"Shh," Bruce said, "he's introducing everybody."

"And my new personal assistant, having given up a career in the aviation industry . . ."

Rayford flopped into a chair. "I hope Buck wasn't behind that."

"Me, too," Bruce said. "That would mean he could have been sucked in, too."

The news of the Stonagal suicide and Todd-Cothran's accidental death stunned them. "Maybe Buck took my advice and didn't go," Bruce said. "I sure hope so."

"That doesn't sound like him," Chloe said.

"No, it doesn't," Rayford said.

"I know," Bruce said. "But I can hope. I don't want to find out that he's met with foul play. Who knows what happened in there, and him going in with only our prayers?"

"I'd like to think that would be enough," Chloe said.

"No," Bruce said. "He needed the covering of God himself."

———

By the time Stanton Bailey stormed into Buck's office an hour later, Buck realized he was up against a force with which he could not compete. The record of his having been at that meeting had been erased, including from the minds of everyone in the room. He knew Steve wasn't faking it. He honestly believed Buck had not been there. The power Carpathia held over those people knew no limits. If Buck had needed any proof that his own faith was real and that God was now in his life, he had it. Had he not received Christ before entering that room, he was convinced he would be just another of Carpathia's puppets.

Bailey was not in a discussing mood, so Buck let the old man talk, not trying to defend himself. "I don't want any more of this nonsense about your having been there. I know you were in the building and I see your credentials, but you know and I know and everybody who *was* in there knows that you weren't. I don't know what you thought was more important, but you were wrong. This is unacceptable and unforgivable, Cameron. I can't have you as my executive editor."

"I'll gladly go back to senior writer," Buck said.

"Can't go along with that either, pal. I want you out of New York. I'm going to put you in the Chicago bureau."

"I'll be happy to run that for you."

Bailey shook his head. "You don't get it, do you, Cameron? I don't trust you. I should fire you. But I know you'd just wind up with somebody else."

"I don't want to be with anybody else."

"Good, because if you tried to jump to the competition, I'd have to tell them about this stunt. You're going to be a staff writer out of Chicago, working for the woman who was Lucinda's assistant there. I'm calling her today to give her the news. It'll mean a whopping cut in pay, especially considering what you would've gotten with the promotion. You take a few days off, get your things in order here, get that apartment sublet, and find yourself a place in Chicago. Someday I want you to come clean with me, son. That was the sorriest excuse for news gathering I've ever seen, and by one of the best in the business."

Mr. Bailey slammed the door.

Buck couldn't wait to talk to his friends in Illinois, but he didn't want to call from his office or his apartment, and he didn't know for sure whether his cellular phone was safe. He packed his stuff and took a cab to the airport, asking the cabbie to stop at a pay phone a mile outside the terminal.

Not getting an answer at the Steeles', he dialed the church. Bruce answered and told him Chloe and Rayford were there. "Put them on the speakerphone," he said. "I'm taking the three o'clock American flight to O'Hare. But let me tell you this: Carpathia is your man, no question. He fills the bill to the last detail. I felt your prayers in the meeting. God protected me. I'm moving to Chicago, and I want to be a member of, what did you call it, Bruce?"

"The Tribulation Force?"

"That's it!"

"Does this mean—?" Chloe began.

"You know exactly what it means," Buck said. "Count me in."

"What happened, Buck?" Chloe asked.

"I'd rather tell you about it in person," he said. "But have I got a story for you! And you're the only people I know who are going to believe it."

When his plane finally touched down, Buck hurried up the jet way and through the gate where he was joyously greeted by Chloe, Bruce, and Rayford Steele. They all embraced him, even the staid captain. As they huddled in a corner, Bruce prayed, thanking God for their new brother and for protecting him.

They moved through the terminal toward the parking garage, striding four abreast, arms around each other's shoulders, knit with a common purpose. Rayford Steele, Chloe Steele, Buck Williams, and Bruce Barnes faced the gravest dangers anyone could face, and they knew their mission.

The task of the Tribulation Force was clear and their goal nothing less than to stand and fight the enemies of God during the seven most chaotic years the planet would ever see.

ABOUT THE AUTHORS

Jerry B. Jenkins (www.jerryjenkins.com) is the writer of the Left Behind series. He is author of more than one hundred books, of which six have reached the *New York Times* best-seller list. Former vice president for publishing for the Moody Bible Institute of Chicago, he also served many years as editor of *Moody* magazine and is now Moody's writer-at-large.

His writing has appeared in publications as varied as *Reader's Digest, Parade,* in-flight magazines, and many Christian periodicals. He has written books in four genres: biography, marriage and family, fiction for children, and fiction for adults.

Jenkins's biographies include books with Hank Aaron, Bill Gaither, Luis Palau, Walter Payton, Orel Hershiser, Nolan Ryan, Brett Butler, and Billy Graham, among many others.

Six of his apocalyptic novels—*Left Behind, Tribulation Force, Nicolae, Soul Harvest, Apollyon,* and *Assassins*—have appeared on the Christian Booksellers Association's best-selling fiction list and the *Publishers Weekly* religion best-seller list. *Left Behind* was nominated for Book of the Year by the Evangelical Christian Publishers Association in 1997, 1998, and 1999.

As a marriage and family author and speaker, Jenkins has been a frequent guest on Dr. James Dobson's *Focus on the Family* radio program.

Jerry is also the writer of the nationally syndicated sports story comic strip *Gil Thorp,* distributed to newspapers across the United States by Tribune Media Services.

Jerry and his wife, Dianna, live in Colorado.

Limited speaking engagement information is available through speaking@jerryjenkins.com.

Dr. Tim LaHaye (www.timlahaye.com), who conceived the idea of fictionalizing an account of the Rapture and the Tribulation, is a noted author, minister, and nationally recognized speaker on Bible prophecy. He is the founder of both Tim LaHaye Ministries and The Pre-Trib Research Center. Presently Dr. LaHaye speaks at many of the major Bible prophecy conferences in the U.S. and Canada, where his nine current prophecy books are very popular.

Dr. LaHaye holds a doctor of ministry degree from Western Theological Seminary and a doctor of literature degree from Liberty University. For twenty-five years he pastored one of the nation's outstanding churches in San Diego, which grew to three locations. It was during that time that he founded two accredited Christian high schools, a Christian school system of ten schools, and Christian Heritage College.

Dr. LaHaye has written over forty books, with over 22 million copies in print in thirty-three languages. He has written books on a wide variety of subjects, such as family life, temperaments, and Bible prophecy. His current fiction works, written with Jerry B. Jenkins—*Left Behind, Tribulation Force, Nicolae, Soul Harvest, Apollyon,* and *Assassins*—have all reached number one on the Christian best-seller charts. Other works by Dr. LaHaye are *Spirit-Controlled Temperament; How to Be Happy Though Married; Revelation Unveiled; Understanding the Last Days; Rapture under Attack; Are We Living in the End Times?* and the youth fiction series Left Behind: The Kids.

He is the father of four grown children and grandfather of nine. Snow skiing, waterskiing, motorcycling, golfing, vacationing with family, and jogging are among his leisure activities.

THE FUTURE IS CLEAR

Left Behind
A novel of the earth's last days . . .
In one cataclysmic moment, millions around the world disappear. In the midst of global chaos, airline captain Rayford Steele must search for his family, for answers, for truth. As devastating as the disappearances have been, the darkest days lie ahead.

0-8423-2911-0 Hardcover
0-8423-2912-9 Softcover
0-8423-1675-2 Audio book

Tribulation Force
The continuing drama of those left behind . . .
Rayford Steele, Buck Williams, Bruce Barnes, and Chloe Steele band together to form the Tribulation Force. Their task is clear, and their goal nothing less than to stand and fight the enemies of God during the seven most chaotic years the planet will ever see.

0-8423-2913-7 Hardcover
0-8423-2921-8 Softcover
0-8423-1787-2 Audio book

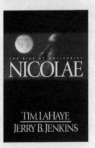

Nicolae
The rise of Antichrist . . .
The seven-year tribulation period is nearing the end of its first quarter, when prophecy says "the wrath of the Lamb" will be poured out upon the earth. Rayford Steele has become the ears of the tribulation saints in the Carpathia regime. A dramatic all-night rescue run from Israel through the Sinai will hold you breathless to the end.

0-8423-2914-5 Hardcover
0-8423-2924-2 Softcover
0-8423-1788-0 Audio book

Soul Harvest
The world takes sides . . .
As the world hurtles toward the Trumpet Judgments and the great soul harvest prophesied in Scripture, Rayford Steele and Buck Williams begin searching for their loved ones from different corners of the world. *Soul Harvest* takes you from Iraq to America, from six miles in the air to underground shelters, from desert sand to the bottom of the Tigris River, from hope to devastation and back again—all in a quest for truth and life.

0-8423-2915-3 Hardcover
0-8423-2925-0 Softcover
0-8423-5175-2 Audio book

Apollyon
The Destroyer is unleashed . . .
In this acclaimed *New York Times* best-seller, Apollyon, the Destroyer, leads the plague of demon locusts as they torture the unsaved. Meanwhile, despite growing threats from Antichrist, the Tribulation Force gathers in Israel for the Conference of Witnesses.

0-8423-2916-1 Hardcover
0-8423-2926-9 Softcover (available winter 2000)
0-8423-1933-6 Audio book

Assassins
Assignment: Jerusalem, Target: Antichrist
As a horde of 200 million demonic horsemen slays a third of the world's population, the Tribulation Force prepares for a future as fugitives. History and prophecy collide in Jerusalem for the most explosive episode yet of the continuing drama of those left behind.

0-8423-2920-X Hardcover
0-8423-2927-7 Softcover (available summer 2000)
0-8423-1934-4 Audio book

Watch for book 7, *The Indwelling,* available spring 2000

Left Behind: The Kids
Four teens are left behind after the Rapture and band together to fight Satan's forces in this series for ten- to fourteen-year-olds.

#1 *The Vanishings* 0-8423-2193-4
#2 *Second Chance* 0-8423-2194-2
#3 *Through the Flames* 0-8423-2195-0
#4 *Facing the Future* 0-8423-2196-9
#5 *Nicolae High* 0-8423-4325-3
#6 *The Underground* 0-8423-4326-1
#7 *Busted!* 0-8423-4327-X (available spring 2000)
#8 *Death Strike* 0-8423-4328-8 (available spring 2000)

Have You Been Left Behind?

Based on the video that New Hope Village Church's pastor Vernon Billings created for those left behind after the Rapture. This video explains what happened and what the viewer can do now.

0-8423-5196-5 Video

An Experience in Sound and Drama

Dramatic broadcast performances of the first three books in the best-selling Left Behind series. Original music, sound effects, and professional actors make the action come alive. Experience the heart-stopping action and suspense of the end times for yourself. . . . Twelve half-hour episodes, on four CDs or three cassettes, for each title.

0-8423-5146-9 *Left Behind: An Experience in Sound and Drama* CD
0-8423-5181-7 *Left Behind: An Experience in Sound and Drama* cassette
0-8423-3584-6 *Tribulation Force: An Experience in Sound and Drama* CD
0-8423-3583-8 *Tribulation Force: An Experience in Sound and Drama* cassette
0-8423-3663-X *Nicolae: An Experience in Sound and Drama* CD
          (available spring 2000)
0-8423-3662-1 *Nicolae: An Experience in Sound and Drama*
          cassette (available spring 2000)

Discover the latest about the Left Behind series
and interact with other readers at **www.leftbehind.com**